Memory and Desire

CARLA SIMPSON

OLIVERHEBERBOOKS

Published by Oliver-Heber Books

0 9 8 7 6 5 4 3 2 1

Praise for Carla Simpson

"MEMORY AND DESIRE is such a wonderful, curl in your chair book I found myself reading it twice to be sure I didn't miss anything. I wish I had written it. *Bravo, Ms. Simpson!*"

Fern Michaels, author

Prologue

FEBRUARY 7, 1856, COAST OF CORNWALL,
ENGLAND

"Regina, you must come away. It's of no use." The elegantly dressed gentleman wore his sorrow and concern in the deep lines etched on his face. He couldn't bear to see his dear friend tormenting herself, hoping against hope as she continued staring out across the ominous sea with stricken eyes. Stoically, she shook her head, pulling the heavy folds of her voluminous cloak more securely around her shoulders.

"I can't give up," she whispered brokenly. "As long as there's even the barest chance one of them may have survived." Lady Regina Winslow turned to her companion in desperation. "Please, Cedric," she implored, "can't you understand? They're all I have left in the world."

Grief hung heavy in her voice, as she turned her gaze back to the churning sea.

Sir Cedric Chatsworth nodded grimly. He knew she'd never cease her vigils on that bluff high above the crashing sea until something was found—something or someone.

An icy wind assaulted the bluff, its cold blasts stealing through their heavy clothing. Behind them waited a stately black coach bearing the Winslow family coronet, and four perfectly matched bays. Heads down, tails and manes blowing in the frigid wind, their dark

1

coats seeming almost black, the horses stood eerily still. The coachman, dressed in the finest burgundy livery, huddled against the cold as the storm-filled sky threatened to burst upon them. He sat rigid, collar turned up almost to the brim of his black silk hat, his eyes nothing more than two narrow slits. And he watched and waited as they'd all done for two days.

"At least come and wait in the coach, out of the wind. What good will it do if you catch your death out here?" Sir Chatsworth implored. His question was met with silence, for Regina continued to gaze over the edge of the bluff which dropped away to the seawall below. One hand reaching to steady his hat, Chatsworth turned and walked toward the coach. The coachman stirred and jumped down stiffly as he approached.

Sir Chatsworth took from the vehicle the thick fur lap robe.

Then he returned to Regina's side and laid it gently about her shoulders. Her trance was momentarily broken as his hand lingered lovingly on her back. "Thank you, Cedric," Regina whispered so softly her words were almost lost on the wind, which seemed to hesitate, then swirl about them with renewed urgency. Her large blue eyes were weary, and lines were etched in the softness of her face. For a moment, she gazed at him searchingly, as if silently begging him for something; then she turned wistfully back to the angry sea that pounded the rocks below with relentless fury.

The villagers of Land's End said it was the worst storm in memory. For two days the sea had seemed to curse and scream, hurling its rage against the coastline, destroying anything that dared venture forth. Days earlier, the waves had roiled and built like avenging demons, and the sky had turned so gray and ominous it seemed that day was night. A howling wind pelted the village with stinging, icy shards of rain, and at noon it was as bleak as night, clouds churning overhead, the ocean heaving and spewing until it and the clouds met and seemed inseparable.

Then, two days ago, a feeble light was seen in the darkness. A ship, struggling against sea and wind and rain, plunged through the teeming waters, sails rigged taut, trying desperately to turn away from the breakwater. Over the roar of the ocean and the howling of the wind, the villagers cringed and offered fervent prayers as they heard the ominous sounds of the wooden hull splintering and cracking on the rock-strewn barrier.

Hearty fishermen braved the night, and crawled, lanterns in hand, to the bluff high above the breakwater. The light they'd seen earlier, bobbing in the storm, hung momentarily suspended like a lone star in the heavens. Then, as the villagers watched helplessly, knowing none dare venture into the stormy sea at night, cries were heard, or was it only the wind?

A few of the strongest men crept down the rocky ledge to the breakwater below. The distant light lingered, flickered, and then vanished, so that none were certain they'd seen it at all. At dawn, the villagers returned to the bluff above the sea.

Out on the breakwater, the crumpled hulk of a brigantine clung lifelessly to the rocks. Splintered pieces of her hull and cargo floated in clouded tide pools. The storm seemed to lessen with the dawn and several men attempted to reach the battered ship. As they drew near, a wave crested and forced them back; but they could hear the ship groaning as she shifted and sank more deeply, until only a portion of her deck and two broken masts remained above water. Her sails hung like a maid's sodden skirts, her stern was completely submerged.

There was no sign of life. It took all their strength and skill to return to the small inlet without capsizing. As they pulled their small craft from the water, one man whispered the name of the ill-fated ship, and the men turned as one to watch solemnly as the brigantine *Venturer* slowly gave up her struggle with the sea.

Lady Regina shuddered and grabbed at her fur robe with gloved hands. The wind, penetrating her heavy clothing, felt like the chill of death stealing over her. She'd waited in Plymouth for news of the *Venturer*; then had made the hazardous journey to Land's End when word had come of the wreck. Her eyes, the deep-dark blue of heather upon the moors, were glazed with unshed tears. Even when she and Cedric had arrived at the inn and she'd heard the ship's name whispered in hushed tones, she'd refused to believe.

James, her dear son, she thought, a sob escaping her. Why had he insisted on returning with his family from the Colonies at this time of year? What was so urgent that it couldn't have waited until later, when the voyage would've been safer?

Her gaze wandered over the deserted bluff which men from the village had descended hours earlier to reach the seawall below. For two days, they'd searched the shoals and tide pools, braving a relentless sea and an equally unyielding wind, searching for survivors. And each time they'd trudged wearily back up the ledge, their heavy woolen coats clinging to their weary bodies like shrouds, the answer had been the same—no survivors.

The sky had turned to slate. If only Richard was with me, she thought, then caught herself. No, it would be no different if her husband were alive and here with her and Cedric. Richard had always been stoic, proud, and faintly overbearing. She smiled faintly at the memory of the friendship between her husband and Sir Cedric Chatsworth, one that had endured since they'd been at Eton together. They were a study of contrasts, always falling into some argument or another over some matter of government or foreign policy. Ceddy, as her husband called his dearest friend, was simply far too practical.

Dear Ceddy, she thought, you've been such a friend to me, so dear all these years I've been alone, especially after James left for the Colonies. Her husband always insisted the United States be called the Colonies. She realized old resentments died hard, even though the matter of the Colonies had been settled decades ago.

Regina's gaze fastened on all that remained of the *Venturer*. Broken masts poked up through swelling waves. James... so dear to her and Richard after their firstborn son had succumbed to the fever. James had held such promise, and he'd so eagerly sailed off to visit the United States, taking it upon himself to personally oversee property Sir Richard Winslow had quietly and unobtrusively acquired over the years. James had met Anne in New York, and they'd fallen deeply in love. Regina's one voyage to the Colonies had been made to attend their wedding.

Family obligations had demanded her quick return, so she'd not been there for the arrival of her first grandchild. But James and Anne had assured her they would make the voyage to England as soon as the baby was old enough. However, Anne quickly conceived again, and that birthing had not gone well. She'd lost the second child at birth and had been confined to bed for weeks afterward. So, the voyage to England had been delayed for almost two years. Tears welled in her eyes. She'd wanted so to see them again, had mentioned it in every letter.

Now, for all she knew, her son was lost, along with his wife and child. Lady Regina caught herself. No! She refused to accept it! Dear Father in heaven, she'd never even seen her granddaughter, Elyse.

Cedric's hand tightened around her arm, steadying her as the first dark figure crested the bluff, followed by several others. Regina looked from one man to the next, her eyes searching their wind-chapped faces, as they trudged past her, shaking their heads wearily, mumbling some vaguely sympathetic words as they rubbed aching hands together. All refused to meet her eyes directly.

The answer was the same as it had been for the last two days. At first, she'd stoically refused to believe the wreck was the ship James and Anne were returning on. But when she'd reached the village of Land's End on the coast of Cornwall, her stoicism had ended.

As the brig broke up on the rocks beyond the breakwater, bits and pieces of her were washed ashore, among them the captain's manifest and a list of passengers. James' name was still decipherable, indicating he'd come aboard the *Venturer* in New York with his wife and child. Upon seeing it, something inside Lady Regina Winslow seemed to die.

As long hours had become one day, and then two, her hope that James and Anne might have survived rapidly faded. Their deaths, along with those of the crew and the other passengers, seemed cruel, but the loss of a child, her granddaughter, was incomprehensible to Regina.

"Reggie, please." Using the nickname he'd given her when they were young, Cedric urged her away. "It's no use, my dear," he gently begged.

She clung to his arm as if all strength had suddenly seeped out of her. Slowly, she nodded.

"It's so difficult. I had hoped that maybe somehow..." she whispered brokenly.

"I know," he soothed, tucking her arm through his and tenderly drawing her away from the bluff. He patted her gloved hand lovingly.

"Perhaps tomorrow... there's nothing more to be done tonight."

A shout stopped them, and Cedric turned, squinting into the growing darkness. One of the men who'd just passed them ran back to the edge of the bluff.

"It's Quimby!" he shouted above the wind. "Come

on, lads!" He cupped his hands, calling to the others. "Give us a hand! He's got something."

"Wait!" Regina pulled back, her fingers tightening over Chatsworth's arm as she followed her companion up the steep rock face.

The man was nothing more than a large, dark shape as he collapsed over the edge of the bluff, strong hands pulling him to safer ground, his friends surrounding him. He fought to breathe, his skin chapped raw from the wind and biting sea spray, and struggled to his knees, clutching the heavy jacket that stretched across his chest.

"Eh, Quimby, what ye got there?" One man threw a blanket around his friend's shoulders while another tried to help him stand.

The man groaned from between chattering teeth, his eyes glassy with cold and fatigue. Then he got to his feet, opening his jacket for the others to see.

"Will ya look at that! Where in bloody blazes did that come from?" one of the men exclaimed.

Regina tore from Cedric's grasp. Her luxurious lap robe fell to the sodden ground and her cloak billowed from her shoulders as she braved the wind at the edge of the bluff. Cedric called out, going after her.

Unable to stand, Quimby collapsed, his legs near frozen from wading in the frigid water below, but he raised bloodshot eyes to Regina, and opened the folds of his coat.

She cried out, her hand flying to her mouth. A small child was bundled inside the sodden folds of Quimby's jacket.

"Dear God!" Regina fell to her knees beside Quimby, clutching at his arm.

"I found her among the rocks, ma'am," he explained brokenly, his breathing labored. "We already looked there. She must have washed up after we moved on," He carefully surrendered the child.

Regina reached for the cold, seemingly lifeless bundle, folding the little girl inside her heavy cloak. She sobbed as her fingers wrapped around smaller, blue ones, almost transparent and rigid with cold.

"What is it? Good God!" Cedric came up behind them.

His cheeks sucked in as he struggled to draw an even breath. He leaned over, eyes widening at seeing the small, blue-tinged face nestled against Regina's ample bosom.

Tears in her eyes, Regina looked up at him, snuggling the child against her own warmth. "Cedric, this is my granddaughter."

"Are you certain?"

Quimby rose shakily to his feet. "It doesn't rightly matter who the child is, guv'ner. We'd best get the wee one out of this weather."

Cedric reached down to take the child from Regina. He knew she must be exhausted. But she met his gesture with defiant eyes, clinging to the sodden bundle.

"I'll carry my granddaughter," she cried out vehemently. However, the hard edge left her voice. "Please, Cedric, she's so small and cold."

Chatsworth nodded, his arm going round her for support. As he held her close, trying to shield them both from the biting wind, he prayed the child, whoever she was, might still be alive.

Settling them inside the coach, Cedric quickly gave an order to the driver. When the door was closed, cutting off the stinging wind, he tapped firmly on the roof of the coach with his cane. The coach lurched forward, the driver setting a furious pace as he sent the horses flying down the road toward to village.

～

Sir Cedric's hand rested on Regina's shoulder as she knelt beside the huge down-filled bed. The child lay motionless in the center, barely visible in the feathery mass with blankets covering her.

The local physician bent over her, his face a mask devoid of emotion. Regina raised desperate eyes to him as he rose.

"It's too soon to tell," he informed them gravely. His mouth was pulled down severely at the corners, as it had been for the two days since he'd been summoned to the inn.

He resented being ordered to remain there when he had other patients to attend to, patients who truly needed his care. But Lady Regina Winslow had been adamant that he stay. Now he looked at her with an expression very near grim satisfaction, as if to say I told you it would be of no use. As he packed his case, he shook his head.

"Where are you going?" she demanded, her fingers protectively pulling the heavy coverlet back over the child.

The physician turned. "There's nothing more I can do. As far as I can see, there are no broken bones. She's alive, but that's about all. There's that nasty bump on her head and all those bruises. She must have been battered about in the water for a long time. It's beyond me how she survived at all. Children that small are usually not good swimmers."

"You can't leave," Regina informed him, her eyes briefly leaving the child. "What must be done when she awakens?"

"I can't be certain that she will awaken," the physician replied. "I've seen it before. Very often they never awaken with a head wound like that." He sniffed indignantly. "You must prepare yourself to accept the worst."

"No!" Regina rounded the bed with purposeful strides, fists clenched. "She's not going to die, and you're not leaving."

"I have other patients in far greater need than this

child. I've a woman waiting to give birth, and several men needing my attention." He implied that she was responsible for the injuries of the men who'd tried to reach the *Venturer*.

But Regina wasn't fooled. She knew the sort of people who lived at Land's End. They preyed on salvage taken from foundering ships, and many vessels sank off this wild and forbidding coastline. It was the promise of finding gold coin that had prodded villagers to search for survivors. And they'd have their gold. She'd gladly pay it. The child's life was worth it.

Regina's eyes hardened. Devil take him, she'd do without the man. She didn't trust anyone who turned away from a stricken child.

The physician stopped beside Cedric. "This has happened before," he told him. "The child is probably not even her granddaughter. She could be from any one of a half-dozen villages along the coast. They wander down to the rocks, disobedient little beggars. We have at least one wash ashore every storm. The next year, their parents replace them with another."

"Get the bloody hell out of here before I throw you out! You're not fit to breathe the same air as that child!" Cedric's eyes glittered with contempt, and he moved toward the physician, the man's words nonetheless churning doubts he hadn't wanted to admit— the child might not be Regina's granddaughter. The physician shrugged and quickly left the room, practically colliding with a young maid on the stairs. The girl squawked, as she re-balanced a tray holding hot broth.

"Watch it, guv'ner. Why's he in such a bleedin' hurry?" She entered the sparsely furnished room, deposited the tray on a small table, and came around the side of the bed to peer at the small face poking through the blankets.

"Not much left of 'er is there?" The maid glanced

uncertainly from Regina to Cedric, then quickly apologized on seeing Regina's stricken expression.

"I didn't mean nothin' by it. It's just that she's so small, and she's gone through so much." She fingered the coverlet, smoothing the fabric. "She needs one of me mam's special potions. It always fixes us up right fine when we come down with a bit of the ague. It has a wee dram of rum in the mix, for medicinal purposes of course," she added.

Regina fixed the girl with a penetrating stare. "Rum?"

The girl beamed. "Right ya are, mum. A good dose of rum, sugar, saffron... "

"And a touch of camphor," Regina finished for her. She smiled at the girl's open admiration.

"Now how would a lady like you be knowin' about that?"

"My mother was from the moors." Regina smiled. "She always swore by the cure. If it didn't kill you, it would cure you. It's a far better cure than any that physician could offer." Regina's contempt for the man was evident.

"Can you find the ingredients?"

"Sure enough!" The girl bobbed her head. "Me mam keeps a good supply at home. I'll have to see if I can get away. Old Harry don't like me sneakin' off during workin' hours."

"You tell the innkeeper I've sent you on an errand. He'll be compensated for his inconvenience," Regina assured her. Then she turned to Cedric. "I'll need your help."

"Anything, my dear." He pushed aside the physician's comments for the moment. Right then, it didn't matter who the child was. The doubts would return later, when the child recovered... if she recovered.

"We'll need lots of wood for the fire." She motioned to the small fireplace, where a meager blaze struggled to warm the room. "It must be made as warm in here as possible." Regina turned back to the girl. "What's your name?" she asked.

"Katy, ma'am." The girl dipped into a quick curtsy.

"I want a big kettle of water boiling over the fire, the biggest you can find. I want this room filled with steam." She shooed the girl to the door. "Move! We've got work to do!"

As Cedric followed Katy from the room, the girl turned and whispered over her shoulder, "Much as I 'ate that old sawbones, he might be right. The child might not be 'er granddaughter. The little ones all go down there. Me own brother Malcolm almost drowned in that cove."

Cedric patted the girl on the arm. "Nevertheless, we'll do as Lady Winslow asks. I've known her a great many years, and there's only one thing in this world or the next I fear more. She can be a formidable force when she wants something."

He sent the girl on down ahead of him. "She can be a mighty determined woman."

Katy nodded, then informed the owner of the tavern that she needed to go to her mum's.

"Hold on there, yer work ain't finished yet." Harry started after her, but Cedric stepped between the man and the hallway that led to the back.

"I'll be needing several things, my good man, and I'll pay well for them." For emphasis, he produced several gold coins from his breast pocket.

Harry stopped, the girl forgotten. "Whatever ya need, guv'ner, I got it."

The small room glowed golden, images of flames dancing on the far wall, as steam curled above the simmering kettle, making the heat damp and thick. When Cedric carefully closed the door behind him, Regina did not notice. She sat on the edge of the bed, spooning drops of a foul-smelling liquid into the child's small, birdlike mouth. Most of the concoction dribbled down the tot's tiny chin. He shuddered, thinking the cure must be almost as severe as the illness. Setting the bowl aside, Regina looked up, her weary eyes meeting his.

"Is there any change?" he inquired softly.

She shook her head. "She's alive and she's warm. I suppose that's all we can hope for right now."

"Reggie, please come down and try to eat something. You've been up here for hours," he begged softly, his heart breaking for the woman he'd admired for so many years. "You can't continue like this. I'll send Katy to watch the child. You must have something to eat, and then rest."

Regina smiled, but her eyes were filled with worry. "I can't leave. I want to be here when she awakens." Not if. She refused to acknowledge that her granddaughter might not awaken. Tenderly, she smoothed the coverlet. "What time is it?"

"Almost daybreak." Cedric came to stand beside her and looked down at the pathetic child. Regina's son had written that the child favored the Winslow side of the family. And Reggie had boasted about her granddaughter, showing the small hand-painted miniature portrait James had sent to anyone remotely interested. Truthfully, Cedric saw no resemblance to Reggie or James in the pathetic creature bundled in the oversize bed, a child so small she seemed to disappear in the voluminous folds of the covers. He supposed it was possible she favored her mother more. He'd never met Anne Winslow. She and James had married in America. Ill health had prevented Cedric from attending the ceremony. The physician's words came back to him. What if the child was from one of the surrounding hamlets? Could Reggie bear to face the truth?

"What about the men from the village?" Regina

whispered brokenly, her fingers tenderly stroking the matted hair back from the child's small face.

"They've promised to take up the search again at first light. Perhaps they'll reach the ship today—" he broke off, not saying what he was thinking. The *Venturer* was almost completely submerged. Even if the searchers did reach the ship, it was certain there was no one left alive.

His gaze fastened on the child. In two days of frantic searching, only this small girl had been found. Each winter along the Cornish coast it was the same. When a ship went down, her cargo was salvaged, but there were seldom survivors. This was a wild and forbidding stretch of land. The crew of the brigantine had made a fatal error and had paid for it with their lives and the lives of their passengers.

Cedric looked down at the child. When they'd brought her to the inn, her skin had been a terrifying shade of grayish-blue, her breathing so shallow it was hardly there. Now, her color had brightened to crimson, and her breathing was hard and labored due to the fever that raged through her small body. He'd seen such fevers and knew even the stoutest of those afflicted often didn't recover. He gently laid a hand on Regina's shoulder, trying to comfort her. Through the long night he'd been trying to think how he could express to her the doubts the physician had left in his mind.

"Regina, you need rest. And we must talk," he coaxed. She spoke as if she hadn't heard a word he'd said.

"I want Dr. Crestwell in London notified. He's the finest physician in England. And I want specialists to look at her, the best. Only the best for Elyse."

"Reggie," he said uncertainly. It was as if her mind was in that same faraway place that seemed to claim the child. She hadn't heard a word he'd said, or if she had, she'd chosen to ignore him.

"I want Mr. Quist to return to London immediately." She asked him to inform her coachman. "And I want the townhouse opened. Everything must be ready when we arrive." She faltered. "I hate to leave. There might be word of James or Anne..." Her voice trailed off, for she knew in her heart there was no hope.

Chatsworth seized this opportunity. "The physician said there are accidents every winter. Regina, listen to me," he implored. "The child may not be your granddaughter. Katy told me children wander down on the rocks all the time."

"No!" Regina turned on him, the storm in her dark blue eyes more threatening than the one beating against the shuttered windows.

"I know my own granddaughter! This *is* Elyse!" She turned back to the child, her shoulders trembling with anguish. Then she crumpled onto the bed, burying her face in the folds of the coverlet.

"Dear Reggie." Cedric reached out to her, but his hand fell limply to his side. He knew her only comfort was to be found in the child, whoever she was. Cedric slowly closed the door. After giving Regina's instructions to her coachman, he slumped wearily into a chair downstairs and kept a vigil beside the fire. When first gray light of a new day seeped through the paned windows, the search party had already left to return to the rocky coastline. He knew they no longer hoped to find survivors. Their interest lay in the cargo that would wash ashore.

For three days and three nights, Regina refused to leave the child's room. Cedric spent long hours with her, placing fresh wood on the fire, conveying messages to Katy through the door, or waiting downstairs for word at the end of each day when the salvagers returned.

Their mumbled replies were always the same—no survivors.

The hours slipped into yet another day, the child's condition remaining unchanged, fever raging through her frail body. But Regina refused to leave her side. Her elegant gown was wrinkled now, spotted with stains made by the foul-smelling medicine Katy prepared in the kitchen. The young maid refused to leave the inn even when her work was completed, saying she wanted to be near the child. And Quimby, who'd found the little girl on the rocks, refused to return to the rocky cliff, giving the excuse that it wasn't fit weather out for man or beast. Though a drinking man, he hadn't touched a drop since he'd pulled the child from the sea.

Cedric jerked upright from his dozing, his blood-shot eyes focusing slowly on the stairway.

"Regina?" His senses cleared. "My God, what is it?"

She smiled wanly, as she slumped into the chair across from him.

"She isn't...?"He couldn't say the words. So many days they'd waited.

"The fever broke almost an hour ago. Katy's with her." Tears welled in Regina's eyes, and she buried her face in her hands. "She's going to live."

Cedric was out of his chair and beside her in an instant. He wrapped an arm about her shoulders. "Has she regained consciousness?" he whispered hopefully. Regina shook her head. "No, but she will." She turned determined eyes up to him, clinging to his comforting hand. "Ceddy, she has to live. After all this time, I know there's no hope for James or Anne, but I couldn't bear to lose that little girl, too."

"Hush, hush." Cedric soothed her, stroking her hair. "We'll just have to wait."

He smiled as he handed her his handkerchief. Never in all the years he'd known her had Regina Winslow had a handkerchief when she'd needed it.

"Did Mr. Quist leave for London?" She wiped her eyes.

"Yes, and he has returned," Cedric confirmed. He frowned slightly at the disturbing news the man had brought back, but he decided not to burden Regina with it at the moment. He knew from the look in her eyes, she couldn't take any more right then. He forced back the frown and smiled gently.

"Everything will be ready when we get there."

Regina nodded, her head snapping up as Katy suddenly appeared at the top of the stairs.

"Come quick, ma'am." The girl gestured excitedly. "It's the little one!" Katy whirled back around and disappeared inside the small room. Regina flew across the tavern and up the stairs, Cedric immediately behind her.

"What is it?" Regina burst into the room, fear lining her face, her eyes wide and stricken.

"Look for yerself, ma'am." Katy pointed to the bed, where the child stirred among the heavy covers.

Crying out, Regina knelt beside the bed. Small and frail, the child weakly turned her head toward them. Her mouth opened and closed, the lips dry and cracked. One small hand reached from the covers. Regina felt her forehead. The child's skin was cool, her breathing regular and even.

"Dear God!" she whispered, her eyes filling with tears. "Oh, Ceddy, she's coming around." She bent over the little girl, talking in the soft, crooning voice she'd used when her son was a small child. There was the faintest trace of color on the child's cheeks, natural, healthy color, not the fiery crimson of fever.

"Sweet, sweet child." Reggie stroked the child's face, holding its small hands in her own. "I'm here, and you're safe. I love you so, and there's so much I want to share with you. Grandmother is here, Elyse."

Tiny fingers tightened around Regina's, eyelashes quivered, lips moved faintly. Then large round eyes opened slowly, searchingly. The little girl blinked once, twice, then stared at the faces looking down at her. As her confusion cleared, the pristine whites of her eyes surrounded blue so deep it was like the heather on the moors. The irises were large and black, fathomless as the ocean that had yielded her so reluctantly.

"Elyse?" Regina spoke softly not wanting to frighten her. The child had suffered a severe blow to the head, the bandage was thick and heavy. Reggie couldn't be certain Elyse's memory would be clear. She wasn't certain she wanted her to remember.

As color flooded the little girl's cheeks, her eyes darted about the room with childish curiosity. She regarded the people hovering over her with a mixture of curiosity and amusement. There was no confusion or uncertainty in the depths of her crystal blue gaze. Her voice was small and breathless.

"Where is he?"

Regina's eyes glowed as she heard these first spoken words which she didn't bother to try to understand. With rapturous delight, she squeezed her granddaughter's small hands, showering kisses on her small face. For her, there had never been any doubt that this was her granddaughter.

Cedric stared in disbelief at the child. His doubts had vanished the moment she'd opened her eyes, for they were as dark and vibrant as Regina's. There was no mistaking the resemblance.

The little girl continued to stare up at them as if wondering what all the fuss was about, and her gaze traveled from her grandmother to Katy, then to Cedric.

"Where is he?" she insisted, struggling up from the coverlet.

Regina smiled uncertainly at the inquisitive child who'd fixed her with such a determined stare, but her smile faded, and she shot a stricken glance at Chatsworth. He?

It suddenly occurred to her that Elyse meant James. Regina's eyes welled with tears. Gently, she smoothed the toddler's thick, dark hair. Her fingers trembled. Anne's hair had been that same color; her father's eyes, her mother's coloring. Elyse would be a striking beauty one day. Regina gathered her granddaughter close, her heart aching.

"They're not here right now, my darling," Reggie explained gently. There would be time to explain later, when Elyse was stronger. Right now, she couldn't be certain of how much the child comprehended of what had happened.

Elyse fought back the covers, her eyes wide, clear, determined. She glanced about the room.

"Where is he? He promised he would come back for me." Her voice was haunting, its aching melancholy tearing into their hearts. She crawled from her grandmother's grasp, heading for the edge of the bed. Tears filled Elyse's eyes as she gazed about her.

"He's been gone so long." Her small voice quavered. "And he did promise, he said he loved me and that he would come back for me."

Katy reached for the child and pulled her onto her lap, cradling her like a baby. "There, there little one. It's all right now. Don't ya be frettin'," she soothed. "He promised he'd come back, and he will. I know he will." Katy rocked the child gently back and forth.

Regina stared in mute silence at Cedric. He patted her shoulder, then firmly took her by the arm, helping her to her feet.

"You're exhausted. The child will be fine now. Come downstairs. You haven't eaten or slept in days." Cedric turned to Katy. "You'll see that the child sleeps?"

"I'll stay right 'ere with her, guv'ner. I gots me seven brothers and sisters. Me mam always said there was nothing like rockin' a wee one when they was troubled. I'll be down to get ya something to eat as soon as she dozes off."

Cedric nodded and then guided Regina from the room. Once she was out the door, she turned and crumpled against his shoulder. "Oh, Ceddy, will she be all right? She seemed so much better when she awakened. But what did she mean?"

Cedric held her close, stroking her disheveled hair. "She's been through a great deal. Give her time. We'll get her back to London and have Tom give her a thorough examination. I'm certain, in time, she'll be just fine. She did suffer quite a severe knock on the head."

"Yes, of course." Regina nodded. Her eyes were red from crying and lack of sleep. "That must be it. I expected too much. I'm afraid I'm greedy. After the last days..." Her voice broke, and she looked up at him, seeking the truth in his eyes. "You do believe she's Elyse?"

Cedric sighed heavily. He had seen a resemblance when the child had awakened. "She has your eyes, my dear. I never met Anne..." He was fumbling badly.

"No, you didn't. She was so lovely, with hair that same color." Her voice trembled. "James loved her so. And he was so proud of Elyse. They couldn't wait for me to see her." She turned and gazed wistfully at the closed door, as if she couldn't bear to leave for even a moment, but Cedric firmly guided her down the stairs.

They sat at the small trestle table in a corner of the inn. Katy had brought them tea, and cakes she'd proudly boasted that 'er *mam* had baked. Then she'd gone back upstairs to watch over Elyse. Every so often, Regina's gaze darted watchfully to the door at the top of the stairs. It was now two days since the child had awakened.

After eating a small meal, she'd slipped into a deep, restful slumber, sleeping for almost sixteen hours. During that time, Regina remained by her granddaughter's bed, fearful that she might yet slip away from them. But with each passing hour, the child seemed to grow stronger.

Sadly, there was no trace of another survivor. Lady Regina Winslow accepted the truth and turned her strength and determination to ensuring Elyse's recovery.

She announced that they would return to London immediately, as if she couldn't bear to remain at Land's End a moment longer. Earlier that morning she'd gone alone to the bluff.

Cedric hadn't asked why; he'd understood. Now he watched her from across the table. She'd donned a clean gown of deep aquamarine that set the color in her eyes to dancing. Her dark blond hair, faintly streaked with gray, was elegantly styled atop her head. The deepened lines at her eyes were the only outward signs of her grieving.

He was again reminded that Lady Regina Winslow was a very beautiful woman. He'd been aware of that for almost forty years, and strongly suspected it was the reason he'd never chosen to marry. There wasn't another woman alive to compare to her. And for twenty-two of those forty years she'd been married to his closest friend.

Cedric rummaged in the pocket of his elegant charcoal jacket, then replaced the cigars. Regina looked up from her tea, a ghost of a smile playing around the corners of her mouth.

"For heaven's sake, Cedric, go ahead and smoke your cigar. You know very well it doesn't bother me. I rather like it. Richard used to smoke them all the time." She spoke fondly of her husband.

"If you're certain?" Most women were given to a case of the vapors or to swooning spells at the first whiff of smoke.

He took out a small cigar and twirled it thoughtfully between thumb and forefinger. He'd hesitated to tell her during the days of the child's recovery, but now that they were returning to London, he knew he could delay no longer.

"We've had news from London," he began thoughtfully, wondering if she was strong enough to hear it now. He preferred she hear it from him rather than one of her household staff upon their return.

"What is it?" Regina reached out and patted his hand. Ceddy had always been such a dear friend, always trying to shield her from life's little unpleasantries since Richard was gone. Her faint smile faded before his silent and somber expression. He seemed to be searching for the right words. She'd never known him to be at a loss to express himself.

"What is it?" she whispered, fear congealing around her heart.

"It's Felicia." He spoke slowly, wishing he could spare her this.

"What's happened?" Regina's voice had a small desperate edge to it as she thought of her dear friend.

"Mr. Quist brought back word... "He hesitated. "I know you were very close."

"She's dead, isn't she?" Regina voiced what he seemed to be having such a difficult time saying.

Cedric nodded.

"Somehow I knew," she replied." She was sick for such a long time, and so very unhappy." She breathed a ragged sigh, no more tears left in her. "She was like my own daughter after her parents died. Her marriage to Barrington was arranged, and, in spite of appearances, not the happiest. She was in love with someone else, but she never spoke of it, not even to me.

"My poor, dear Felicia," she continued. "She was a true friend. I hope she's at peace now." Regina sighed. So much sadness. So much loss. When did it happen?"

"The evening of the fifth," he told her. "The night the ship went down. According to Mr. Quist, within the very same hour."

Regina only nodded sadly. If the coincidence registered at all, she showed no sign of it.

Katy interrupted them, jauntily coming down the

steps. "I swear that wee child has two hollow legs, she does. Why she eats more than me brother, Simon, and he's five goin' on six."

Regina smiled, heartened by the good news. "Katy, you've been a godsend. I can't think what I would have done the last two days without you. I've been considering something." She hesitated. "How would you like to come back to London with us? You could help me care for Elyse."

"London? Me? What would I do there? Me mam says the place is dreadful wicked and there ain't a job to be had." She jerked her thumb over her shoulder toward Harry the innkeeper. "Ole Harry might not pay much, but it's steady work. Men is always wantin' their ale."

"Elyse has become very attached to you the last few days, and I'll need someone to help me with her. I'm a bit old to be starting with a child," she admitted.

"Right ya are, mum." Katy nodded, completely unabashed. "But there is me mam and me sisters and brothers to consider!"

"You'll be well compensated. You'll live in London with us at the town house, and at the country house in York." Regina reached out, taking the girl's hand.

"You're gentle and caring, and the only other person I've met who knows about saffron and camphor. Please, say you'll come. You'll make more money in a month than in an entire year here at the tavern. And I would like someone such as yourself around my granddaughter. She's going to need a great deal of love and caring."

Katy's eyes widened as she considered Lady Regina's offer. Then she nodded and set her mouth in a firm line, her decision made. "I guess I'd be a fool to turn down an offer like that. Besides, who could refuse a position carin' for a pretty little thing like 'er." She shook Regina's hand very businesslike. "Ya got yerself a deal, ma'am." Then she blushed and dipped into a deep curtsy. "Sorry, yer ladyship. I gotta be honest with ya, I don't rightly know how I'm gonna fit in. Me mam says me manners are right fine for a tavern, but not rightly what you be findin' in a house in London."

Regina smiled. "You let me worry about that. It'll be refreshing to have someone with your honesty around. And I want to learn more of your mother's recipes, especially that broth you fixed the other evening. I think we both have a great deal to learn. I just hope I haven't forgotten how to raise a child."

Katy waved her off. "Ah, there ain't nothin' to it, ma'am. Ya just love 'em and squeeze 'em, and give 'em a swat or two on the bum just to let 'em know when they get a bit rowdy. That's what me mam always says. I best get home and tell her the good news. When are we leavin'?"

"First thing in the morning," Regina informed the girl.

Katy's eyes widened. "Boy, Harry is sure gonna have a fit when he hears this." She waved, curtsied, and waved again, not quite certain what to do with herself. Then she giggled and sped out the back of the inn.

Regina looked up as Mr. Quist came through the front door of the tavern, a large man in tow.

"Excuse me, ma'am." Mr. Quist took off his hat and nodded his head.

"Good morning, Mr. Quist. Will we be ready to leave in the morning?" Regina asked her driver.

"Aye, yer ladyship." He twisted the silk hat in his hands. "This here is Mr. Quimby. He's the one that found yer granddaughter."

Regina stood, immediately seizing the large man's hand. She hardly recognized him. His face was all but hidden behind a growth of whiskers, heavy jowls, and a moth-eaten muffler.

"Mr. Quimby, I'm forever in your debt. I hoped we might have a chance to speak before I left."

The man bobbed uncertainly and shuffled his feet,

obviously uncomfortable. "She's a fine little girl, ma'am. I wish the best for her, and you."

"Thank you, Mr. Quimby. I'd like to do something for you in appreciation. Do you have a family here at Land's End?"

"Me?" Quimby's eyes widened in surprise. "Lord, no, ma'am. Beggin' yer pardon." He winced at his lack of manners. "It's not every day we have a fine lady like yerself so far from London."

Regina smiled. "It's quite all right. My late husband, the Earl of Larchmont, used to swear quite a lot." She gestured to his jacket. "That's a fine coat you have, Mr. Quimby." She eyed the shabby and torn fabric. "Perhaps you'd like another. When I return to London, I'll instruct my solicitor to open an account for you. The weather is severe here. Perhaps a new scarf too. She suggested carefully, not wanting to offend the man.

"I don't need such fancy trappings, ma'am. Not such as me." Quimby shuffled his large bulk. "It's enough just knowing the little lady is doin' well."

Mr. Quist intervened. "Quimby here is real handy. We had a loose coupling on the coach when I got back from London, and he fixed 'er right up. Folks say he can do almost anything with his hands."

Cedric coughed loudly to gain Regina's attention.

"Perhaps you should have some of Katy's broth," Regina suggested. "Are you feeling ill?" Then she smiled. "I do quite a bit of traveling back and forth from London to the country. I seem to remember having the coach repaired just last October. Isn't that correct, Mr. Quist?"

"Quite right, ma'am." His eyes lit up.

"Then I think perhaps we should have someone who could take care of it on a regular basis. And, of course, there will be other responsibilities." Regina smiled.

She liked this big gruff man who found words so difficult. When all the others had given up searching for survivors from the *Venturer*, he'd stayed behind and continued. His unselfish gesture had meant the difference between life and death for Elyse.

"I hope you'll consider joining my household staff in London, Mr. Quimby."

The man was completely speechless. What little of his face was visible through beard and muffler quickly turned a bright shade of crimson.

"I'd like that real fine, ma'am, er, ah yer ladyship."

"We'll cover that later," Regina reassured him. Mr. Quist grabbed the big man by the arm, and quickly led him out of the tavern.

"Regina, have you completely taken leave of your senses? You have more than enough staff in London, and at the country house." Cedric gaped at her. "I was about to offer to place Quimby with one of my associates."

"He wouldn't have accepted it," she informed him flatly. "Mr. Quimby may be lacking in a good many things, but he's obviously a man of strong principles. He'd be completely out of place working for one of your friends."

"And he won't be with your staff in London?" Cedric questioned.

"Not at all. For you see, if any of my people say a word against Mr. Quimby, they'll find themselves immediately discharged," Regina announced firmly. Then her voice softened.

"I value a man with a courageous heart more than all the finely spoken words in the world. He risked his life to save my granddaughter. That's all I need to know about him."

"You're a remarkable woman." Cedric enfolded her hand in his.

"No," she answered simply. "It's just that I understand what it is like to live in a place like this. What future would a girl like Katy have here? And Mr. Quimby?

God knows how the man lives. These people gave me back my granddaughter. Now I want to give them something, a chance at life."

Cedric took her hand in his. There was a spark of the Regina he remembered in her eyes. "You're right, of course."

"Thank you," she murmured. Slowly drawing her hand from his, she laid her palm lovingly against his cheek. "Thank you for being my friend."

She turned and climbed the stairs, wanting to be with her granddaughter. She needed family about her to ease the ache of the grieving that had only just begun.

~

Mr. Quist tipped his hat, the sharp wind rustling his thin hair. "We're all ready, your ladyship."

Regina nodded and drew her cloak around her to block the wind.

Their few bags were already loaded in the boot of the coach. The innkeeper had been paid handsomely for his hospitality, farewells had been made, and Mr. Quimby sat atop the coach.

He quickly scrambled down. Cutting off Mr. Quist, he bowed low, sweeping his woolen cap from a balding head in a grand gesture of respect as he moved to open the coach door.

Cedric assisted Regina into the coach, settling himself across from her in the warm protective interior. Katy beamed at her from the corner in which she was carefully cradling Elyse. After the door was firmly latched, the coach dipped slightly under Quimby's weight as he climbed atop. Mr. Quist followed and, seizing the reins, gave a shrill whistle, and snapped leather just over their heads.

Regina pulled the heavy velvet curtain back from the window. Rain had begun to fall. How she hated this place, longed to be away from it. Her pain eased as her gaze went to her granddaughter. There was no doubt in her mind as she looked at the sleeping child. The eyes, the shape of her face, the curve of her mouth were her father's. But her fair skin, finely shaped brows, dark hair, and small, straight nose were definitely Anne's. She was a treasure, a mixture of the parents who'd loved her so.

Glancing out the window at the bleak coastline, Regina tapped on the roof. The coach rolled to a stop.

Cedric watched silently as she gazed out the window at the churning ocean that still raged against the forbidding coastline.

A tear slipped down Regina's cheek. Somewhere out in that vast darkness, two souls she loved had been lost. Somehow, by some miracle or act of God, the tiny child nestled in Katy's arms had escaped.

What had she endured? What fears and pain were locked deep inside her? She seemed to remember nothing of the storm or the loss of her parents. Whatever memories she had were tucked away, perhaps never to emerge.

James' or Anne's name brought no response. She was unafraid, not a hysterical child, but it was as if the life she'd known before the accident was a slate wiped clean. She had no memory of her mother or father.

The child stirred, yawning softly and rubbing her eyes before she sat up. She smiled first at Cedric, who had become an immediate favorite, then at Katy, who tucked a woolen coat about her shoulders.

"Why have we stopped?" Elyse's small mouth curved almost into the shape of a bow. "Is he here?"

It was the same question she'd asked when she'd first regained consciousness. Regina gave Cedric a startled look. She reached out to Elyse, stroking her sable curls.

"You've been dreaming again, sweetheart."

Elyse glanced expectantly to the door, intelligence

burning in her large blue eyes. "He promised he would come back for me. He promised."

Regina gathered her granddaughter against her side, tears filling her eyes. "It's all right sweetheart. He'll come back for you," she said soothingly.

Elyse turned her face up to her grandmother. "But when?"

"Not now, but one day he will come to you," she promised, thinking of James and believing with all her heart that somehow loving bonds did survive death. She smiled lovingly down at Elyse.

"He loved you very much, and he'll find you one day." She kissed the top of her granddaughter's head, more than ever convinced of the power of love. It was indefinable and enduring. Hadn't she found it again in this small, beautiful child?

Cedric tapped a signal to Mr. Quist, and the coach lurched into motion.

One

"And just what do you think you're doin', miss!" Katy's mouth thinned into a disapproving line. The gray silk of her skirts crackled as she ascended the wide curving staircase.

Peeking through two spindles of the curving balustrade, Elyse looked at her, then pulled back into the shadows. Caught!

She could try to reach her room, but what was the use. Katy had already found her out. The maid reached the landing, her cheeks puffing from the exertion of racing up the stairs. It was a full minute before she was able to speak between gasps for air.

"And don't think I'll be acceptin' any of your excuses, sittin' up here like a common servant, actin' like you have no manners or breedin'," she scolded.

Standing her ground or rather sitting on it, Elyse fastened Katy with a beguiling smile that could charm pennies from a pauper. "I wouldn't think of offering any excuse. And it serves you right, being out of breath," she retorted playfully. "You shouldn't run up stairs."

She was repeating a rule she'd heard cited countless times.

Katy's soft brown eyes narrowed as she wagged a

finger at her young mistress. "Yer supposed to be restin' before the party."

"I can't possibly sleep." Elyse sprang to her feet, slipping her arm through the maid's as they turned toward the top of the stairs. "You know how I love Christmas, and Grandmother made me stay up here all afternoon."

Walking with her to the bedchamber, Katy fixed on her a reprimanding look. "It's because you always poke all the packages and shake them. Then you guess what's inside and spoil the surprise." She opened the door to Elyse's chamber, pushing her inside.

"And I'm usually correct." Elyse clasped her hands together as she whirled across the room, her dressing gown softly brushing the floor. The brilliant, peacock blue fabric set her eyes to dancing.

"What do you think Grandmother gave me this year?" Taking Elyse firmly by the shoulders, Katy pushed her gently down onto the seat before the dressing table, and picking up a brush, she waved it menacingly at her mistress. "It would serve you right if she gave you nothing. Sittin' at the top of the stairs like a common street urchin, in nothin' but your dressin' gown. Your behavior is appallin'. What would Master Jerrold say to see you acting like such a hooligan?"

"Indeed." Elyse fixed an innocent smile on her beautifully curved mouth, but the light in her eyes danced. She was anything but contrite. "What would he say?" She burst into laughter.

Katy forced her mouth into a thin line of disapproval. It wouldn't do for her to break out laughing. "Yer too bold fer yer own good. Yer grandmother has spoiled you rotten. Maybe marriage will settle you down." She shook her head, as if she sincerely doubted that possibility.

The pout returned, only to tilt into a breathtaking smile. "I don't see why," Elyse announced brazenly; then she grew more thoughtful.

"Why is it the moment a woman marries she becomes insipid and boring?" It was obviously something she'd given a great deal of thought.

Katy's surprised expression was caught in the mirror. "Now, whatever gave you such an idea? Yer grandmother is not insipid or boring," she directed the admonishment to the reflection of an exquisite beauty in the mirror.

"Grandmother is not married," Elyse hastened to point out. "She's, how do you say... keeping company with Uncle Ceddy."

"Don't be so bold. She and Sir Cedric are old friends. He was a good friend of yer grandfather's as well."

Elyse refused to be distracted from her train of thought. "Why is it that, when a young lady is seen about with a young man, she must have a chaperon? Who's to be grandmother's chaperon?" Mischief danced in her brilliant eyes, daring Katy to come up with an answer for that one.

The maid fumed. "Yer the ornery one today, aren't ya?

"It so happens that a lady of yer grandmother's position and age does not need a chaperone."

"But why?" Elyse persisted, warming to her subject. "After all, she's capable of a physical relationship. Surely such things don't end when you get older."

"Good Lord!" The hairbrush clattered from Katy's hand. "Whatever put such ideas into your head? It's not for you to be wonderin' what older folks are up to! Now, come along." She crossed the room toward the wardrobe. "It's time you dressed for the party. Sir Cedric arrived over an hour ago."

"I know. I waved to him from the stairway." Elyse laughed as she rose from the chair. Hands folded behind her back, rocking on firmly planted feet, she grinned, amusement dancing in her eyes. "I think age has little to do with it. Grandmother and Uncle Ceddy have been on very intimate terms for quite a while. There was one time I almost walked in on them."

"Shame on you!" Katy whirled around. "Sayin' such things and eavesdropping on yer grandmother. You're an ill-mannered chit." She wagged her finger until Elyse was certain it might fall off.

"If her ladyship heard you sayin' such things..."

"God's nightgown, Katy!" Elyse burst out laughing. "Grandmother is the one who told me all about it afterward."

"Good heavens, what is the world comin' to?" Katy collapsed on the dark blue satin coverlet draped across the bed.

Elyse crossed the room and knelt before the stricken maid.

"Grandmother thought I should have one of those conversations that all brides have with their mothers when they become betrothed. One thing led to another, and well I just asked... "

"Asked?" Katy was too horrified to believe it was true.

"Well, you and Grandmother always said the best way to find out something was to come right out say it."

Katy groaned, her eyes rolling heavenward. "You did ask her! Lord have mercy, what will she think of me and what I've been teachin' ya?"

Biting her lip, Elyse practically choked from holding back laughter. "She thinks you're a good influence on me. She said just the other day that you keep me from becoming too serious about myself."

Katy fretted. "She'll ship me back to Land's End, I just know it."

"No, she won't," Elyse assured her as she rose and went to the small writing desk that stood before the window. She opened the center drawer and took out an envelope. "I suppose I should save this until Christmas morning," she said, "and you were perfectly rotten to me on the staircase." Her mouth curved into an enticing smile. "But I never could stand the anticipation of waiting." Crossing back to the bed, she thrust the gold embossed envelope into Katy's hands.

"What is this?" Katy eyed it suspiciously. "Me severance pay?"

"Of course!" Elyse teased. Dropping down onto the thick carpet at the maid's feet, she tucked her dressing gown around her long legs. Despite the grim expression on her face, lights danced in her eyes.

"I persuaded Grandmother to keep you on until after the holiday. I thought it would be cruel to toss you out before Christmas." She watched Katy from the corner of her eye.

"You're an impudent girl. It's a wonder young Lord Barrington offered his proposal." Katy teased her back, completely unruffled.

Elyse rolled her eyes and waved her hand through the air in a gesture of abandon. "How could he refuse? You know how determined Grandmother can be when she wants something."

Katy frowned. "I've changed me mind. Yer not impudent, yer just plain rude. I think that knock on the head when you was a wee thing addled yer common sense. Master Barrington won't be pleased with a sharp-tongued bride!"

Elyse's eyes widened in mock horror. "Undoubtedly. He'll probably lock me away in the country and take a mistress here in London."

The maid discreetly refused to respond to this reference to what had been common knowledge about Jerrold Barrington before his engagement to Elyse. She couldn't meet her young mistress' gaze, having heard from some of the other servants that the situation hadn't changed.

"I believe mistresses are supposed to be quite fashionable. And don't frown at me so," Elyse admonished. "I know of the rumors about Jerrold's activities. There's no need for you to look like a prune-faced old crow?" She fixed Katy with the wide-eyed gaze that more than once had caused the maid to wonder if there wasn't someone much older lurking behind it. "Well, are you going to open it, or must I do it for you?"

Frowning, Katy slipped a finger beneath the wax seal. It was obvious that Elyse was aware of the rumors, so she tried to lighten the mood that had suddenly descended on the room.

"If I'm to be cast off, I might as well start preparin' meself fer it."

She reached out and lovingly pressed a hand against Elyse's cheek. A filmy piece of paper fluttered out of the envelope clutched in her other hand. Katy picked it up and began to read. Then she thrust it into Elyse's hands. "Well, I don't see me final pay. You read it; you know I'm not so good on me letters."

Taking the paper, Elyse rose to her full height. "It's a deed," she announced with great ceremony.

"Deed? To what, in God's name?"

"Katy, darling," Elyse chided teasingly, "you really must try to do something about your language." She then became very serious, her dark sable brows drawing together slightly.

"It's the deed to a house in Cheltingham, not far from here."

Upon seeing Katy's confused expression, she continued. "You see, I have been eavesdropping just a little." She sat down beside the young woman. "I know that practically everything you earn goes to yer family."

Katy nodded. "It's been hard on me mum ever since Pa died. He was a good man, always did his best to provide for all of us. But there was always a new mouth to feed. There were four new babes after I left. Then, after he died... well, mum just couldn't do it alone. The older kids try to help out, but there's just so much they can do."

Elyse squeezed Katy's hands lovingly. "That's why I'm giving you this deed. I know how you miss your mother." She stopped, drawing in a deep breath. "I know how I would feel if my mother were still alive and very far away." Her eyes glistened with sudden emotion. She wiped at them, silently scolding herself. She certainly hadn't intended for this to be a somber occasion.

Katy patted her charge's hand. She still didn't fully understand the meaning of Elyse's gift, "You've been as dear to me as my own since the day Quimby found you in that tide pool. I understand what yer feelin'."

"I know you do, and that's why I want you to have the house."

Elyse wiped a tear from the corner of an eye. Then, laughing at her own foolishness, she rushed on to describe the house. "It's quite large with several rooms, and an ample kitchen with a good stove. I remember you telling me how your mother likes to cook. And Grandmother still raves about her special soup."

"Aye, me mum's always been a good cook." Katy nodded. Then her eyes widened, as the full meaning of the gift finally took hold.

"Good heavens!" She clapped her hands to her cheeks. "You're most serious about this!"

"Perfectly serious," Elyse reassured her. "And there's more than enough room for all the children and any guests." She became very thoughtful. "Of course, you may decide to live with her as well." There was a touch of wistfulness in her voice, but she hid it behind a bright smile. She wanted very much for Katy to be completely happy with the gift. "I know Grandmother would insist that you have the use of the carriage whenever you need it to get back and forth." She folded Katy's hands around the deed, hating the idea of losing a dear friend but understanding Katy's desire to be closer to her family. She'd considered asking her to go to Barrington House with her after she married, but that decision must be Katy's.

"But why...?" Katy stammered. "This is so much. Whatever possessed you?"

"Because you've been a dear and wonderful friend. And I want you to have your family near you. I know what it means to feel alone."

Katy's eyes filled with tears. "Does yer grandmother know about this?" She smoothed the deed with trembling fingers.

Elyse sat down beside her on the bed, wrapping an arm lovingly around her shoulders. "Of course," she admitted smugly. "She helped me find it, and Uncle Ceddy made the necessary arrangements. She's been so excited about the whole thing; I didn't think she'd be able to keep it a secret until Christmas. "I did it because I love you, and you mustn't refuse." She squeezed Katy affectionately, then fixed tearful eyes on her.

Katy nodded, momentarily unable to reply. "Thank you, darlin'." She laid a hand against Elyse's cheek. "Thank you from the bottom of me heart. You're the dearest child. It'll mean so much to me mum. But I won't be leavin' here," she announced, sniffing loudly. "This is my home now, as long as you and your grandmother want me. Besides," she hesitated. "As much as I love me mum, I don't think we could live in the same house together. She still thinks I'm fifteen years old." She dabbed at her eyes with a handkerchief.

"I was hoping you'd say something like that." Elyse rose from the end of the bed. "Then it's settled. After the holiday, I'll help you make the arrangements necessary to move your family. It'll be fun." She whirled across the room, as excited as Katy about the gift. A loud shriek stopped her dead in her tracks.

"What is that?"

Elyse whirled back around, her dressing gown

swirling open below her knees, and her gaze followed Katy's to the muddy toes of the riding boots protruding from beneath her hem. She quickly pulled the gown closed. "Perhaps the latest fashion from Paris?" she suggested weakly, wincing at the ridiculous notion. Just how was she going to get herself out of this one? She'd been so excited about the preparations for the party and about Katy's gift that she'd completely forgotten about the boots until they'd poked incriminatingly from beneath the dressing gown.

"You've been out ridin' again!" Katy exclaimed, her gift now completely forgotten. "And by the looks of them boots, it's been real recent!" She threw her hands up in a gesture of frustration. "What will yer grandmother say?" She inhaled deeply, preparing to deliver a lengthy tirade on proper conduct for young ladies of society.

But Elyse whirled away, cutting her off. Once Katy got started, there'd be no end to it. "Katy darling, do you think the blue gown is right for this evening? Or perhaps the red one?" she questioned innocently, deftly changing the direction of their conversation.

Katy's eyes narrowed. "The red is scandalous." Her mouth snapped shut; she had been outmaneuvered. "No young lady should expose so much of herself in public. You'll fall right out of it. And quit tryin' to change the conversation around!" she scolded, her finger coming back into action. "You don't fool me a bit. I know what yer up to."

"Oh?" Elyse raised her delicate chin a defiant notch as Katy took a deep breath. "I suppose you're right, of course." Devilment sparkled in her eyes. She reached for the blue gown and heard an audible sigh of relief. Her mouth twitched with suppressed merriment as she stuffed the blue back into the wardrobe and seized another gown.

"I'll wear the red," she said. Behind her, the sigh became a startled gasp.

"Oh, no, you won't! You'll wear the blue!" Katy announced flatly, handily retrieving the blue gown. Whirling around from the wardrobe, she stood with feet planted as if ready to do battle, the expression on her face one of utter determination. Nothing less would be needed to see that her mistress wore the blue gown.

"Now, Katy darling..." Elyse cajoled.

"Don't you Katy darling, me. I know what yer up to, and I won't have it! I won't have it!" Katy's eyes narrowed.

Elyse swept down the wide staircase, brilliant in the red silk gown clinging to her slender figure. She stopped, taking a shallow breath and then quickly releasing it.

Katy was right, of course. With every breath she took, she feared her dire predictions would come true, and she would spill out of the low-cut neckline. It was scandalous, and she loved it.

She greeted a distant cousin, and her smile deepened as she caught sight of her grandmother and Sir Cedric. Disengaging herself from her enraptured cousin, she crossed the room.

"You've outdone yourself, Grandmother." Elyse clasped her hands together in delight as her gaze swept the decorated room. "Everything is so beautiful."

Her eyes glowed with excitement. Red and gold candles shimmered in every corner, and the mantel above the fireplace was draped with garlands of waxy green holly dotted with clusters of crimson berries. A fire crackled merrily at the hearth, its golden flames reflecting off polished wood. And the Yule log waited, decorated with ribbons. It had become a tradition for Cedric to place the gigantic log on the fire just before midnight so that it might burn through the night, leaving warm embers for Christmas morning, when he joined them for a large breakfast celebration.

A gleaming brass kettle simmered over the fire, a mixture of pungent spices steaming in the bubbling liquid it held. The concoction filled the room with fragrant scents, and spicy pine boughs hung at every window sash, bordered every table. But by far the most spectacular sight was the huge evergreen tree in the center of the drawing room that opened off the parlor. With almost childish delight, Elyse approached for closer inspection. Her eyes glistened as she gazed up at the huge tree.

Years before, Uncle Ceddy had explained the Christmas custom of the German people. Each Christmas at Yuletide, they cut pine trees in the forest and brought them into their homes to be decorated. Candles were carefully placed on the tips of branches decorated with bows, strings of colorful beads, and hand-painted toys. Enraptured by the story, Elyse had pleaded with her grandmother that they have just such a tree for their next Christmas.

Now she inspected every decoration. She'd made most of them herself as a child. Hand-stitched dolls and toy soldiers clung to the branches along with the hand-carved wooden animals Quimby had made for her one year. They competed for space with fresh apples and oranges, while white candles in small gold holders winked from the ends of the branches. Atop the tree was a shining gold star. And below, peeking from beneath the lowest boughs, were colorfully wrapped packages.

"They're not all for you, my dear." Lady Regina smiled lovingly. "How would it look if I spoiled you, by giving you everything?"

As he silently watched their exchange, Sir Cedric coughed behind his hand. "I'm afraid you don't have to be concerned with that, my dear," he said to Lady

Regina. "You've already done it." Humor danced in his eyes as he pressed a kiss against Elyse's cheek.

"You look ravishing. I propose a toast." He took three goblets of champagne from a nearby tray and raised his ceremoniously. "To the two most beautiful women in all London. One I consider as dear as my own daughter," he said, his eyes twinkling beneath the sweep of frosty white brows. "The other," he hesitated, a devilish gleam sparkling in his eyes. "I should like to call my bride," he announced softly, his gaze fastened on Regina.

"Bride! Good heavens, Ceddy, have you taken leave of your senses?" Regina pressed her hand against her heart as the champagne threatened to go down the wrong way. Several of her guests glanced in their direction.

"Not at all!' Sir Cedric smiled back at her, knowing the advantage was all his. "I've asked you several times, and I've decided it's now or never.

"Is that so?" Lady Regina recovered quickly. "You know very well I don't like ultimatums," she responded.

Elyse headed off the impending confrontation. Both Ceddy and her grandmother could be unreasonably stubborn.

"I think it's a grand idea," she announced. She'd like nothing better than to see the two dearest people in her life together. "It's about time you made an honest woman of her." She smiled as she sipped from her glass.

"I can see whose side you're on, my dear!" Regina replied. "I think this is hardly the time or place to be discussing such matters. And I'll tell you both right now, I won't be manipulated into a decision."

Cedric ignored her last remark. "It's precisely the time and place." He reached for a nearby bottle of champagne and refilled their glasses.

But Regina begged off. "Please, you know how it

affects me. I can't have you talking me into something when I've had too much champagne."

Filling her glass with bubbling liquid, he would have none of that. "I want it to affect you, my dear. And I think there's no better time to discuss this. After all, Elyse is to be married in June. Then what will you do with yourself?"

"I hadn't thought about it. There's been so much to do lately. And there are still plans to be made..."

"I'm afraid that won't do, Reggie," he informed her matter-of-factly. "You see, it's not a matter of my making you an honest woman, but of your making me an honest man. My dear, you've absolutely ruined my reputation, keeping company with me as you have the last several years."

He shook his head as Regina's mouth dropped open at his outrageous announcement. He pressed his argument.

"Therefore, I insist that you accept this now." He slipped his hand into the pocket of his waistcoat, producing a small box.

Elyse watched in delight as he opened it, revealing the ring inside. A large gleaming emerald was set amidst smaller diamonds.

"I can't think of anything I would like more than for you two to be married," Elyse replied as her grandmother wavered. Then with sudden inspiration, she added, "We could make it a double wedding! Wouldn't that set London on its ear." She whirled around. "I must find Katy and tell her." She was off in a swirl of red silk.

"Elyse, wait!" Lady Regina called helplessly after her granddaughter. Then she turned on Cedric, her eyes, so like Elyse's, narrowing. "You did that deliberately. Now everyone will know about it," she accused.

"That's what I'm counting on, my dear. It's a sorry situation when a man is forced to beg a woman into

marrying him." He smiled in spite of himself, quite satisfied. "But there you are. Now you dare not refuse."

Lady Regina fought back a smile, her eyes sparkling.
"I should be angry with you."

He wasn't fooled. "You should, but you won't. Because, my dear, " he took her arm, pulling it through his
as he lifted his glass in a toast to her. "You know as well
as I that it's time to get on with our lives."

Regina smiled softly. "You're right, of course. And I
do love you, Ceddy."

Her gaze wandered across the parlor to where Elyse
was laughing at something someone said. Her granddaughter was beautiful, and Regina so wanted her to be
happy. Her expression became pensive.

"I had hoped Jerrold would be here by now." She
frowned, wondering what diversion kept Elyse's fiancé
from her side at this time. "There are times when I
wonder if I'm doing the right thing in allowing her to
marry him," she mused aloud.

"Allowing her?" Sir Cedric almost burst out laughing. "My dear, I've never seen a campaign to match yours
in arranging this marriage. I thought it was what you
wanted."

"I only want for Elyse to be happy." Regina watched
her granddaughter thoughtfully.

"She seems happy enough." Cedric's gaze followed
hers.

"Yes, so it seems," she replied hesitantly. "I just wish I
could be certain. I wish she were more concerned about
Jerrold's absences. It's as if... " the rest went unspoken.

"She wouldn't have accepted his offer if she wasn't
certain. Elyse is a strong-minded girl. I can't imagine
anyone forcing her to do anything. She reminds me of
someone else I know."

Regina smiled at his last remark, but she was still
troubled. "I lay awake nights wondering if she's doing
this for me. Jerrold's mother was a dear friend of mine,

but that's not a reason to agree to this. She's been through so much with the death of her parents..." she said, thinking of that tragic day years before. "I just want her to be happy.

"There are times when I look at her, or hear something in her voice when she speaks of Jerrold or the wedding," she continued. "Almost as if she's resigned herself to it. That's not how a bride should feel."

"I would hardly call her resigned. Look at the girl, she is positively radiant."

Regina nodded, unconvinced. "Yes, she does seem happy, but still... " Regina knew that the dreams still woke her at night.

"She's taken to riding early in the morning and refuses to take anyone with her. I'm at a loss to understand this restlessness in her. And, every once in a while, I find her looking out the window, as if she is watching for something..." Or someone? she thought to herself.

"Have you tried talking to her about it? I can't see Barrington tolerating that sort of thing."

"Yes, but she insists that if she can ride in the country, she can ride when we're here in London. I've had Quimby follow her at a discreet distance. I'm not certain if she knows it."

"Then what have you to worry about? She's safe enough with Quimby about." Cedric tried to ease her concerns.

"You're right of course," she admitted. "Still..."

"Are you worried about how it looks for the future Lady Barrington to be out alone about London?" he teased, knowing full well Regina had never given a fig about what other people thought. It was one of the things he loved about her.

Since Elyse had come to live with her, she had made an effort to observe certain rules of propriety, determined that her American-born granddaughter would take her rightful place in society.

"I want the very best for Elyse. Look at her." Lady Regina's eyes glowed with pride and love. "She is lovely, isn't she?"

"Almost as lovely as her grandmother."

She squeezed his hand affectionately, but her worried expression remained. "Perhaps after the holidays, she'll take more interest in the wedding."

"Speaking of weddings," he hinted. "I should like you to consider ours. Don't worry about Elyse. Jerrold will make her a good husband." Any doubts he had, he kept to himself. He was not family, yet. "After all, Lord Barrington wants this marriage almost as badly as you do."

Lady Regina smiled as she looked down at the ring he'd given her. She prayed Ceddy was right. Jerrold did seem to care for her granddaughter, and it did seem that lately he was curtailing some of his more indiscreet activities. In his circle, membership at White's, one of London's more elite men's clubs, was expected, as was occasional gaming or betting on horses at the private jockey club.

That didn't bother her. What did bother her were the rumors of various liaisons since the betrothal was announced. It might have been old-fashioned, but she had hoped that Jerrold's affection for her granddaughter might curtail such activities. Ceddy tried to assure her that these were most likely nothing more than a man's dalliances before settling into marriage and family.

"Have you given Elyse the gift we spoke of?" he asked.

"Not yet. I do hope she'll like it," Regina replied. She had kept it for her granddaughter. Now, with the wedding only months away, it seemed like an appropriate time to give it to her.

They crossed the formal parlor together. Elyse looked up and smiled.

"I have been keeping this for you," Regina said,

handing her the small, wrapped package. She laid a hand against her granddaughter's cheek. "It's very precious to me, as you are."

"Shouldn't we wait until Christmas morning?" Elyse asked.

"I've waited long enough for you to have it. Go ahead, open it," Regina smiled.

Elyse removed the gold paper to reveal a small box much like the one Ceddy had given her grandmother. She opened it, her eyes widening at the sight of the pendant on the gold chain.

She'd seen the pendant once as a child. She had come upon her grandmother in her room and found her staring at it. There had been something in her eyes and on her face, a sadness she hadn't understood. She had quietly left without saying anything. Now, she stared down at the piece of jewelry that she knew meant a great deal to her grandmother.

"It's beautiful," she said.

The design was old-fashioned with twelve small blue diamonds encircling a large pearl at the center. It was attached to a gold chain. Elyse looked at her grandmother.

"I saw this once, a long time ago, and then you put it away," she told her. "I know how much it means to you. Why are you giving it to me?"

"You're right," her grandmother admitted. "It does mean a great deal to me. It was a gift from a very dear friend of mine, Jerrold's mother."

Surprise filled Elyse's eyes. "Felicia Barrington?"

She knew her grandmother had been acquainted with Jerrold's mother, but she hadn't known the pendant had once belonged to Felicia.

"She was very much like a daughter to me. I admired the pendant once. Then, after she became ill, she had it sent to me, insisting that I accept it. Within a matter of weeks... " she hesitated and then seemed to shake off the sad memory. "She was gone very quickly."

"I added the chain with the thought that you should have it one day," she continued. "And now that you will be marrying Jerrold, it seems appropriate for you to have it."

She watched Elyse, seeing something in her that for a moment reminded her of her dear friend, and she experienced the same feeling that had come over her when she'd watched her earlier as she came down the stairs. She had been convinced that, if she closed her eyes and opened them, she would find Felicia standing on the stairs. But, of course, that was impossible. Elyse bore no physical resemblance to her friend. Still, there were times in the past when there was something in her eyes, and expression, and she had the strangest feeling...

Get a hold of yourself, Regina silently scolded herself. It means nothing. You're just a sentimental old woman.

Perhaps she should accept Ceddy's offer. It was time to get on with life and the time they had left.

Now, as she looked at her granddaughter, she tried to shake off the feeling once more. And yet, as she watched Elyse's reaction to the pendant, she felt as if she were seeing someone else. Then it was gone.

Elyse caressed the large pearl—she couldn't refuse something that meant so much to her grandmother—and thanked her.

"We should rejoin our guests," Cedric reminded them. "Others have arrived, and Mrs. Halverson is insisting we sit down to supper. I would not want to anger the woman."

"Has Jerrold arrived?" Regina asked. The invitations had been sent weeks earlier. Surely he wouldn't miss Christmas Eve supper, she thought.

"I'm certain he'll be along," Cedric assured her, having also wondered what was keeping the man.

"Come along then," he told them, taking her arm and then Elyse's to escort them into the formal dining room. "By all means, let's join your guests."

~

It had been a long time since she had the dream, or, if it was there, she didn't remember it afterward.

It was the same when it came, filled with shadows and terrifying sounds—a ship with broken masts, the wind lashing the decks. Lightening slashed the sky as the ship was battered against the rocks. But it wasn't the child that looked back at her, terrified.

It was like looking into a mirror, as the rain lashed at her, the water pulling her under... and the man who reached out to her.

"Take my hand!"

Two

Eyes filled with pain and loss searched the land as evening stole across the fertile valley, the last light of day glistening off the silvered ribbon of the river. Faint tendrils of mist shrouded the trees, making them seem like mournful women, draped in widow's weeds. The wisps clung to the earth, stealing through gullies and hollows, guarding secrets, whispering to him with a soft rustling of leaves, the message unintelligible. Beneath his feet, the ground cooled as night slipped over all.

The scorching sun was gone now, hiding deceptively. Only in those last few moments of daylight, when the night air crept on cat feet and faint breezes stirred, did the land seem less harsh, almost peaceful. In moments like these, he could almost hear the voices.

The Aboriginals said they were the voices of their ancestors, speaking to them through the darkness of Dreamtime. For the natives, *nanga mai,* to dream, was the basis of all thought and practice. It was their cultural, historical, and ancestral heritage. It was an age that existed long ago and yet remained ever present as a continuing, timeless experience linking past, present, and future.

For them it was the dawn of all creation, when land,

rivers, rain, wind, and all living things first began. Born and raised in this land, he accepted their beliefs, and now hoped they were true. He needed to believe that something from this life continued beyond the grave.

Shadows moved across his chiseled features as his strong brows drew together over his silver eyes that appeared almost catlike above the planes of his pronounced cheekbones. His straight nose hinted of aristocratic ancestry, his mouth was thinned, uncharacteristically, into a tight line. A muscle flexed at his stubborn jaw line.

"I should have been here for her." Zachary Tennant flattened his hand on the freshly turned earth, regret sharp in his voice. He smoothed the mound, as if he might still reach out to the woman buried there. Then his fingers closed, gathering the dry loam, trying to hold back death a little longer. Haunted eyes squeezed back tears. He wouldn't cry. Damn! She wouldn't want him to.

"Don't be so hard on yourself, lad." The voice came from the shadows beneath the gum tree. "She understood that you couldn't be here. The fight against the Crown means survival for Resolute, for all of us. You were needed elsewhere. She accepted that, just as she accepted this land."

"So far from her beloved Ireland," Zach lamented. "And she loved this land so much," he whispered brokenly.

"Aye, that she did, as your father loved it." The owner of the disembodied voice separated himself from the shadows, and Tobias Gentry, physician, stepped forward to bid silent farewell to a woman he'd respected and admired, and loved in his own way.

"Why, Tobias?" Zach fought the emotions that churned inside him. "How could she love a land that took so much from her?" He stared out at the vast expanse that stretched away from the river, looked to the large white house framed in the growing twilight, as if he might find the answers there.

Resolute. It was a word that defined the land and the people.

Tobias straightened against the infirmity in his back. He grunted.

"It didn't matter that the land wasn't her native Ireland. She loved your father, Zach, and everything that was him, including this land. She put her roots down deep, boy, and raised you here." Tobias laid a hand on the younger man's shoulder.

"Mourn her loss, boy, but don't mourn her love of Resolute. She pledged herself to this land just as she pledged herself to your father. It isn't likely she had any regrets." He fell silent, remembering the fair-haired young lass who'd come to Sydney so long ago.

They'd all begun in Sydney—he, Megan, and Zach's father, Nicholas. Had it really been so many years? He rubbed his hand thoughtfully across his chin, grizzled with silvery whiskers. Time had a way of slipping away from you. He watched the boy, then smiled gently. Zachary Tennant was no longer a boy. He had to remind himself, more often than not, that he was twenty-seven now, a man full grown, very near the same age his father was when he'd arrived from England in the early years.

Zach swallowed, emotion thick in his throat. As earth fell from his fingers, his gaze returned to the valley. Herds of sheep swelled across the landscape, their bodies lean from clipping and recent lambing. He loved this land; loved its harshness, the unrelenting beauty and starkness of it. He knew Tobias was right. He could almost hear Megan's reproval of his anger. She'd loved Resolute almost as much as she'd loved his father.

Zach stood, eyes closed as he breathed in the pungent camphor of trees damp with early evening dew. This land was home, his parents were buried here in the wild place they loved. He understood the sadness of that and accepted it. But the restlessness he'd felt since Megan's death was less easily understood. Some vague thought, half-formed, nagged at him. He should have come back when he'd first learned she was gone. But Tobias was right, it would have served no purpose. Not then.

She'd always been Megan to him, never Mother or Ma. Just Megan. Perhaps it was because she had to be both mother and father to him. She and Tobias and Resolute had formed the core of his life. And then, when she'd needed him, the one time he should have been there, England had denied them that, just as it had denied them so many freedoms.

Tobias waited silently. There was a time to mourn and a time to heal, a time to all seasons according to the Bible. He knew he must give Zach his time. And then he must fulfill an old promise. He shifted, feeling all of his sixty years as he watched the man beside the three graves, one new, the other two different in size and one of those marking the death of a small child, Megan's firstborn. Tobias sighed heavily.

Had Nicholas really been gone so long? Yes, yes of course, he thought. He'd been gone since just before Zach was born. The lad had never known his father, except through Megan's memories and stories. But then, Megan hadn't known everything.

He looked up as Zach walked toward him, brimmed hat in hand, the early evening breeze gently lifting golden hair so like his mother's.

"Come on, Tobias. Megan wouldn't want us wasting time. Minnie should have supper waiting, and I want to meet with Jingo first thing in the morning. There are stray lambs to be brought in." He wrapped an arm around the older man's shoulders. The bond between them was deep. Tobias had been like the father he never had, making his home here at Resolute. They'd made an odd family; a widowed woman with a son to raise, an assortment of itinerant workers, and Tobias.

"Aye, lad." The older man nodded brusquely. "Yer mother never did hold with grievin' for long. She used to say the land couldn't wait for such things. It just goes on bein' what it is. She got that from yer father."

Together, they walked from the small hill above the house, the wild grass damp and pungent beneath their boots.

Inside the dwelling, the smells of the evening meal bolstered them, reminding both men that, like the land, appetites didn't understand the need to mourn. A robust woman emerged from the kitchen, steely hair pulled sharply back from her face into a neat bun. A ladle was clenched in the hand she propped against an ample hip. Clad in men's work pants and clean white shirt, Minnie scrutinized both men.

"Dinner's gettin' cold," she announced. But her soft brown gaze lingered on Zach. "You all right?"

Minerva Halstead had been at Resolute since Zach was a small boy. Almost as wide as she was tall, she was chief cook and housekeeper. The two women in the house had been an odd pair, Minnie's robust girth overshadowing his mother's slender height.

She'd arrived at Resolute over twenty years ago, a child tucked under each arm and no husband. She'd informed everyone she was a widow, although no one had ever bothered to verify that fact. She just arrived, went to work, and never went back *to* wherever it was she came from. It had been Megan's policy never to ask about a person's past. She'd always said nothing mattered but today and what tomorrow could bring.

Zach nodded, his smile not quite reaching his eyes, eyes different from Megan's soft blue ones. "Yeah, I'm all right. She wouldn't want me wastin' time."

"Right ya are. I never knew a woman like yer ma for work. Yer the same way?" Minnie nodded. Suddenly, thoughtful, she stared down at her boots. "I suppose you won't be stayin' long this time."

"We've got wool for the ships in Sydney harbor. The Queen's Navy will be startin' their regular patrols, so I want to get two more ships out, and a very special cargo." Zach nodded. "I think Resolute is in safe hands for a little while."

"Megan wouldn't want you riskin' yer neck like the last time," she reprimanded with motherly affection. "Besides, my Tess is comin 'up from Adelaide." Her eyes sparkled with old mischief.

"She's turned into a right proper young lady in spite of herself."

Zachary laughed. "Still the matchmaker, Minnie?"

"My Tess would make you a fine wife. She's got a temperament to match yours, and it's about time you thought about settling down. It just ain't right for a handsome man like you to be shying away from the ladies," she scolded.

Zach watched her with amused eyes. It was a frequent topic of discussion, and she was right. He and Tess were of the same temperament. That was precisely why he was convinced life with someone as volatile as Tess would be pure hell.

As long as he could remember, Minnie had been scheming to get them together. He tried imagining the high-spirited Tess complete with proper manners. The last time he'd seen her, she'd had her skirts hiked practically over her head, and was astride a nervous brush pony that threatened to unseat her at any moment. He'd ordered her off the beast for the animal's sake.

Tess had a wildness about her he found difficult to believe anyone could tame. He remembered how she'd followed him into the barn that sultry hot afternoon. There in the cool shade she'd stripped down to bare skin without so much as a flush appearing on her adolescent body. Raising her dampened, long blond hair off her sweat-beaded back, she'd calmly proclaimed she was hot all over. It was almost more than any man could be expected to endure. Yet Zach had endured it and politely refused, heaving her into a stall and covering her light body with scratchy hay. He could still hear the obscenities that had followed him all the way to the main house. Two days later, Minerva had bundled Tess off to a distant cousin in Adelaide and what she'd hoped was a proper education. With a faint twist of a smile, Zach wondered just who had been the instructor and who the pupil. It might be interesting to see what changes Tess had gone through, but more urgent matters demanded his return to Sydney.

The local parliament was allowing itself to be dictated to by the home government in London, on matters including the raising of impossible tariffs on all imported goods. As for exports, such as valuable cargoes of high-quality wool, Mother England was rapidly taking the final steps toward monopolizing all shipping, the Barrington Shipping Company out of London being their approved carrier. All independent shipping lines were forbidden to carry any cargo for export to Europe. Slowly, but surely, the Crown was imposing an economic stranglehold on the colonies in Australia, and vast profits were making their way into the pockets of the powdered and pompous overlords in London.

Zach and others he knew felt it was time to loosen that stranglehold. Some would call what they did in secret off the coast of Australia acts of piracy against the Crown. But loyal colonists considered it a bid for independence every time a ship of the Barrington line was attacked and sent to the bottom of the ocean along with its cargo.

It would mean his life and those of every one of his crew if they were ever caught, or their identities discovered. They'd accepted that from the very beginning, and they carried that with them each time they sailed against an English ship. But their attacks had worked.

In the past two years, they'd sent an impressive amount of shipping to the bottom of the sea. And they'd gotten the attention of the Crown. The penalties were high. Every man who sailed with Zach had a price on his head. But Zach was undeterred. He'd strike and strike again, until the mighty English lion was ready to listen to the colonists' demands. Until that day came...

"Sorry, luv."

Zach smiled at Minnie.

"So, what are you waitin' for? My Tess is as close as you'll find to perfection."

"Maybe I'm not looking for perfection," he argued playfully, and leaned around the large woman for a better glimpse of supper.

She slapped, at his shoulder. "You'll not set foot in my kitchen smelling like range critters." Her eyes sharpened, just what are you lookin' for in a woman? Those fancy sportin' women in Sydney aren't for you. Yer mother would turn over in her grave if you tried to bring a woman like that onto Resolute."

Zach almost burst out laughing. "Sporting women are for sporting, not marrying." His stomach grumbled at the delay of supper. He laid hands on her ample shoulders.

"I'm waiting for the one woman meant to share my life." He pressed a finger against her mouth as she started to question just who that might be.

"I don't know who she is. I haven't met her yet." A smile teased at one corner of his mouth. "But I'll know her when I meet her."

"Well, it can't be for not lookin' that you haven't found her yet," she admonished. "Every woman in Sydney under the age of sixty and old enough to say yes is after you."

He winked at her. "One of these days, I'll return to

Resolute with my bride flung over my shoulder and surprise everyone."

"Quit eyein' them biscuits. They're for supper." She motioned to Tobias. "Go on and get washed up."

Zach nodded, then gave her an affectionate peck on the cheek. "Besides, you've always been my favorite girl," he teased.

"Go on with you." She swiped at him with the ladle. "Don't you go bein' cheeky with me," she grumbled.

"Damned bossy woman!" Tobias muttered as he followed Zach to the closed-in porch off the kitchen, where a pump gleamed over a metal sink. "You'd think she owns the place."

"At times, I do," Zach admitted. "I don't know what we'd do without her."

Tobias rolled his sleeves. "Just don't go tellin' her that. She's impossible to live with as it is." He thoughtfully scrubbed his hands and arms; a habit he'd acquired when he'd been a physician, though many doctors had ridiculed the practice.

"There's something I need to talk with you about, but it'll keep till after supper." He cast a thoughtful glance at Zach as he reached for a nearby towel. "There's several things need to be discussed now that Megan..."His voice trailed off. "I'll meet you in the dining room. I need something from upstairs." He turned down the hallway and made his way to the stairs that led to the second-floor rooms.

Zach cut through a tender lamb chop, hardly tasting it as he popped it into his mouth. But he smiled his compliments to Minnie anyway. Then he drained the coffee from his cup and thoughtfully contemplated Tobias who was entering the room.

His old friend hesitated as if considering something of importance. Then, apparently having made a decision, he crossed the dining room, dropped into one of the straight-backed chairs, and set a small traveling case on the table.

Zach motioned to the satchel that looked much like a medical bag. "You thinking of starting' up your medical practice again?" he teased gently. Over the years, Tobias had provided medical care for the workmen at Resolute and other families across the valley. The library was filled with medical texts, most of them brought with him from England years ago. Occasionally he ordered a new book from Sydney, but it took months to reach New South Wales from Europe. In all those years, he'd never chosen to set up practice in the bustling port town. It was another of those unexplained secrets from the past. Just as Zach had learned never to question Minnie's past, he'd never questioned Tobias about his. Someone's past was no one else's business.

Tobias gave him a thoughtful look, then shoved the bag across the table.

Zach waved him off, thinking he meant to teach him some new medical technique. "I don't have time. Those lambs need to be brought into the feeding pens or we'll lose them. And there's wool to be loaded on the flatboats down at the river. The warehouse in Sydney is empty, and I want to get those ships out before Barrington Shipping and the Crown see fit to close us down." There was contempt in his voice.

Tobias patted the trunk solemnly, then took a cup of strong coffee from Minnie. "This won't wait, Zach. I promised to give you this once Megan was gone." His saddened eyes shifted down to the table.

Zach pushed his plate back. Toying with his coffee cup, he glanced across at the small satchel. "Promised who?"

Tobias' gaze met his. "I promised your father, before you were born. I've kept this all these years. Megan never knew about the trunk."

Zach's gaze fastened on the scarred leather case. The

aching emptiness he'd felt earlier, returned. They were both gone now Megan and the father he'd never known. Nicholas Tennant had died before he was born, but Zach knew him as if they'd shared a life together. Tobias and Megan had seen to that, by telling him stories of the early days at Resolute, when his father had brought his new bride to the sheep station from Sydney.

The old man nodded. "Nicholas kept a journal, beginning on the day he left London. I imagine it's inside. There's a great deal you never knew about your father, a great deal none of us ever knew, not even Megan. That's the way it was in the early days. No one asked questions and no one volunteered information."

It was impossible for Zach to tear his eyes away from the satchel with initials etched in the cracked leather. It was old and scarred, its corners worn away. It had endured much handling.

"Minerva! Where is that woman when you need her?" Tobias bellowed.

"Right here, you old fool. Calm down; you'll get apoplexy." Without being told, she retrieved a bottle of whiskey from the kitchen cabinet. It was kept there for medicinal purposes on orders from Dr. Tobias Gentry. She poured a healthy draught.

Tobias looked up at Zach. "Megan and I told you about the years after he came to Resolute. But I first met Nicholas Tennant in Sydney. He never spoke about the past, felt it was best forgotten. Then those last months before he was killed, he seemed to change his mind, especially after he knew Megan was carryin' you.

"He hoped for a son," he continued. "I know he'd be real proud of you. He told me about the journal. He said if anything ever happened, I was to make sure you got it after yer mother was gone. He felt you'd have a need someday to know about all the years before he came here." Tobias took a liberal swallow of the *medicinal* coffee. Reaching out, he thumped the trunk.

"It's all in there; everything about when he was a young man. You read it."

"Megan told me everything." Zach's gaze impaled the case as if he might see the contents without opening it. A shiver throbbed along his nerve endings, almost as if he were reluctant to know what might be inside.

The old man rose from his chair, setting the drained cup down hard on the table. "She told you what she knew, what she'd been told by your father, what life was like after she came to Resolute. But it wasn't everything." Tobias slowly came back to the table. Leaning across it, he braced his weight on his knuckles.

"There's a great deal you don't know about Nicholas Tennant because he never told anyone else. I only knew bits and pieces, as much as he wanted me to know, and I never questioned him. We all had our secrets in those days." He ran a hand over the trunk, regret lining his face; regret for the old wounds he feared the truth might bring.

"When you've finished, I'll be down at the barn. That mare's gonna foal anytime. Horses or babies, it doesn't make much difference." Grabbing his hat, Tobias shoved it down hard on his head. But he stopped at the door to the dining room and held out his hand. Frowning her disapproval, Minnie nonetheless held her tongue and handed him the whiskey bottle.

Zach stared at the satchel. After draining his coffee, he reached for it and twisted the latch. It opened freely.

The dusty journal lay on top, its leather binding cracked and worn, the pages slightly faded. Zach read the opening entry:

London, England June 7, 1839

I begin this journey into hell. One day I will return and have my day of justice for the crime of which I am accused.

I will reclaim my birthright from those who have accused me. And, God willing, Felicia will be waiting for me. I shall now be called Nicholas Tennant.

Zach stared hard at the neatly scrawled words of a man taking on a new identity. Turning the pages, he slowly began reading about the man he'd never known, his father, Nicholas Tennant. The words pulled at him, drawing him back to another time and place. Her name appeared again—Felicia. The night breeze stirred the drapes at the windows. Already, mist slipped heavily across the land, bathing it in unnatural light. Felicia. Her name was like a whisper across his soul.

He looked up. The soft glow of the lamp was creating golden pools in the room. His eyes ached from reading. The opening passages began with the voyage from England, and a detailed description of the squalid conditions aboard ship. Again, that name appeared, almost like a litany spoken to ward off the suffering and longing of the young man who'd made the entries so long ago. As he read, Zach's fascination grew. Who was Felicia? And what was the crime his father had been accused of? Before, he'd believed his father was a settler who'd arrived like so many in the early years of the colonies. But the entries he read were hardly the words of a man at peace with his life or the land where he'd been thrust. Anger and the desire for revenge leaped at him from the pages.

Zach sat back in his chair, the chair his father had once used.

The name haunted him. Felicia. Who was she? Zach slammed the journal shut, not yet fully read. He reached for a thick bundle of neatly folded papers at the bottom of the satchel. They were official government documents.

One was an unconditional grant of land. Zach set it

aside, knowing it was the deed to the land at Resolute. Scanning the other documents, he found one that was torn into several pieces.

His eyes narrowed as he tried to decipher the elaborately scrawled words on one piece. Then, as he held several pieces together, hard lines formed between his brows. The words *Form of Conditional Pardon* leaped off the paper at him.

The kitchen door slammed behind him as he stormed across the yard, mist swirling in his wake. Not finding Tobias in the barn, he rounded the paddock, throwing the door to the small office back hard on its hinges. Eyes blazing, he heaved the journal down on the desk. It hit the hard surface with a damning thud.

"My father was a convict!"

Tobias winced, the whiskey having failed to completely dull his senses. The accusation echoed in the small office, bringing back a flood of memories filled with secrets. He pushed himself back in the hard chair, squinting to focus his weary eyes. He sighed heavily.

"Megan's mare threw a fine colt," he replied dully. "That line will produce some good horses."

Zach descended on the desk and the man behind it. Hands twisting the front of Tobias' shirt, he hauled him upright. "It's true, isn't it!"

"Aye, it's true," the old man acknowledged, pulling himself free. "As were a lot of us sent to serve out our sentences."

The full impact of his response slowly registered with Zach. He let Tobias fall back into the chair. "You were a convict?"

Tobias nodded as he slumped wearily, shoulders sagging. "Aye," he admitted gruffly, his gaze dropping to Zach's clenched fists. "Those were hard times, harsh penalties."

"Why? In God's name, what was your crime?"

Tobias rubbed his bloodshot eyes. "My crime?" he

repeated thoughtfully. And then he laughed cynically. "My crime was my profession." He waved the next question aside.

"I was trained to be a physician at the Royal Academy of Medicine, a most prestigious school." With an almost conspiratorial air, he leaned forward in his chair.

"You see, one must have connections even to be admitted to the school." Laughing to himself at some private joke, he leaned his head into his hands. "My father wanted me to be a country gentleman, marry well. I had delusions of a profession, to the great horror of my aristocratic family." There was a note of derision to the last words. "But they finally relented. After all, I was not the firstborn son, merely the second. I was allowed to enroll at the Academy, where I quickly earned my degree. A most promising career loomed ahead of me.

"That is," he paused, "until the day I accepted a very prominent and influential gentleman and his family as my patients." Tobias shifted, uncomfortable with the memory as he continued.

"The son was taken ill with a severe fever. The family delayed in contacting me, refusing to accept the seriousness of the boy's illness. When I was finally summoned, he was already very weak. He died two days later. Suffice it to say, the family was deeply grieved at the loss of their only son and heir. As a result, I was brought up on charges before the local magistrate. Because of the man's position in the House of Lords, I was tried and convicted of contributing to the boy's death. A brilliant career was shattered, a family ruined." With an absent wave of a hand, he continued, only the faintest trembling of his fingers giving any indication of the emotions that still held him prisoner.

"Because of my family's position, my sentence was reduced from hanging to a seven-year term at the penal colony at New South Wales, and permanent exile from

England. I arrived in Sydney in the spring of 1817 to begin my sentence. I met your father there. We were men of a similar past. He told me only that he'd been wrongly accused of a crime. I never questioned him about it, and he never chose to speak of it again." Tobias opened a drawer to rummage for another bottle of whiskey.

"You're drunk," Zach accused, wondering how much he should believe.

"And I plan on getting a lot more so before the night is over," Tobias announced, finding the bottle and turning it over appreciatively in his unsteady hands. "As a physician of dubious reputation, I'm certain of one thing," he said, squinting an eye. "This is the only thing that dulls the pain."

Zach grabbed the bottle and heaved it against the far wall. "No you don't!" He pulled Tobias out of the chair, dragging him across the office and out into the open yard. Hauling him to a stop in front of a large wooden trough, he shook the old man until his head wobbled back and forth on his shoulders.

"I want some answers and I want you sober enough to give them!" he spat out the words with choking fury. Ignoring Tobias' feeble protests, he plunged him head-first into the cool water, holding him under until bubbles frantically broke the surface.

Tobias' arms flailed wildly as he tried to free himself. Finally, Zach jerked him up, coughing and spewing, allowing him only enough time to inhale a small amount of air before plunging him back in again. He dunked the old man three more times, until his arms hung limply at his sides. Relenting then, Zach jerked him out for the last time and dropped him into the dust at his feet.

Gasping for air, Tobias clutched at his throat. "You tried to drown me!" he rasped between gulps for air. His reddened nose held the only distinguishable color in his face. The rest of his skin was a sickly, pasty green. Finally, drawing a deep breath, he fell silent. Then his eyes widened. Scrambling to his knees, he crawled as fast as he could across the yard and rounded the corner of the horse barn.

Zach listened in disgust as Tobias was sick again and again behind the shelter of the barn. When he heard nothing but silence for a couple of minutes, he started around the barn, suddenly afraid he might have been too hard on the old man. Rounding the corner, he was stopped by a well-laid punch that caught him in the midsection.

The air slammed out of Zach's lungs in a whoosh. Surprise quickly turning to anger, he staggered backward into the dirt.

"What the bloody hell...!" His gray eyes turned the color of slate.

Tobias stood over him, legs spread, chest puffed up like a rooster. His clothes were soaked, his hair rumpled, but he'd obviously fully recovered from the unexpected bath Zach had given him.

"Just remember, boy," he roared, his head beginning to clear, "I can still take you any day of the week!"

"Is that right?" Zach propelled himself up out of the dirt. "Right!" The older man stood his ground as they came nose to nose, or rather nose to chest; he refused to be intimidated by Zach's height. "I seem to recall takin' yer father down a peg or two in me youth. I'm not too old that I can't put you in yer place as well," he shouted.

Zach reconsidered, knowing he could beat Tobias in a fair fight. But what would it prove? That he was stronger and younger? He shook his head. "Not today, old man. I want you in one piece to answer some questions." He turned away, unaware that Tobias' shoulders sagged in relief.

Tobias followed Zach back to the barn, keeping a cautious distance between them. They collapsed into chairs on opposite sides of the desk. More stubborn than cautious, Tobias reached inside the bottom drawer, retrieving a third bottle. He held it up. "Drink?"

"Don't mind if I do." Zach winced faintly as he felt the bruised ribs that had taken Tobias' punch. He shook his head. "You throw one helluva punch for an old man." He frowned as he accepted the bottle, taking a healthy swig. He and Tobias had shared more than one bottle over the years. This was the first time they'd ever shared one as a peace offering to one another.

"You've got a wee bit more muscle than the last time I took you on," Tobias conceded. "I'll have to remember that next time." Taking the bottle back, he raised it in salute.

"You drink too much," Zach told him.

"Aye," Tobias agreed, "that might be true. I can't seem to throw as good a punch as I used to. A few years back, if you'd tried that stunt at the trough, you'd have been picking yerself outta the dirt."

"I did pick myself out of the dirt," Zach reminded him with a wry smile, picking at the stained cloth of his shirt. His expression sobered.

"Who was Felicia? What did she have to do with my father?" Tobias' eyes widened at the name. "Your father always spoke of returning to England, until the day a letter arrived from her. Her name was Barrington. I never knew the contents of that letter, but after that your father changed. He never spoke of her or England again. It was as if that letter cut off any ties he had there. But she meant somethin' important to him. I'm certain Megan never knew about her."

"The letter wasn't in the trunk."

"He destroyed it. I watched him as he tore it into pieces and burned it. I think most of your father's dreams must have been destroyed along with that letter. Not long after that, he accepted a post on a journey inland over the mountains from Sydney. He talked me into going with him. We traveled for months. Then we found this place, and your father named it Resolute. The provisional government saw to it he had an unconditional, full deed of title to as much land as he wanted out here. I suppose they thought, if he was buried in the interior, they were well rid of both of us. And your father was content to remain here, except for occasional trips to Sydney. I think it was all because of her. Lady Felicia Barrington."

Zach leaned across the desk, retrieving the whiskey bottle. He took a long drink, then reached into his shirt pocket.

"What do you know about this?" He opened his fingers, revealing a diamond and pearl pendant. The fine metal and sparkling stones seemed to burn into his skin.

Tobias shook his head. "It never belonged to your mother. If your father had given her something like that, I'd have seen it."

Raking his long fingers through his hair, Zach stood. He stretched his long body, against the pain of bruises that could be seen and those carried deep in his soul, those that couldn't be seen. The pendant was clutched in his hand.

"Was my father serving his sentence when you met him?"

"Aye, seven years. The same as me. We were both given conditional pardon by the territorial government; we were free men, so long as we never attempted to return to England."

The brilliant diamonds and luminous pearls glowed with hidden light. Zach's cold fingers closed over the pendant, the glow stealing into his aching flesh. Felicia Barrington. Some half-formed thought lingered just at the fringe of memory, like something he'd once known and had now forgotten. It was the same feeling he'd had when he'd first seen her name in the journal, like a memory that refused to be remembered but teased at him, nevertheless. It was like the night voices he often heard out in the wilds of Resolute, carried on the wind. The voices of Dreamtime.

He shook his head, unable to understand the nagging restlessness that pulled at him. Now that he'd come home, he realized the answers weren't here. He slammed the door of the small office behind him, the loud snap distant and remote, like the closing of another door, in another time and place.

Something indefinable turned his gaze in the direction of the mountains and beyond, to the sea. He'd promised... something. What, and to whom? His fingers slowly uncurled, and he stared at the pendant, wondering about the woman it had once belonged to. Retracing his steps to the main house, he climbed the stairs and slumped across his solitary bed. Visions of a beautiful young woman filled his imagination and claimed his Dreamtime, echoing the promise.

"Yer daft, clean out of yer mind!" Tobias burst into the wood-paneled office in the main house. The collar of his shirt was askew, his thinning hair was mussed, and his skin had a blotchy pallor due to the whiskey he'd consumed the night before. Bloodshot eyes fixed on the object of their attention across the monkey-wood desk.

"You can't go to England! Yer a wanted man!" He clutched at the desk edge, weaving slightly off center of firm footing as the room suddenly seemed to move uncertainly about him.

"Sit down before you fall down," Zach commanded gently. Reaching across the desk, he pressed a signed voucher into the hands of his foreman, Jimmy Nymagee, known by most as, simply, Jingo. "That should cover any expenses for Resolute while I'm gone. If anything else comes up, you're to see my solicitor in Sydney."

Jingo nodded, grunting out a response only Zach would have understood.

"When ya comin' back?" he mouthed, his speech an odd mixture of English and his native language.

He was full-blood aboriginal and the best foreman Resolute ever had. His ancestors had roamed this valley for generations.

Zach Tennant had saved him from hanging at the hands of the Queen's regulars when both men were young, and he'd hidden Jingo at a remote herder's cabin high in the hills. Loyalty ran deep among the natives. As Jingo saw it, Zach had saved his life, so he was bound to return the favor. Not wanting Jingo to risk life and limb, Zach had convinced him to stay on at the station. And so, Jingo was another who came to Resolute and never left. With Megan's approval, Zach made him foreman at the sheepherding station, and there was no one more knowledgeable about this valley or the mountains beyond. Over the years, Jingo proved his loyalty ran blood deep. He taught Zach the ancient tribal customs of his people, and Zach taught him how to twist the tail of the Queen's enforcers.

"It's a long voyage. We'll have good wind this time of year, but we'll be to sea at least four months. It may be as long as a year before we can get back; that is, if they don't catch me." Zach's twisted half-smile could have meant he was perfectly serious, or sharing one of his many jokes with his friend. Tobias came up out of his chair.

"You can't go to England," he exclaimed. They'll hang you fer certain!"

Zach chose to ignore him for the moment, giving Jingo final instructions. "Minnie will be here to supervise the house. Justin and Rufus will help you with the ranch."

"What about that next season wool? Ya want for me to ship it downriver to Sydney?"

Zach shook his head. "It's too dangerous. When the shearing's done, have the wool processed for storage and transported to MacDonald's warehouses in Adelaide. The British will never look for Resolute wool that far from Sydney.

"It's a longer trip, but I want things to quiet down while I'm gone. That will make the damned watchdog fat and lazy. And make certain you keep the men working on that new area. Post guards if you have to. Just don't leave any witnesses if things go bad with the authorities."

"Right ya are, boss." Jingo tipped his sweat-stained hat, another expression fastening on his face. "Wish I be goin' with ya to that bloody England," he grumbled.

"I need you here, my friend. I can't trust anyone else with Resolute now that Megan's gone."

"Yeah, boy, she sure one fine lady. I'll take care everything here!" He nodded, tucking the voucher inside his shirt pocket. Then he turned and left.

"Now, you were saying?" Zach turned to Tobias and settled into the chair behind the desk, carefully rechecking the list of instructions he'd made for the running of Resolute in his absence.

"Just what the bloody hell do you think yer doin'? You can't go to England! Have you lost all reason, man?" He groaned at his own words, pressing the heels of his hands against his aching eyes.

Zach turned in the chair behind the desk, to stare out the wall of windows. He only half-listened as Tobias continued to argue. His gray eyes, weary from lack of sleep the night before, scanned the valley.

Felicia. In the light of day, the name still haunted him. What had she meant to his father? As he read the journal through the long hours of the night, he felt himself drawn by some intangible force behind the neatly scribed words on the faded paper.

Questions with no answers. Instead of providing him insight to the man his father had been, the journal had only raised more questions. He turned the chair back. Tobias had finally worn down, the effects of the whiskey draining him of all energy.

"Yer a wanted man," the old man pleaded with outstretched hands. Then he slumped into a chair opposite the desk and hung his head, shaking it slowly from side to side.

"They'll hang ya, if you so much as set foot on English soil. It's too dangerous." He raised his head, bloodshot eyes fixing on Zach.

"It's the Raven they want, not me," Zach responded with a smile.

"Then yer determined to go?" Tobias ran fingers through his sparse gray hair.

Zach nodded. "I've sent word ahead to Sydney. The *Revenge* will be ready to sail when we arrive. We'll escort the other two ships to Lisbon and then continue to London."

"We?" Tobias stared, trying to focus his eyes.

"Of course." Zach rose from his chair, a gleam sparkling in his gray eyes. "I've never been to London. I'll need someone to show me about if I'm to learn about my father's life there. You must still have friends in England."

"I was exiled, banished from England forever! I'll be sent to Newgate if I return!" Tobias exclaimed.

"Only, if you get caught." The smile deepened, glowing in Zach's eyes. Then he sobered. "I have to go, Tobias, with or without you."

"It's because of that bloody journal, isn't it!?"

"Partly," Zach admitted. "But it's more than the journal." He reached inside the small carved case on the corner of the desk, his fingers closing over the pearl and diamond pendant. It wasn't the most expensive piece of jewelry he'd ever seen, although obviously quite valuable, but it was by far the most fascinating. Intricately designed and of great beauty, the pendant intrigued him, its diamonds winking at him, its pearls glowing.

"My father had another life, one we never knew about. I have so many questions and I want answers," he admitted, his voice filled with an emotion unusual to him, as his hand rested on the journal. He cleared his throat.

"I never knew him. It seems no one knew him completely, not even you. I have to go. Besides," Zach's mood suddenly lightened, "I think it would be great sport to tweak the nose of the English lion in its own lair. Don't you?"

It would take another day before the *Revenge* and the other two clippers were ready to sail. He hoped in that time, with Alice's usual passionate attentiveness, he might purge his soul of the restlessness that had possessed him since he'd first read Nicholas Tennant's journal.

A shadowy image had emerged from the pages, telling of a man neither his mother nor Tobias Gentry had ever spoken of. Perhaps more revealing were the events of this man's life that remained untold.

He dropped the pendant into a soft leather pouch. "And I need to pay a visit to someone."

~

Zach stirred beside Alice. She was a comely creature, enough to satisfy any man, her legs twined wantonly around his waist. She fastened him with a long gaze.

"Didn't I please you, luv?" Her pleasure had come easily, as it always did with Zachary Tennant. But it didn't take an expert to realize that it hadn't been the same for him.

Zach threw back the covers and slipped from the bed. Dousing water on his face and shoulders, he gave her a long look.

"It's not you," he told her, running a hand across the stubble of beard on his chin. He turned back to the mirror over the dressing table.

He was a fool, and he knew it. Any number of men in Sydney would like to fill her life as well as her bed, yet over the last two years, she'd contented herself with the rare visits he made to town. He knew she saw others when he was away. It didn't matter. In fact, he encouraged her to do so.

He caught the reflection of Alice's sad expression in the mirror. She slipped from the bed, draped in pink satin. Her covering slipped as she came up behind him to wrap her arms around his waist and press her bare breasts against his back.

"Why do I always feel as if there's someone else in that bed besides you and me?" she whispered, for the first time voicing the doubts that had haunted her for the last two years.

It hadn't been easy loving a man like Zach Tennant, having to content herself with the three or four days each month that he spent with her. And then, there were times when he was gone for months at a time.

Zach turned, wrapping his arms loosely around her, regretting that he hadn't been more attentive to her. He liked Alice, she was a beautiful, exciting woman. Any man would give his right arm just to be with her, but he wasn't in love with Alice Mulroney, or any woman. He pressed a kiss against her forehead.

"And just who might be in that bed with us? There wasn't room for anyone else last night," he teased, trying to bring a smile back to her face.

She pulled back, her gaze somber as she studied him, looking for the truth behind the casual conversation.

"I don't know. I wish to God that I did." She tightened her arms around him, laying her cheek against his chest.

"It's not just last night," she continued. "It's happened before. You're here, with me, and then somehow..." she paused, closing her eyes, almost afraid to go on. "It's as if you've left me. You're still here, you seem to go away somewhere. There are times when I look in your eyes, like last night and now, and you're not really here, you're someplace else." She placed her hands at each side of his face and shook her head.

"You've gone away from me again, Zach. Even now, you want to be away from here. What are you searching for?"

He wrapped an arm around her shoulders, and they stood silently for the longest time, both gazing out the window.

Alice's small house was on a hill, looking out across the harbor, and Zach's gaze fastened on the expanse of restless ocean that waited.

His arms dropped. "I have to go."

Alice bit off her response. She couldn't send him away with harsh words and risk losing him forever. "Where this time?"

Buttoning his pants, Zach looked up. He could trust Alice, she had no more love for the British than he did. Still, he held back telling her everything. "I have cargo to deliver to Lisbon."

"When will you be back?" She silently cursed herself, even as she asked it. He didn't like to be questioned, and she knew the reasons. If she didn't know anything about his activities, she couldn't answer any of the magistrate's questions.

Pulling on boots, Zach tucked his shirt into his pants. It was always the same. He'd never spent a full night with Alice. Something always compelled him to leave, a restlessness that he didn't understand. He'd come to her only a couple of hours ago and was now anxious to leave again.

He hesitated, knowing he should say something to her. But the words refused to come. He feared, if they did, they'd only be lies. "I'll be back." He kissed her brusquely, and then slipped from the room, his boots treading softly on the hall carpet. Downstairs, the door closed with an impatient thud.

Alice Mulroney leaned against the wood post of her bed, already feeling the emptiness of his leaving.

"Somehow, I doubt that this time, Zach Tennant," she said with regret.

The blue-green water sliced beneath *Revenge's* hull as wind filled her sails. Zach stared across the harbor, the masts of the other two clippers barely outlined in the dawn light. Within a short while, they would be on the open sea and beyond the reach of the Queen's enforcers.

Their course was set, orders had been given to the crew by the second mate. Zach smiled at the news that Tobias had come aboard sometime during the night, even though he'd sworn he'd never set foot on deck again. One of the crew had informed him that his old friend was below decks sleeping off the effects of a long night spent in one of Sydney's finer gambling establishments.

Zach took the wheel, fatigue slipping away. Beyond the horizon lay endless miles of open sea, and the energy of the sea beat like the heart of a restless creature as it carried them toward the rising sun, and England.

Three

"Yer courtin' the hangman's noose if yer caught!" Tobias stomped the length of the captain's cabin, hands balled into fists of impotent rage.

"I promised yer mother I'd look out for you. How can I do that when you insist on sailing right into London harbor? For God's sake lad, there's still time for us to be away! We can unload the cargo. There's no need for you to even go ashore," he implored. "We'll take on fresh supplies and be on our way. Think! What yer plannin' is madness!" His face was crimson, large veins prominent in his neck.

"*Here come the lobster backs!*" came the squawked warning from the next cabin.

With a faint smile pulling at his mouth, Zach closed the journal. He'd come this far; he wasn't about to leave London without answers.

"I won't leave, Tobias. We're here and I intend to find out about my father. At any rate," he downed the last of the strong coffee, fastening his old friend with a grin. "I've always wanted to see England. "He became thoughtful, a wicked gleam lighting his gray eyes.

"It'll be great sport dealin' directly with the Crown, without paying the usual import tariffs they impose on the colonies. And just maybe, it'll give me the opportunity to learn what the God-almighty English have planned for us in Australia." His eyes lowered, scanning the ship's manifest.

It would take several days to unload the cargo. Already, his first mate was ashore, locating warehouse space where they might store the wool from the *Revenge's* hold.

Tobias shook his head. "This is no game. We could both end up in prison."

Again, that voice mimicked their conversation. *"Lash the bastard to the yardarm!"*

"Will you shut him up!" Tobias thundered, patience gone from too much whiskey and too little sleep the night before.

Zach ignored Tobias' and Sebastian's gloomy predictions. "You know as well as I that Sebastian says exactly what he pleases," he said of the parrot in the next cabin.

"And with his temper, I'm not about to tell him otherwise and lose some skin for it. Now. if you're quite through, I want you to go ashore."

"Not bloody likely!" the old physician blustered, Sebastian and his dire warnings momentarily forgotten. "I'm an exile! Do you know what they do to exiles who try to sneak back into the country?"

"They can't do anything if they can't prove anything. Haven't we learned that about the English?" Zach's smile deepened as he warmed to his plan.

"What do you mean by that?" Tobias failed to follow his line of thought.

Zach rose from his chair and, going to stand before the open porthole, gazed out across the harbor. "It's been over thirty years since you left England. You're not the same man you were then. You've changed."

A smile lifted the corners of his mouth as he turned to his friend. "You've put on a few stone the last few years." His amused gaze traveled over Tobias' portly frame.

"Insolent upstart!" Tobias glared at him, but there was a definite twinkle in his eyes. "So, you don't think anyone will recognize me, eh?" He passed a hand over the stubble on his chin.

"It's not likely any of us will be recognized. We're different men with different identities. Exactly as it was when you and my father first went to Sydney."

"You could be right there."

Zach nodded. "You'll notice when you go topside that I took the liberty of changing the colors. *Tamarisk* now flies the flag of Spain. I thought it a safeguard against too many questions."

"And you think we can fool the bloody boys in red?"

Zach winked conspiratorially. "I've been lucky so far." He grinned and, crossing the cabin, slapped a hand on Tobias' back.

"The British fleet is far too busy searching every harbor town in New South Wales for the Raven. They'll not be concerned with the likes of us."

"Yer too bold, lad." Tobias shook his head. "Sometimes I think you like playing games with the devil."

Zach threw back his head and roared with laughter. "Why, Tobias, don't you know?" His silver-gray eyes narrowed dangerously. "I am the devil." Then he sobered and went back to his small desk. "Now, we must make a plan for you to go ashore. You have some memory of London, whereas I have no knowledge of it whatsoever."

"I don't like it," Tobias complained, shaking his head.

"But you will go," Zach informed him gently.

"Aye, I'll go. But only because I know if I don't, you'll do it yourself and probably end up in some kind of trouble. London is no town for a stranger." The old man sighed resignedly. "What is it you want me to do?"

Zach sat down at the desk, opening the journal. "I need information." He pushed back thoughtfully in the chair, his fingers lightly drumming the worn pages of the leather-bound volume. "I need to know everything about the Barrington family, particularly Felicia Barrington." His voice hardened. "And find out what you can about Barrington Shipping. It's time to corner the lion."

Tobias shook his shaggy, gray head. "Yer always reading that damned journal. I wish I'd never given it to you. Felicia Barrington has become an obsession with you. For God's sake, it all happened over thirty years ago!" He waved an arm in frustration. "You don't even know if she's still alive! And what are you going to do when you find her? She's a Barrington, remember? They'll not exactly roll out the red carpet for us!"

Zach sighed, his gray eyes traveling back to the open porthole with an expression of inexplicable longing.

"I don't know," he whispered, lost in his own thoughts.

She was out there, somewhere. He could feel it, but even he was at a loss to understand his obsession with a woman his father had once known.

"Aye, Tobias," he agreed, "she has become an obsession." He picked up the sparkling pendant, twirling it in the sunlight that poured in through the porthole. The rays invaded the stones, reflecting deep hidden facets, hinting at other secrets concealed within. "A magnificent, elusive obsession. And I won't rest until I find her."

~

"Suck it in, my dear," Katy managed from between clenched teeth as she pulled hard on the corset strings.

"You're cutting me in half," Elyse gasped, trying to breathe.

"Yer dressmaker said we have to get it down to seventeen inches for that dress to fit." Katy pulled harder.

Elyse clung to the post of the large bed, eyes closed painfully. Behind her, Katy wound the strings of the corset more tightly around hands reddened from pulling.

"Just a little bit more," she coaxed.

Elyse groaned. "A little bit more and I won't be able to walk."

"It's necessary," Katy gritted out, pulling the strings, a fraction of an inch tighter.

Elyse's cheeks drained of all color. "Enough!" She swore inaudibly under her breath. Then, jerking away, she swung around, drawing a deep breath as the strings loosened and the garment gaped open down her back.

"No more!" she warned with an outstretched hand. "I refuse to be trussed up like a Christmas goose." Determination glittered in her brilliant blue eyes as she backed away from the maid. "Eighteen inches will just have to do." She tossed her auburn hair defiantly over one bare shoulder.

Katy sucked in her cheeks. "Madame Duquesne won't like it."

"I don't care if France declares war on England!" Elyse told the girl. "No one will ever know it's eighteen inches and not seventeen."

"Eighteen won't fit," Katy announced. "Madame said it would have to be no more than seventeen or you'd never get the back of the gown closed."

Holding the front of the corset against her firm breasts, Elyse strode across the bedchamber. "Then I won't wear it." Head held high, she threw open the wardrobe. "It's as simple as that," she declared, surveying an array of gowns.

Katy threw up her hands. "Yer grandmother paid a fortune for that dress. The seamstress has been working on it for weeks." A satisfied smile tilted her mouth as she added a final comment, knowing the effect it would have. "Master Jerrold approved the fabric himself. He's expectin' you to wear this gown to the engagement party. I heard him say the lady who's to be the future Lady Barrington has to be properly dressed."

That did it! Elyse whirled back around. "I don't care if Queen Victoria herself selected the fabric! Can't I be allowed to choose anything for myself!"

She jerked first one gown, then another roughly aside, the lace-trimmed corset falling to the floor.

"Good heavens, but yer an indecent chit." Katy swooped across the room, seizing the corset and wrapping it about Elyse's bare body.

"What if someone were to come in just now?"

"And who might that be?" Elyse demanded. "My fiancé, perhaps? I think not." She answered her own question with more than a trace of sarcasm.

"He's far too occupied responding to all the gifts we've received, or," she finally took a deep breath now that she was free of the corset, "visiting his mistress at Brookfield Court!" Her color, now fully restored, spread vividly across her cheeks.

"You don't know that," Katy warned. Her mistress really had her temper up this time.

"Oh yes, I forgot. If we don't speak of *those* things, then perhaps they'll go away. Dearest Katy," Elyse squared her slender shoulders, "mistresses don't go away, they merely remain discreet. Or perhaps not so very discreet."

"You shouldn't say such things about the man yer to marry. Why, if anyone were to hear you, they'd think you didn't love him," Katy scolded, concern knitting her brows together.

"Would they now."

Elyse remembered the evening at the opera several weeks earlier, when Jerrold's supposedly *former* mistress had approached them.

Katherine West had been more than a little intoxicated, and Elyse had felt sorry for her escort. He'd truly seemed like a nice gentleman. But the realization that she hadn't felt the slightest twinge of jealousy at the time was disconcerting. In fact, she'd been amused. After all, how often could a woman actually claim to be socially acquainted with her fiancé's mistress?

She remembered the livid expression on Jerrold's face at her reaction. He'd been cool and distant the remainder of the evening, and she knew the reason. He liked dictating her responses to such situations, just as he liked dictating the gowns she was to wear.

Katy gave her a thoughtful look. "That's it, isn't it?" she asked in a quiet voice.

"What is?" Elyse remarked absently. Her hand closed over a new gown she hadn't yet worn. She pulled it from the wardrobe and turned to Katy.

"I'll wear this one," she stated emphatically. "It's *my* favorite."

"Yer ignoring me," Katy said accusingly.

Elyse smiled, her eyes turning a darker blue with the lie. "That's impossible."

"You don't love him." Katy pinned her charge with an insistent gaze.

It was pointless to lie. Katy would see the truth despite any excuses she tried to give.

Elyse sighed heavily, wishing there were an easy answer. There just wasn't. "I don't know what I feel, Katy. I wish I did."

Katy shook her head. "It's wrong marrying a man ya don't love, even if he is one of the richest men in all England. All the money in the world can't buy happiness."

"It really doesn't matter, does it?" Elyse replied. "After all, a proper lady would never break her betrothal simply because she wasn't certain of her feelings. Now, bring the gown, and be sure to lace me up—*eighteen* inches."

The humor in her smile was forced. "After all, I have another party to attend. And please, work some of your magic." There was an odd catch in her voice, as she turned for the corset to be laced. "After all, everyone always expects the bride to look radiantly happy."

"You may be able to fool everyone else, including yer grandmother, but yer not foolin' me. I've known you since you were a small child. Have you forgotten? I know everything about ya. And," Katy added, lacing the corset to eighteen inches, "I know you've been havin' that dream again."

This time Elyse didn't even try to disguise the truth. "Why is it always the same?" she asked, more to herself. She closed her eyes, leaning her head against the post of the bed.

"Who is he, Katy? Who is the phantom of my dreams?"

"Yer grandmother always thought it must be your father, because losin' your parents was such a dreadful shock." Katy held out pantalets for her to step into.

Elyse shook her head. "There are portraits of him and of my mother. He's not the man in my dreams. It's someone else. Someone I know... " If only she could remember. She closed her eyes, experiencing again the overwhelming peace she always felt with the dream, and.... the passion.

"I feel so safe, as if I've finally come to the end of a very long journey." Her voice was sad with longing. "And when he kisses me... "

Katy's head came up, a startled expression on her face. It was the first time Elyse had ever mentioned anything so intimate being in her dreams.

"It's natural to dream of the man yer to marry." Her voice was hesitant as she tied the strings at Elyse's waist.

Elyse wrapped her arms about herself as she crossed the room to stand before the windows. She stared into the early evening darkness as if searching for something beyond the glass.

"I can almost see him." But it wasn't Jerrold. Of that she was certain.

Her throat tightened with inexplicable longing. Sadness always accompanied the dreams, like a foreboding of some loss she couldn't understand.

"You had a saying when I was little—*if wishes were horses, then beggars would ride*. Well, it seems, Katy my love, that I'm without my horse. I've lost him and can't seem to find him."

Elyse smiled then. "It'll be all right, Katy, I promise. I won't spoil this for Grandmother?"

The maid frowned, unable to dismiss the nagging doubts that had plagued her since Elyse's betrothal was formally announced. It was not her place to interfere. What did she know of arranged marriages?

All she was certain of was that a young girl, no matter her station in life, should have the right to make a choice of the heart. Perhaps, she thought to herself, it was one of those things a girl gave up when she became a proper lady. Still, Katy couldn't help feeling it was wrong.

"Come along," she whispered. "Let's finish getting you dressed. Master Jerrold and his father will be here soon. Which jewelry will you be wantin' to wear? How about the diamond and sapphire necklace he gave you for your birthday?" she suggested.

Elyse shook her head. There was only one piece she would wear that evening. She almost felt as if it were a good luck talisman.

"I'll wear the pendant, Grandmother gave me." After all, she thought, tonight was to be a very special night. She should have shared that feeling, but didn't.

~

Zach forged the elaborate signature on the contract. At least now he would have a place to store his wool. Only he and his second mate knew the true value of those tightly bound bales, for inside each was a heavy leather pouch containing something far more valuable—gold. It was a deception of course, hiding the gold at the same time, almost keeping it in plain sight.

He looked up as Tobias carefully made his way up the gangplank to step down on the more secure deck. Wiping beads of perspiration from his brow, the older man sat on a nearby barrel.

Zach nodded to his second mate. "Make certain guards are posted, but not conspicuously." He turned to Tobias. "What were you able to find out?"

"Give me a minute to catch me breath," Tobias puffed. Removing the top of an adjacent barrel, he seized a ladle and dipped into the cool water. He took a long drink.

Zach had waited long enough. "Good God, man! What did you find out about the Barringtons?"

Tobias shifted his stout frame. Taking another sip, he narrowed his gaze thoughtfully.

"I found out that if you mention the Barrington name anywhere about London, you're bound to find out something."

"Such as?" Zach shifted impatiently.

Tobias' gaze dropped to his hands. "London hasn't changed much in thirty years. Most of the businesses are still here, though the faces have changed a bit." He smiled ruefully. "They're all younger." He chuckled to himself.

"Over thirty years," he murmured. "An entire lifetime. God, I didn't realize how much I missed England." There was an odd catch in his voice as he blinked back emotion.

"What about the Barringtons?" Zach repeated.

Tobias' eyes narrowed. "They're a powerful family, old money, impeccable lineage. The name carried a great deal of power when I was a young man. They're not limited to shipping. They own a piece of the rail system, and mining operations in South Wales."

"I didn't ask for a banker's report," Zach replied and didn't bother to hide the sarcasm. "What about the family?"

"Old Lord Barrington died several years ago. The son inherited the family fortune, and the grandson will inherit everything he's built up, the title and the fortune."

"And made from the sweat and blood of our people at Resolute and the other stations back home," Zach replied, contempt in his voice.

Tobias continued to reveal the information he'd gathered throughout the morning. "They have a large town house here in London. The Barrington offices are on Regent Street. Most of the family business is handled there. And there are several country estates. The largest is in Lincolnshire. And," he paused, "they own practically every warehouse on this waterfront. You're probably renting space from them for that wool." He watched Zach carefully for a reaction to that last statement.

A dangerous smile lifted the corners of Zach's mouth. "As you would say, my friend—'not bloody likely'! I had Sandy make certain he found an independent owner. I'm not about to pour any more money into Barrington's fat purse. Where is this London town house?"

"Highgrove," Tobias replied. "It's not likely you'll get an invitation to visit. Their usual houseguests include the nobility, even a member of two of the royal family."

"There's always a way, Tobias. Have you forgotten how charming I can be when I want something?" His eyes darkened to cold slate. "After all, we have something in common—Felicia Barrington."

Tobias wiped the perspiration from his upper lip with a handkerchief. There was no point in holding anything back. If he didn't tell him everything, Zach would find out for himself. It was always that way. The man had an uncanny ability to ferret out things, as if he could see beyond what a person was telling him... or leaving out.

"There's a fancy get-together this evenin' in honor of young master Barrington," he added, replacing his dampened handkerchief in his vest pocket. He glanced at Zach speculatively from beneath the sweep of frosty eyebrows.

"What sort of get-together?"

The chill in those silver eyes could cut into a man's soul. It had been the same with his father. Tobias remembered that same look, long ago in Nicholas Tennant's eyes. The memory sent an uneasy chill down his spine. The conversation held on that day had become too personal. He'd pressed too hard, freely giving information about his own past, then asking the same of his friend, to receive only that cold stare in response. He'd never asked again.

"Lord Barrington's son is to be married according to what I was told. The engagement is being celebrated," Tobias replied, knowing full well what the next question would be.

"And where is this get-together being held?"

"The bride's grandmother is hosting the event. Lady Regina Winslow is well-placed in society. I believe the girl was American-born, so I hear." Tobias straightened the fabric of his vest. "It's to be the social event of the season."

"No doubt," Zach nodded. "It would be the perfect opportunity to meet Felicia Barrington. What shall I wear?" His gaze met Tobias' squarely, a glint of challenge in it.

His old friend very nearly fell off the barrel. "It's impossible!" He was thunderstruck. "You must be daft, boy! Haven't you heard a word I've said? These are powerful people! Invitations aren't handed out to common people, much less ex-convicts, or the son of a convict."

"Ah, yes. The bloody class structure." Zach squared

his wide shoulders, fixing Tobias with a deadly gaze. The light in those gray eyes hinted at a trace of deadly humor.

"Then I suppose we shall just have to be certain an invitation is extended. Certainly an exception might be made for a member of the nobility visiting London."

"What the devil are you talking about?" Tobias came up off the barrel. "We don't know anyone like that! Impossible!"

Zach arched a brow. "That's what the Crown and Barrington Shipping said when the Raven lured all those ships out onto the Barrier Reef. They said it was impossible that it could be the work of just one man."

"Yer mad! Yer bloody mad! You'll be caught and hanged."

"For attending the social event of the season? I think not." Zach winked at his friend. "I merely want to give the happy couple my fondest wishes, and to find out what I can about Felicia Barrington." Zach straightened as a thought came to him.

"I'll need a place to live while we're in London, perhaps in Highgrove," he suggested. "You mentioned it's a fashionable place to live."

"You think you can just bloody walk in and buy a place? Those are old family homes of the aristocracy. They don't sell them unless there's a very great need."

"I have a very great need. But I have no desire to own property in England. With the wealth of these people, surely one house can be found vacant, its owners possibly vacationing elsewhere. Find such a place. And servants," he added as an afterthought. "Everything must be perfect."

"Is that all?" Tobias roared. "Surely there must be something else you'll be wanting?"

Zach nodded. "I'll need a carriage and horses. Sandy will be my driver." His enthusiasm gained momentum as he laid out his scheme. "And I'll have need of a tailor. The rest can be taken care of tomorrow."

"Tomorrow? How generous of you!"

Zach raised amused eyes to his friend. "Inform the tailor that we'll need evening wear for two gentlemen. And pick out suitable fabric for yourself, *your grace*."

"My what!"

Zach stood back, studying his friend.

"Yes, a marquis will do quite nicely. You'll go as my uncle, although some may question the family resemblance." He forced back a laugh. "Do you think you can handle the accent? Anything will do, so long as it's *not* English."

Tobias was incredulous. "A marquis? Now, I know you're mad! It won't work, it just won't work! Even if your scheme had some merit, there's not enough time to accomplish everything. The get-together for Barrington is tonight! Only a few hours away!"

"Precisely so, my friend. But you've forgotten how arrogant the English can be." He smiled coldly. "I intend to make certain the Barringtons are aware of the arrival of Sir William St. James, newly arrived from Macau." He savored the title he'd bestowed upon himself.

"Yes," he said with great satisfaction. "A title and a little deception will get me exactly what I want."

His thoughts returning to the present, he sobered. "And in plenty of time to attend the special occasion of the engagement of young Lord Barrington."

"Barrington will have people there who will no doubt tell him there is no William St. James."

"And by that time, I will have accomplished what I want, and disappear."

~

"Elyse, my dear, you disappoint me," Jerrold Barrington whispered discreetly, as he smiled congenially at the grand duchess.

"I had hoped to see you wearing the gold satin. Was there something wrong with the gown? Perhaps Madame Juliette and her seamstresses were negligent," he suggested, an annoyed tone at his voice.

Elyse laid a gloved hand on his arm in what must have seemed to others an intimate gesture. "I'm sorry you're disappointed." She smiled up at him. "Madame is not to blame. Her work was perfect, as always. I chose not to wear the gown. It seemed... " she paused, searching for the right word. "Extravagant."

"Extravagant? My dear, of course it's extravagant, as I wanted. You must remember that, once we're married, you will be a titled lady with all the social recognition that accompanies such a title. It is expected of you."

Her reply hid the irritation that always seemed to dominate their discussions lately. "I already have that," she reminded him. "And I *will* wear what I please."

A muscle worked at his clenched jaw. "Of course. It's just that the Barrington name carries a great deal of importance. People in society look to us to maintain certain standards."

"Do you find my standards lacking?" she coolly asked. His fingers tightened around her arm.

"Elyse, darling," he added the endearment almost as an afterthought. "You're beginning to draw attention."

She fastened him with a look of wide-eyed innocence. "But I thought you liked attention."

His grip tightened, bruising beneath her long gloves.

"You're hurting me."

His fingers immediately relaxed, the expression on his face suitably contrite. "I'm sorry, my dear. It's just that you have the most irritating habit of challenging me at the most awkward moments." His hand slipped to her waist, pulling her against him. "But I suppose that is why I desire you so completely."

Desire. Is that what it was, she thought. Lately, he'd

become much more demanding of her affections when they were together. This was not the first time Jerrold had made certain she was aware of his feelings. Her gaze lowered as she brought her churning emotions under control.

She should have been flattered. Instead, she found his *attentions* as bothersome as his criticism of her selection of a gown.

What was wrong with her for God's sake? After all, in less than two months they were to be married.

Elyse pushed that from her thoughts with almost silent desperation, as she had done numerous times over the past year, as if she could will it away by ignoring it. But in her heart, she knew it wasn't that simple. With each passing day. she was fast approaching that moment when they would be husband and wife.

She smiled as she put what would be considered a respectable distance between two unmarried people. "We must be careful, someone may be watching."

She reached up a gloved hand, touching his cheek, trying to feel some essence of the desire that leapt into his eyes, masking her own disappointment as her fingers curled into a fist.

"Elyse, my dear."

Her grandmother approached and she fixed a smile on her face. This was, after all, something her grandmother had campaigned for.

"You and Jerrold must come along and greet your guests. Lucy Maitland has been looking for you. She mentioned something about a guest newly arrived from Macau. I believe the name is St. James." Regina smiled, trying to lighten her granddaughter's mood. She turned to Jerrold.

"It seems he's an acquaintance of your family."

He smiled. "Of course, Lady Winslow," he took her arm with the grace and dignity of a perfect gentleman.

"We should attend to the guests. After all, this is the very important night." He extended his other arm to Elyse.

Lucy Maitland smiled radiantly in greeting as they joined her. "You look absolutely stunning tonight," she whispered discreetly to Elyse from behind her satin brocade fan. "But you really should try to smile. People will think you're not enjoying your own engagement party."

Elyse flashed her a pleading glance as Jerrold left to converse with an acquaintance.

"Oh, Lucy, what am I going to do?" she whispered miserably.

Lucy caught her by the arm and drew her away from prying glances. "What are you saying?"

Elyse smiled. "It's nothing, probably just the excitement of the party."

"I've seen more excitement from you over studying French essays from our tutor," her friend commented.

They'd attended academy together, and suffered over French as well as mathematics, going through it all with undying loyalty to each other. In the past, she could tell Lucy just about anything. But how could she possibly tell Lucy about the doubts that nagged at her now?

Elyse shook her head, "I don't know..." She made a gesture toward the brilliantly decorated room. "I should feel differently about all this."

"What's wrong?"

"I want to feel the way you do about Andrew. That's how it should be between a man and woman, isn't it?"

Her friend drew back in surprise. A playful smile twitched at the corners of Lucy's mouth. "Well, let me tell you. He is off limits," she declared. "And I'll scratch out the eyes of any female who thinks otherwise."

Elyse groaned. "You know what I mean."

Lucy nodded. "Yes, I know precisely what you mean." She wrapped an arm around Elyse's waist as they walked together. "You're probably just nervous about all this. After all, the Barrington name has been known to strike fear into the hearts of mortal men. That's quite a title you're marrying."

"A title," Elyse responded somberly. "Perhaps that's it." She shook her head, trying to find a way to explain her feelings. "When did you know you loved Andrew?"

"I must have been about seven years old." Lucy tapped the tip of her closed fan thoughtfully against her chin. "Yes, I'm certain of it." Her eyes widened. "Do you promise not to laugh, if I tell you about it?"

"Seven years?" Elyse laughed, astonished. It seemed incredible that her friend, who'd been known to be rather wild, unmanageable, and unpredictable as a child, could have loved anyone for more than a week at the most, much less since she was seven years old.

"I warned you not to laugh."

She fastened an appropriately solemn expression on her face. "Yes, of course."

Lucy looked at her skeptically, then decided she could be trusted to keep her word.

"Andrew and his parents were visiting us at Shelbourne. I was riding my pony and fell off, right into the middle of a mud puddle at his feet. I'll never forget the expression on his face. He laughed so hard."

Elyse couldn't restrain herself as she imagined Lucy sprawled in a mud puddle. It came out in a most unladylike fashion and was quickly muffled behind her gloved hand.

"You must have been furious," she managed to say, forcing back laughter until her eyes watered. "You've always had a dreadful temper."

Lucy glared at her. "I was, of course. But he just kept right on laughing. Well, he just has the most infectious laughter. How could I possibly resist? No one ever dared laugh at me before. I decided right then and there, he was the man I was going to marry. Anyone who would dare laugh at Lucy Devereaux was as crazy as I was... or had a strong sense of himself." She tried to bolster Elyse' spirits.

"Not everyone falls into love and a mud puddle all in the same day. Usually, it's accomplished in much more conventional ways. It's just not the same for everyone," she said encouragingly. "Now, if you were to ask Andrew, he'd come up with an entirely different explanation. Our first meeting wasn't like that at all for him. He thought I was an impossible, demanding child." She winked wickedly. "Now, he knows how demanding I can be."

"But you fell in love in spite of everything," Elyse bemoaned. "Why can't I feel that way about Jerrold? Do you know what he'd say if I fell into a mud puddle?" She tilted her head and assumed a stern, disapproving expression. *My dear Elyse,*" she mimicked, her mouth pursing into a thin frown. *"Whatever will people think? After all, you have a position to think of. You'll be the laughingstock of London. How will I ever live this down?"* For added effect, she rolled her brilliant blue eyes in an exact imitation of Jerrold's most reproving glare.

Lucy choked back her own laughter. She'd known Jerrold Barrington a long time. They all moved in the same social circles, but despite that, Jerrold always considered himself a notch above everyone else.

"Oh, Lucy." Elyse sighed, wiping tears of laughter from the corners of her own eyes. "Here I am making a joke about it." She smiled sadly. "It's no joke at all. I should feel something...more, something like... "She paused, searching for the right word. It was there, from her dreams, but she wondered if Lucy would consider her completely mad.

"Like a bolt of lightning?" Lucy suggested, arching her brow. "I feel it every time Andrew and I are together. I'd die if I didn't," she whispered solemnly, rare for Lucy Maitland. Her gaze wandered across the ballroom to where her husband was involved in lively discussion with an acquaintance. "It's as if we were meant to be together." She laughed at the foolishness of the notion and made a joke of it.

"You know, destined, written in the stars," she said making an elaborate gesture through the air with her hand. Then, struck by a sudden thought, she seized two champagne glasses from a nearby tray, and handed one to Elyse.

"A toast, between friends," she proposed as she raised her glass. "To your happiness, and lightning bolts." Crystal rang with false gaiety against crystal.

Elyse drained the glass, her eyes widening as Lucy coaxed her to enjoy just one more toast.

"I can't!" she declared. "Champagne affects me strangely."

"Strangely?" Lucy swallowed back her astonishment. "What happens? Do you change into some sort of wicked creature, casting spells on everyone?"

Elyse giggled. "If only that were true. Maybe I could cast a spell on Jerrold."

"And turn him into a frog," Lucy suggested, quickly handing Elyse another glass of champagne before she could protest.

"But then, I suppose you would have to start with a prince first. And my dear," she leaned discreetly forward as if she were sharing a secret.

"Jerrold is no prince."

"No, he's not," Elyse replied.

She knew Jerrold would disapprove of such behavior, and conversation. Ladies simply did not discuss such things even though men surely did.

But why shouldn't she share another glass of champagne with her dearest friend?

Tobias tugged at Zach's sleeve. "We'll never pull it off. It isn't enough that we've lied and bribed our way this far,"

he muttered, casting a worried glance at the English gentlemen and their ladies who filled the enormous room.
"Oh, no. You insist on wearin' that damned eye-patch.
Be subtle you said, blend in with the crowd! We stick
out like whores at a church social in these fancy clothes.
There isn't enough gold in all of New South Wales to
buy our way out of this if we're caught."

"Easy, old friend." A smile pulled at Zach's mouth as
he separated from Tobias. "And stay away from the attendants tonight. I want you sober."

"Sober?" Tobias whispered in his wake. He made a
move to follow, then thought better of it. If one was
caught, the other might still get away.

He turned with an appreciative eye toward the elegant, embossed silver serving bowls set upon linen-cov-
ered tables along the wall. He frowned. The last thing he
wanted was some weak punch. He needed a real drink!

Zach's gaze swept the room, taking in the under-
stated wealth of the immaculately dressed men and their
elegant but overstated ladies.

He'd inquired discreetly about Lady Barrington,
but had received only vague responses. Now, an uneasy
feeling slipped down his spine. Perhaps Tobias was right.
Felicia might not be alive after all these years. He hadn't
been able to learn anything about her since their arrival.

Contrary to his suggestion to his old friend, Zach
took a glass from a tray offered by a passing servant.
When he made a remark about something more substantial than champagne, the servant disappeared with a
nod to reappear a few minutes later with a bottle discreetly wrapped in fine linen.

The amber-colored liquid splashed reassuringly into
a heavy crystal tumbler. As fine French cognac slipped
into Zach's stomach, he looked over the rim of the glass,
and saw her.

He would have known her anywhere. Now where the
devil had that come from, he thought? Still, it was there

—some past memory, in the slender arch of her neck, the delicate features of her face as she turned in conversation.

It teased at him, then became something more. Something he couldn't name or fully recall.

Drawing a deep breath, Zach turned away, trying to bring his thoughts back under control. Something white-hot slipped across his senses.

Impossible! He knew none of these people. He didn't know *her*. Yet, even as he denied it, he felt himself turn and search for her almost with desperation.

It was insane! He'd known countless women, some as forbidden to him as England. Yet he crossed the room, compelled by something he could neither understand nor escape.

He heard the whispers following him across the room as he threaded his way through the guests, the black worsted wool of his dress coat that had been hastily completed by the tailor brushing against satin and lace.

Several elegantly coiffed heads turned in his direction, and glances, no longer discreet but openly appraising, stared at him, but his gaze was only for *her*.

Like music reaching through darkness, her voice was low, silky. Her soft laughter slipped inside him. As he reached out, his fingers brushed her arm, and something very like an echo of memory moved like a whisper through him.

The touch was so faint, Elyse might not have felt it. It was like the feather-soft brush of the wind, or the touch of a feather.

"Lady Barrington?" Zach said.

Not yet, she thought as she heard the name and turned. She was about to say just that, in spite of the reason everyone was there, that ripple of irritation at what everyone assumed—that she must be absolutely thrilled. After all, wasn't Jerrold the most sought-after bachelor in London?

When she would have explained that with a polite smile, the color drained from her face. Everything and everyone else in the room suddenly faded away. Light conversations of those around her ceased, it was as if she had stepped into another room that was softly lit, and there was the man who stood only a few feet away. And she knew him...

Her hand went to the pendant she wore, the pearl and diamonds warm at her fingers, even as she heard her name, pulling her back.

If she were to describe it afterward, she would have told Lucy that it was as if she went away for those few moments to some other place that she'd never seen before... and there was someone there, someone she knew, and he was waiting for her.

Lucy would have laughed and told her that it was just her imagination, nervousness over all the details of the wedding, or perhaps too much champagne.

The room seemed to right itself again. Everything was as it had been—voices, sounds, the tinkling of a champagne bottle against a crystal goblet as she finally took a deep breath. And the man was still there, something in the gaze behind the startling eye-patch over one eye.

He was tall and handsome, in spite of the eye-patch or possibly because of it, his overlong sun-streaked hair curling slightly at the collar of his waistcoat and pristine white shirt with gray cravat, immaculately polished boots, and the intense expression on his face.

Her first impression was that he seemed perfectly at ease and out of place at the same time, a gentleman and someone who could be dangerous if one let down their guard, someone capable of restraint at the same time the word wouldn't even exist for him, a man of sharp contrasts that sent a tingling across her skin.

Four

That sense of familiarity Zach had first experienced washed over him again. The feeling was disturbing, and he carefully masked it as a dark-haired man with dark eyes appeared at the young woman's side, the expression on his face reflecting several emotions.

"Here you are," Jerrold said as he joined them. Then, with a look at Elyse, "Are you feeling unwell? You're quite pale. I hope you're not thinking of fainting."

Thinking of fainting? How did someone *think* of fainting? She wondered. "I never faint," she replied.

That intense gray gaze fastened on her with a mixture of amusement and genuine concern, and something else behind that black patch across one eye.

"Ah, yes," Jerrold said with that same air of aloofness as he made introductions. "St. James, I heard someone say."

Her striking blue gaze met Zach's. "I don't believe that we've been properly introduced, sir."

Zach's concern for this beautiful young woman shifted to amusement with her smile. "Is there an improper way?"

Whatever had caused her first reaction certainly wasn't affecting her now. She seemed to have fully recovered as she laughed at his comment. He wished he could say the same for Barrington.

Jerrold frowned at the off-hand comment. "Allow me to introduce myself," he said, inserting himself once more.

"Jerrold Barrington," he announced.

Zach smiled as if he found something amusing in Jerrold's manner.

"William St. James," he introduced himself and took her hand.

His smile deepened. Taking her gloved hand, he raised it and gently dropped a kiss across the back of her fingers. As he did so, he turned his head slightly for a glimpse of the man who had suddenly appeared at her side as if to rescue her. Or was it something else in the way the man frowned, almost as if he intended to reprimand her?

Barrington was tall and dark, with the sort of looks that were almost too polished, too perfect, as if he spent a great deal of time making certain they were just that. Unless Zach missed his guess, the heir to Barrington Shipping and other assorted enterprises was more than a little displeased with the lady's comments.

His lips curved into a secretive smile. So, it seemed Mr. Jerrold Barrington was a man given to propriety and appearances, as well as greed and ruthless business dealings. As Zach knew only too well, it was easy to act the part of the perfect gentleman. But the young lady who'd captured him with her unpretentious greeting was less easily understood.

He held onto her hand, knowing how it must look to those who stood with them, and couldn't care less. Unless he missed his guess, she must be Elyse Winslow and the man beside her and the assorted guests had gathered to celebrate their forthcoming marriage.

He saw the play of emotions on her face, surprise, followed by embarrassment, then curiosity, as pink spread across her high cheekbones. Those magnificent eyes rimmed in dark lashes tilted faintly at the corners as she met his gaze.

"Miss Winslow is soon to be Lady Barrington." Jerrold Barrington elaborated, setting boundaries much like an animal.

'Soon to be' fixed in Zach's mind as he nodded. "Then congratulations are in order." That was the reason his inquiries earlier that evening had met with such surprise. He glanced down, unable to understand his disappointment at learning that she was to marry this man.

The smile he gave him was as much a mask as the one he wore over his eyes and hid his contempt for the Barrington name. For now.

"We've never met, sir, but we've had business dealings."

"You're not English," Jerrold commented.

Elyse stiffened at Jerrold's biting comment. It was maddening how much pleasure he got from belittling people, yet fascinating that this stranger seemed completely unaffected by it.

Zach smiled to himself. So, the soon-to-be Lady Barrington wasn't easily manipulated by her fiancé.

"I have widespread business dealings," he said coolly, but his eyes never left hers.

"And some past dealings with your company," he added. "And by what I hear, it seems that you have crossed paths with that fellow who goes by the name of the Raven. I understand you've lost substantial cargo, not to mention several ships to this devil!'

"Ah, then you've had some dealings in the Pacific and the colonies of New South Wales, dangerous territory. I do hope you weren't a victim of that pirate."

"Many have suffered at the hands of the Raven." Zach carefully maneuvered the conversation. "He seems to be such an elusive fellow that I'm given to wonder if he truly exists. Perhaps the difficulty you've had in the South Pacific is due to your inexperience in dealing with the people there."

"The people!" Jerrold laughed incredulously, "I would hardly give the inhabitants of New South Wales the courtesy of that description. They're nothing but convicts and savages, the dregs of humanity, if you will. Of course, we anticipated certain difficulties in dealing with such people. But we can and will control the situation.

"After all," he continued, "there is a great deal of wealth to be obtained from the place. It's beyond me, how those insufferable Australians can even consider themselves equal to an Englishman, making demands for their own home government."

"I've heard of their intense dislike for all Englishmen," Zach replied.

"It is a temporary condition, I assure you," Jerrold continued. "In time they will come to appreciate what Britain has provided them when a good many of them should have gone to the gallows," Jerrold assured him.

Elyse drew in a sharp breath at his cruel remark, but St. James seemed unaffected.

"You are to be complimented for your sense of grace and humility, Lord Barrington," Zach told him. "You are a true example of an English nobleman."

Only Elyse seemed aware of the biting edge of St. James' remark. Like his words, his gray gaze sparked with something that seemed almost threatening.

Jerrold smiled, thinking that perhaps he might have missed something in the exchange but unable to find anything in St. James' response to take offense.

Zach hid the anger as he smoothly replied, "It is most fortunate for me that we have met. I should like to discuss business with you. At your convenience, of course. It is a most rare and precious cargo, one I'm certain you will find of great interest. Certainly someone who has your expertise with the colonials of New South Wales might be able to advise me on a purchaser for it."

"Yes, of course, and you seem to have arrived unscathed," Jerrold commented. "When a good many of us have experienced substantial losses on the high seas."

Elyse watched St. James. He seemed to be praising Jerrold, but she knew for a fact how disastrous the last two years had been for Jerrold and his father. They had lost several ships to a man known only as the Raven.

Their latest loss had been ships heavily laden with cargo at some remote place called the Barrier Reef. Most of the crew had escaped, but the financial loss of the cargo had been devastating. She knew of the details only through Jerrold's manager, who had shared the news with her grandmother's solicitor.

Elyse had used the heavy financial loss as an argument to persuade Jerrold that they should wait until the following year to announce their engagement. But he'd adamantly refused, informing her that it was nothing for her to concern herself with. He had been irritated with her for even suggesting it, informing her that he fully intended to take measures against any further losses. He hadn't elaborated how that would be accomplished.

She was aware that a good many marriages were often made for financial advantage. Until that moment last winter when she'd confronted him about the trouble in New South Wales, it had never occurred to her that Jerrold might consider their marriage just such a financial arrangement in consideration of her grandmother's considerable wealth.

St. James seemed well informed about Barrington difficulties, however. She could see the superiority waver in Jerrold's eyes and couldn't smother a feeling of satisfaction as he extricated himself from a conversation where he no longer had the advantage. She remembered how she'd once thought of him as commanding and confident. Now he often seemed little more than arrogant.

"We have many ships." Jerrold struck a polite pose. "Traveling to virtually every port in the world. Undoubtedly, we've carried your cargos as well. I should like to discuss it more with you." He turned to Elyse.

"Come along, my dear, we have other guests. "He effectively cut the stranger from their conversation.

Elyse begged off. She wasn't in the mood for polite conversations. "I need to speak with Lucy about something...You do understand?"

For a moment the air almost crackled with tension. Then Jerrold nodded. "Of course, '*women*' things, no doubt." He kissed Elyse on the cheek. "Don't be too long, my dear." He turned and left.

She caught the look Lucy gave her, familiar from their days escaping unwanted suitors at one event or another, then her frown.

"I must find Andrew before he starts to worry where I've gone to," she improvised. And she was off, leaving Elyse alone with St. James.

A smile played at the corner of Zach's mouth. "We haven't yet had our dance of the evening. Surely that wouldn't be inappropriate since we've already been introduced and you are already spoken for," he said. He gave her a disarming smile. "Soon-to-be Lady Barrington," he added.

There was something in his voice and his eyes, and again she experienced the feeling that they had met before.

Zach turned his full attention on Elyse Winslow. He still had many questions he wanted answered, and Miss Winslow might prove an excellent source. Not only was she lovely, but she was intelligent. Which raised the question what was she doing with Barrington? However, it could be advantageous to use Jerrold Barrington's fiancé to learn what he wanted to know.

"Congratulations are in order," he told her. "You must be very happy..." He heard the mockery in his own voice and wondered where the devil that had come from.

"Yes, of course," she replied, but the ease with which she said it didn't reach her eyes.

He reached for her gloved hand, determined to play out his game and learn what he could from her.

It was a simple gesture, it shouldn't have meant anything other than the simplest courtesy, there shouldn't have been the heat that burned through that simple contact. He saw it in her eyes and realized that she had felt it as well, and they suddenly darkened.

Something appeared just beyond her circle of vision, as if it was there, then gone, that sense that they might have met before. Elyse stared at a man she didn't know, couldn't remember, and yet felt an inexplicable heat in the touch of his hand.

Good heavens, what was the matter with her? she thought as she pulled her hand from his. She should have been relieved. Instead, she felt that same sense of loss and emptiness she experienced after her dreams.

Everything in the ballroom seemed suddenly different, as if she were standing still, and the entire room and everyone in it, spun about her.

No, not everything was out of control, she realized. *He* was there, like the calm in the middle of a storm. She pressed her fingers against her forehead. The room had become unbearably warm.

She closed her eyes, hoping she could open them in a few moments and find everything as it was before... before Sir William St. James had appeared.

"Perhaps a walk outside for some fresh air," he suggested. He slipped his arm through hers. It fed his sense of recklessness to steal her away from all of them, including her fiancé.

She was a few steps ahead of Zach as he guided her

through the doors and out onto the veranda. She stopped abruptly. "I'm really feeling much better now. It's not necessary for you to remain with me," she informed him with a shaky voice.

"I wouldn't dream of abandoning you." His voice was low, almost intimate. "How would it seem if I retreated too quickly? Someone might assume that we exchanged more than idle conversation."

"I don't really care what people might think," she replied. To be perfectly honest, the only thing she'd thought about since they were first introduced was curiosity and that feeling that they had met before.

"You really should. It might be the beginning of something very scandalous. And Lord Barrington seems very conscious of such things," Zach teased, reaching to hold her gloved hand in his.

She'd met many foreigners on the Grand Tour, but this one certainly qualified as the most...interesting. She composed herself, forcing her eyes away from the black eye-patch he wore.

Was he badly scarred with only a gaping hole beneath the slash of his brow? How had it happened? Was it an accident or something else? Was he once with the military and suffered the wound in some far-off place?

There was something about it that bothered her. It wasn't the idea of scarred flesh. What she felt was more like sadness that he might have suffered great pain for it.

"A penny for your thoughts." Zach smiled down at her, unable to resist the temptation of knowing what she was thinking at just that moment.

"I'm afraid a mere penny wouldn't do." She hid the sadness with a faint smile. "It may very well cost you an entire fortune."

There was something elusive about her smile, something almost lost and mournful in her eyes.

"It would be worth losing a fortune, I think," he said then.

A man who wanted to know her thoughts? It was quite amazing. She took a step back as she changed the topic of their conversation. "I really should return," she informed him, then struck a light note. "I thank you for asking, but I don't dance with pirates. It could be dangerous."

Zach burst out laughing, to cover his reaction at just how accurate her comment was. "Oh, I think you will. It would be very bad form for you to refuse."

Her chin angled slightly; her eyes filled with humor.

"Do you always get what you want?"

"Always." Zach smiled down at her. "You see," he said, and took a step toward her, closing the distance between them once more. "I don't like losing, but winning... " He paused.

"I didn't realize it was a game?"

"Everything in life is a game," he replied, his gaze darkening to slate as he thought of many prizes to be sought and won. "Winning is everything."

He knew the exact effect his words would have on her. And he was right as alight sparkled in her eyes. She liked a challenge. Zach smiled. Barrington was twice a fool. He had no idea.

She most definitely felt better. It might have been the night air, or the challenging conversation. Or possibly both.

"Everything?" she asked.

Jerrold felt the same way, but she disliked his overbearing, competitive nature. There was nothing overbearing about St. James. He could be competitive, she sensed that about him. Perhaps even dangerously so, but it was vastly different.

There was no cruelty in this man. Instinctively she knew it. She'd felt it in the gentleness of his hand. As she thought of that touch, and the feelings it had aroused, she was curious. Who was he really?

"It isn't necessary for you to remain here with me,"

Elyse informed him. "I'm really much better, and I can take care of myself."

"Yes," he admitted, his fingers slipping beneath her chin and tilting her head up so that he could look directly into her eyes, "and you never faint. "His tone was teasing.

"Never." Her gaze lowered to the curve of his smile. Color crept into her face as she found it impossible to break away from the humor she saw there. "Why did you call me Lady Barrington?"

"Why did you think that we might have met before?" he answered her with a question of his own.

"It was a simple mistake." She dismissed it, but knew the question went unanswered for both of them. For the life of her, she couldn't understand why she'd said what she had. Still, she was curious.

"You thought I was Lady Barrington?" she replied. Jerrold's mother had been dead for many years.

"As you said," he replied. "A simple mistake. "But still there was the pendant. "Your fiancé has excellent taste. The pendant you're wearing is extraordinary."

Her hand went to the pendant. "A gift," she replied, but didn't elaborate. The pendant was very special to her.

"It's very much like the color of your eyes."

That seemed a bold thing to say, and yet... Her fingers tightened around the pendant. The clasp separated and the pendant fell to the flagstones at her feet.

Zach bent over, his fingers closing over the cool of diamonds and pearl intricately set in an old-fashioned design. The muted light from the ballroom illuminated the stones, the large pearl glowing softly.

She stared at the pendant in his hand. How was it possible that she felt as if she had done this once before? Her gaze met his as she reached out to take the pendant, her fingers brushing his.

"It's most unusual." His voice softened, as he caressed the large pearl. "Like the one who wears it. "His gaze shifted then. "A gift from your fiancé?"

"Jerrold?" She laughed softly and shook her head. "No. He prefers more simple jewelry. He's given me several other pieces."

And still, he thought, she'd chosen to wear this particular piece.

"I'm sure he has," Zach remarked. "Why aren't you wearing them?"

"I prefer the pendant." Elyse smiled softly. "It holds a special meaning for me." Her voice had softened. "It was a gift from my grandmother. It was given to her by a friend many years ago, Felicia Barrington."

Zach's gaze changed at the sound of the name that had brought him thousands of miles across oceans and continents to a country he loathed.

"Lady Felicia Barrington," he repeated the name.

"Yes," Elyse answered uncertainly. The night had suddenly grown cold, and she shivered at the way he said it, as if there was something else that wasn't being said. After all, what did she know of this man? Watching his gaze, partially hidden behind that eye-patch, she felt that first impression all over again.

"Who is she?" he asked.

"She was Jerrold's mother."

"Was?" he asked. "What happened to her?"

"She died many years ago. I remember my grandmother telling me she died the night of the... " She hesitated. "The night my parents died." She asked herself why she felt compelled to tell him that? Or to explain anything to him at all for that matter?

She should have left then, but she didn't.

"I would like some answers as well," she told St. James.

Zach's smile returned. "Fair enough," he acknowledged, hiding his disappointment at learning that Felicia Barrington was dead.

Tobias had tried to prepare him for that possibility. After all, everything that had happened to his father before he'd arrived in New South Wales had taken place over thirty years ago. It was a long time.

"Who are you?" Elyse fastened that blue gaze on him. "I don't remember Jerrold mentioning you." Not that he would necessarily, but she wanted to know more about him.

"And you're not English," she informed him. "Your accent is... different."

"All right. Then, who am I?" Zach countered, wondering just how much she thought she knew. He was curious since she seemed to be so certain.

"You're possibly from one of the colonies," she began. "Perhaps Burma or Hong Kong. You obviously sustained an injury, perhaps in the Queen's service."

"Go on," he told her.

"I don't recall anyone of the name St. James. For all I know, you might be a pirate come to remove everyone's valuable possessions."

When he didn't respond or offer any argument, it seemed it was more a matter of what he *was* than what he was not.

If she was right, she might very well be venturing into dangerous territory. He was a maddeningly handsome man with the aggravating air of someone who didn't give a damn about anything or anyone. And the eye-patch only heightened the air of mystery and danger about him, in spite of the spotless shirt and the formal black waistcoat and pants. He slowly shook his head.

For heaven's sake! She hadn't meant to embarrass him. Then, he raised his head, and she realized he wasn't embarrassed at all. He was laughing!

"I don't see what's so amusing," she announced. But he only continued laughing, as if he found something she'd said amusing. "What are you laughing at, sir?" Oh, what she wouldn't give to wipe the smile off his handsome face.

"I'm sorry," he apologized, reaching to wipe what appeared to be a tear from the corner of his eye. Then he cleared his throat and tried to hold back another fit of laughter.

"It's just that you've found me out," he confessed.

Elyse drew back in surprise. In spite of her observations, this was not at all what she expected.

"And you're quite right, Miss Winslow," he said, bowing low from the waist.

"I'm not at all what I appear to be," he said, his manner now teasing. Zach delighted in the way her mouth twisted thoughtfully.

Most women would have given him some wide-eyed, simple look and then played the confused, naive young virgin.

He found Miss Elyse Winslow, soon-to-be Lady Barrington, a breath of fresh air. She didn't give a damn about appearances, or she wouldn't have come out on the veranda with him in the first place. And, as it was, she had no idea just how close she'd come to the truth.

Leaning toward him, as if to share a secret, her eyes sparkled. "With that patch, I'd say you're a pirate."

Zach watched her, only a trace of a smile lingering at the corners of his mouth. "A pirate?"

"Of course. Which would explain why you found the pendant so fascinating. And," she hesitated, "why you still haven't given it back to me." She leaned closer. "You sir, are undoubtedly a blackguard and a scoundrel, probably with a price on your head."

Taking another step toward him, Elyse's hand shot out, her target the pearl and diamond pendant that dangled from his fingers.

His fingers closed around her wrist, and his other arm stole around her slender waist, pulling her against him.

"And you, dear lady, are a thief." His breath was warm against her cheek.

She was very definitely a thief. But he doubted she understood his meaning. She could steal a man's heart with those eyes that promised something elusive. And unless he missed his guess, that something was desire, but he doubted Barrington was even aware of it. No, this was something she kept to herself, holding back, almost as if she was waiting.

He reached up, stroking the back of his fingers against her cheek.

"Please don't," she whispered only to find herself drawn more intimately against his muscular body.

He sensed something deep inside as he held her, and he felt the trembling that had her hands pressing against him as if to push him away.

"What are you afraid of?" he whispered.

"I'm not afraid."

Who was this man and why was he having such a devastating effect on her? More importantly, why had she allowed it. "Please stop."

"What is it that you want me to stop?" Zach teased, his lips brushing the curve of her jaw, feeling the small muscles that clenched and unclenched as if she would have said something, but didn't. Unable to resist tasting her, he turned his head, until his mouth lightly touched the corner of hers.

She'd ceased breathing. Her hands curled in the folds of his shirt, determined to push him away, instead pulling him closer, as her lips parted.

Lys. The name whispered as he caressed the soft angle of her face, then slipped into the silken mass of her hair, stealing the pins, freeing the dark mass until it tumbled at her shoulders, then lowering his mouth to hers once more.

It was reckless, they might be discovered, and she wanted it to never end. It was dangerous and she'd never felt so safe. Then he slowly stepped away from her.

"No," he whispered. "I won't hurt you," he said, unable to understand where the thought came from for someone he'd just met, a beautiful woman when he'd never walked away from one before.

The cool night air moved between their heated bodies, leaving Elyse confused as much at herself as him, and angry at something she had never felt before.

She slapped him. "You're a cad and a lowlife!" The pendant was all but forgotten. "And I want you to leave, now."

Zach nodded, marshaling the feelings that churned inside him, a desire that formed with a need to protect her, escaping once more behind a different mask.

"My apologies if I offended you." He, who never apologized to anyone. "Good evening, Miss Winslow."

Five

"How long did you say you would be in London?" J. Hollings, Esquire, looked down the narrow twist of an incredibly long and disdainful nose.

"I didn't," Zach replied, causing poor Hollings to jump as he fixed him with an icy stare.

Tobias shifted uncomfortably. His head hurt, his eyes ached, and his mouth felt as if it were stuffed with wool. The collar of the damnable shirt cut into his neck, his shoes pinched miserably, and he had the feeling that Zach was taking great pleasure in drawing out this meeting unnecessarily.

"Mr. Hollings assured me there would be no problem in using the house while we're in London," he said. "I might add, I hope our stay will be brief." He irritably forced the words from between clenched lips. If he didn't sit down soon, he'd fall down.

On second thought, maybe that might teach the young upstart a lesson, set all of London abuzz about *Sir William St. James.* Of all the idiotic, addlepated ideas! The longer Zach kept up this charade, the greater the chance they were going to get caught at it. But the longer it continued, the more deeply immersed his young friend had become in the deception. It was as if Lady Felicia Barrington had some sort of hold on him.

Zach left the library, continuing his inspection of the first-floor rooms. The elegant manor house bespoke position, respectability, and wealth. He only had a need of the first two. His decision made, Zach turned abruptly to return to the library.

"It will do quite nicely," he told Hollings." We only have need of the rooms on the ground floor. Our stay in London, will be... brief." He fixed on the solicitor an expression of cool disdain that was heightened by the black eye-patch obscuring part of his face.

Mr. Hollings straightened his coat with a thoughtful nod. There was something about this elegantly dressed gentleman with the odd accent that intrigued him. The name was not known to him however he'd learned early in his career the rewards of discretion. He never questioned the motives of his clients, but this was a most uncommon situation.

"It is unusual that Lord Vale left no instructions that you would be visiting, your grace," he ventured, hoping to learn more. "We've handled many transactions for him in the past. It seems somewhat unusual..."

"He wasn't aware of my precise plans. However, if you wish, we could send word to him that you prefer I remain aboard my ship until the matter is settled." Zach fastened the man with a cool stare.

Hollings blanched. "Oh my, no! We couldn't have that! It wouldn't be proper... that is, what if his grace were to learn of the matter?" Removing a handkerchief from his coat pocket, he blotted at his upper lip. "No indeed. I wouldn't want Lord Vale to think we were remiss in our responsibilities to a member of his family."

"If everything meets with your approval, I will make the necessary arrangements for the household staff to return immediately," he added.

Zach smiled "I will rely on your expertise, Mr. Hollings. And upon my cousin's return, I will convey my compliments regarding your excellent service."

It was amazing, he thought again, how people fawned over the titled, amazing how much could be gained with just the nod of a head or the raising of an eyebrow—amazing and loathsome.

"I would like to move in immediately. I'll have my things transferred from my ship." His gaze wandered over the richly paneled library.

It was elegant. Dark wood, dark velvet fabrics, and equally dark carpet. Elegant and the walls closed in worse than those of the cabin aboard the *Revenge,* making him silently long for the vastness of Resolute.

He pushed the longing back. Soon enough he would have the answers he'd come for and would conclude a very special "transaction" with Barrington. Whether she realized it or not, Lady Elyse Winslow would help him accomplish those ends. She would make the perfect pawn to get at Barrington.

His mood carried an edge of anger. He turned to the solicitor who was hesitating as if there were something else to be said but he was afraid to risk it.

"Is there something more?" Zach asked, controlling the anger. After all, this man had nothing to do with it. He told himself it was merely anticipation at being so near the truth about his father. But just this morning, he'd turned his anger on Tobias and had felt badly for it afterward. His friend was suffering his own demons, drinking himself practically unconscious each night and then enduring the after-effects the following morning. He hated Tobias' weakness, but he understood the reasons for it.

He supposed his old friend was entitled to want to forget the past. As he knew only too well, the past was often a harsh taskmaster.

"Was there something else you wished to discuss, Mr. Hollings?" he asked then, wishing to be done with the matter.

"Not at all, Sir William." The solicitor dipped and

bobbed like a puppet controlled by invisible strings. "I'm certain I'll be able to have the servants here before end of day."

"Excellent." Zach preceded him to the front door.

"Good God!" Hand clasped to his sweat-beaded brow, Tobias collapsed into a nearby chair draped with a dustcover. "I'm certainly glad that's over." His eyes closed wearily, his head rolling back against the Queen Anne chair.

"And you standing there as if you couldn't quite make up your mind about whether you wanted the house or not! If that little pipsqueak starts snooping around, the constable will be our first caller."

Zach leaned casually against the doorframe, hands thrust deep into the pockets of his worsted pants. His mood was deceivingly calm.

"Mr. Hollings won't ask questions. People always see what they want to see."

"God help us if he investigates that information you gave him. A bank account in Switzerland of all places!" Tobias muttered, rubbing his eyes.

"Which shows how much you know, my friend. The most reputable international businessmen, and even royalty, utilize such accounts. The Swiss are known for their expertise and more important their discretion in financial matters. The account exists," he assured him.

"It does?" That seemed to sober Tobias somewhat. He sat upright with a jerk, paying a severe price for moving so quickly as he winced at the throbbing at his head.

Zach nodded. "I took the liberty of establishing it several years ago. I thought it necessary to secure certain funds that no one would be able to find."

"That explains a good many things," Tobias mumbled. "I always wondered about all those account books you kept in the safe at Resolute."

Zach smiled. "There's a great deal you don't know, my friend."

"Eh, what's that you say?" Tobias raised bleary eyes to stare at him a little unsteadily.

"I've been thinking about the coincidence of things that come in twos—gloves, shoes, and pendants." He changed the direction of the conversation.

"Pendants? What are you talking now? I see only one." Tobias closed his eyes. He could have sworn Zach held only one pendant in his hand. He groaned. "Even my hair hurts."

"It should, considering the whiskey you consumed last night." He held the pendant that he'd taken from Elyse Winslow the night before, fascinated by the light that gleamed on the diamonds. Blue diamonds, very rare.

"Yer daft, there's only one. Unless me eyes are playing tricks on me." Tobias squinted at the sparkling object Zach held aloft. He rose on unsteady feet only to slump back wearily into the chair.

"I think maybe you'd better go on without me to that appointment. I'll stay here and wait for the ones that Mr. Hollings said he'd send over."

He rested his forehead in his hands. "I wish Minnie were here with one of her tonics. Better yet, I wish we were back at Resolute."

"Soon enough," Zach replied. He shrugged off the same feeling he'd had when he'd first met Elyse Winslow two nights ago, as if he were somehow seeing her again...

The deep rumble of snoring filled the library. Tobias' head nodded forward onto his chest. Zach crossed the room to his friend. Lifting the older man's feet onto a stool, he tried to make him more comfortable.

"Rest easy, my friend," he told him. "I'll have the answers I want and then we can leave England."

∼

Zach paused at the steps of the imposing building. Austere brick towered overhead a full six stories. Gold leaf lettering on a bronzed plaque announced, Barrington Shipping.

The building and the name spoke of old money, old family, and power. If he'd been anyone else, he might have been impressed—might have. Still, there was a vague feeling of familiarity about the building, as if he might have been there before. He shrugged it off.

Trapping the lion in its lair. The thought he'd first shared with Tobias months ago came back to him. This was the lair, and the lion was inside.

Jerrold Barrington rose in greeting as he entered the formal office. A faint smile played across his lips. It must be an affliction of the nobility, to surround themselves with rich furnishings. This office, like the library in which he'd left Tobias, was richly appointed to the point of being grotesque.

"Good to see you again," Jerrold Barrington declared. "Please, make yourself comfortable."

"The pleasure is mine," Zach responded. More than he could know, he thought.

Jerrold came around the desk. Lifting the lid on a hand-carved wooden box, he offered his guest the finest of rolled cigars.

"I hope you had no difficulty finding our offices."

Zach shook his head. "None at all." He declined the offer of the cigar, preferring one of the thinly tapered cigarettes he carried inside his coat pocket. The gesture was a small one, but it had the desired effect. Barrington's brows rose at the refusal. He was obviously a man who wasn't accustomed to being refused.

"Your company is well known in many ports of the world. I decided long ago that my business would be best served by dealing with you when I reached England. That is," Zach continued. "If we can reach a mutually satisfying agreement." His statements carried far more import than the other man could possibly know.

Jerrold resumed his position behind the desk. "I find it somewhat surprising that a man of your obvious station would concern himself directly with matters of business."

Zach's smile deepened. "As with yourself, I find there are certain matters that I prefer to handle myself." Standing before the sweep of windows that opened onto a view of the business district, he maneuvered the conversation.

"Certain transactions are best handled by me. I think you understand my meaning. The fewer who know of them, the better." He turned, leveling a speculative gray gaze on the watchful man behind the desk.

Barrington was careful, in his choice of words and his reactions. "You spoke of just such a cargo the other evening when we met at the celebration for myself and my fiancée."

His hands, spread on the desktop, betrayed only the faintest tremor of anticipation. After that evening, he'd sent one of his men to learn what could be found out about St. James. The man had returned with little information. It seemed the man was a mystery. He had only learned that he was apparently distantly related to Lord Vale.

"Ah yes," Zach replied, carefully masking what he felt deep inside. "A lovely young lady. You are most fortunate." He forced himself to get beyond the loathing he felt for Barrington.

"Yes," Barrington admitted. "It almost seemed as if you might know each other."

"A simple mistake. I knew of Lady Felicia Barrington through a friend some time ago."

"My mother has been dead for many years," Jerrold replied.

"Yes, so Lady Winslow informed me. I am deeply

sorry. She must have been a very fine lady. My friend spoke highly of her."

"Who is your friend? Perhaps I know this person."

Zach turned to him. "It was someone I knew in the colonies."

"New South Wales? Such a wretched place. I sincerely doubt that, although I do have friends there because of my business dealings, and there are many English people there. It's possible one of them might have been acquainted with my mother."

Zach's gaze narrowed. A man like Jerrold Barrington wouldn't dirty his feet walking across the street to exchange pleasantries with a colonial, much less one who was a convict. He concentrated on the framed etchings of various Barrington ships that filled one wall as he slowly brought his anger under control.

Gypsy Moth came to mind. The name seemed to leap into his thoughts. Why in the devil had he thought of it? He knew of no ship by that name. He continued his slow perusal. A ship's sextant was encased in glass on a mahogany table. He was drawn to the sextant as another thought, vaguer, remained just beyond his grasp. Then, as clearly as a memory, his father taught him to use the sextant when he was a boy.

Zach blinked as he stared at the sextant. That wasn't right at all! His father had died before he was born. An old sailor by the name of McAndrew in Sydney had taught him how to sail and use the sextant to chart a course. What the devil was wrong with him!

As easily as the thought came, it was gone and Zach turned to Barrington, hoping to learn something more from their conversation.

"I became acquainted with this man in New South Wales. His name was Nicholas Tennant." He watched carefully for any sign that Barrington recognized the name and hid his disappointment when there was none.

"You said *was*?"

"He's dead now." Zach continued his slow tour of the office, feeling a restless need to keep moving. He pretended to study the etchings of ships. Most were of clippers or the slower frigates, although a more recent sailing vessel also boasted a steam engine as evidenced by the single smokestack protruding from her main deck.

His gaze narrowed at the sight of a smaller sailing vessel. The artist had caught it at just the right moment, revealing the two-masted ship heeling over hard almost white-capped waves. The name *Gypsy Moth* was neatly scribed underneath, and the year 1814.

Jerrold Barrington rose from his chair and crossed the office. Standing very near Zach, he noticed the direction of his interest. "I first learned to sail aboard her. Wretched, beastly little craft to handle in rough seas."

"Where is she now?" Zach's voice was hollow as he fought off something vague that hovered at the edge of some memory. How could he possibly have known the name of the vessel?

"At our summer place near Dover. Father goes there quite often. I haven't been in years. But as you can see," he went on boastfully, "our interest lies in bigger ships, and their cargos."

"The other evening it seemed you might be acquainted with Miss Winslow," Jerrold probed.

"A most delightful young lady. But no, I'd never met Lady Winslow before that evening," Zach assured him.

"That's strange. She seemed to think she knew you," Jerrold mused, unable to suppress a nagging irritation that perhaps this man wasn't telling him the truth.

"A simple mistake," Zach smiled. "I'm often mistaken for someone else."

Barrington frowned. Mistake indeed. Only a fool would mistake this man for anyone. He wanted to know a great deal more about him, and the business transaction he'd spoken of.

Jerrold Barrington smiled, reminding Zach of a venomous snake he'd seen in the Outback before it moves in for the kill.

"You mentioned a business matter the other evening," he continued. He tugged on the satin rope mounted on the wall beside the desk, and then looked up as an older man entered.

"Hobson, we'll take brandy in the library." He turned to Zach. "If you'll join me. The library is much more comfortable and is a discreet place for discussing business." Indicating a door in the mahogany-paneled wall, he led the way into the library.

"Since you seem so well acquainted with Barrington Shipping, you're undoubtedly aware that we are experienced in handling a variety of cargoes for both import and export to virtually any port in the world."

It sounded like a well-rehearsed speech he gave often. When the brandy was brought, he dismissed his employee and poured the amber liquid into squat glass tumblers.

Zach smiled as he accepted the proffered drink. He had Jerrold where he wanted him. Barrington was curious and greedy. He would not turn down the offer Zach was about to propose. And it was all so perfect. A precious cargo was carefully disguised and quite safe. What Barrington didn't yet know was that it was actually his cargo, first sold to him in New South Wales for a mere fraction of its true value.

Barrington controlled all shipping, and thereby controlled prices on all commodities. It was a lucrative arrangement that had the effect of maintaining an economic stranglehold on the colonies.

But this particular cargo had a unique history. It had first been sold to Barrington Trading Company, then loaded in the hold of a Barrington ship bound for England. Mysteriously, the ship never made her destination. Her crew, as well as her cargo, were lost off the treacherous coast of Australia, as were so many ships over the past two years. Now that cargo had just as mysteriously reappeared in the hold of the *Revenge,* to be resold to Jerrold Barrington at an exorbitant profit. It was a scheme the Raven would envy.

Zach smiled secretively. "As I explained, I am a stranger to England. But I thought you might be able to acquaint me with someone who might be interested in a certain cargo."

Jerrold's demeanor was almost condescending. "I will try. Of course, there is the possibility my company might be interested as well. That would depend on the cargo, and whether or not there is a ready market for it."

"Of course. There's always a market for this particular cargo. I acquired it from a man in the colonies; however, I'm not at liberty to divulge his identity." It was a game of cat and mouse, and Zach loved it.

Jerrold nodded, as he lifted an etched-crystal tumbler of brandy to his mouth. Contraband. But then it wasn't the first time his firm had dealt in such commodities, and it wouldn't be the last. There was a great deal of profit to be made in it. "What is the cargo?"

Zach lifted his own glass in a faintly mocking salute. "Four and a half kilos of raw, unrefined gold, taken from one of the richest ore deposits in the world." He suppressed a faint smile as he revealed the exact amount of gold lost aboard that Barrington ship off the coast of Australia only months earlier.

Jerrold Barrington broke into spasms of coughing. When he had sufficiently recovered, his dark eyes narrowed as they studied his guest. "I think perhaps we might be able to strike a deal, *senor.* Where did you say you came by such a large amount of gold?"

"I didn't."

There wasn't a trace of warmth in Barrington's smile. He reminded Zach of a sly wolf.

"It hardly matters. As you said, there is always a

market for such a cargo. What price did you have in mind?"

Barrington never flinched when Zach named a price that was just below the market price in London, and over ten times the amount he'd originally paid in New South Wales.

"You drive a hard bargain, *senor.*" Jerrold lifted his glass, carefully scrutinizing the man before him. Four and a half kilos of gold. What he wouldn't give to have that amount of gold, especially after his heavy losses this past year in those damnable colonies. But perhaps he could bargain the price down. He smiled as he thought of various methods he'd used in the past. Every man has his weaknesses. He had only to find out what this man's were, then use them to advantage and perhaps acquire the gold for substantially less.

"Nonetheless, I'm certain we can arrive at a mutually satisfying agreement," Barrington assured St. James.

He pulled a watch from his vest pocket as if only just realizing the time. "I hadn't realized the lateness of the hour. I hope you will excuse me. I have another appointment. But I would like to discuss this further. I'll be getting together with a few friends, evening after next, at my private club. If you're free, we could do so then."

Zach smiled graciously, masking his keen satisfaction. Barrington had reacted just as he'd thought he would by stalling for time. The man wanted to see what he could find out about Sir William St. James and a cargo of four and a half kilos of gold.

Jerrold rose, extending his hand. His cool smile stiffened when the man only nodded curtly.

"Until Thursday evening."

Pulling on his gloves, Zach smiled as he stepped down onto the cobbled sidewalk. His meeting with Jerrold

Barrington had gone just as planned. Barrington was careful, but he was also greedy. If he looked up now to the sixth floor set of windows, he would find Barrington watching him. He tipped his hat to a fashionably dressed lady who passed by. The trap had been baited.

He nodded a greeting to Sandy, across the cobbled street snarled with coaches and hansom cabs. The second mate from the *Revenge* looked faintly out of place atop the elegant gleaming black coach sitting around the corner. He'd given him instructions to be there promptly at twelve noon, when he'd sent him out before dawn on specific errands. As Zach threaded his way through the congestion of conveyances, the mate jumped down to greet him.

"Mornin', Cap'n." He tipped his hat with an awkward gesture that would have been out of place aboard ship.

Zach corrected him. "Not Captain, Sandy. We must be careful."

"Sorry, your grace." He beamed as he got it right.

"Did you get the information I wanted?"

"Yes sir." Sandy opened the door to the coach, lowered the folding step, and stood aside. To anyone observing, they seemed to be exchanging only the customary greeting and response of employer and servant.

"What did you find out about Miss Winslow?"

"I went to the house just as you said, Cap'n." He winced. "Sorry about that."

"Go on." Zach climbed the step, paused to adjust his hat, and took a seat inside.

"With the weddin' only a couple of weeks off, there's all kinds of people comin' and goin' at the house, but I talked to their coachman. He was a real talkative fella. Miss Winslow has been real busy with all the plans."

"What about Barrington?" Zach discreetly watched the street to make certain he wasn't being followed.

"He hasn't been around. But one of the maids at the

market first thing this mornin' said its common knowl-edge Barrington's keepin' a mistress. Some actress, I think. He's been spendin' most of his evenin's with her or at that private club of his."

"Does Miss Winslow ever leave the house? She must have appointments to keep. Most ladies do."

For days Zach had been trying to find some way to meet her again. But after their last encounter, he knew it would have to appear to be an accidental meeting. He was certain she wouldn't accept an invitation. Still, he mused thoughtfully, he did have something she wanted to have back.

"No appointments the last two days, but she left the house anyway. She went out ridin' again this morning, just like yesterday."

Zach looked up from beneath the brim of his hat. He swept it off, glad to be rid of it. "Where did she ride?" An idea was beginning to take shape. He knew it was reckless; still, he wanted to see her again, felt almost compelled to see her.

"A place called Kensington Gardens, usually. There's a big fella always follows along behind."

"Protection?" Zach mused with a smile.

"So it seems. But she usually manages to give him the slip. He's not very good with a horse."

"You've done a good job, Sandy. Does she ride at the same time each morning?"

"Same time every day. She slipped outta the house before dawn this mornin'. I never seen a proper-born lady who likes riding that time of day. And you want to know somethin' else real strange?" Sandy refolded the single step into the coach. "I almost missed her both times."

Zach's gaze narrowed. "What do you mean, missed her? She's not exactly the sort of woman you'd overlook."

"Right ye are, sir," Sandy quickly agreed. "She's one

beautiful lady. But that's just it. Both times, when she left the house, it weren't no lady I saw. It was a man!"

He had Zach's full attention now. "What are you talking about?"

"Just that. She weren't a lady at all. She was a man."

"Sandy, what the devil do you mean, she was a man?"

The second mate from the *Revenge* shrugged. "She was dressed up just like a man, with fancy breeches, jacket, and fine leather boots. And she had her hair all tucked up inside a black cap. Darnedest thing I ever did see. But she sat astride that horse like she knew what she was doin'."

Amusement deepened Zach's gray gaze. "Astride?"

"Yes sir! Full astride, just like a man. You don't think maybe...?" He left the implication unfinished.

Chuckling, Zach met his questioning stare. "No, Sandy. I don't think so at all. She's a woman all right. In every way possible." He sobered. "Let's get going. There's a great deal to be done before tomorrow morning. Suddenly, I have need of a horse."

He came to her... No words were spoken. None were needed. It was as though any words would only give unnecessary voice to that which they knew in their hearts. Elyse turned to him, her questions falling away before the answering promise in his eyes. This moment was as it had been a thousand times in the past and promised to be in the future. But now they came together slowly, almost as if they both feared it might be gone again too quickly.

Her eyes were filled with love as he reached out to her. Hands touched, fingers slowly entwining as he drew her to him. All the fears and the emptiness of yesterday slipped away as her body brushed against his. Slowly, his arms enclosed her, and the shadow of his face fell across hers. Her lips parted in silent longing. And then, in a whisper of time, his mouth closed over hers, filling her with tender warmth. His breath slipped through her, freeing her from the aching loneliness of the past.

"Lys," he whispered, his lips beginning a journey that followed the column of her throat to the soft, taut flesh of full breasts. The restraints of her clothes fell away beneath those familiar hands as they swept away eons of loneliness.

She cried out softly, his nakedness moving across hers with the promise of tender possession. Memory as infinite as passion engulfed them, taking them once more into that void where only they existed.

"I knew you would come back to me," she whispered, knowing an aching need as they slipped to the soft coverlet across the bed.

They might once have been lovers carried on a barque bound for ancient Thebes, or a knight and his lady in a flower-strewn meadow far from the conflicts of war. Or they might have lain beneath a night sky on a high plain, watching as stars burst overhead in a magical shower of light and promise.

They came together slowly, his body moving over hers, his lips whispering against her fevered skin as he had loved her before. Her cries against him were softly sweet with the pleasure of his name, then urgent with loving him. She'd waited a lifetime for him.

It was like the first time and the next time all as one, fulfilling a promise made long ago.

Loneliness filled her even as she struggled to hold onto the dream. Only a dream.

Passion and desire slipped into the far place of memory and unspoken thought until she couldn't remember at all. *In time,* his voice whispered to her, aching in its tenderness. *In time...*

Elyse sobbed as the dream slipped away, playing across her thoughts in fleeting images that made her ache with longing. In the darkness that remains just before the dawn, she threw back the covers of the bed, feeling the staggering jolt of morning air against her bare flesh. She sat up, eyes wide with something very near fear as she wrapped her arms around her naked body. The pale blue gown she'd donned only hours ago as she'd dressed for bed lay on the floor. The covers were in wild disarray and her pulse still raced.

She stared across the room as if she could see the apparition from her dreams, almost hoping she would. Instead, the shapes and forms silhouetted in the early gray of dawn were dearly familiar. Elyse struck a fist against the pillow, venting fear, anger, and frustration. The dreams came every night now.

"Who are you?" she cried desperately into the half-light knowing no one remained to answer her. She flung back the covers. With something very near desperation, she swung her feet to the floor. Crossing the room on shaking legs, she seized the cloth beside the pitcher and bowl on the commode. With almost vengeful desperation, she scrubbed the heat from her skin, then drew the cloth across her breasts sharply at the lingering ache that remained deep inside.

She turned, half-expecting to see her phantom lover watching her from the bed, still feeling him.

Everything remained as she'd left it, including the throbbing pulse of passion deep in her woman's softness. How was it possible for her to feel these things when she'd never lain with a man? How?

It was three nights since the ball, and each night the dream came back to her with a persistence that was becoming frightening, almost as if it were connected to something, or someone. And now this last dream had seemed so real, so intimate... She shuddered with the longing that still remained.

Her smile faded as she probed her temple where the telltale ache that always accompanied the dream still lingered.

"My mysterious phantom lover." The feeling of helplessness shifted to growing anger. "Who are you!"

She flung the cloth into the basin, sending a wave of water sloshing over the side. She needed a ride more than ever this morning! If she left now, she'd be back before anyone was aware she'd been gone. Elyse whirled around. Stark naked, she crossed to the wardrobe.

A driving restlessness made her impatient. Three days!

It was three days since she'd met St. James and lost her pendant. And each day, she'd sent Katy to market to try to find some bit of gossip about the elusive man who'd mysteriously appeared at the engagement party without invitation, and then had disappeared just as mysteriously.

Elyse silently cursed each button at the closure of the slim men's pants. She shoved the buttons of the shirt through maddeningly small holes and then tucked the voluminous tails in at the waist.

Barefoot, she crossed back to the bed, riding boots tucked under one arm while she struggled with the loose ends of the tie. Her fingers tangled hopelessly. Tossing both ends of the tie, as well as her heavy mass of her hair, impatiently over one shoulder, she pulled on first one boot and then the other, wriggling her toes into the soft leather. Grabbing a man's cap and riding jacket, she slipped out of the bedchamber.

The hall was dimly lit by one gas lamp at the far end. One of the maids put it out when she came upstairs to wake her grandmother each morning. The space under Katy's door was still dark. She had been completely exhausted the night before, after spending the last three days trying to learn something of St. James.

Elyse knew Katy wouldn't be up for at least another hour, and walked quietly down the hall, to the door leading to the servants' quarters on the first floor. It was much closer to the back entrance of the manor and the carriage house beyond. Stepping over a creaking floorboard in the middle of the top step, Elyse stole down the narrow stairway. Upon reaching the bottom, she stopped, inhaling the delicious aromas that drifted from the kitchen as cook prepared food for the day. Her stomach grumbled a nagging reminder that she'd been able to eat very little the last three days.

Checking to make certain no one was about, she ducked inside to steal a handful of warm rolls pungent with buttery cinnamon. Taking a fortifying nibble of one, she quickly slipped to the outside door and stepped into the fresh morning air.

A short walk along the hedgerow took her to the far end of the carriage house where Mr. Quist and the stable boy slept. Quimby's room was across the hall; stables, coach, and day carriages were housed at the far end. She could easily slip by undetected, leaving Quimby to follow her as she knew he was instructed by her grandmother, but today she desperately wanted him along. She'd decided on a different route for her ride this morning. She knocked lightly on his door. A loud snorting was the only response, followed by incoherent mumbling.

"Eh? What's that? Who's there?" he finally grunted, obviously not wanting to know.

"Good morning, Quimby." Elyse poked her head inside his quarters, giving his rumpled countenance a tremulous smile. "It's time to be up and about, if you're going riding with me this morning."

"Good God!" was his only discernible comment. The rest were muffled by a mound of bedcovers.

"I'm not decent!" Quimby roared, coming more fully awake.

Leaning against the door opening, Elyse popped another bite of pastry into her mouth. Cook's splendid pastries always seemed to cheer her up.

"You're never decent, Quimby," she quipped. "But

you'd better hurry if you want to catch me. After all, Grandmother has ordered you to follow me on all my morning excursions." A playful smile finally appeared at the corner of her mouth. She dearly loved Quimby. He was gruff and a bit cantankerous, but he was a steadfast friend and a trustworthy confidant. On top of that, she owed him her life.

"See you in the stables." She left his door open, knowing he'd turn over and go right back to sleep if she closed it, and she very much needed him along today. She had something she wanted him to check up on for her, or rather someone.

"I have fresh cinnamon rolls from Mrs. Halverson," she called back over her shoulder, bribing him. That ought to do it, she thought, as with a knowing smile she grabbed bridle and blanket.

"What's that!" Quimby came up off the bed. He wasn't wrong.

He had smelled fresh pastry! "Be right with ya, lass." He rolled out of bed, reaching for pants and boots.

Tightening the cinch strap on the saddle, Elyse slapped the rump of the large roan gelding. Quimby always rode the roan, while she preferred the more spirited bay, aptly named Deliverance.

Quimby found the roll she'd left for him on the small table in his room. Licking buttery syrup from his fingers, he shrugged into suspenders as he strolled down the length of the stable.

"What's this?" he grunted suspiciously, eyeing the additional horse.

"I've saddled him for you." Elyse smiled.

Quimby was immediately wary. Hot rolls, no doubt stolen from Mrs. Halverson, for which they would both suffer a good tongue-lashing, and now she'd saddled his horse as well. He shifted his massive bulk uncomfortably. She'd long ago given up trying to slip furtively into the stables. And almost as long ago, she'd taken to calling a morning greeting to him as she passed his door. From there, it was often a contest to see if he could dress and saddle his horse in time to catch her before she reached the end of the lane on her own mount and tried to leave him behind. One eye narrowed speculatively. Unless he missed his guess, she was up to something this morning.

"Cinch strap tight?" He grumbled, not putting anything past her. She could be as devilish as they came when she wanted to put something over on him.

"Check it yourself, if you're uncertain," she offered, an amused smile playing at the corners of her mouth. Stepping beside the bay, she reached for the reins and nimbly pulled herself into the saddle. "I think I'll ride in the Woods this morning. If you don't hurry, you'll get left behind," she teased playfully. Devilment danced in her soft blue eyes.

"The Woods? You haven't ridden there in a long time. Why today?" He was immediately suspicious. It would be just like her to tell him where she intended to ride and then choose another location.

"Quimby!" She pretended to be terribly hurt. "I don't think you believe me." Then she grew somber. "I have to ride as much as I can. My future husband doesn't approve of such things."

"Neither does yer grandmother," Quimby observed with a grumble. "That never stopped you."

"True enough," she admitted. "But today I have need of some company. Now, are you coming, or are you going to argue with me all morning?"

"Aye, I'm comin'." Satisfied she hadn't deliberately left any of the harness loose, he unsteadily swung his mountainous frame atop the tall roan.

"Damned fool beast!" he roared as the horse sidestepped, practically unseating him. "They're stupid, foul smelling and unpredictable," he yelled at her. "Couldn't you settle for a carriage?" While trying to bring his horse under control, he threw her a beseeching look.

"Good heavens, no. We'd look far too conspicuous." She favored him with the devastatingly beautiful smile that invariably got her what she wanted. "The whole idea is not to draw attention to our little ride." Laughter bubbled inside her. Conspicuous indeed! What could be more conspicuous than an oversize giant astride a horse whose sole purpose in life was to be riderless?

On more than one occasion, Elyse was forced to double back from her ride in search of Quimby. Once she'd found him painfully extricating himself from a bramble bush. Then there'd been the time he'd landed in a stream and moss was clinging to his head like tendrils of green hair. Another time she'd found him dangling in midair, frantically clinging to a low-hanging branch the roan galloped under to remove him from the saddle.

He gave the roan a murderous glare. "The beast hates me. Sometimes I think you're tryin' to do me in with these mornin' rides."

She leaned over, patting his arm lovingly. "You know perfectly well the roan is the only horse capable of carrying you. Grandmother selected him especially for you."

"With a little help from a certain young lady, I'll warrant," he accused.

Elyse turned the bay toward the open doors. "Well, I will admit I did influence her decision. I assured her he was a strong, intelligent animal."

"Intelligent!" Quimby spouted. His mouth clamped shut as he was practically unseated before even leaving the stables. "Cursed, good for nothing—"

His description of the roan was cut off as the lunging horse whirled first in one direction then the other, trying to unseat him. Elyse guided the bay into the soft gray light of early morning, smiling to herself.

Sooner or later, Quimby would follow. She pulled her horse up, turning about just as the roan emerged alone from the stables. She snatched at his reins as he tried to dart past her.

Following on foot, Quimby mumbled something inaudible, as he massaged his backside. He fixed Elyse with a withering glare, took the reins from her, and swung into the saddle.

Six

Elyse guided the bay past the Winslow house, down the cobbled lane that ended at Pont Street.

It wasn't a lane at all, but a square enclosing several of the statelier London homes. Pont Street led to the heart of London, including Victoria Station. They took the train when her grandmother decided to close the London house and retreat to the country for the warmer months of the summer. Uncle Ceddy's small stately manor house was near the business district and the Houses of Parliament. An elegant day carriage passed, the occupant nodding a stiff acknowledgment, one man's greeting to another.

"Good day, Lord Chesterton." Elyse fixed a somber expression on her face, one that was faintly disdainful, and nodded a greeting to her grandmother's acquaintance. Then she promptly broke into a giggle after he passed by. He'd have a devil of a time trying to decide just who the "young man" coming from Lady Winslow's drive was.

Instead of following the carriage down Pont Street, she cut across the end of the lane, guiding the bay down an embankment, and across a narrow strip of Regent's Park. Skirting the perimeter, she urged her horse across the footbridge that spanned the Boating Lake. The

Woods bordered the park to the north. Crossing the indefinable barrier that separated the two was like stepping into another world. One moment she was traversing meticulously manicured grass, the next she'd slipped into shaded, lush greenery allowed to grow unrestrained. It was almost primitive, dark, and secretive; and she loved it.

She preferred the overgrown, unkempt trails of the Woods. Footpaths crisscrossed several hundred wooded acres, filled with wild game, rippling creeks, streams, and hidden hollows. Rail fences intersected at unpredictable locations, testing a rider's ability to jump them, relegating those incapable of doing so to taking a long circuitous route back to one of the main trails. The Woods was a magnificent overgrown maze. There were rumored to be three paths that led into it and exited on the far side, but Elyse had been able to find only two of them.

In years past, the Woods had been a hunting preserve for members of the royal family. It dated back to King Henry VIII, and according to legend, that robust king liked nothing better than to lead a party of friends into the park, declaring they must find their own way out.

And, of course, there was Jane's Folly, the source of an even more outrageous story that dear old Henry, contemplating a new wife, had deliberately sent young Jane Seymour down a badly marked trail in the Woods. Mistress Seymour was not known to be the brightest of Henry's wives. Needless to say, she failed to find her way out, but good old Henry managed to find her. From then on, Jane's Folly referred to the trysting place of the third queen with old Henry VIII. It was a secluded glen, where the King supposedly first bedded his future wife. Hearing of the episode, the Queen, Anne Boleyn, lost her temper, and within a very few months, her head.

Elyse had found the Folly two years ago. Whenever she rode in the Woods, she dared Quimby to find her.

And each time she was forced to double back over the path in search of him. It was on one of those occasions she found him picking himself out of a thicket and cursing a blue streak.

The Woods was secluded and was now frequented only occasionally by more adventurous riders. She knew she was unlikely to see anyone except for Quimby, if he ever managed to catch up with her.

She heard the faint staccato of hoof beats behind her and smiled.

"Very good," she complimented him. "You're getting better." A soft smile turned up her lips. She would be glad for his companionship this morning. As the dream from her childhood occurred with increased frequency, she found herself filled with inexplicable loneliness. She slowed her horse to a walk. Faint smudges of sleeplessness rimmed her eyes, and a restlessness thrummed along her nerve endings. Three times the dream had come to her...

And it was exactly three nights since she'd lost the pendant. Her hand wound more tightly around the reins. It wasn't exactly lost, she thought, her irritation mounting. Stolen was a more accurate description!

"Fool!" she hissed at herself, causing the bay's ears to flicker back and forth. She soothed him by running a calming hand along his well-muscled neck, just how the devil was she to get her necklace back without her grandmother or Jerrold finding out about the incident.

The hoof beats were closer now, a rhythmic pacing. Elyse frowned. Quimby wasn't an accomplished rider. It occurred to her that he was taking the trail much too fast. She pulled the bay to a halt and turned in the saddle, but was unable to see anyone on the overgrown trail behind her.

A flash of black streaked through the distant trees and then disappeared, but the hoof beats continued, drawing closer with each passing moment.

A prickling of uneasiness caused the hair at the back of her neck to prickle. Tightening her grip on the reins, she urged the bay on, keeping watch behind her. The sounds of an approaching rider were closer now. She'd given Quimby ample time to follow, but it wasn't like him to take unnecessary chances with a horse. He simply wasn't that confident astride. And the rider bearing down on her at a steady pace was competent as well as confident.

The subtle pressure of her ankle sent the bay ahead at a faster pace. At the intersection of trails, she took the one to the left. As the hoof beats continued with unrelenting determination, she decided to leave the trail. Only a fool would dare follow her through the densely wooded forest.

Elyse reined the bay hard, sending him down an embankment to the right of the trail. She checked him only once as they crossed a stream and plunged up the far side. Not more than a few paces behind, she heard the faint splashing of another rider crossing the water. Whoever it was, it wasn't Quimby, and he was gaining on her. Flattening herself low over the saddle, Elyse ducked a low-hanging branch. Such a bough would've been Quimby's undoing. Still the rider persisted.

Ahead, the undergrowth broke, revealing a span of crisscross fencing. The jump was not a difficult one, but Elyse knew a hedgerow loomed less than a full stride on the other side. She smiled to herself as the bay nimbly took the jump. Only a rider experienced in the Woods, or a very lucky one, would know he must cut hard left as soon as his mount touched down to avoid careening into the hedgerow.

The bay cleared the fence, his ears immediately pricking forward at the familiar jump. She guided him hard left, negotiating the turn with ease. Here another surprise waited. The trail sloped up sharply. It took a strong, agile mount to recover from the jump and the hard turn, and to possess enough energy to make it up the incline of the softly mounded embankment. They were very near Jane's Folly now. At the top of the embankment, Elyse pulled the bay to a stop and whirled in the saddle.

She smiled victoriously at the lingering rush of distant hooves, waited out the momentary silence as the other horse left the ground, breathlessly expecting a telltale crash into the hedgerow. Instead, the relentless beating resumed.

"Damn!" she said under her breath and whirled the bay hard about. Fear tingled down the length of her spine, and beads of moisture slipped down between her breasts. As her mount lunged down the trail, Elyse glanced back over her shoulder, unable to resist a glance. She hesitated a moment too long, waiting for the rider to appear, then felt the sudden tensing in the taut muscles beneath her thighs. The bay's even tempo had changed abruptly. A moment too late, she checked his pace. She gasped at the sight of the large fallen oak that loomed before them across the entrance to Jane's Folly. A brief thought flashed in her mind—*Elyse's Folly*. It was too late to do anything except cling to the bay and pray he made the jump.

At one moment the morning sky held the promise of a brilliant golden day, the next it exploded in a burst of blinding light. Elyse felt the bay stumble beneath her. Instinctively, she released the reins and relaxed her body. There was nothing more she could do as the ground in the clearing seemed to reach up for her.

Elyse roused slowly. There was a dreadful buzzing in her head, and she felt as if a great weight were on her chest. She couldn't seem to breathe. She tried to move her head, only to have the pressure at the back of her neck increase, immobilizing her.

"Not yet," a man's voice told her. "Don't try to move. Keep your eyes closed."

She felt the faint pressure of hands moving slowly over her entire body. When the man, whose hands they were, seemed satisfied that nothing was broken, he instructed her again.

"You took a pretty nasty fall. Just relax and breathe deeply."

Elyse couldn't move if she'd wanted too, and the buzzing at her ears made it difficult to hear clearly. Her arms felt as if they were attached to lead weights. And something else prevented movement.

As her vision cleared, the ground seemed to come up at her with amazing swiftness. She closed her eyes again.

"You just had the wind knocked out of you. It'll take a minute to get it back. Breathe slowly," the voice commanded again, and she obeyed, the shadows in her immediate vision disappearing as the world righted itself once more.

She blinked, confused by what she was looking at. Her vision finally cleared. She tried to pull back but felt the firm pressure once more at her neck.

"Not too fast. Take it slow or you'll faint. Take a deep breath."

"I am breathing!" Her response was oddly muffled. Her head was buried in her knees for God's sake! "At least I'm trying to breathe." She pushed back against the strong hand and this time felt gentle release. Everything tilted crazily as she moved too quickly. She snapped her eyes shut in an attempt to stop the unsettling motion. Her head seemed to think it was still astride the horse, while her body was firmly earthbound.

"You had a good knock on the head. Take another deep breath."

Elyse gritted her teeth. "If you say that one more time..." The threat ended abruptly as she finally recognized her rescuer.

"You!"

"I've been called a great many things," he admitted with faint cynicism, "but usually something more memorable than that."

Elyse groaned as she tried to sit up. "Give me a moment, I'm certain I can come up with something."

"Undoubtedly you can," Zach assured her.

"What are you doing here?" she groaned, her sudden movement sending pain knifing through her head.

"It seems I'm picking you up off the ground."

He was dressed all in black, the only contrast being windblown waves of golden hair that spilled recklessly over the collar of his elegant shirt. Elyse jerked away as he reached to help her stand.

"I can do quite nicely for myself." She struggled to her feet, then suddenly thought better of her remark as the ground tried to come up to meet her again. Gloved hands immediately seized her arms and guided her to the tree she'd jumped only moments before.

"You seem to have a penchant for being unsteady on your feet, Miss Winslow." A smile produced a faint dimple at the corner of Zach's mouth. She'd given him a scare with that jump, but she was obviously feeling much better now. "Everything seems to be in its right place," he said, his gaze warming appreciably. "There don't seem to be any broken bones."

Elyse's head came up. "I suppose you're going to tell me you're a physician as well as a pirate," she commented, remembering their argument the night of the ball.

Devilment danced in his gray gaze. "I haven't been one recently."

He was playing along and with maddening charm. "But then there hasn't been the need until now."

Elyse's eyes narrowed. There was something different about him. She couldn't quite put her finger on it. Or maybe she had taken a worse knock on the head than she'd thought.

Retrieving a handkerchief from his coat, Zach wiped at a smudge of dirt on the end of her nose. "Are you always so reckless when you ride?"

"Do you always run people down?" Elyse responded tartly. Just speaking set her head to pounding.

"I didn't exactly run you down. Until that last jump, you seemed to be doing quite well. You almost lost me at that hedgerow." His smile flashed white amidst dark, bronzed skin. "At any rate, you didn't seem to be about to stop, and I did want dreadfully to see you again."

He was being a perfect gentleman. But the teasing light in his eye hinted at something else. "I don't suppose it occurred to you to call on me at my grandmother's house," she suggested.

"That thought did occur to me," he admitted with a rueful smile. "But it also occurred to me that after the other evening you might not see me."

"That depends." She looked up at him from beneath the curve of the hand still at her forehead.

He leaned forward, resting his weight on one arm propped against his knee. One booted foot was braced beside her on the fallen tree. His smile softened dangerously, and there was a languorous air about him that could only be described as unsettling.

"On what does it depend?" His voice was faintly husky as he leaned very near her, his gray gaze holding hers with subtle persuasion.

Elyse tried to swallow. She'd been afraid of whoever might be following her, then vaguely relieved to find it was someone with whom she was acquainted. Now the fear returned as a faint warning that tingled across her skin. But this was an entirely different fear. Letting out a slow steadying breath, she moistened her lips.

"It would depend on whether or not you returned, the pendant." He watched her, something unreadable in his eyes.

"Ah yes, the pendant." With maddening calm, he

stepped away from her and went to check his own horse. Her horse was nowhere in sight.

Elyse placed a cool hand on her aching forehead. At least now she was seeing only one of everything.

"I assume that's the reason for this little encounter." She watched him closely as she waited for his answer. Yes, a pirate, she thought as she watched him check the cinch strap. An elegant, handsome pirate with that flash of black eye-patch covering one eye. He swung effortlessly up into the saddle.

"I'll see if I can find your horse. Stay where you are." Not waiting for a reply, he whirled his own horse around and headed down the trail.

She couldn't move if she wanted to. There might be nothing broken, but every muscle ached from the fall.

She watched as he rode off, his hand was sure on the reins, and the firm angle of his boots in the stirrups denoted a man who accepted nothing less than perfect control. With a snort of disgust, she acknowledged that a man such as St. James would never have allowed himself to be thrown from his horse.

Zach guided the stallion past the next twist in the trail, then turned back. The bay Elyse was riding had cleared the jump and had kept right on going after her fall. Eventually he'd find his way back to his stall. There were two of them and only one horse. A faint smile twitched at the corners of his mouth when he returned to find her standing a little unsteadily beside the fallen tree.

She was just as beautiful as he remembered, but so completely different from the elegant young woman he'd met the night of the ball. Sandy would have no doubts if he saw her now. Soft brown pants were snug over slender thighs, glistening boots encased her calves. Her jacket was unbuttoned, exposing the flowing softness of a white shirt left open at the collar. And the black riding cap was gone. A disheveled mass of glistening sable-colored hair cascaded over her shoulders and down her back. And her eyes... large and soft, with secret shadows that betrayed a woman's thoughts, they were a haunting blue that seemed to go right through him, almost as if she were seeing inside him. The skin across her high cheekbones was pale, the color only now just beginning to return. Her mouth was full, too full for her to be anything but a woman, and faintly downturned in the beginning of a frown. The illusion of the clothes ceased where the collar ended.

"It is a lovely day for a ride," he teased, knowing full well by the look that sparked in those magnificent eyes that she was in no mood for it.

"Won't you join me, Miss Winslow? It seems your mount is nowhere to be found." He held out a hand, offering to help her astride his own horse.

Elyse hesitated. "What about my pendant?" she persisted, regarding his outstretched hand as if it were a snake.

"You certainly are single-minded." He deliberately avoided a direct answer.

"Do you have it with you?" Provoked by his maddening evasiveness, Elyse felt color rise in her cheeks.

"Actually, there is just one tiny problem." His gaze took in the finely chiseled planes of her face, then slipped down the elegant column of exposed throat to the voluminous man's shirt left open at the collar, plunging to the alluring darkness between the thrust of her breasts. He wondered if she was aware of how beautiful she was at that moment, her hair in wild disarray, twigs clinging to her pants, and a faint scratch across one cheek.

"I see no problem," Elyse's voice quavered. "Simply return the pendant." She tried to disguise her amazement. My God, he was practically undressing her with his eyes, or rather, quite effectively with his one eye.

"I would really like very much to return it to you, but I haven't got it with me."

A look of such boyish innocence came to his face that for a long moment Elyse was caught off guard. But the throbbing pain in her head gave her focus.

"If you don't have it, then what are you doing here!" She stomped a booted foot.

"It seems I'm rescuing a fair maiden."

Her head came up, her gaze locking with his. All the anger and pain seemed to seep out of her. *Rescuing a fair maiden.* A flash of something from her dreams returned and was quickly gone. Shaking her head, Elyse tried to brush away her confusion.

Zach dismounted. "You should take it easy. And since there is only one horse, we'll have to ride double."

Elyse frowned up at him. "I don't suppose you'd consider lending me your horse since you are responsible for my being without one," she suggested, as his arm slipped around her waist, and he guided her to the tall stallion.

"That's right, I won't." When she stubbornly tried to pull away, he nimbly placed her one foot in the stirrup and gently boosted her into the saddle.

For a brief instant, Elyse considered leaving him right where he stood but as her gaze locked with his, she realized he knew exactly what she was thinking.

"I wouldn't try it if I were you." He swung up behind her. "You wouldn't want a bruised backside to match your head."

He pulled her back into the curve of his body, then smiled as he felt her stiffen in response.

"You wouldn't dare!" she replied.

"Wouldn't I?" A smile teased at his lips, which were very near her cheek, but in his gaze was a steely promise. "I always get even when someone tries to pull something on me. And I pay back in triplicate."

Elyse swallowed back a stinging remark. He was just

arrogant enough to leave her there without a horse. As for the spanking he'd threatened, she didn't really believe he would do it. Still...

"What is this place anyway?" He cast a speculative glance around them as his arms encircled her waist, and the reins were gathered in his maddeningly strong hands.

"It's called Jane's Folly. It was named after Jane Seymour, the third wife of Henry the Eighth."

"Henry the Eighth?"

His warm breath brushed her ear. Far too close.

"He was the King of England," she reminded him.

"Oh yes, of course," Zach responded vaguely. "And this place was named after his third wife?"

"Well, actually it was named before she became his wife," Elyse informed him matter-of-factly.

"Really?"

There was the faintest hint of disdain in that maddeningly low voice, that was almost familiar as it slipped over her senses.

"I suppose there's a reason it was named Jane's Folly."

Elyse glanced at him, so close behind her that his body wrapped around hers.

"Henry was determined to have a son and when his previous wives had not produced one, he'd gotten rid of them. Jane was his third wife. It's said that he courted her here in secret while he was still married to the second Queen."

"Didn't he have six wives?" Zach mused, trying to remember what he could about the English royalty. Tobias had seen to it that he had a rudimentary education in such things.

Elyse frowned. "Yes. And I suppose someone like you would approve of such things." She bit at her lower lip, unable to understand what caused her to be so outspoken with a man she hardly knew.

He chose to ignore her comment.

"Did he ever get it right?" he asked.

"Get what right?" Elyse turned to face him. She immediately realized her mistake. She had thought him dangerous the night of the ball. It was still there, only more intensely so.

"Did he ever get the son he wanted, or did he merely wear out six wives?"

"You are beyond a doubt the most arrogant, insufferably rude man I've ever met. Yes, but she died shortly afterward."

"Ah, I see, and left poor Henry to take three more wives. I wonder why he didn't just set up a harem. He'd have had his son in much shorter time, perhaps two or three. And English history might have been different."

"What did you call it?"

"A harem." Zach guided the stallion over fallen limbs toward the trail. "The chieftains of the desert tribes have harems. They choose women and make them their concubines. They can claim as many women as they can provide for. That way a man increases his chances of producing many sons." He watched her out of the corner of his eye. "Of course, there are several very pleasant advantages to such a system," he added, forcing back a smile.

"I see!" If he was trying to shock her, he'd succeeded. Color spread across her cheeks as pain throbbed in her head.

"You really are the most maddening man. For someone who claims to be of the nobility, you have no manners. You're—"

"I think we've been over that already." He cut her off and urged his horse onto the main trail.

"Please stop!" Elyse breathed out angrily. "I want to get down."

"Not yet." Zach urged the stallion on at a gentle pace.

"I want to get down! Now!" she demanded, twisting around in the saddle and practically slipping over the side of the horse. His hands gently prevented her falling.

"And take your hands off me!"

Zach inhaled the windblown freshness of her hair as it gently blew against his cheek. "I can't do that. You see," he began to explain, "if I let go..." And for emphasis he did-just-that.

Without his arms about her, she fell backward from the saddle. She grabbed at his riding jacket.

A smile appeared on his lips as his arms closed once more around her. "At any rate, it's not safe for you to be out here alone."

"Not safe!" She turned to looked up at him. "And I suppose riding with you is safe?"

Her coolness at their first meeting returned. It was like an invisible barrier.

"Perhaps you could best answer that question, Elyse. Is it unsafe to meet a man in a secluded place? After all, you are to be married soon. What would people say if they knew you were meeting me like this?" He smiled maddeningly.

"And don't forget about Jane's Folly. She ended up marrying the King."

"Meeting you!" Elyse flung back at him. "You followed me!"

"Actually, you're right," he conceded. "I did follow you. And it was fortunate I came along when you needed me."

"If you hadn't pursued me, I wouldn't have fallen. Exactly why did you follow me?" Her fingers slowly entwined about the reins. If she could just get control of the stallion.

His gloved hand closed over hers. "I explained that before; I wanted to see you again. After all that was quite a memorable greeting you gave me the other evening. It intrigued me. Where was it you thought we might have met?"

"I explained that it was all a mistake."

As Zach easily loosened her fingers from the reins, something very near a memory filled his thoughts.

"You should never ride without gloves," he said, and carefully spread her fingers, exposing lightly callused skin. Tenderly, he kissed the palm of her hand, his lips brushing the raised flesh.

In spite of the growing warmth of the morning sun, Elyse shivered. Her fingers curled tightly as something deep inside knotted and tightened at that innocent contact. What was the matter with her?

She'd been kissed before. But never in her life could she remember being kissed with such infinite tenderness. It was like a breath of wind across her senses, like a whisper of something once remembered but now forgotten. As her startled gaze met his, her fingers clenched protectively over her exposed palm.

"I'll ride whenever and wherever I please, and without gloves. I certainly don't need your approval," she informed him coolly. "Now, if you don't mind..." She drew her hand from his. "I should be getting back. If my horse returns before I do, my grandmother will be terribly worried."

Zach snapped ramrod straight in the saddle, saluting her. His gaze darkened and became unreadable.

"Absolutely! And if anyone questions me about this morning, I'll deny anything happened."

"Deny what? For God's sake, what are you talking about?"

Elyse turned, her hand still tingling where his lips had touched it. Her breath caught at the nearness of his face. As her gaze fastened on that slash of black satin across his eye, she was suddenly seized with a desire to pull it away and see him fully. She stared at the arrogant sensuality of his mouth, only inches from hers. She wet her lips, for they were suddenly dry at the memory of the exquisite heat of his mouth when he'd kissed her the night of the ball.

The arrogance in his gaze shifted to something equally unsettling. "I'll never tell a living soul that I took advantage of you in a secluded, dark place. I'm afraid your reputation could never stand the rumor and speculation. Nor could mine for that matter."

"Took advantage?" Elyse almost laughed at him. She would have if she could have breathed. She fought to control the wild hammering of her pulse. "I think your reputation will survive anything you do," she whispered, mesmerized by the downward turn at one corner of his mouth, forgetting whatever else she'd intended to say.

Staring into those wide blue eyes, her lithe body against his, Zach felt everything about him slip into some nether world as if everything had ceased to exist except for this moment, except this woman, whose slender body enticed even when disguised in masculine clothes. He wanted to kiss her and then walk away from her without regret, just as he wanted to believe he had done the night of the ball. He needed to prove to himself that she was nothing but a pawn he would use to get to Barrington, that she meant nothing to him. But staring into her soft blue gaze he felt something quicken deepen inside, betraying all his well-intentioned plans. Never before had he lost control with a woman—never, until this moment and this woman.

Everything suddenly seemed changed. They were no longer in a shaded hollow of the forest, nor were they in any dimension of time or reality. It was just the two of them, as there had always been.

Elyse's eyes closed at the touch of his gloved hand against her cheek.

"Lovely Lys."

The mocking laughter was gone from his voice. It was as if the game were suddenly over and they the last two players. The stallion stood quietly beneath them. And time seemed to stand still.

Zach ran his fingers through her disheveled hair, slowly stroking the silken mass.

"You promised you'd always wear your hair long for me."

An inexplicable fear made her shiver. "Please don't." She tried to pull away from him.

"I don't want... "

His hand gently brushed her chin, angling her face toward him. Any further protest was cut off as he kissed her.

Elyse jerked away. "No!"

She tried to retreat further but there was no escape, confined by the saddle. She was trapped and she knew it.

His other arm encircled her waist, pulling her to him as he gently drew her head back. "I'm going to kiss you the way you were meant to be kissed and need to be kissed." His lips caressed hers.

It had nothing to do with his arms around her, holding her, preventing any retreat. It was a deep raging need, a hunger that had waited too long. A soft sound escaped the back of her throat as the kiss deepened, his lips tender against hers, his tongue plunging between.

"I knew you would come back to me."

She didn't try to understand how or why the thought came to her. She only knew that it had, like a litany from her soul. There was only this man and the lean, hard strength of his body bruising hers with such tenderness.

Desire slammed through Zach. He was out of control and knew it. He didn't like being out of control, or... vulnerable. And instinctively he knew the one went along with the other. He'd never allowed it with any woman. He especially didn't like that feeling now. She was betrothed to Barrington, as off limits to him as England itself.

Holding her in his arms, Zach knew it was all a lie. But he needed the lie as a barrier between himself and this young woman. She was as good as a Barrington, and because of that she was the same as Barrington, not to be trusted any further than it might serve his purpose.

Even when he was certain he believed that it took every last shred of control he could call up to close his fingers over her slender wrists and pull them from around his waist. Slowly, he pushed her from him. When he looked down at her passion-filled eyes, his gaze once more held the sting of cold mockery.

He pushed her away. The change in his mood was swift, like a cloud engulfing the sun. Coldness replaced the heat in that cold gray gaze, and the corners of his mouth lifted in a cruel smile.

"Is that what you wanted, my lady?"

She flinched at his stinging words, and inhaled sharply, choking on pain and humiliation.

"I was right about you. You're no gentleman. Damn you! You're nothing but a... "

He cut her off. "I'm certain you'll think of the words in a moment, Miss Winslow."

"You pompous, overbearing...!"

"Of course." His smile was cruelly mocking. "I get the general idea of what you're trying to say. Now, if you don't mind, I don't think I care to hear the end of your tirade."

Elyse couldn't think of anything bad enough to call him. Cheeks aflame with humiliation and embarrassment, she blazed with cold fury. Jerking one wrist free of his grasp, she drew back her arm, intending to strike him as hard as she could. Instead, the sudden movement completely unbalanced her.

She gasped as she landed on the trail with a sickening thud. Then she raised cool eyes to St. James. "Bastard!" she hissed.

Equally stunned by her sudden fall, Zach checked his first instinct to dismount. He certainly hadn't intended this. But the murderous look in those vivid blue eyes told him she wasn't about to listen to any explanations. Inhaling deeply, he forced back regret and a feeling of self-loathing. She had every right to be angry.

"Obviously, you're not seriously injured," he commented as he turned his horse about.

"Injured? I might have been killed! Where are you going?"

"I'm certain you can manage quite well on your own. You seem to be a young woman of great resourcefulness."

"What about my pendant?" Elyse demanded. She held her breath when he hesitated, turning back in the saddle.

"You may have your pendant back whenever you like. You have only to call at my house for it," he announced.

"That will be a cold day in..."

"Miss Winslow, soon-to-be Lady Barrington, whatever will people think of your choice of words?" And with that, he turned back around. The faintest pressure of his heel sent his mount down the trail, leaving her behind with her bruised ego and an equally painful backside.

"I don't give a fig about what anyone thinks!" Elyse shouted after him. For emphasis, she pounded the ground beside her bruised hip. Mud splattered into the air, peppering her pants and jacket. It streaked the white shirt and plastered her hair and face.

She groaned as she looked down at her soaked pants. Of all the places for her to fall. The entire trail was dry except for this one place where rainwater from the light shower just before dawn had pooled.

"Of all the damnable luck!" She struck at the mud puddle again, completing the damage. Then she rose slowly, wincing at the pain in her bruised backside as she walked toward the stream.

If Lucy could see me now, she thought morosely. "And he still has my pendant." Tears pooled in her vivid eyes. She hated him. Oh, how she hated him!

Her head came up at the sound of hoof beats on the trail. She hastily wiped her tears with the back of her sleeve, excitement sending her heart racing. It quickly died as Quimby rounded the bend in the trail.

"Damn!" she whispered, to no one but herself.

Seven

Elyse fumed as she slammed the heavy door on the heels of the servant who'd delivered the message from Jerrold.

Swirling into the parlor in a wave of crackling, sea green silk, she flounced into a chair, wincing painfully. She looked up, meeting her grandmother's bemused gaze.

"Was that Jerrold's man, Chivers, at the door?"

"Yes! Honestly, he has some nerve!" Elyse crumpled the elaborately scrawled note, at the bottom of which Jerrold had signed his initials with a flourish.

"Chivers?" Regina Winslow looked up from her cup of morning tea, unable to comprehend why a meek toad of a man such as that amiable servant had sent her granddaughter into such a fit of ill temper.

"No, of course not!" Elyse bounded out of the chair to pace the width of the parlor with restless energy. It was preferable to sitting; she was still smarting from that fall she'd taken in the Woods two days earlier. Actually, she'd taken two falls. And St. James was responsible for both of them. Now this! She waved Jerrold's note through the air like a banner.

"We were supposed to attend the opera tonight!"

Lady Regina set down the delicate bone-china cup,

giving her granddaughter a long look. "I take it, that you're speaking of Jerrold."

Elyse looked up. "Of course." She resumed her agitated pacing.

"I seem to remember you sending round word yesterday that you didn't feel up to attending any social functions," Lady Winslow reminded her.

Whirling about in front of the fireplace, Elyse tapped a foot in frustration.

Quimby had done his work well. He'd managed to find out a few very interesting things about the Sir William St. James. Just that morning she'd sent Jerrold a message stating that she wanted to see him about something important, and now his return note informed her that he was attending his private club that evening, with none other than St. James.

"I take it Jerrold has canceled your plans for the evening," Regina said.

"He's invited the man to attend his private club." Having unfolded the message and read it for the second time, Elyse tore it into tiny pieces that she scattered on the cold hearth.

She'd learned from Katy's excursions at the market that St. James was staying at the London town house of Lord and Lady Vale. Supposedly, he was related to them. But of even more interest was the information Quimby had acquired at the docks. It seemed that St. James had arrived only days earlier, and though his ship was flying a Portuguese flag, there was something very peculiar about an entire crew that spoke not a trace of that language. The harbormaster was unable to provide any further information except that the *Revenge* carried a cargo of wool which had been brought ashore and was now stored in warehouses at the docks.

"I think it's very generous of Jerrold to be so hospitable to the man. After all, he is newly arrived. And I did find him to be such a charming man," Lady Regina confessed.

"Charming?" Elyse replied incredulously, remembering the episode on the veranda. "The man is nothing but an arrogant, rude, ill-mannered..."

"Yes?" Her grandmother watched her skeptically. "You were about to call him something?"

"Impostor!"

"Impostor? My dearest Elyse, I can name several things he is, but impostor is not one of them. Why, anyone can see that the man has exceptional breeding. His manners are impeccable. I have it on good account that he speaks several languages including French, which you refused to learn, my dear," she pointed out.

"And you cannot deny that he cuts a dashing figure with that eye-patch covering one eye." She tapped a bejeweled finger against her chin. "I wonder how he came to lose the eye. Quite exciting, don't you think?"

Elyse rolled her eyes heavenward. Please, not her grandmother, too. Ever since the night of the party, it seemed every woman in London was quite taken with the mysterious, Sir William St. James. The man was an impostor! And she was determined to prove it.

"What do you think?" Elyse turned from the mirror at the dressing table in her friend's bedchamber. She put the finishing touches to the makeup she'd artfully applied. It was late afternoon and she'd just been to the costumer's shop that provided clothes for actors at the theatre.

Lucy's house had been her second stop of the day. Fixing her friend with a coolly disdainful look, she tried to smother a fit of laughter.

"Do you want the truth?" Lucy shook her head, a skeptical expression at her face.

"Of course."

"I think you've absolutely gone round the bend," Lucy informed her.

Elyse choked back laughter. "Do you mean I'm addle brained?"

"The question is, my dear," Elyse fastened her friend with an expression of pure devilment, "Can *we* pull it off?"

"We?" Lucy shot back a look of complete amazement. "You can't mean...?"

"Of course that's what I mean." Elyse turned back to the mirror. "It won't work unless we both go."

"You are crazy!" Lucy looked back at her with astonishment. "No woman has ever been inside White's before. At least no woman who's a lady. The only women allowed inside are... Well, it's only a rumor, of course."

"Yes, I know," Elyse replied. She had heard the rumors as well. "Don't you think it's about time a lady did see just what goes on in an exclusive men's club? Or perhaps two ladies?"

Lucy's eyes widened. "Andrew would never allow it... "

"Which, is precisely the reason you're to say nothing to him about it." She saw the objection on her friend's face.

"Haven't you been just the least bit curious to know what goes on at those clubs, or what Andrew does when he goes there?" The expression on Lucy's face was her answer.

"What time do we go?" Lucy asked with growing excitement.

"Chivers told me that Jerrold usually leaves for the club around nine o'clock. We should plan to arrive around ten o'clock."

Lucy's hands trembled with the boldness of their plan. "Aren't you just a little bit nervous about this?"

Elyse smiled. "I think it's exciting. A little like that trapeze act we saw at the circus last summer, don't you think? Besides, it's all very harmless. We'll go for just a little while, and then leave. After all, Jerrold claims it's all quite boring.

"Supposedly the men play a few games of cards, talk, smoke their cigarettes, and discuss whose horse won at the races. He claims I wouldn't possibly be interested in any of it. Still," Elyse mused thoughtfully, "it does make you wonder why they all go if it's so boring." A mischievous gleam danced in her eyes.

"What happens if we're caught?" Lucy asked. "We need an escape plan."

"We won't be caught. Andrew won't even know about it," Elyse replied. "You'll be home and in bed before he leaves the club. But just in case, if anything does go wrong, we'll split up and leave by separate doors. I found out there are two back entrances as well as an employees' entrance out the back alley. What do you think?"

"Think!" Lucy gaped at her reflection in the mirror. "I think you're insane."

"But you will go." Elyse turned to her friend.

Lucy sighed. "We're going to regret this," she predicted, but the light in her eyes matched Elyse's for excitement. "Still, I wouldn't miss it for the world!"

Elyse smiled. "You'll find clothes for yourself in that box." She indicated the box on the bed. "They should fit quite nicely."

Lucy pulled the man's coat from the box and tried it on. It was a perfect fit.

"You were obviously fairly certain that I would go along with your plan," Lucy commented.

Elyse smiled. "Haven't we always been partners in every little escapade since we were small?"

"Yes. And I keep remembering the disastrous results of your last plan, exchanging places at my own wedding just to see if Andrew would notice the difference. He was on to us and said nothing, and you practically ended up married to my husband. I would never have forgiven you for that," Lucy replied.

"You have to admit, it worked, for a while. Andrew kept waiting for one of us to end it, and we kept waiting for him to say something."

"What could I say?" Lucy's eyes widened innocently. "I was the farthest from the altar and the bishop."

Elyse laughed. "Remember the bishop's face, when he finally realized he very nearly married the wrong bride to the groom?"

"I thought the poor man would have apoplexy. And dear Anne almost fainted." Lucy sighed a small twinge of concern for the stepmother she'd never gotten along with. Then her mouth twitched with delight.

"But you'd never have gotten through the wedding night, my dear. Even if he were a blind man, Andrew would have known the difference."

Elyse turned, her eyes widening at the revelation of a secret she'd not known until this moment. "Lucy! Do you mean to tell me that you and Andrew...? That you... before you were married?"

Lucy smiled as she realized that she'd finally managed to shock Elyse. "Of course. How do you expect anyone to endure a betrothal that lasts an entire year? I'd have come unraveled if I'd had to wait a year to make love with him. Certainly, you and Jerrold...?" she stopped as Elyse glanced away.

"Do you mean to tell me that you and Jerrold have never made love?" She was completely aghast.

Elyse's blue eyes darkened. "No," she answered simply. "I'm certain that he's wanted to, he said as much. There never seemed to be the right moment, or the right place," she made the excuse.

"The right moment?" Lucy watched her thoughtfully. "My dear, when you're head over heels in love with a man, there's no need for the right place or moment. Somehow every place, every moment is the right one. I speak from experience in that regard." She arched a brow knowingly.

Elyse's eyes narrowed. "What do you mean, every place and every moment?"

Lucy casually crossed the room, a smug expression at her face.

"There was the time in the stables," she casually said. "Of course, I was picking hay out of my clothes for days. And then there was the time in the coach during an afternoon ride through Kensington Gardens. I would caution you against coaches. There's never enough room, and your legs get all tangled up. But where there's a will..."

"I don't believe for a moment that any of this ever happened," Elyse replied.

"And then there was my cousin Charlotte's country party," Lucy continued. "Andrew and I couldn't bear to be away from each other for an entire week. He disguised himself as my driver.

"The entire week was wonderful. I pretended to have a cold so that I could be excused from the family activities. Then when everyone was out of the house, I'd meet Andrew. Do you remember that little gazebo in the gardens at Charlotte's?" She turned inquisitive eyes on Elyse.

"You made love in a gazebo? The stables and a coach? Lucy, whatever possessed you?"

Lucy smiled. "Surely, you've felt it."

She turned away, not wanting her friend to see the uncertainty she felt.

"Yes," she admitted, "I've felt it..." *Once, a long time ago...*

"What did you say, dear?" Lucy crossed the room, picking up stray garments strewn across the floor.

Elyse smiled sadly. "Nothing," she said, then suggested, "Shall we eat at Winslow House? Grandmother is dining with Uncle Ceddy this evening. We'll have the entire house to ourselves."

Lucy looked at her, wondering why she had changed the subject but said nothing more.

"Yes, of course. Then we can play with the makeup you purchased. I want to get my disguise just right."

"My dear." Again, Elyse lowered her voice dramatically. "By the time I'm through, no one will recognize you." She laughed, some of her good humor returned.

"Have you ever smoked a cigarette?" Elyse asked her.

The night was cool and held an air of expectancy after the warmth of the late spring day. Open carriages passed an occasional closed coach. Drivers called to their teams of horses. The faint clip-clopping of hooves grew louder as a carriage approached, then gradually faded like the faint ticking of a clock.

White's was known to every gentleman of breeding and wealth in London society. The membership was exclusive, catering to a specific clientele. There was no gold-lettered name plate beside the door, not even a street number with the exact address.

Though no plaque restricted members and their guests, there was no need of one. Anyone who was anyone about London, from the lowliest hack driver to the most impeccably liveried coachman, knew the hand-carved mahogany doors on the tree-lined street just one block over from the theater.

The rented black coach pulled to a stop at the curb. Immediately a liveried doorman emerged from one of those impressive doors and greeted the most recent arrivals.

"Good evening," the raspy voice greeted the doorman.

"Good evening, sir." There was a faint questioning note in George's voice.

The first gentleman to alight from the carriage nodded a brief greeting while waiting for his companion. A second gentleman of approximately the same slight stature emerged and stepped down. His face was concealed in the shadow of his silk hat.

"We're joining Sir Jerrold Barrington this evening," the first gentleman announced. "Has he arrived yet?"

"He and another guest arrived a short while ago."

"Ah yes, that would be Sir William St. James." The young man smoothed his lapel with a gloved hand. "A splendid fellow and quite interesting with that eye-patch."

The doorman nodded, satisfied that these two young gentlemen were indeed well acquainted with Sir Jerrold and his guest.

"This way, please," he said as he stepped aside to allow them through the elegant, carved doors.

"Do come along, *Lucien*," the first gentleman called to his companion. "We don't want to miss anything." He was answered only by a cough as his companion joined him.

"Lucien!" Lucy whispered beside her. "Where the devil did you come up with that?"

"I couldn't very well go around calling you, Lucy. Our disguises would soon be undone." A trace of a smile appeared at the corners of a mouth disguised by an impeccably groomed mustache.

"We're both crazy," Lucy whispered again with a look about. "This will never work."

Stepping through the double doors into the foyer of the exclusive club, they were greeted by another man who offered to take their hats and capes. Lucy looked at her with rising panic.

"Come now, old chap," Elyse told her, keeping with

their disguises. "They'll give it back to you when we're ready to leave."

"Which just happens to be now!" Lucy muttered as coat and hat were surrendered, revealing a head full of gleaming black hair, a wig she wore, while Elyse wore one in a blonde shade.

Elyse glanced down at the polished toes of the boots just there at the cuff of the perfectly fitted trousers and tried to smother back a fit of laughter.

"Do come along," she said with a lowered voice.

Together, they followed a young attendant to a single door across the hall. And together, like the two perfectly dressed *'young men'* they appeared to be, entered the elegantly furnished, faintly smoky, male domain of White's Exclusive Club.

"We're both out of our minds!" Lucy whispered. "And this damn glued-on mustache is driving me crazy." Her upper lip twitched back and forth.

"Everything will be fine. No one will ever know it's you underneath all that makeup. People see what they want to see. And those whiskers look quite marvelous," Elyse teased.

Then, as they passed a large adjoining room, "Look at this," she commented. "Have you ever seen anything like it?"

Gold-embossed paper covered the walls above the wainscoting, while below it was crimson velvet. Several small alcoves were sectioned off around the perimeter of the room with heavy, crimson velvet drapes edged with gold satin and bound back with braided satin cords.

There were tables in the alcoves with anywhere from four to eight chairs around each one. In some, gentlemen could be seen enjoying conversation along with their drinks. In others, a lively game of cards was underway.

A few were hidden from view, heavy drapes discreetly closed. Only an occasional movement of the drapes indicated that anyone might be behind them.

Immaculately dressed young men wove in and out of the tables in the main room, entering the secluded alcoves, replenishing containers of brandy and whiskey. Gas lamps gave just enough light to the tables but left the remainder of the room in shadows.

Elyse recognized several gentlemen. Faint streamers of cigar and cigarette smoke, curled into the air to mingle with the fragrance of pipe tobacco. She hardly saw anything to cause any excitement. It all seemed quite boring.

"Oh, dear!" Lucy said with rising panic.

"What is it?" Elyse turned, trying to see what it was that had managed to upset her.

"Jerrold is coming this way. Someone must have told him about us. Why on earth did you have to use his name?"

"I had to use a name that would get us in the door," Elyse told her. "I could have used Andrew's," she reminded her friend.

Lucy only groaned. "Well, it's too late to do anything about it now. We'll be found out. I just know we will."

Elyse smiled from beneath the sweep of the fake mustache she'd painstakingly applied. It perfectly matched the wig that concealed her hair.

"Now is as good a time as any to find out if this will work?'

Rolling her eyes heavenward, Lucy seized a tumbler of whiskey from a tray as a uniformed young man passed nearby. Whoever belonged to the drink would just have to ask for another. It was quickly downed, causing her to breathe in sharply.

"Good evening." The polite greeting came from behind Elyse.

She hesitated as Lucy was seized with a fit of coughing due to the hastily downed drink. With a gesture she'd seen more than once, she clapped her friend heartily across the back.

"I say, Lucien, you've really done it this time. You must be more careful," she pretended to admonish her.

"Is there anything I can do?"

If they were going to be found out, it would be now.

"Not at all," Elyse replied in that same lowered voice without turning around. "Everything is under control. My friend has a tendency to over-indulge. I do have to keep an eye on him, promised his wife I'd have him home early."

"I don't believe we've met, sir," Jerrold said, coming round to stand beside her.

The uncomfortable moment drew out as she opened her coat and reached inside, retrieving a gold cigarette case. Her concentration wavered for only a moment as she saw another man coming toward them from across the room.

There was only the slightest trembling in her fingers as she flicked open the case and retrieved a cigarette. Beside her, she heard Lucy's sharp intake of breath.

They hadn't rehearsed this part. Elyse hadn't wanted to leave the scent of smoke in her grandmother's house which surely would have raised questions. She pulled out an elegantly rolled cigarette and tapped it against the gold case as she'd seen Jerrold do on several occasions.

"Of course, you remember," she explained. "I was with Sir Laughton at the races last month, his cousin from York," she began what she had rehearsed. "You said if we had the occasion, we should join you at your club in London." She glanced around as if giving the interior of the club inspection.

"We've just come up from the country."

She knew he'd been seen with the Laughtons at the races. In fact, had been seen with Lady Laughton on several occasions. She saw the confusion at Jerrold's face as he signaled one of the club's attendants. He'd undoubtedly been so caught up with Lady Laughton he didn't remember meeting anyone at the races. It had been slightly irritating when she'd found out about it. Now she used it to keep their disguise.

The young man appeared at Jerrold's elbow, quickly producing a match and striking it.

"Ah yes, the races." Jerrold responded vaguely. He turned as St. James joined them.

"May I present the cousin of an acquaintance..." He hesitated.

Elyse nodded. "Stephen Mortimer," she said, pulling a name out of the air. "And my companion, Lucien de Villiers."

She quickly made the introductions, knowing what her grandmother's reaction would have been to her using the name of an author of one of the French language texts she'd studied with such disastrous results.

The French language had practically been her undoing. Lucy, on the other hand, had an impressive command of it. She hoped that she remembered enough of it in her current state of distress.

Jerrold curtly nodded to them both and introduced St. James.

Elyse inclined her head as she'd seen gentlemen do when greeting each other. "A pleasure, of course." She held her breath when St. James seemed to hesitate a moment longer than necessary.

"Have we met before?" Zach's gaze narrowed slightly as he studied the young man before him.

"I'm certain I would remember, sir."

The reply was polite. And the second young gentleman seemed to be afflicted with great nervousness. Barrington apparently didn't notice.

"I am pleased to make your acquaintance," Lucy greeted him in flawless French and he responded in the same language. That look narrowing on both of them.

"Well." Jerrold smiled. "Since we are acquainted,

please join us. And a little later, there will be some exciting... entertainment."

Elyse caught the slightly bemused expression of Sir William.

Preceding them across the large room, Jerrold turned and leaned toward them both.

"Several young ladies will be joining us. I think they will prove exciting even by French standards, monsieur. Tonight," he said, glancing toward St. James, "is a night to forget all other women you have ever known. I guarantee, the young ladies who will be joining us will be like no others you have ever experienced."

Young ladies? Elyse thought. She ignored Lucy's look of panic, her thoughts scrambling for a way to extricate them from this. She had hoped to observe St. James from a distance, and possibly learn more about him. This was not part of the plan.

"Lord Barrington has been teaching me the basics of a game known as Battle," he explained as they reached a table. "Have you played before?" He reached for the deck of cards that lay there and spread them fanlike.

Elyse shook her head. "I don't believe I've had the pleasure," she replied, continuing their deception.

He smiled. "It's a fascinating game, filled with all manner of traps and deceptions. One must be very careful in order to play." He watched the *young man* across from him and his companion who stood behind him.

Elyse immediately learned two things. The first was that she had to pay quick attention to the rapid exchange of cards as the hands were dealt, and the second was that she'd worried needlessly that Jerrold might recognize her. There was far more danger with this man who played cards as if he were out for blood.

She'd dreamed up this mad scheme to expose St. James for what he was—an impostor. But over the course of four hands of Battle, she felt as if the tables had been turned. And now she was uncertain whether her suspicions were correct.

He laid out the cards of yet another winning hand. "I believe that is my game once more. Shall we try something else? Our host seems to have found other diversions."

It was over an hour since Jerrold had disappeared, saying that he must see to the evening's entertainment. She then caught sight of Lucy who stood at a discreet distance from Andrew.

Playing her role of young gentleman to perfection, Elyse sipped at the brandy placed beside her a few moments ago.

"Is there something wrong with the brandy?" he asked.

Elyse glanced up. "Not at all."

A faint smile twitched at the corners of his mouth. He'd accepted this invitation so he might get to know Barrington better. But the evening offered surprising twists and turns. Reaching across the table, he pushed the full tumbler of brandy toward his young companion.

"Then, drink up, my friend. The evening is still young. And our host would be displeased if he thought you weren't enjoying yourself."

Elyse's startled glance met his briefly, then fastened on the tumbler. She took a deep breath knowing she had no other choice but to drink. Bracing herself, she quickly downed the amber-colored liquid as she'd seen the other gentlemen doing all evening.

The brandy burned in her stomach and back up again. If she breathed, Elyse was certain flames would leap out of her mouth. Her eyes watered. She tried to swallow. She tried to breathe and was seized by a fit of coughing.

St. James was beside her in an instant, thumping her on the back until she thought she was being pounded to death. She clasped a gloved hand over her mouth as she tried to draw another breath. When she pulled her hand away, her eyes widened in horror. There, in the middle of the table, was the immaculately groomed mustache that she had taken pains to apply. It lay on the rich velvet like a giant raised eyebrow.

She reached across the table and grabbed it, bending over as if still seized by that fit of coughing, she pressed the mustache back into place and prayed it would stick.

Across the room, the other gentlemen seemed oblivious to her. They rose, one by one from their chairs and gathered at the far end of the large room.

Elyse rose from her chair as she composed herself. "What is all the excitement about?"

St. James turned to her. "It seems... " He stopped midsentence and looked at her, an odd expression at his face. Then it was his turn. The coughing seemingly contagious. However, he quickly recovered.

"It seems the entertainment is about to begin. I've met these people before. I think you'll find this most unusual." With a slight bow, he motioned for her to follow him across the room.

Smiling uncertainly, Elyse looked across the room for Lucy, but her friend seemed to have disappeared as music unlike any she'd heard before filled the room. The buzz of expectant conversation around them quieted and all eyes were focused on the source of the music. Pushed forward by others equally eager to see the entertainment, Elyse was helpless to do anything but move with them.

Her eyes widened in stunned surprise. Under the glow of light from an overhead chandelier, a young woman whirled and danced. But it wasn't the music that held Elyse fascinated, or even the woman's movements. It was the scanty costume adorning the dancer's, voluptuous body. She wore nothing more than several transparent silk scarves that whirled in the air with each undulating movement, threatening to expose her naked body underneath.

Amusement darkened St. James' gray gaze as he watched the brilliant display. But he was more fascinated by the *young man* beside him. Fatima of the Thousand Veils did promise exotic and tantalizing pleasures. She claimed to be from a Bedouin chieftain's harem, but she was in fact a Gypsy. He'd seen her perform before in Lisbon.

He leaned over his young companion's shoulder. "Rather interesting muscle control, wouldn't you say? I've heard it said she can hold that gem in her navel indefinitely."

Elyse's gaze remained fixed on Fatima, wondering just how the woman moved her body like that. So this was how Jerrold managed to entertain himself when he came to White's! Card games indeed!

A half-dozen other dancers joined the woman. They whirled and gyrated around the room in frenzied abandon. Their lithe bodies soon glistened with a fine sheen that only seemed to heighten the men's appreciation. The decorum of distinguished gentlemen was gone, replaced by loud calls of encouragement and some rather vague comments that Elyse thought she was probably better off not understanding.

At that moment, as the woman whirled around right under her nose, the gentleman to Elyse's left decided to add his own interpretation to the dancing. He joined the silk-clad girls. One by one, the girls continued their rhythmic flight about the room. With each full circle, every dancer selected one scarf from the myriad assortment attached to the waistband that circled low over her hips and tossed it out into the gathering. The dance continued, more and more silk tossed into the crowd of men who gathered, each one of them catching one and smiling as if they'd just won some grand prize.

The music abruptly ended, and the performers

posed before the leering men. Only two scarves remained about each performer. One dangled between the legs, the other from the back of the waistband. Absolutely nothing covered the women's breasts. They stood in a circle of gleaming flesh.

"My God!" she exclaimed, fascinated by the performance and the unabashed sensuality of the young women.

Zach waited expectantly. "I told you Fatima possessed captivating talents." His mouth twitched with suppressed amusement that was quickly masked behind a bland expression.

"She most certainly does!" Elyse declared, in her own voice. Realizing the mistake she'd just made, she excused herself. "I really must find my friend. It's quite late, must be leaving."

"Leaving so soon?" St. James looked disappointed. "The evening is just beginning."

He seized his companion's arm and quickly steered *'him'* through the circle of gentlemen who mingled with the dancers.

Elyse noticed that several other young ladies appeared, their costumes as scant as the dancers. Just as quickly, each disappeared, a gentleman's arm looped through hers.

"As you can see, everyone else is leaving. It seems the entertainment is through for the evening," Elyse insisted as she searched the room for Lucy. She caught sight of her friend and started to make her way across the room.

"Not at all." St. James gently restrained his young companion. "The entertainment has only just begun." He gestured across the room, to where a distinguished gentleman, whom Elyse knew to be the husband of one of her grandmother's acquaintances, disappeared through crimson velvet drapes that led to a stairway. A scantily clad young woman clung to his arm. They paused, the woman leaning forward to press her body against his and whispered something. His laughter could be heard across the room as he climbed the stairs with her.

"Where are they all going?" Elyse kept her voice deliberately low as she watched several other gentlemen disappear with similarly clad young women.

"To be entertained, of course. You are rather young and inexperienced in these things, aren't you?" St. James commented. "I think I know just what's needed in your case."

Before Elyse could turn around to respond, St. James disappeared. She immediately seized the opportunity to find Lucy. Crossing the room, she wound her way through the assorted tables and chairs, now completely deserted. Stepping around a man and his female companion, she caught a glimpse of Lucy moving toward the main entrance with a great deal of urgency, a man beside her, a hand around her arm.

They paused briefly as they reached the entrance, and Elyse stared into the infuriated gaze of Andrew Maitland.

"Come along, *'Lucien'*." Andrew's hand tightened on his wife's arm. "We have much to talk about," he added. The expression on his face was one of barely suppressed rage. Throwing a murderous glare in her direction, Andrew escorted Lucy toward the double doors at the entrance.

With her scheme up in smoke, she decided it was probably best if she left as well. But she was stopped by a familiar voice.

Jerrold stood nearby with one of the dancers she'd just watched perform. The woman was pressing her large breasts against the front of his jacket. He laughed at something she said. He glanced briefly over her head, his gaze scanning the room before he pulled her into his embrace. Then he turned, pulling the woman with him up the stairs that led to the second-floor rooms.

He had looked straight at Elyse and not recognized her. She almost wished he had so that she could see the reaction on his face at learning he'd been found out about the night's entertainment.

There was vague disappointment but surprisingly nothing more. Elyse didn't pause to examine the reason.

Several other 'gentlemen' lingered about the enormous room. She started for the door. If her disguise had fooled Jerrold, it was good enough to fool these last few.

"You can't leave now."

She almost collided with St. James. The expression on his face was amused, almost as if...

"As I said," he continued, "you seem rather inexperienced in these matters. Therefore," he pulled the woman who had begun the dance from behind him. "I've arranged for you to enjoy some very special entertainment tonight."

She stared at him, not understanding at first. "Special entertainment?" she asked, keeping to her disguise.

"Exactly so." He smiled graciously. "Fatima will show you to a chamber. She's very accomplished in these matters. I assure you it will be a night to remember."

"You don't mean...?" Her gaze locked with that of the seductive Fatima. The woman seemed to radiate sensuality. A warning whispered in her thoughts.

He couldn't mean... She thought of those she'd seen climbing the stairs including Jerrold. Limited as her experience was in such matters, more the result of rumor and gossip, she had a fairly good idea what happened in those upstairs rooms.

Why wasn't Lucy here when she needed her? Because, she told herself, Lucy's husband had discovered their game and had taken his wife home, leaving Elyse to fend for herself. She glanced at St. James. He seemed to be enjoying all of this a little too much.

"That's most considerate of you, sir, but I couldn't

possibly." She turned and would have walked away, determined to find a way out of the club.

"Of course, you can." He seized her by the arm and propelled her toward the stairway.

"I've taken care of everything," he assured her as she turned to protest. "It's the least I can do after winning all those games of Battle." He turned to Fatima, speaking with her briefly.

Elyse hardly had time to think about what that meant as Fatima took her by the arm and led her up the stairs. They stopped before a set of double doors at the end of the hallway.

"You don't understand," Elyse protested. "I really must leave." Any further discussion ended as Elyse was forcefully led into the room.

"You will wait here." The woman told her, then left.

Elyse collapsed back against the door as she took in the room, lushly appointed with crimson velvet and gold satin braid. A single gas lamp cast golden light onto the room, flooding across the large, bed covered in crimson velvet.

White's Exclusive Club for men was nothing than a high-class brothel!

"God's nightgown!" Elyse breathed out. "What am I going to do now?"

Somewhere a clock ticked with maddening slowness. She also caught the sound of laughter somewhere down the hallway.

She'd really gotten herself into a difficult situation. Of all the hare-brained ideas she'd ever come up with for her and Lucy, this one was possibly the worst. She had to find a way out of here.

Jerrold! Where the devil was he when she needed him? But she already knew the answer to that. She gave a very unladylike snort. He'd been one of the first of these so-called gentlemen to disappear with the evening's *'entertainment.'*

Elyse flung aside the elegant drapes that covered the windows on the far wall. For a second, she considered going out a window. But one look at the drop to the street below convinced her otherwise.

Eyeing a second door, she quickly crossed the room. It opened onto a closet filled with an array of garments and other curious items she chose not to inspect. After trying the first door once more, she paced the room.

Eight

Zach downed another brandy as he wondered just what the young *'man'* upstairs was thinking right about now. Several minutes had passed since Fatima had led the startled *"fellow"* up those stairs.

His eyes narrowed as he saw her return. She was preceded by several of the girls who'd performed earlier. She didn't look as though she intended to stay for the remainder of the evening. A heavy black shawl was wrapped about her body, and she seemed more than a little nervous as she glanced in first one direction and then another, urging the girls to the back of the club. Zach set down the empty brandy glass.

"Where are you going?" His hand closed around her arm.

"I am leaving," she told him. "And if you are wise, you will do the same," she cautioned, her gaze darting about the large room.

"What is it? What's happened?"

He knew the Gypsies well. They lived by cunning and stealth. Over the past few years, he'd acquired those traits himself. He'd learned them quickly as a matter of survival.

"The local constables are on their way here!" she replied.

"This is a private club," Zach replied. "What would the authorities want here?"

Fatima leaned closer, her words urgent. "There was trouble earlier this evening, down near the docks. A young girl was found dead. Before she died, she gave information about her attacker. He was a very rich and powerful man."

"There are many rich men in London." Zach was inclined to doubt what she was saying.

"But how many rich men strangle a woman with this." Reaching around Zach to the heavy velvet drapes, she seized the distinctive gold satin braid bordering one.

She leaned in closer. "A length of it was found around the girl's neck. And your host for the evening was gone for several hours before you arrived."

"Barrington?"

She shrugged, then looked past him at the sudden pounding on the doors at the front entrance. "I am leaving," she announced. "You'd be wise to do the same."

"What about my young friend?"

"He is not worth the trouble."

"Where did you leave him?" Zach insisted as he started toward the stairs.

"The first room on the left. But there isn't time," she called after him.

"What about a way out of here?"

"At the back of the kitchen is a large cupboard. The wall behind is fake. It leads into a passage that adjoins the next building."

"You've used it before?"

"When necessary," she replied.

Zach thanked her and climbed the stairs two at a time as the knocking at the entrance doors continued. Upstairs, doors were being thrown open. Downstairs, pandemonium broke out among the 'guests' as some fool opened the front doors.

He reached the top landing as the alarm went out to

the rest of the club members. This would be a night to remember.

He was relieved that Tobias had insisted on staying at the town house. He was going to have enough problems getting his young card-playing companion out of here. At the moment, he had no idea how he was going to get both of them back downstairs to the kitchen.

Elyse turned at the sound of the door opening as she heard sounds from the hallway. But the figure that emerged from the shadows was not Fatima.

Elyse stared at the tall man with fair hair, slightly too long, hanging over his elegant collar. A swath of black eye-patch slashed his face. It was St. James!

"I told you this evening would be special, Elyse," he remarked wryly.

Her mouth fell open at the sound of her name. "How did you know?"

His expression was amused. "As charming as I'm certain the young women would have found you in that disguise, there are vast differences between men and women. No matter how you tried to disguise your walk or flatten your breasts," he gestured to her jacket front. "There are still differences. You, my dear, have a very nice bottom. I remember it well, from our little ride the other day. And there is that other thing."

What other thing? she wondered as she took a step back in an attempt to leave. He reached out, fingers closed over her wrist in easy restraint. Then he seized her by both shoulders.

"Let me go!" Elyse protested then gasped as she caught sight of her reflection in the large mirror. The mustache she'd worn, lost, and then hastily reattached was upside down!

"Oh."

"Is that all you have to say?"

The long evening, the brandy, Fatima, and now this.

She could think only of how ridiculous she must look with that mustache. And Jerrold hadn't noticed?

The giggling began as she turned back around to inspect the mustache.

"It was a good disguise."

"You can compliment yourself later," Zach told her. He reached up and pulled the mustache from her upper lip.

She cursed him as her eyes watered and the skin above her lip reddened.

"Such language, but I think you'll survive," Zach informed her, and then, because he couldn't resist, he bent over and kissed her, slowly and thoroughly, then seized her by the hand, and pulled her toward the door amid loud protests.

At first too surprised to react, she quickly recovered. "What about Fatima?" she snickered, then rubbed the tender skin above her lip.

"Shouldn't we wait for her?" she added sarcastically.

He fixed her with that maddening gaze: "Were you thinking of a threesome?" he quipped with a trace of irritation. "Sorry to disappoint you, but Fatima's already left and we're about to have other company, if I don't get you out of here first."

"Who?" She had no idea what he was talking about.

"The London constabulary. It seems there's someone here they'd like very much to take in."

"What are you talking about?" Elyse started past him, only to have herself flattened against the inside wall.

"This is not a game." He looked at her hard. "It seems Barrington wasn't here all evening."

She looked up. She didn't trust him for a moment, but she was aware that Jerrold had been conspicuously absent during a good part of the evening.

"What are you talking about?"

"I'm talking about a bit of trouble down at the

docks. It seems a certain young lady of questionable reputation managed to get herself killed tonight," he informed her.

"What has that to do with Jerrold?" The laughter was now gone from Elyse's voice. But no matter how angry she was at Jerrold, she didn't see how he could be connected to such a thing.

Zach watched for her reaction. "It seems the girl wasn't quite dead when her attacker finished with her. She was unable to provide a description of the man, a rich gentleman."

An uneasy feeling slipped down Elyse's spine. My god, it wasn't possible that Jerrold had anything to do with that. Was it?

"The authorities are here. It seems they have proof the man who killed the girl was a member of this club. They intend to question everyone."

Elyse's eyes widened. "You can't mean...?"

"They will want to question everyone." He repeated and glanced once more out into the hallway. "That is unless you're willing to leave with me now."

Sneaking into White's in disguise was one thing. But this was an entirely different matter. If she was questioned, she would be found out and that could cause all sorts of embarrassing questions for her grandmother, as well as others. And she couldn't risk Jerrold knowing she had been there.

However, depending on this man to get her out didn't sit well with her. He was completely unpredictable and, as she had pointed out on more than one occasion, certainly no gentleman. His prank with Fatima had proved it. She wondered just how long he would have left her in this room if circumstances hadn't changed.

Clearly, he didn't want to be questioned by the London police any more than she did. Which only piqued her curiosity all the more.

"All right," she agreed. "I'll go with you."

Zach smiled. She might be angry at him, but she'd go along to keep from being questioned by the police. He nodded. "I know a way out of here, but we first have to get downstairs." He took her hand and led her out into the hallway.

It was a mass of confusion. Up and down the hall, doors stood ajar. The respectable and wealthy gentlemen she'd seen hours earlier now hurried about in various states of undress.

A young woman cursed from inside one of the rooms and then emerged from it with her partner.

"I thought you knew a way out of here," she complained. Zach pulled her into one room and then another, searching the closets. When they again emerged into the hallway, it was clear time was running out. Voices came from the bottom of the stairs.

"It's got to be here somewhere."

"What the devil are you talking about?"

He pulled her with him toward the stairway.

"What are you doing? They're coming up the stairs. We'll be caught!"

Reaching the end of the hallway, Zach ran his hands over the paneled wood. It had to be here. The voices below grew steadily louder.

"What are you looking for?" Elyse bit at her lower lip as she kept an eye on the landing. She could just see the look on her grandmother's face at hearing she'd been taken in for questioning after being found disguised as a man at the notorious men's club.

"This!" Zach announced as a section of paneling swung away from the wall, revealing a compartment. "Every respectable establishment has one. After you." He gestured to the wall as a panel opened.

Elyse stared. A set of cables were at the back of the compartment. It was approximately four feet deep, of the same width, and somewhat greater height. At the moment it was occupied by a silver service cleared no doubt from one of the rooms. It was a servant's lift!

"There's no way we can both fit in there."

"Then you can wait until I send it back up," Zach informed her as he climbed inside, ducking his head.

The sound of voices was much closer now. She knew perfectly well there'd be no time for her to escape if she didn't get in immediately. Whoever belonged to those voices would be at the top of the stairs within a matter of seconds. And she was certain they weren't club members returning to resume their activities.

She climbed into the lift and found herself pinned against him. He immediately tucked her legs in and closed the panel, plunging them into complete darkness. When he pulled on the handle attached to the cables, the compartment immediately began a slow downward descent.

Elyse fumed in the cramped darkness of the lift. "Please move your hand," she said sharply, and tried to shift her position. "There's no need to hold onto me. I can't possibly go anywhere."

Zach smiled. "I was merely trying to reassure myself that you weren't a man, after all. And please quit wiggling around."

Elyse tried to sit up straight, so that they had as little physical contact as possible, and cracked her head on the ceiling of the lift.

"I must be crazy to let you talk me into this."

"Crazy perhaps, but I assure that you managed this situation all by yourself." Zach shifted, enjoying her soft curves. He smiled, trying to visualize the expression on her face as she let out an exasperated sigh.

He knew there was no question about the way her eyes looked at that moment—brilliant blue and undoubtedly ablaze with anger. The lift bumped to a stop.

"I think we've arrived," he announced with maddening humor. "Shall we stay in here the rest of the night, or take our chances outside?"

Struggling from her cramped position, Elyse braced both feet against the door and pushed. What if someone had seen them crawl into the compartment and was waiting for them even now? They could hardly return to the top. She pushed again and tumbled out into the dimly lit kitchen.

Zach crawled out after her, feeling a twinge of regret that their intimate ride was over. Confined quarters in total darkness did have its advantages.

His eyes quickly adjusted to shadows in the kitchen and found the storage closet Fatima had spoken of. Locating the brick wall, he leaned his weight against it. It slowly moved aside.

"An escape tunnel for the members of the club," she exclaimed. "I wonder how many times they've had to use it." Including Jerrold? she thought.

"Evidently not all the members were informed about it," he dryly remarked of the half-naked gentlemen left scurrying about upstairs.

"Where does it lead?" Elyse poked her head inside, sniffing air that was oddly dry. There wasn't a trace of the damp coolness she'd expected.

"Hopefully a safe distance away." Zach turned to her. "By the way, do you usually prefer men's clothes?"

"Only when it suits me," she replied. "Actually, I find it's a great advantage when I want to move about unnoticed."

"In disguise," he added with that hint of humor.

"Exactly." When she tried to move past him, Zach reached out and snatched the wig from her head. Her hair tumbled past her shoulders.

"Impostor!" he accused, a devilish smile curving his lips as he moved past her into the passage.

Elyse followed, and he moved the wall back into place behind them. She abruptly came right up behind

St. James in the darkness. A hand reached for hers. She took it and hoped that he knew where they were going. He moved quickly through the narrow passage, taking her with him.

"You're very good at this," she remarked, her words spoken into his back as he came to an abrupt halt. "This is not exactly the sort of skill a nobleman would come by in his usual activities. I'd almost think you've done this before."

"Or a proper English lady for that matter?" he replied. "And be quiet. I'm listening."

"For what?" Her response was immediately muffled by a hand across her mouth. She jerked it away.

"I can't breathe!"

Zach smiled. "I think I found it."

"What?"

"A door. This passage has to lead somewhere." His hand closed over hers in alarm.

"What was that?"

Elyse swallowed back her own panic at the grating sound. "It came from behind us!"

He released her and felt along the end wall for some sort of release mechanism. His fingers eventually brushed a metal handle. He pulled it and the wall opened into a chamber in another building. Elyse quickly scrambled after him, blinking uncertainly in the meager light.

"Come along," he told her. "It's time to get out of here." He swung the stout door back into place and shoved a thick bolt into place. Whoever was behind them wouldn't be able to follow from this end, but it might be only a matter of time before the constables entered this building and searched it. He seized her by the arm and headed toward a wooden stairway.

"Wait!" Elyse hissed frantically, pulling back on his hand.

"What the devil?" Zach demanded.

"I'm caught!" Her pants, a little too big for her slender build, were caught fast in the bolted door.

"There's no time," Zach told her as she frantically tried to free the woolen fabric. He pulled on the back of her pants.

"You're not going to leave me?" she demanded.

Their eyes met. There was something in the words that slipped inside him, and for just a moment... Just as quickly as it came, the moment was gone amid the sounds of their pursuers on the other side of the door.

"You'll have to take them off," he told her.

"I beg your pardon?"

"Your pants. And I'd suggest right away by the sounds coming from beyond that door. It'll only take them a moment to figure out we locked it from the other side and then come round here."

"Take them off, or I'll take them off for you."

She had little time to dwell on her anger at him, as the pounding on the door became more persistent. She pulled frantically on her the leg of her pants in a last effort to free them. Then she looked up with startled eyes as St. James turned and headed for the stairs.

It took some effort, but she managed to slip out of the pants. She frowned as she glanced down at her bare legs. Refusing to go without undergarments, she'd worn a pair of the under drawers she usually wore on her early morning rides. They were made of silk and reached just to her knees, and left little to the imagination.

Barefoot and barelegged, she came up behind St. James, carrying her boots.

Zach glanced briefly in her direction and forced back a smile. He wasn't wrong. Miss Elyse Winslow was a very beautiful woman and she had exceptionally long and beautiful legs.

He'd seen many women in various states of undress, including the exotic Fatima just that evening during her performance, but none could compare with the young woman who clung to him like a shadow.

"Have you thought about what you're going to do when we get out of here?" she asked.

Getting out of the building was much easier than either of them expected. Judging by the offices they passed in the hallway, it was obviously some sort of professional building. Light from the streetlamps outside spilled through windows and lit the way. In a matter of minutes, Zach guided them away from the front of the building and out through a service entrance at the back. Elyse stepped out into the dark alley after him.

"What now?" she whispered.

"You're going to stay here," Zach informed her, stepping away from the back of the building into the alleyway.

"You're leaving?"

"I have to find a coach. I don't think you really want to be seen parading about the streets of London at this time of night in your silk underwear."

"If you'll remember, it's your fault I don't have my pants. Wait!" she called frantically after him when she realized he really did intend to leave her.

Zach turned and quickly retraced his steps. Without a word, he stripped off his jacket and wrapped it around her. He hesitated for a moment, and then, as if he'd suddenly decided something, lowered his head down and brushed his lips across hers. He caught the startled look on her face, that matched his own at... something he felt in that brief kiss.

"I'm going with you," she informed him, not trusting him in spite of their kiss. To a man like St. James, it meant nothing. After all, he'd left her in the Woods without a horse. What was to stop him from leaving her now?

"There's no telling what I'll find out there." He indicated the street that fronted both buildings. "I'll be back. You have my word."

"A promise from a pirate?" she replied. There was nothing light or playful in his gaze when he briefly looked back.

"You don't trust me?"

"Of course, not!" But strangely enough, she did.

He smiled that maddening smile. Then he was gone, blending in as if he were nothing more than another shadow. Elyse pulled his coat more tightly about her.

It seemed an eternity before he returned. She'd almost believed he had gone off and left her again. He took hold of her hand.

"Come with me."

"Did you find a coach?"

Without answering, he pulled her down the alley and then another one. It seemed they wound their way blindly before they turned into another alley and almost came face to face with two uniformed officers, gas lanterns in their hands. He pulled her into the shadows of a recessed doorway, and they both held their breath as the officers passed by without noticing them.

She had only a moment to catch her breath as they ducked down another alley. Emerging at the end, they rounded the corner and practically ran right into a team of horses.

"That you, Cap'n?" came a low voice.

"Aye, Sandy."

Captain? The greeting caught her by surprise. And he'd responded with such easy familiarity. The man called Sandy turned up the wick of the coach lantern to light their way.

"That's the last of em, Cap'n. I heard one of them say they was returnin' to that fancy club."

"Good." Zach stood aside and held the door open for her. When she hesitated, she was quickly assisted the remainder of the way into the coach. Just as he was about to enter the coach, there was a warning shout from down the street.

"Get us out of here, now!" Zach ordered, pushing her unceremoniously to the floor of the coach.

She felt the forward lunge of the coach, and then she was smothered by a strong male body as St. James crouched low over her. Anything she might have said was buried against his shoulder as they lay together on the floor, pinned between the seats.

Something Lucy had said flashed through her mind as she struggled to right herself and was rewarded by the pressure of his shoulder against her breast. She wondered if this was what her friend had meant when she'd referred to making love in a coach.

Their legs and bodies were hopelessly entangled. She should have been angry. At the very least, she should be afraid they might still be stopped and questioned. Instead, all she could do was laugh at the ridiculousness of it all. The evening hadn't turned out at all as she'd expected.

"What the devil are you laughing at?" Zach tried to untangle his legs from hers and instead became more hopelessly tangled with her as the coach careened down the street.

Any response was muffled against his chest. Grabbing the edge of the seat, Elyse struggled to sit upright and immediately realized the danger in doing so as she came up atop and fully astride William St. James.

"I can't say much for your methods, but I applaud the results," he quipped, a devilish gleam in his eye. His arms closed around her slender waist even as her hands flattened against his chest, trying to wedge distance between them.

"I'm afraid it's no use," he told her. "Sandy is not the best driver in the world. You might as well give up and enjoy the ride."

"Let go!" She struggled further, only to be flattened

against his body as the coach swung around a corner. She finally gave up, deciding there were worse things than being in close proximity to a maddeningly arrogant man, worse things such as the broken bones she would surely have if she tried to move around.

The coach turned again, then around the next corner, then ground to a bone-jarring stop. Elyse groaned as she tried to push away from him. But she wasn't quick enough. The driver jerked open the door.

Sandy coughed loudly. "Er, ah sorry, sir," he apologized.

Elyse wanted to die. She wanted to crawl into the nearest hole and pull the sides in after her. As it was, she could do neither.

"Let me up!" she ground out, her mortification complete, for she could well imagine the full view the driver had been given as he'd entered the coach.

"I'm trying to," Zach winced at the sharp edge of the seat cutting into the back of his shoulder.

"What are you doing?" Elyse gasped at the intimate thrust of his knee between her legs.

"Trying to let you up. Lie still!" he commanded.

She twisted under him, only managing to wedge their hips more tightly together, aware that the coachman stood just outside, probably enjoying the best performance he'd seen in years.

Leaning over, Zach fastened her with a cool smile.

"I'd like nothing better than to lie with you like this for the rest of the night. But there is the matter of your reputation. Now, if you will please move your bottom." His hand closed over her hip. He lifted her, freeing his pinned knee.

"There. Easily done."

"Easily done," she whispered, still affected by that intimate contact, her anger now replaced by something confusing. His hand lingered at her hip, the fingers fanning out across the curve of her bottom. Zach breathed out slowly.

Every time he was near her, he found it impossible to keep his hands off her. His voice was tight as he rose up on one knee, cool air rushing between their bodies as he offered his hand.

"What's happened?" a voice greeted them.

Elyse emerged from the coach as a portly man came down the steps of an imposing house, lantern in hand. She immediately recognized the residence as the London home of Lord and Lady Vale.

"What in the name of...?"

The man was immediately cut off by St. James

"There was a bit of trouble this evening. I believe you've met Miss Winslow." He made a brief introduction as he escorted Elyse to the house.

"Winslow?" The older man was left to ponder in their wake. "Good God! You don't mean Barrington's fiancé?"

She could have died right then and there, but she wasn't even given the time to contemplate doing so. Instead, she was pulled up the stairs and through the front doors.

"Where are the servants?" he demanded.

"Asleep at this time of night," the man answered. Elyse remembered he'd been introduced as St. James' uncle.

"Nothing is to be said of this to anyone! Is that clear?"

"Of course."

After giving more instructions, St. James turned toward the staircase. Any objections she might have voiced were quickly forgotten as Elyse struggled to keep her feet under her and navigate the stairs without falling.

As they reached the top landing, St. James paused, then pulled her along behind him, opened a door, and propelled her into a room. She immediately whirled around.

"What do you think you're doing?"

He turned up the gas lamp on the wall, that gray gaze locking with hers and then slowly lowering to take in slender bare legs before traveling back up to her face.

"You'll have to spend the night here," he informed her, as if it was nothing unusual for him to return home at the end of an evening with a woman and then drag her up to his bedroom.

His long slow perusal had done nothing to improve Elyse's humor. She squared her slender shoulders. "No. I won't," she responded with equal determination. "I appreciate your getting me out of there this evening, but I now insist upon returning home."

"Home?" Zach mused thoughtfully. "Dressed like that?" He gestured to her odd costume.

"I can't believe that you're concerned for my reputation."

"Not at all," he told her.

Elyse's eyes flashed with anger. "I want to go home. Now!"

"I assure you, I'd like nothing better. But under the present circumstances, it's impossible. Unless, of course," he added, with a maddeningly arrogant lift of his brow, "you've made other arrangements for the evening." Then added, "Just what were your plans for returning home this evening, Miss Winslow?"

She stiffened at the condescending tone in his voice. "Lucy and I were to return to her house," she informed him. "But that was before you intruded with that ridiculous scheme involving Fatima."

"And I suppose you hold me to blame for everything else that happened this evening?" St. James replied.

"If you hadn't interfered, I would have gotten out well ahead of the police."

Zach leaned back against the doorway. "Is that so?"

"Yes."

A maddening smile curved his handsome lips, and despite their tumbling about in the coach the eye-patch was still firmly in place and emphasized the impression of a pirate.

"That's where you're wrong, my dear," he informed her calmly. "When I arranged that little scene with Fatima, Maitland had already discovered his wife's part in this little game of yours."

Elyse swallowed. He had obviously overheard their exchange as Lucy and Andrew were leaving.

"He didn't seem amused by your little escapade. There's every possibility that you won't be a welcome guest in his home this evening."

He was right, of course. It would be weeks before Andrew spoke to her again. The evening was a complete fiasco. She'd have to make it up to Lucy. But not tonight. She had another problem, a very serious one.

"Then, you'll just have to take me home," she insisted, aggravated by his arrogant attitude and by the fact that he was absolutely right about the outcome of the evening.

"And return you to your grandmother's loving arms dressed like that?" He gestured to her bare legs and his once-immaculate evening jacket, now soiled from their crawling along hidden passages and running through dingy alleys.

"I hardly think so," St. James continued. "She'll take one look at you and Barrington will be over here with a pistol to defend your honor. No thank you. I have business with Barrington, and I'll not see it jeopardized simply because you haven't more sense than to go where you're not invited."

He continued when she would have argued that point. "And furthermore, the streets of London are crawling with police. They're questioning everyone they see, trying to find the murderer. If I tried to get you home at this time of night, I guarantee we'd be stopped, and I don't want to have to explain your current state of undress to the authorities. So, you see, you have no choice but to remain here for the night." He turned in the doorway, one hand resting casually on the knob.

"I think you'll be comfortable, and we'll see what's to be done about you in the morning."

With that, he turned and left, the door closing behind him, ending their conversation. Or rather his conversation, she thought angrily. She'd hardly been able to get a word in edgewise.

The most aggravating part of it was that he was right. Arms folded, she sat on the bed and pulled her knees up. Looking at her bare legs, she groaned. She had no clothes. She was in St. James' house. The evening couldn't have gone more wrong.

Elyse almost laughed out loud at the absurdity of it all. She'd really gotten herself into a fine mess. And like it or not, there was no one else she could blame for the way everything had turned out, not even William St. James.

"Impostor!" she grumbled into the silence of the room. And he had the nerve to call her one!

She wondered what had become of Jerrold, then snorted out loud, as she recalled that he'd seemed to be doing very well for himself right up to the point where she'd been forced to go upstairs. He'd been far too occupied with the young woman in his arms to give her a second glance, and he hadn't been among the half-naked men running about when the police had arrived.

No, she thought, experiencing a feeling that was part disappointment, part anger, Jerrold was far too clever to be caught in a compromising situation, either by the authorities or anyone else. And with that thought, she was forced to confront something she'd ignored during the past months.

Jerrold had been calling on her for several months.

Her grandmother had been certain a proposal was imminent, and it had been clear Lady Regina was ecstatic at thinking her granddaughter might marry the son of her dearest friend. And Elyse had to admit that, at first, she'd been flattered by Jerrold's attentions.

But that had ended the day he'd taken her riding in Kensington Gardens and finally proposed to her. He'd spoken of family honor and duty, and of all sorts of ridiculous notions about preserving the Barrington lineage. She'd ignored most of it, but the part she hadn't been able to ignore was the fact that he'd never once mentioned his feelings for her. Oh, he cared for her, and as she'd learned on several different occasions, he desired her. But love?

Love came slowly, her grandmother had told her. Lucy had refused to comment about all of it, but Elyse knew her thoughts on it. Worse, she had the feeling that this marriage was more of a business arrangement. Jerrold needed a wife, a lady suitable to bear the title of Lady Barrington and the sons he wanted.

This was how many marriages came about within the circle of her grandmother's acquaintances. Alliances of families were made for titles and the fortunes that went with them. It was expected that she would marry well, as others she knew.

Admittedly, she had grown bored with the endless rounds of parties during the social season—all for the purpose of finding a proper husband. In the end, when Jerrold had proposed, she'd almost found it a relief to think she wouldn't be subjected to them any longer.

She told herself that, when she became Lady Barrington, everything would be different. But as the months passed and rumors of Jerrold's dalliances were whispered, Elyse realized that not *everything* would be different.

Like so many she knew, she suspected there were those who simply accepted their husband's private activities. Her dear friend? She hoped not, for Lucy was in love with Andrew and she would hate to see her hurt by such an arrangement.

Ironically, she was in the house of another man. But she could hardly have returned home half-naked after the disastrous evening. What would her grandmother think? What would Jerrold think?

Elyse almost laughed at the thought that he would even know about it, so occupied was he at the club that night.

She stood at the glass doors, staring out into the storm, not unlike the one that she' dreamed about since she was a child, the wind lashing at her hair. In just a little over a week, she and Jerrold would be married.

Was that what she wanted?

Having said good night to Tobias, Zach paced the formal parlor. After tossing down a third brandy, he reclined in a chair, rolling his head back against the chair back.

Tonight could have been disastrous for his plans if he'd been stopped by the authorities and questioned. He smiled faintly as he thought of their escape. Staring up at the ceiling, he tried to imagine what Elyse was doing and thinking at that moment.

She would be angry; he was certain of it. He'd seen the anger in her eyes when he'd delivered his little speech upstairs. Admittedly, he hadn't given her any choice. He hadn't wanted to, knowing she'd probably have wakened the entire household if he had.

He sat up and held his head in both hands. What was he doing here, hobnobbing with Barrington and the men who made the decisions that controlled his life, and had controlled his father's?

The answer was in the question, but it seemed he was no closer to learning the truth than when he'd first arrived in England. The only thing he knew for certain was that Jerrold Barrington's mother had once known his father. But what did it mean?

He poured another brandy and downed it, rolling his neck against the tight muscles that were a constant presence.

Felicia Barrington, a name, someone he'd never known. A name, a presence that if he turned suddenly, what would he find? What did it mean? Was it even real, or something he imagined?

An apparition, a ghost? He didn't believe in them.

A guardian angel, as a priest once suggested? He didn't believe in those either. There was no guardian angel watching over him, certainly not with the things he'd been through and done.

A spirit, as the Aboriginals believed? The people at Resolute believed in them. They believed in a beginning that never ended and in mysterious spirits that had the ability to change into wind, rain, and thunder. He'd grown up with it, but never believed in it. Still...

The voyage from Sydney, the stories of ships becalmed for weeks near the Cape of South Africa, Tobias' dire warnings that never came to be as the wind continued to fill the sails of the *Revenge*.

A spirit that brought him to England? He didn't believe in any of it. He believed in what he could hold in his own two hands, in what he'd built at Resolute, stone by stone making a place for himself, and the loyalty of trusted companions.

He stared into the glass tumbler and the brandy shimmering in the light from the fire at the hearth.

Lys. A name that no amount of drink could dull. And a woman he should never have met and shouldn't want. But since that first meeting, not a moment had passed that he didn't find himself thinking about her, drawn to her, wanting her and knowing the risk.

Elyse Winslow, soon-to-be Lady Barrington, represented everything he despised—England with its iron-fist over the colony, the nobility with their entitlements that took away people's history, the ability to provide for their families, and for many—their names and who they once were.

He heard the sound from somewhere inside the house, a distant thumping sound as if a door had been left open. He heard it again and set the empty tumbler aside on the table beside the chair.

The downstairs lights had all been extinguished except for the light in the parlor and at the foyer. The sound came again from upstairs.

He climbed the stairs to the second-floor rooms and heard it again from the room Elyse Winslow occupied. He hesitated, his hand on the latch, then slowly pushed the door open.

She stood before the open glass doors, the only sound the bump of one of the doors against the wall as wind filled the room.

She wore the shirt she'd worn earlier, the wind whipping her hair about her shoulders, and stood motionless in the opening as the rain began. She didn't move, didn't seem to be aware of him or the rain. She might have been a ghost spirit the Aboriginals believed in, a creature that came with the wind and rain.

Lys. Was it only the sound of the wind, or something else as she stared out into the storm-filled night, and the memory of another storm at sea a long time ago? And she was so cold as those memories wrapped around her. Then, the warmth of a hand on hers.

She turned from the window opening as lightning lit up the night sky and the expression on her face, her eyes wide and dark, rain soaking her hair.

Was it a dream as the Aboriginals believed? Or something else? All he was aware of was that he knew her...had known her before, something that was deep inside him as he reached out and touched her face.

Elyse didn't pull away, couldn't breathe as his head lowered and she felt the faint brush of his mouth against hers. A small sob escaped, and she closed her eyes as he deepened the kiss, and a memory slipped out of the past.

The rain lashed at them as they stood there, soaking them both as she reached for him, and his arms closed around her. Then he was looking down at her, her breathing ragged, almost painful as he stared at her.

Who was she? Zach thought as he traced her face with his fingers... A dream? Dreams weren't real, but the young woman who stood there, her hand in his, was very real, tears mingling with the rain on her face, that gaze that fastened on his, and the taste of her. He whispered her name as he picked her up and carried her to the bed. *Lys.*

She didn't protest, but instead reached for him as he laid her on the bed and a memory slipped out of the shadows in the room, of another time and place, of a man and woman... as he slowly made love to her.

A touch, a kiss, the feel of her hand in his hands, the sound as her breath caught into the deep hours of the night, surrounded by the whisper of memories as their bodies joined.

Nine

"Have you lost your mind?" Tobias confronted Zach in the library of Lord Vale's home.

"She's Lady Winslow's granddaughter, engaged to Lord Barrington, and you bring her here? Good God, man! What were you thinking?"

Zach slammed the cup down so hard on the saucer that it shattered beneath his hand. He never even winced as blood seeped between his fingers.

"And where exactly was I to take her? The streets were filled with police. It was after midnight. I couldn't simply take her home and explain to Lady Winslow that her granddaughter had spent the evening with me at an exclusive men's club."

For the first time in weeks, Tobias was sober, just when Zach wished his friend were upstairs sleeping off the effects of the night before.

"And what do you presume to do this morning? How do you think you can explain to her grandmother and Lord Barrington that she spent the night in this house? Yer in too deep, lad. It's too dangerous. And do you think Miss Winslow will play along with whatever explanation you come up with?" He bellowed at the younger man, not caring that lack of sleep and this new problem made Zach's mood dangerous.

"And what good will it do if you bleed to death?" Tobias argued. Seizing a linen handkerchief from the silver service he'd brought in earlier, he bound Zach's hand.

Memories of the night before returned and regret was sharp. He must have been insane to go to her last night. Even now he didn't understand it. He was angry, angrier than he could ever remember being before. But not even anger could explain everything. It was as if a madness had come over him, driving him to her. If he could only have those hours back...

No, if he had them back, he'd make love to her all over again. And if he did, he knew he'd never be able to walk away from her. He pressed his fingers into his eyes, trying to drive the memory of those last hours from his thoughts.

He looked up as Tobias deliberately jerked the makeshift bandage tighter.

"She'll cooperate because she doesn't want anyone to know she was at that club last night." His gaze hardened. "She especially doesn't want to jeopardize her betrothal to Barrington. The man's wealth and title mean far too much. That' s why I want you to talk to her."

"Me?" Tobias' gaze narrowed. "What makes you think she'll listen to me?"

Zach fixed his eyes on the distant wall, images of the recent hours of passion playing across his thoughts. "She'll have her reasons for not wanting to see me this morning!" His gaze returned back to Tobias', but he did not quite cover his emotions quickly enough. His smile was ironic.

"She thinks I'm an impostor."

He didn't need to say what he was thinking. It was written all over his face.

Tobias scrutinized his young friend, just what did happen between you and that young woman last night?"

Zach's gray gaze leveled with his. "That, my friend, is

none of your business," he replied. He was tired, this situation with Elyse Winslow had only made the stay in London more precarious, and he still didn't have the information he wanted.

Somehow, he had to meet with Barrington again. He was confident the man had managed to elude the police the evening before.

"What do you want me to do?" Tobias asked, knowing that it would do no good to argue the matter.

"When she awakens, I want you to make arrangements for her return to Lucy Maitland's home. She was to spend the night there. Explain to the Maitlands that I entrusted her to your care and spent last night aboard my ship. That should protect Miss Winslow's reputation." Zach crossed the room and poured coffee into another cup. He hadn't slept the entire night. He hadn't wanted to and could still feel the heat of her skin.

Seizing a decanter, he added a liberal amount of brandy to the steaming coffee. "I'll be leaving shortly. As far as any of the servants are concerned, I returned to my ship last night." He reached inside the pocket of his pants and threw several hundred-pound notes down on the table.

"She'll need clothing before she returns, the finest you can buy." His voice was harsh. "After all, a lady must look the part."

A lady. Yes, she was a lady, in spite of the man's clothes, in spite of her independent nature. And she was as far removed from him as the truth about his father.

"All right," Tobias replied. "I don't like it, but I'll do it. And pray she goes along with the idea. I'll check her myself, then make the necessary arrangements. The sooner she returns home the better, for everyone." He took a drink, his first drink in over twenty-four hours, then shuddered. "I must be getting old. I swear that stuff doesn't taste like it used to." With that, he turned, leaving Zach to his tormented thoughts.

His thoughts were filled with the memory of her in that massive bed, her slender body curled against him. Why did he want her even now? he asked himself.

Elyse clutched the satin coverlet against her naked body. Slowly, like the mist in her dreams, the night before receded until there was only herself. She was alone.

She gazed about the room, the events of the previous night slowly coming back to her, the sight of her clothes on the floor beside the bed. She hadn't been dreaming.

She squeezed her eyes shut as she remembered everything. How could he...? How could she have been such a fool to allow it...? What was she to do now?

The house was completely silent except for the ticking of the clock. Five o'clock. Everyone, including the household staff, would be asleep. She had to leave. But she needed clothing and a way to get home.

She left the bed and crossed the room. She searched the large armoire.

It was empty, as were the dressing table drawers. As she looked about the room, she realized with the lack of personal items this was undoubtedly one of the many guest rooms.

Lord and Lady Vale were gone, but she might be able to find something to wear in Lady Vale's rooms. She stepped silently into the hall, listening for any sounds of movement from the floor below, then slipped down the hall toward the closed doors on either side.

She smiled to herself as she found the room that was obviously Lady Vale's private suite of rooms. There was just enough light that came in through the windows for her to make out the large wardrobe in the adjoining room. The wardrobe was overflowing with clothes.

Pink was obviously Lady Vale's signature color.

Gown, slippers, hat, and stockings of the same pale color that decorated the walls of the room.

Why couldn't it be something subtle, gray or blue? she thought as she searched for something she might wear.

The gown she finally chose was a shade of deep wine color with pink at the bodice and at a panel down the front of the skirt. The gown fit well enough across the bodice, and she was able to button it herself. She returned to the room she'd found herself in that morning and gathered the remnants of her clothes and the boots she had worn.

At a sound from the hall, she flattened herself into the shadows at the edge of the room at a knock at the door and then a portly man walked into the room.

Tobias looked first to the bed, then went to the adjoining room. He quickly returned to the bedchamber. Both rooms were empty. She was gone!

Elyse quickly stepped from the shadows at the edge of the room as the door slammed shut. The man was undoubtedly on his way to inform St. James that his guest was nowhere to be found. She had to get out of this house!

The main staircase was her only hope for escape. Running to the landing, she leaned over and listened. Downstairs, a door slammed, the echo reverberating up to her.

It was foolhardy and she knew it, but there was no other choice. She quickly ran down the staircase, past a formal parlor on one side and a set of closed double doors on the other.

"I tell you she's gone!"

Elyse raced across the entry hall. There wasn't time to try the front doors. If they were locked, she was caught. As the man she'd just seen emerged from a doorway, his back to her, she ducked around a massive, long table into the shadows.

"That's impossible!" St. James replied.

"See for yourself," his companion suggested.

A curse split the air as St. James emerged from the library. "She has to be there!"

Elyse pulled back against the wall, closing her eyes. He was just as she remembered—the soft gold of his hair and the sharp planes of his face now tense with anger.

Both men raced up the stairway, St. James' longer stride taking the steps two at a time. Elyse didn't have time to consider what had happened the night before. As soon as both men were out of sight at the top of the stairs, she quickly crossed the entry to the front door and escaped.

She found a hansom cab only a half-block from Lord Vale's home. The driver looked at her strangely but said nothing. He easily found the address for Lucy's house.

Andrew Maitland was punctual to a fault. Unless she missed her guess, he had already left their fashionable home at Bainbridge Square for his office. That is, unless he was still angry with Lucy about the previous evening at White's.

She had the driver pull into the circular driveway. She was met at the door by their butler and asked to see Lucy. She waited in the front parlor then whirled around at the sound of rustling skirts as her friend joined her.

"Good heavens!" Lucy flew into the parlor. Glancing quickly about, she discreetly shut the cream white doors, then immediately crossed the room and took Elyse's hands in hers.

"I couldn't believe it when the butler announced you. I've been frantic since last night. What happened after Andrew and I left? How did you get out of there?"

How indeed, she thought. She couldn't tell Lucy the truth about what had happened.

"I was able to find a cab and left." She could tell by her friend's expression that she didn't believe that was all of it, but she had the good grace not to ask. At least not for now.

"You have every right to be angry with me," Elyse was determined to clear the air.

"You're right, I should be," Lucy admitted. "But it was my own fault for letting you talk me into such a ridiculous scheme, and it was exciting. It's good that Andrew left earlier. I don't think he's ready to see you just yet."

Elyse confessed. "I had hoped that he'd already left for his office. Do you think he'll ever speak to me again?"

"Maybe in forty or fifty years." Lucy shook her head and then burst out laughing. "I tried to convince him we should go back for you last night, but he thought being left was just what you deserved." Lucy pulled her to a nearby settee.

"I argued until I was in tears. Finally, he turned the carriage around, but when we returned there were police everywhere."

"I don't know how I would have explained it to Grandmother if we'd been caught." She wasn't certain how to explain what had happened afterward to herself.

"Was Jerrold terribly angry?" Lucy asked.

"I didn't see Jerrold last night after the police arrived."

"Oh. Well, I suppose he was able to leave discreetly," Lucy replied. "You're looking a bit wan. Are you feeling all right after our little adventure?"

She needed an excuse, any excuse. "I left before breakfast this morning, perhaps some coffee or tea?" She simply didn't elaborate where she had left from.

"Brunch," Lucy decided." Then you can tell me about all the excitement after Andrew and I left."

Excitement, Elyse thought. That was one word for what had happened afterward. She had deliberately left out any mention of what had happened after St. James had taken her to Lord Vale's residence.

"What about St. James?" Lucy asked about the previous evening over biscuits and assorted cheeses. "According to Andrew, he is such a blackguard. I can't imagine that he would allow himself to be caught in such a situation."

"What's he like? I mean really like? He seems so overbearing, impossibly rude, but impossibly handsome with that eye-patch!"

"I suppose one might think that," Elyse replied vaguely.

"It's just that, in all the time you've been engaged to Jerrold, you've never—well you know what I mean. Now this man comes along and in a matter of a few weeks... "

"Lucy, please!" Of course she couldn't keep the secret from Lucy for too long.

Her friend wasn't about to be put off. "I saw it the first time you met him," she said. "There was something between you. Have you met him before?"

"Of course, not. I never met him before the night of the party."

"And there is nothing between us. It was all a mistake. I want to forget it."

A thought suddenly occurred to Lucy. "Did he force himself on you?"

"No! It wasn't that way at all!"

"Very well," Lucy told her. "But there is something you may have to face whether you like it or not. If he..." Lucy began hesitantly.

For all their candor with each other and their years of friendship, they'd never discussed this particular aspect of relationships before. "That is, when you were together... "

"For heaven's sake. What are you trying to say?" Elyse demanded.

Lucy bluntly replied, "If two people are together and the man finishes, there's every chance you could get caught."

"I know," Elyse whispered. "But it doesn't happen every time, or every woman in the world would be constantly with child. You and Andrew have been married for nearly two years and you haven't had a child."

"True," Lucy admitted, "but there are certain measures that can be taken when a man and woman don't want to have a child just yet. I have to admit, they often fail, but they usually work. I know this is difficult." She tried to put it as delicately as possible while trying hard to accept what her friend was *not* saying.

"Did he?" she asked in a quiet voice.

Elyse breathed out slowly. "It will just have to be all right. And remember, you have promised not to tell anyone. Grandmother would be heartbroken if she knew."

Lucy reassured her. "But I think you're making a mistake in going ahead with the wedding. Not just because of what happened. It's just that I've always thought Jerrold was not the right man for you. You're not in love with him, and he won't change his ways."

"Lucy, please!" she begged. "I don't want to talk about it anymore."

"It serves Jerrold right, though," Lucy added. "It's no secret what happens at White's."

At the look Elyse gave her, she changed the subject. "All right, what are you going to do next?"

She'd thought about it. "I have to get home. I left word with Katy last night that I intended to spend the night here, but it's late and there's packing to be done for the trip to the country with Jerrold's family. His father is planning a round of parties for all the local people before the wedding." She ignored the look her friend gave her.

"Then we must get you home, and act as if nothing unusual happened," Lucy replied.

"What about Andrew? Does he suspect anything?"

Lucy shook her head. "He's too concerned that I might slip and mention something to the wife of one of his friends. I must say, I love the man desperately and he was completely faithful to me, even before he found out my disguise, but I'll hold this over his head for a few weeks. It makes him so much more attentive." She smiled confidently.

Late that afternoon, Elyse bid her friend farewell and swept into Winslow House as if it were all part of the original plan for the previous evening.

Chivers delivered a message just before supper. It seemed Jerrold had missed her dreadfully the previous evening and was looking forward to their trip to his family's country estate the following day.

There was nothing in his note to indicate that he might have seen through her disguise the evening before at White's. She wondered who he'd spent the night with, and then realized she no longer had the right to criticize him. Never-the-less, the last part of his note suddenly stopped her. He briefly mentioned that he'd invited St. James to join them at Fair View.

"Was that Chivers, my dear?" Lady Regina swept down the staircase and greeted Elyse at the landing. At her granddaughter's brief nod, she continued her chatter, adjusting a coil of silver hair. "I swear that man comes and goes without being heard or seen. I think he must have been a thief in another life."

Elyse looked up, paying only vague attention to her grandmother. "What were you saying?"

"Chivers," Lady Regina went on to explain. "He moves about so quietly, it's sometimes frightening. I was thinking he must have been a thief in a past life.

Are you feeling all right, my dear? You're as pale as a ghost."

"It's nothing," Elyse blurted out a little too quickly. She tried to smile casually. "Jerrold has invited some other guests to the country, that's all. He says he'll call for us around ten o'clock tomorrow morning so that we'll arrive early at Fair View."

"I'm so looking forward to seeing it again." Lady Regina stepped down the last few steps to the main floor, looping her arm through Elyse's. "It's been almost twenty years since I was last at Fair View, and of course you've never seen it at all. It's a grand place.

"Jerrold's mother was so happy there. She loved going to the country. I think it held special memories for her," she continued. "She once confessed to me that she would have stayed there year-round but Jerrold's father wouldn't hear of it. His business interests and friends were here in London. You'll love it, my dear." Lady Regina patted her hand.

Elyse only murmured a faint response. She didn't want to discuss either Fair View or Jerrold.

What was she to do now? Her wild scheme of the night before had ended in disaster, and she'd hoped to avoid all further contact with St. James. There would be a great many guests, of course. Perhaps she could avoid him completely, or at least avoid being alone with him. All she had to do was get through the next three days.

She changed the topic of the conversation. "What were you saying about Chivers? Something about his past life? I didn't know you believed in such things." She forced a smile as they entered the dining room and took their places at the table.

"Past lives?" Lady Regina looked up. "Well, of course there's no proof of such things, but there are cultures that believe in them." She chatted gaily about a notion popular among certain of their friends.

"Naturally the church is against such thinking, but

I've always thought it to be a most fascinating notion that we don't die but merely pass from one life to another. A lot like cats with their nine lives." She placed a damask napkin across her skirt.

"I wonder if that's how the saying came about?" she added. "Perhaps someone had proof of multiple lives. Wouldn't that be marvelous?"

Her grandmother took a sip of wine. "Think of all the people you could meet. I suppose a person might love someone different in each lifetime. Good heavens! I had a marvelous marriage to your grandfather, and now I have Ceddy. If I kept that up through several lifetimes, it could be quite confusing trying to keep track of all those men."

In spite of the shock she'd had over Jerrold's note and her uneasiness about the next few days, Elyse laughed until her eyes watered. Past lives, future lives... and lovers in each one. It was an interesting notion, of course, and her grandmother managed to make it all seem quite humorous.

"Or perhaps it's the same person in all those lifetimes," she suggested.

Lady Regina thought long and hard about that one. "Then that would mean I might possibly find your grandfather again in the next life," she concluded. "Oh, dear!" Regina looked faintly bemused. "However am I going to explain Ceddy to him? He just won't understand at all."

The wine with their supper was having a calming effect on her badly shaken nerves. "But it's an interesting thought. Once you've found the person you truly love, you would never be parted. Two people would simply find each other again."

"Of course, the opposite might also be true," Regina suggested. "You might keep meeting up with the wrong person and never be happy. Such a dreadful thought."

Elyse was suddenly very quiet. "Yes, there is always

the possibility that we could just go on and on, through one lifetime after another, never finding the person we truly love."

What if people were destined to meet over and over again, time after time? she thought. Did that mean that she and Jerrold were destined to be together not only in this lifetime but in others? And if so, would her feelings always be the same?

She hoped that it wasn't true. If she couldn't have what Lucy shared with Andrew or what she knew her grandmother felt for Ceddy, then she didn't want to go on to another lifetime with that same person.

The trip took over five hours by coach, but the time passed quickly. Jerrold rode with Elyse and her grandmother. He kept up an animated conversation, pointing out places of interest as the city gave way to rolling green countryside. He seemed to be in a particularly amiable and attentive mood. Elyse vaguely wondered if the events at White's had anything to do with it. Nothing he said or discussed gave any indication that he knew she had been anywhere except at Lucy's home that evening.

Though she would have dearly loved to see the expression on Jerrold's face at finding out she was at the club, that would lead to other questions she couldn't afford to have asked. Even with Jerrold's past indiscretions, she couldn't risk his knowing where she'd actually spent the night.

She wasn't fooling herself. Surprisingly, it wasn't because of any regret that he should find out. Like her grandmother, she didn't give a fig about what other people said or thought. What did matter to her was her grandmother. She wanted only to make her happy, and if this marriage would accomplish that, then so be it. And as for the night she had spent with William St. James, that was for her to keep secret.

Gazing out the window of the coach at the lush countryside, Elyse hoped she would be more fortunate in love in the next lifetime and her thoughts wandered where they shouldn't have. What might her life be like with a man like St. James if the circumstances were different?

Early afternoon, they passed through a small town lined with shops and houses and cobbled streets. Townspeople stared with curiosity at the gleaming coach and the accompanying carriages and wagons. It was obvious the Barrington family held a position of great importance there.

Beyond the town, the coach turned off the main road and swung up a long drive lined with mulberry and yew trees, then swept past a lazy stream and lush meadows, the storm of the night before gone.

"Elyse, you must see Fair View from here." Lady Regina urged her from the corner of the coach where she'd carried on a lively conversation with Jerrold for most of the journey.

"It is rather magnificent, Elyse," Jerrold boasted, insistently taking her arm and drawing her forward so that she could look out the window.

Fair View, the Barrington family's country estate, lay like a magnificent crown at the end of a small, verdant valley. Elyse stared at it as if transfixed. It was a massive Tudor creation of stone and leaded glass. Intricate pathways crisscrossed gardens and led to sprawling lawns, while the house seemed to go on forever in wing after imposing wing, each like a different facet of the crown.

A glass-walled conservatory lay to the right; it was attached to the main house. To the left, the lawns rolled to the stables and beyond them was open pastureland and a heavily wooded forest. They circled a large pond to reach the main entrance. It was filled with graceful black and white swans and inquisitive geese. This was by far the most impressive house Elyse had ever seen, easy rivaling any of the great estates in London for size and magnificence.

Their coach slowed and came to a stop before the wide stone steps. Jerrold's father had preceded them by two days, and he now came down the front steps followed by several servants. Jerrold was the first to descend from the coach. After greeting his father, he turned back to assist Elyse's grandmother. As she gazed at the imposing stone facade of the house, Elyse realized that several guests had arrived earlier. They appeared from the gardens. Atop horses, they called greetings to the new arrivals.

For some inexplicable reason Elyse hesitated, held back in the cool seclusion of the coach. She wanted just a moment longer to look at this wondrous house before the peacefulness and beauty of her first moment here was completely shattered.

Her gaze wandered over the intricate stonework and the expanse of leaded glass that formed the massive front wall of the main part of the dwelling. The bottom rows of glass were made up of the smallest panes, probably only two feet by three feet. The next rows were made up of panes that appeared to be twice those dimensions. And the very top pane of glass spanned the entire width of the opening.

Brilliant sunlight glistened, in prisms of color, off the glass.

Shading her eyes, Elyse realized the profusion of colors wasn't caused by the sun at all. In several panes, stained glass could be clearly seen. And the largest pane was of such intricate design it could only be considered a work of art. It was by far the most impressive thing Elyse had ever seen. Without conscious thought, Elyse found herself searching the bottom row of smaller panes. At this distance the smaller designs of stained-glass were almost indiscernible, and yet her gaze was drawn to the bottom left corner.

It has to be there, she thought to herself. It has to be! Her gaze fastened on the last pane. She held her breath as wispy clouds passed before the sun, momentarily darkening the entire wall of glass to a somber, slate shade, obliterating the colors. Like an expectant child she held her breath, waiting for the sun to emerge and light the wall of color. And, as if moved by her desperate hopes, the clouds skittered past, and the sun illuminated the windows once more.

"It is there!" Elyse whispered joyously, tears coming to her eyes. "The rose. I knew it would be there." She stared, transfixed, as the image of a single crimson rose appeared in the leaded design of that last pane. It was like a gift, just waiting to be found by her, a gift of memory and something more.

"Elyse?" Her grandmother looked back at her hesitantly. "Are you coming, dear?"

"Yes!" she breathed out, her heart quickening. An almost uncontrollable exhilaration ran along her nerve endings. Home...

It was insane, or perhaps it was fatigue after the strain of the last two days; but for some unknown reason, Elyse felt she had truly come home. It was as if she'd returned from a very long journey, and now the house welcomed her. But that was impossible. A house wasn't like a person, with feelings and emotions. Yet she felt it just the same; a sort of beckoning in the craggy stones and shining glass, a warmth of familiarity that left her almost weak. Even before she'd looked out the window, she'd known exactly what the house would look like.

"I've been here before," she whispered to herself, convinced of it. She heard Jerrold's impatient reminder and reached for the handle of the door. Inexplicably, she felt angered by the intrusion. Then she silently chided herself. Of course, she knew what Fair View would look like. Surely Jerrold or her grandmother had described it to her. As she stepped from the coach, her gaze immediately went to the paned window and the crimson rose patterned in the glass.

The rose was his promise to me. Unbidden, the words filled her thoughts.

"You promised," she whispered, staring transfixed at the single fragile bloom. Without knowing the reason, it occurred to her there was something wrong with the design in the glass pane. She stared up at it, trying to understand what it was that bothered her about it.

"Elyse, please. My other guests are waiting!" Jerrold reminded her impatiently.

"Yes, of course," she murmured in response, reaching down to lift the hem of her gown as she stepped forth. All at once, she remembered what it was that disturbed her about that single pane of glass. Her head came up, vivid blue eyes fastened once more on the simple leaded design.

"There was supposed to be a white rose," she said, causing several heads to turn in her direction.

Jerrold quickly retraced his steps and firmly seized her elbow.

"What the devil are you talking about? Everyone is watching." He leaned close, and his voice was tight.

"Elyse, please come along. Now!" he instructed from between thinned lips.

Memories, bittersweet and illusive, whispered across her soul. A red rose was symbolic of passion. A white rose represented love that was true and enduring.

There should have been a white rose entwined with the red one. He promised me the white rose, symbolic of his love.

"Elyse! Try to get hold of yourself. Are you feeling ill?"

"Ill?" She looked at Jerrold as if she were only just seeing him for the first time.

Jerrold forcefully pulled her up the steps.

It was hardly necessary. She wanted to see everything. This land, this house, the ancient stones and glass were somehow still dearly familiar, were reaching out to her with illusive memories from another time and place.

"Do come along," he muttered under his breath.

"Yes," Elyse whispered, her eyes again going to that glass pane with the single red rose, almost as if she were looking for something...

Or someone.

Ten

Elyse squeezed her eyes shut. *I must have been insane,* she thought as she hid deeper in the thick downy coverlet of the bed.

She could hear Katy moving quietly about the room, putting away the last of her clothes, straightening things, and then the faint clink of the silver service from last night's dinner as it was picked up for removal from the room.

Good heavens! Why did the woman have to be so slow. Usually, she flew about like a whirlwind, accomplishing in a very short time what normally took anyone else several hours. Elyse silently ground her teeth. If Katy didn't finish soon, she'd come right out of that bed and give everything of her well-planned charade away.

Then where will you be? she chided herself. The answer came quickly enough. You'll be out with everyone else, riding to hounds this morning and very possibly meeting up with St. James. That possibility was the only thing keeping her snug in bed, pretending to have a dreadful headache and a case of the sniffles.

Earlier, when she'd had Katy inform her grandmother that she wasn't feeling at all well, the response from all camps had been predictable. She'd never lied, discounting little childhood fibs, and hated deceiving her grandmother. Lady Regina had immediately come to her room.

Elyse had seen the worry and concern on her lined face and had felt dreadful for it. But Jerrold was an entirely different matter.

He'd insisted on seeing her to express his concern. Now, she might be good at disguises, but outright lying was a different matter. Jerrold was attentive and solicitous, yet underneath the pleasant demeanor she'd sensed his irritation. And while they were alone for a few minutes, when her grandmother went downstairs to find Katy, he'd very bluntly informed her that he was disappointed in her. After all, he'd said, she was always so healthy and vital. With a disdainful sniff, he'd told her in no uncertain terms that he sincerely hoped this wouldn't continue after the wedding. His mother had been sickly for a long time, and he openly admitted that suffering through the same thing in a wife was completely unacceptable.

The nerve of him! Standing there in her room and handing down edicts like some pompous, imperious ass! A thought flashed through her mind; the shorter the time until the wedding, the more overbearing and downright supercilious he was becoming. In short, he was almost rude to her now.

If she felt any twinges of regret for her deception of Jerrold, they went right out the window at that moment. She would pretend to be at death's door for the next three days just to irritate him!

But as Elyse lay in the bed, wrapped in her downy cocoon of deceit, she heard the muted sound of the call to the hunt, and she wondered who was more irritated at that moment. She'd give anything to be out of this bed and riding with them, to feel the wind rushing against her face.

Only one thing kept her bound to the bed now as

she listened to Katy moving about—the presence of Sir William St. James. Three days!

The thought of staying cooped up in this room for that amount of time made her want to scream. She seized the opportunity Katy provided by closing a drawer a little more loudly than she'd intended. With a performance that would have rivaled any on the London stage, Elyse turned over slowly, letting out a long, low sleep-filled murmur.

"I'm sorry, darling, I didn't mean to wake you. Did you manage to get more sleep after Master Jerrold was here?"

"A little." Elyse almost winced as she forced pretended weakness into her words.

"You seemed restless last night," Katy observed. "I heard you movin' about in here long after everyone had gone to bed. Was it the dream again?"

Caught off guard by the woman's comment, Elyse opened her eyes. The dream. No. For the first time in months, she hadn't had the dream! She quickly recovered and resumed her charade, dropping her eyelids wearily.

"It's just a headache." She sighed heavily, turning back over under the covers so that she faced away from Katy. If she had to look the woman in the eye, Katy would know she was lying.

"Have all the guests arrived?" She asked, a tremor in her voice. Even she heard how bad it sounded.

The maid rounded the end of the bed. She frowned faintly as she neatly folded her mistress' dressing gown.

"So it seems. There may be one or two who haven't arrived yet." Good heavens, Elyse thought. She decided to chance just one more question.

"I think Jerrold was expecting Sir William St. James. Has he arrived yet?" She had to know if that man was already at Fair View.

"Sir William? I believe there was a message came

from London. He wasn't able to make the trip at the last minute. Master Jerrold seemed quite agitated about that. But don't worry your pretty little head over it," Katy said soothingly.

"Now, I'm going downstairs and give the cook the recipe for that special soup of me mum's that you always liked so much. It'll fix you right up. After all, we have to get you well. You can't be ill for your wedding."

"That would be wonderful," Elyse told her, greatly relieved at the news.

"I'll be back as soon as I can with that soup," Katy added.

Elyse immediately came out of the bed. She threw open the heavy drapes and the filmy sheer under curtains. Then she pushed open the windows and leaned out into the morning air.

From the past, she knew the soup will take at least a couple of hours, and by then she would have made a miraculous recovery. She turned to the wardrobe where Katy had hung her clothes for the next few days. She reached into the bottom of the closet and retrieved the bag she'd carried with her on the trip from London.

She pulled out gleaming black riding boots, sleek pants, an immaculate man's shirt with stock, and the brown jacket cut far too slim for any man. She quickly dressed, then ate the biscuits left on the plate from breakfast.

She sliced it and tucked a piece of ham between, then glanced out the window once more. Jerrold and his guests had already left for the hunt. It would be hours before they returned. She swept her hair back and tied it. She smiled faintly at her reflection in the mirror.

"Impostor," she said. Now to find a horse.

~

Zach tapped the carved ivory head of the walking stick against the roof of the coach. He shook his head. At least there was something this ridiculous affectation of a proper Englishman might be used for.

He ordered the coachman to halt at the crest of the hill that descended into the small valley, then stepped down from the coach. It was like stepping into another world, another time and place.

The air was cool and refreshing in contrast to the stifling, coal smoke and heat of London.

Something indefinable came over him. He closed his eyes and breathed deeply, the scent of fresh field flowers and pungent grasses stealing through him. He was filled with the oddest sensation that if he kept his eyes closed a little longer and then opened them, he would suddenly find himself home.

He breathed in, listened, and felt the land around him. When he finally opened his eyes, he almost laughed at his own foolishness.

There was nothing in this lush, green countryside that even remotely reminded him of Resolute, except perhaps the openness of it, and even then, it was a complete contrast to the stark, wild, beauty of the ranch in New South Wales.

He almost laughed, but not quite. He couldn't rid himself of the feeling he had been here before, had stood in this exact spot and looked down at the spreading greensward dotted with cottages and farms, brown cattle and white sheep grazing in the fields.

"Ya ready guv'ner?" the driver he'd hired to bring him from London broke into his thoughts.

"Aye, I'm ready." Taking hold of the center post, Zach swung back up into the coach. Earlier feelings of uneasiness about this trip came back to him as he closed the door and the coach lurched down the road.

Tobias had warned him against coming here. "Finish

the business with Barrington when he returns," he'd argued. "Don't go!"

It was almost if his old friend feared his going to the Barrington estate. And perhaps Tobias was right. After all, it wasn't necessary to meet Barrington at Fair View to conclude their business. That could be handled when he returned to London. But like the intangible feeling that had stolen over him at the top of the hill, something lured him there. And, if he were truly honest with himself, he knew it was more than that. It was Elyse Winslow.

Two nights ago, when he'd taken her back to Lord Vale's London residence, something had happened between them. He could no more explain it than he could explain the events that had destroyed his father's life in England, or Nicholas Tennant's connection to Lady Felicia Barrington.

Of all the women he'd known, Elyse was the one he could never, would never, have. And yet, in spite of the fact that she was forbidden to him, or maybe because of it, he'd gone to her that night.

If he believed in the possibility of a man being possessed by the devil, he would have believed she'd taken hold of his soul.

It was almost the same with his need to come to Fair View. Not waiting for the driver as the coach rolled to a stop, Zach thrust the door open with sudden impatience to see it.

His gaze wandered across the imposing Tudor facade of stone and wood. Late morning sunlight shimmered off the gleaming span of windows. He stood motionless for the longest time, just staring, the muscles across his chest tight and painful.

"Are you all right, sir?" the driver asked as he stepped down from atop the coach.

Zach forced himself to draw a deep breath. His smile was brief.

"Yes, of course. See to the horses and find a place for yourself with the other groomsmen. I'll be returning to London day after tomorrow," he instructed the man.

The driver nodded and pulled his bags from the boot of the coach as a servant came down the front steps of the manor. Carrying Zach's two cases, Barrington's man led the way to the front entrance. It was then that he saw her.

She was walking quickly across the sloping greensward from the stables. He knew her even though her head was down and she was dressed in a man's riding costume. The sun just caught the gleam of sable hair she'd pulled back.

Perhaps he had come here to prove something, to prove that after the night they'd shared she meant nothing to him. But as he watched her, he felt the familiar tightening of desire, and longing, and knew the only person he was fooling was himself.

"Sir?" The reminder came from the servant who carried his bags.

"Yes, of course," Zach responded vaguely, unable to shake off the feeling that he knew this house.

He was shown to his room and informed that the other guests, and Lord Barrington, would be returning later from the morning ride. He smiled faintly at that. So, it seemed that Elyse had chosen not to ride with the others.

He wanted to see more of the house. Pausing at the top landing, he watched Elyse as she crossed the main entry hall.

She hesitated momentarily and then turned toward the large floor-to-ceiling double doors that opened onto what appeared to be the great hall.

Zach knew many of these old country manors dated back several hundred years. Fair View was no exception. He was silently impressed by the interior as he followed Elyse.

The manor house was large and sprawling. Several times, Elyse had lost her way and had doubled back trying to find the staircase to the second-floor rooms.

Instead of a formal parlor, Fair View had a great room that had once served as the main hall, formal dining room, and receiving room.

According to what her grandmother had told her, over the years the rooms had taken on the functions of formal dining room and reception hall. But the great hall, as it was still called, still served many purposes, including holidays and special celebrations.

It was filled with overstuffed furnishings: chairs, and settees, and elaborately woven tapestries, with a massive chandelier in which countless tiny candles were mounted. A portrait of a Barrington ancestor in a hunting scene from another era covered an adjacent wall. But by far the most imposing sight was the one that seemed to draw her.

Zach watched as she went to the wall of glass and stood before the massive stained-glass panels and stared at the images there—two roses, one red, one white entwined. He watched as she reached out and traced the images.

'The red rose is for passion. The white rose is for my promise that I will love you forever.'

Elyse suddenly stopped, then turned.

"You," she whispered. Somehow, she knew that he would be there, in spite of that message from London.

"Do you make it a habit to go around sneaking up on people?" She bit the words off sharply, trying to bring her emotions under control at suddenly finding him there, especially after... she pushed the thought back.

"I didn't sneak up, as you put it. I saw you returning from the stables."

He ran a finger along the lapel of her riding jacket, amusement at one corner of his mouth. "I see you're still *sneaking* around in disguises." His gaze softened. She was so close to him he could see the pulse that beat at her throat.

"Didn't you learn the trouble you could get yourself into playing such games?" he asked.

She knew perfectly well what he meant, but he was the last person on earth she'd admit it to. She pushed his hand away.

They were alone, but there was no telling when he might choose to bring up what had happened after they left White's. It would be just like him to embarrass her in front of Jerrold or her grandmother.

"Please let me pass," she coolly replied.

That half-smile again. "You should be more pleasant. Especially when I have something of yours that you might want returned." His gaze darkened. "Your pendant."

She remembered that night in the garden. The clasp had broken, and he'd retrieved it, then she had left.

"You have it with you?"

That smile deepened. "I thought that might change your mind," he replied. "But I want something in return. You will have to earn it."

"Earn it!" This was preposterous. Everything she'd heard about was true. "When the pendant is mine in the first place? You can go straight to the devil!"

"Or I can simply return it to Lady Winslow," he suggested. "And you can provide whatever explanation to your grandmother about how it came to be in my possession. However, that might raise other questions."

"You wouldn't dare!"

"I think you know that I would. Do we have a bargain, Elyse? Or are you afraid?" He saw the way her eyes darkened. "You weren't afraid the night of the storm."

She swallowed her indignation and anger, neither would gain her the pendant. "Very well," she replied. "What do you want in exchange for the pendant? I warn you that I have no money of my own. Everything belongs to my grandmother."

He wasn't the least put off. "You are very rich in what I want." His voice softened as he watched emotions play across her lovely face.

"I want a kiss, Elyse. Not the ones you give Barrington, much like kissing one's brother I would imagine." He shook his head when she started to protest.

"I want the kind of kiss you shared with me two nights ago before leaving without saying good-bye."

"Of all the...!" To remind her of that! "I wouldn't kiss you if you were the last man on earth." Again, she was cut off.

"No bargain, no pendant. It's very simple."

"And just what do you think you'll prove with that?" she demanded.

"I'm not trying to prove anything."

She felt as if there was sand under her feet and water was washing it away.

"Nevertheless, that is the offer—a kiss, in exchange for the pendant. Not a bad bargain. Some might think that you have the better of it." Zach stroked back a tendril of hair that had come loose from her face.

Elyse wanted to tell him exactly what he could do with his condition for returning the pendant, but if she didn't accept, she was fairly certain she'd never get it back. At least she could make some stipulations.

"Very well," she finally accepted. "But I want you to agree to my terms."

He should have known she wouldn't simply accept the offer. "Please continue." He was enjoying this very much.

"Our agreement is to be handled very forthright," she insisted. With the other guests about, he'd not dare kiss her with anything more than a polite peck on the hand. He'd be a fool to do otherwise, and she was certain he was no fool. "And," she continued, "when the terms of the agreement are met then you will stay away from me. Is that clear?"

Zach thought about that for a moment. He knew exactly what her game was. She was certain, if he agreed to settling the agreement with others around, the kiss would have to be a fairly innocent one, much-like the gesture of a friend. As for her second condition...

"A hard bargain, Miss Winslow. But there you have it."

Why did she have the feeling that she hadn't won that at all.

"Since we've settled on the terms, I think after supper this evening would be appropriate, even though there will be several people about." There, she thought, enough people to thwart any other thoughts he might have.

"My grandmother will be there as well several others and my fiancé."

"Most appropriate," Zach commented. Then, without warning, he bent over her and caressed her cheek.

"You promised!" Elyse put more distance between them.

"I promised that after our bargain was met I wouldn't go near you again. I said nothing about now."

"You arrogant, rude impostor!" Elyse almost cried out as her arm was drawn up so sharply she feared it would snap.

"One impostor to another? Playing games dressed again?" he reminded her with a look at her riding costume.

"I saw you without the eye-patch," she reminded him. "You weren't wearing it that night..." Her voice broke off.

"How can you be certain? He replied. "It was dark after the storm. We didn't bother with lighting any candles."

She vividly remembered as something tightened deep inside her. She refused to look at him now.

Zach smiled. "I say you're wrong. But perhaps you should visit me again in my bedchamber. Perhaps tonight, just to make certain."

He was staying over?

Abruptly freeing one wrist, Elyse drew back her hand and would have struck him for the suggestion. But he blocked it, his fingers closing around her wrist. They slowly loosened as he stared at her, then focused on her mouth.

Surely not! she thought. Not here, and yet drawn by that his gaze behind the mask, she felt herself drawn to him, wanting to strip that eye-patch away, and...

They both heard the sharp tread of boots crossing the stone entry hall. She was slower to recover, and he steadied her with his hand on her arm, then politely stepped away from her.

"Here you are," Jerrold announced as he entered the great room. He turned to St. James." And I see you've arrived as well."

Zach inclined his head in greeting, the smile on his lips thinning.

Jerrold looked from him to Elyse.

"The house is quite magnificent, don't you think. It's a pity that I haven't been able to be here more often, but that will change after we're married," he said pointedly with a look at her.

"After supper this evening, you must take the grand tour of the house. It has been in our family for almost six hundred years. Though the house is only about two hundred years old." Jerrold's gaze fastened on St. James.

"Of course, you must be able to trace your family lineage back almost that far," he said to his guest. He gave Elyse a concerned look as she was suddenly seized by a fit of coughing.

"Surely you don't intend to spend the remainder of

our stay closed away in your room, my dear," he suggested. "It would be a shame."

At that moment, Elyse would have joyfully retreated to her room. But that wouldn't be acceptable for Jerrold.

"Not at all," she replied. "I've quite well recovered."

"Obviously recovered sufficiently to take a ride?" He gestured to her unusual choice of clothes and riding boots with a frown.

"I thought I might join you. But here you are," she added, her smile not quite reaching her eyes.

Jerrold slipped an arm through hers. "Dinner will be at eight," he informed St. James.

"It's to be a costume affair. We're all to dress as a famous person out of history," Jerrold explained as he led the way from the great room.

Elyse turned to him. "I've nothing to wear for a costume party."

They both looked over at St. James as he was suddenly seized by a fit of coughing.

"Are you all right, sir?" Jerrold looked at him uncertainly.

Zach forced back his smile at the memory of that evening at White's and then after. "I was just thinking that Miss Winslow would enhance any costume she chose to wear."

When she would have protested again, Jerrold patted her hand in that annoying way he had, much like quieting a retriever.

"Not to worry, my dear. We have closets filled to overflowing with all manner of costumes. This used to be an annual event at Fair View, as you will learn. I'm certain we can come up with something for you. And St. James also, of course."

"Of course." Zach acknowledged. He wondered if Elyse would like to borrow his formal jacket and pants for the evening. She did cut such a fascinating figure in a man's formal attire, and equally fascinating out of it.

"Until this evening, Miss Winslow," he said, thoroughly enjoying her discomfort at the direction the conversation had taken, as well as the curve of her bottom under the riding pants. The evening did promise endless possibilities.

~

"I thought perhaps an Egyptian queen. What do you think?" Lady Regina stood swathed in yard upon yard of diaphanous silk. A tall headpiece adorned her head, another length of silk trailing from it. Row upon row of bracelets adorned her arms. She did look positively stately, and very Egyptian.

"And you haven't listened to a word I've said. What has you so distracted?"

Her granddaughter looked up from the elegant escritoire set beside a window in her suite of rooms. "I'm sorry." She turned to Regina and gave her an apologetic smile. "I think your costume is absolutely stunning. You'll be the belle of the ball."

Lady Regina's hands fell to her sides. "But you're supposed to be the belle of the ball, not me. I'm just an old warhorse who happens to be the grandmother of the bride. Have you decided what you'll wear tonight?"

"After Jerrold's little tirade this afternoon over my choice of clothes for my ride, I thought of going as a sailor, or perhaps a pirate," Elyse remarked wryly.

She was unable to stir up much enthusiasm for a costume ball, rather put out that Jerrold hadn't told her of it so that she could have brought something to wear from London. As it was, all she had were her gowns and party dresses. And then there was the looming encounter with St. James.

She was a fool to have made that bargain when she

should have simply forced him to return the pendant and be done with the situation. However, she had to admit she had no idea how she would have gone about that. The man was not the sort to be manipulated by sweet words or trickery.

"Sweetheart?" her grandmother cajoled, "you must be patient with Jerrold. He's simply not used to your ideas about things. But that's the marvelous part about marriage I suppose," she said encouragingly. "Two people, often quite different, coming together, and they complement each other like two marvelous halves becoming a splendid whole."

"Did it ever occur to you that not all married people share what you had with Grandfather, or what you have now with Uncle Ceddy for that matter?"

"Good heavens, no!" But her grandmother was brought up short nevertheless and grew thoughtful. "Of course, most matches among those we know are arranged, but they seem to work. You certainly don't hear much about divorce. It seems everyone manages to work things out rather well."

"There aren't divorces because the parties involved aren't about to jeopardize family fortunes," Elyse pointed out. "It's much easier to take a mistress or a lover and keep the jewels and estates intact."

"Good heavens!" Lady Regina replied. "Wherever do you pick up such absolute notions?"

"You know as well as I what goes on in some of the finest families in England." She thought of the persistent rumors about Jerrold. "Men taking mistresses and lovers seems to be common practice."

Lady Regina sat down at the upholstered bench at the end of the bed. "I know it happens, but I believe there are many happy marriages. I certainly had one, and look at Lucy Maitland. Her husband is absolutely infatuated with her. And the Queen had Prince Albert."

Elyse rose and crossed to her grandmother. She

leaned over, planting an affectionate kiss on her cheek. "Yes, but what about all the others? The simple truth is that many of my married friends share their husbands with mistresses in Coddington Square. There's quite a colony of kept ladies established there. It's no secret that Jerrold has frequented the place." And then there was the recent evening at White's.

"That is well over and finished," her grandmother stated confidently. "I have it on good faith that everything ended months ago. After all, a man in his position and about to be married must keep up appearances."

Appearances? As much as she loved her grandmother, that wasn't convincing by what she had seen for herself. And then there was the disturbing fact that it somehow hadn't bothered her other than the fact that it was a deception. How many more were there?

They both looked up in response to a knocking on the door to the suite.

Elyse was silently grateful for the interruption. How could she possibly explain to her grandmother that she desperately wished she could have the devotion and love of the man she was to marry?

"That must be Mrs. Evers, the housekeeper. Jerrold mentioned that there were several costumes I might choose from." She was across the room in an instant.

Lady Regina smiled, but couldn't help feeling there was a great deal more she should discuss with Elyse on the subject of marriage.

She frowned slightly as her granddaughter greeted the housekeeper. When Elyse returned briefly, to give her a tender kiss on the cheek, Lady Regina caught her hand in her own.

"You've brought me such joy. I hope you know, all I've ever wanted is your happiness. If I thought you weren't happy or if you were going forward with the wedding for my sake..."

Elyse smiled. "There you go, worrying." She gave her grandmother a smile.

But behind the smile, she had her doubts. She loved her grandmother. Regina Winslow had been both mother and father to her, giving her unconditional love and care. She would never do anything to hurt or disappoint her. Squeezing her grandmother's hand affectionately, she swept out of the room in the wake of Mrs. Evers, in pursuit of a costume for the ball that evening.

Eleven

J errold Barrington pushed back the leather chair behind the mahogany desk.

"When you give this draft to my man in London he will arrange for the transfer of funds." His smile was brief, then gone. "After he's verified the shipment, of course. I'll keep the draft here in my safe until you leave for London." He looked up.

"How long will you be staying?"

Zach met Barrington's dark, hooded gaze evenly from across the desk. This man was being very careful. He must be even more careful.

"For the next few days, if that's agreeable with you, of course," Zach replied, his tone one of faint boredom. "London is so warm." He favored Jerrold with that lazy smile he'd practiced to perfection. "I'm glad to be done with this business. There's always the risk that someone might try to steal it." He gave particular emphasis to this last statement, watching for Barrington's reaction.

Jerrold looked. "Someone such as the Raven?" he suggested with a tightening around his mouth.

"So it seems," Zach agreed, shrugging his shoulders. "You must admit the fellow has played a devilish game in Australia. From what I hear, no one has caught him yet. He's very clever."

"Not clever enough." Jerrold straightened in his chair, just thinking of the Raven tightening every muscle. "I promise you, the man will hang from the yardarm before I'm through. And every one of his men with him."

Zach slowly smiled. He enjoyed playing this game with Barrington, much like a cat with a mouse. "Ah, but first you much catch him. So far, it would seem you've been less than successful."

"Until now. But I have a different strategy," Jerrold replied. "As soon as the fellow shows himself again, he will find out what it is. Until now, my ships have been easy victims. But if it is war the Raven wants, then it is war he shall have. And not only he will suffer for it, but the colonies as well." He rose from his chair to lean over the desk, almost as if he were directing these threats at his guest. His eyes gleamed with an unnatural light, his lips thinned, and a muscle in his cheek twitched with long-held frustration over the matter.

His fist suddenly came down on the desktop, rattling the feather quill in the inkwell. "I will destroy the man, and then I will destroy this trade rebellion of the colonists. The Crown learned a lesson from the American colonies. We will not lose control again. The colonies in the Pacific will submit or they will be brought to their knees by force if necessary."

The atmosphere in the room was electrically charged, like the sky at sea before a storm. Zach's gaze locked with Barrington's. He didn't blink as he slowly rose, having decided it was time to end this conversation.

"It seems you've already set the example." He nodded courteously. "I'm certain you'll give it your best effort." Zach was sincere in making that statement. However, he was equally sincere that Barrington's best effort would gain him nothing.

Barrington followed him to the door of the library.

"I do apologize. The Raven has been most elusive. I find the situation very... annoying."

He chose his words carefully, not wanting to give the Raven too much importance or to appear less than confident of the eventual outcome. "I can see that it would be, but I believe the Crown can rest easy. It has the very best man to deal with the situation."

Barrington smiled and adjusted his coat front over his puffed-up chest. "I appreciate your confidence, sir."

"Indeed." Zach smiled, greatly enjoying this little game. Barrington might be the best, at least in his own opinion, but this was a case where the Crown's best wasn't good enough.

"When did you say you were leaving? I do hope you can at least stay for a few days." Jerrold asked.

"Even now my crew is seeing to the cargo for our return voyage. That should take only another two or three days at the most."

"What a pity you can't remain longer. I should like you to attend my wedding to Miss Winslow. It promises to be the grand occasion of the season."

Zach nodded but inside, his thoughts churned. How the devil could Elyse be interested in a pompous ass like Jerrold Barrington? He almost laughed out loud. She'd called *him* that very same thing on more than one occasion.

He felt it again, that whisper of memory he'd first experienced months ago when he'd discovered his father's journal and the pendant at Resolute, identical to the one Elyse had worn. It was the same feeling that had come upon him repeatedly ever since he'd arrived in London. It was always there, just beyond his grasp, elusive. Like a beautiful woman, he thought wryly, and his next thought was of Elyse.

She was a lovely, passionate, and unpredictable creature that he found to be fascinating. But he'd known many equally beautiful and passionate women. What was it about her that continued to haunt him?

Why the devil did the fact that she was marrying Barrington leave him with a feeling of contempt, even anger? It shouldn't matter. A few weeks ago, it wouldn't have. Even now, he told himself he'd made love to her that night only to prove to himself that he could do so and not be affected by her, but he was wrong and knew it.

It was ridiculous, of course, and he put the thought away. He had only one goal, to find out the truth about his father and to sell the gold, for the *second* time, to Barrington. That thought made him smile as he turned to Barrington.

"I'm looking forward to this evening's party. It promises to be most... interesting." He chose his words carefully.

"Then you've selected your costume," Barrington concluded.

"One that I think you will find especially amusing. I trust Miss Winslow will be wearing a costume as well?" Zach inquired.

"I'm certain she'll be able to find something appropriate. Could I interest you in a card game or two to pass the time?" Barrington extended the cursory invitation. "My other guests seem to have found their own diversions while we were concluding our business."

Zach eyed the open safe and made a mental note of its location. "With your permission, I think I will take a ride about your estate. I didn't have a chance to see it earlier."

"Then I will see you later." Barrington nodded.

"Of course," Zach promised, giving his host a cold smile as he left.

Barrington closed the door to the safe, then nodded to the huge man who stepped quietly from a panel behind the heavy tapestry that covered one wall.

"You're to go to London," he told the man. "I will keep St. James here. The ship is the *Revenge*. You will need several men to get the gold. Be back by tomorrow night and do not fail me."

There was a grunt of acknowledgement, then the man disappeared into the shadows.

When Zach stepped into the cool, immaculate stables, he once more experienced the feeling that he'd been there before. He couldn't shake it off.

Selecting a tall, well-conformed jumper for a mount, he emerged into the late afternoon sun, enjoying the lean animal strength of the gray.

He was familiar with this particular breed of horse even though there was no need for this finely bred an animal. The horses at the ranch were lean and strong, bred for endurance in an unforgiving climate and in a land that took a toll on both man and horse. But not so the one he kept in Sydney.

"You sure you want to take him out, sir?" The stable master said, eyeing Zach skeptically. "There are very few who can ride him. Master Jerrold takes him out once in a while, but not since he took that last fall."

Zach stroked the stallion's heavily muscled neck. "I prefer a horse with spirit. This one reminds me of a stallion at home. He has the same fire as my Domino." An expert rider, he kept gentle but firm control of the reins.

"Eh, what's that you said? What do you call yer horse?"

Zach looked up. "Domino. He's as black as night except for... "

"A blaze of white down his head?" the old man added.

"Yes." Zach gazed down at the man uncertainly. "How did you know that?"

The stable master dismissed the question. "Just a

guess, sir. There's very few horses that don't have some kind of distinctive marking. A patch of white here and there, is common on blacks."

"True enough," Zach acknowledged as he turned the gray about.

"Still, there is the matter of the name," the old man commented. "I knew a horse called Domino once, just like you describe your black. He was a fine, high-spirited beast. He was here at the stables when I first came on with Lord Barrington."

Zach's gaze narrowed. "Barrington?"

"Aye, Lord Barrington, Master Jerrold's father, sold him off. Said he didn't want him around."

Zach had no idea why he felt the need to know what had happened to this other horse. "Was it someone nearby?"

"No. That was the sad thing. He gave him to a band of Gypsies that always used to camp out in the meadow during the warm months." He shook his head sadly. "And after his father had had him bred for the line he wanted to have. But after Lord Clayton died, young Master Charles insisted on getting rid of him. Said he wanted to be rid of the black devil. That's what he called him—a black devil."

"What became of the animal?"

"When the Gypsies came through the year after, they no longer had him. Such a fine animal," he reminisced. "Sure is a strange coincidence him bein' so like your horse and with the same name." The stable master shook his head.

"How long ago?" Zach asked.

The man removed his cap and scratched his head. "Well, as close as I can remember it must be well over thirty years ago."

Zach nodded thoughtfully. "Thank you for telling me about this other Domino." He turned the gray away from the stables.

"The man called after him. "You won't be wantin' to go that way this late in the day. The woods get dark early, and you don't want to get lost."

"I thank for your concern. But I'll be quite all right," Zach assured him.

Sunlight spilled through the treetops and shimmered like molten fire through pine and oak branches. It cut across his vision, momentarily blinding him and was then gone. When he looked again, everything seemed oddly familiar.

What was it about this place? Zach wondered again as he guided the gray through quiet hollows that led deeper into the forest.

He seemed to instinctively know where it was he wanted to go, yet knew he hadn't consciously chosen this path. There were no answers in the sigh of the wind in the trees.

The trail stopped and then started again in several places, and he realized that the stable master was right, one could get lost if they didn't know where they were going.

The warmth of the afternoon faded, and the only sound came from the horse's hooves on the trail as he guided him through gullies and thick stands of trees so dark it seemed as if it was already night.

He pushed the gray to a quicker pace, one that might have been dangerous in the fading light for one who didn't know the way. They were both winded when they finally halted at the crest of the hill looking down over the valley, lights from Fair View gleaming in the near distance. He'd been here before, he thought as he stared across the greensward. But that was impossible.

He mentally shook off the thought.

Tobias would swear he'd taken to drinking if he told him of it.

"What do you think?" He stroked the gray's damp neck. The stallion snorted.

"Yes, my fine friend. I think so too. It's time to go home." He thought of Resolute. He'd chosen the name because of what it meant—determined, as he had been determined to carve out a place for himself.

He needed only a little more time.

Here, he might be able to learn something about Felicia Barrington from the people who'd known her. Perhaps they might have heard of a man named Nicholas, even though he had no last name to go with it.

Then he and Tobias would leave. He had part of what he'd come for—the voucher Barrington had given him for the gold. He'd made a very lucrative deal, selling Barrington's own gold back to him. Perhaps that was all anyone could hope for, even the *Raven*.

Elyse dismissed Mrs. Evers with a smile and stood before the long wardrobe. She pushed aside first one costume, then another. None seemed to catch her interest. She dismissed the gown of a Greek goddess, then considered the costume of a Roman centurion. A smile played at her lips. She stood back, unimpressed. Then her gaze fell to the suit of armor standing at the end of the closet.

She could imagine the looks she'd get walking into the party and raising the face plate to reveal her identity.

"Jerrold would never forgive me. And it would be a bit cumbersome when it came to dancing," she admitted as she continued to search through the costumes in the wardrobe that filled an entire wall in the room that had been opened for the purpose of finding a costume to wear.

The room was decorated in tones of blue with odd pieces of furnishings at one end, all covered with dust cloths with several old trunks stacked against a wall, including what appeared to be a large framed painting that stood draped in the far corner.

She'd seen the family portrait gallery earlier in the day, along with other paintings that hung on the walls of the manor. Jerrold's family was brilliantly displayed throughout. She wondered why this one had been stored away and covered?

There had to be some reason why this painting wasn't displayed with the others. Perhaps it was unfinished, or by the looks of some of the Barrington ancestors, someone had decided this particular one was too frightening to put on display.

The painting was at least four feet wide and eight feet tall. She pulled off the cover, then gasped.

"Lady Barrington." She immediately recognized the young woman in the painting as Jerrold's mother. It was a pastoral scene with the gardens beyond the house in the background. Roses were in bloom, and Lady Barrington held a long-stemmed red rose in her fingers.

Her other hand was spread across the voluminous skirts of the most exquisite gown Elyse had ever seen. It was midnight blue, the same color as her eyes with a wide row of lace across the bodice. The shoulders of the gown swept daringly low across her shoulders, and her dark hair was worn long down the middle of her back. But what caught Elyse's attention were the earbobs Lady Barrington had been wearing when the portrait was painted.

They were an elegant design of pearls and diamonds. Exactly the same as the pendant her grandmother had given her! She read the name plate at the bottom of the portrait—Felicia Seymour, on the occasion of her betrothal, 1837.

She stood back, staring at the portrait. It was neither incomplete nor ugly. It was breathtakingly beautiful, and she was suddenly filled with a feeling of such sadness. But there was no sadness in Felicia Seymour's eyes. She looked incredibly happy.

"I wonder why you were closed away in here." She laughed at her foolishness, as if she expected an answer.

"I don't suppose you have a suggestion for my costume for tonight," she commented. She looked up thoughtfully. "I wonder what you would have worn."

"There will undoubtedly be a Greek goddess or two. Everyone always wants to be a goddess." She paused with her hand on the centurion costume, then shook her head.

"Grandmother would love it, but I fear Jerrold might come undone." She opened another wardrobe—surely she'd be able to find something in there—and stared in amazement. No centurion costume or suit of armor to be found there. Here, neatly arranged from one end to the other, was the most stunning array of gowns she'd ever seen.

There were taffetas, satins, and brocades. Every color was there. There were long-sleeved gowns, more daring evening gowns, hats in boxes on an overhead shelf, shoes lined up precisely along the bottom, along with capes, long and short, lightweight and fur lined. And at the far end were drawers, at least a dozen of them, filled with gloves, delicate hand-stitched underwear, satin evening bags, shawls, and stockings.

One drawer that contained delicate handkerchiefs. The one on top caught her attention. Elegant scrolled letters were embroidered in gold threads—F.B.

"Felicia Barrington."

This was Lady Barrington's wardrobe. These were her things, everything meticulously cleaned and pressed, as if they only waited for her. She'd never seen anything like it before in her life and wondered why Lord Barrington had kept everything.

"He must have loved you very much," she whispered. Still, this discovery left her feeling unsettled.

Her grandfather had been dead for years, her parents as well. Portraits of them adorned her grandmother's house, but Lady Regina certainly hadn't kept their clothing closed away, except for a few infant's garments from when her father was a baby. That was quite common, she supposed. But an entire wardrobe?

Elyse reached to close the far door. She didn't have time to wonder about Lord Barrington's reasons. She still didn't have a costume and absolutely refused to be another Greek goddess at the party. Then she stopped, her hand on the other door as her gaze fastened on a particular gown. She opened the door to more allow light.

"Oh my," she whispered as she turned to the painting then back to the wardrobe. The gown was the very same one Lady Barrington had worn for the portrait.

She removed it from the satin-wrapped hanger and held it against herself. She looked over at the smiling image of Felicia Barrington.

"I hope you don't mind, but I think I've just found the perfect thing to wear tonight." She pulled the pins from her own hair.

"It will be perfect," Elyse declared. Then she frowned faintly. The only thing missing would be the earbobs. She wondered what had happened to them. Probably tucked away in a safe somewhere in the house, as they would have been quite valuable.

There was certainly no need to worry about that now. Her frown turned into a smile. She intended to wait until the other guests had gone down to the party before making her entrance. Jerrold and his father would be so pleased.

"Thank you," she whispered to the painting.

Zach tied the wide band of silk behind his head. A smile pulled at his mouth as he deliberately positioned it over his left eye. Standing before the full-length mirror in his chamber, he inspected his costume, dressed entirely in black silk.

"Ah yes, a pirate. Especially for you, Elyse." He pulled on black gloves, and in one practiced move placed a steel blade into the narrow scabbard at his hip. After all, every pirate worth his weight in gold had a sword.

Tonight, however, he wasn't out to rescue damsels in distress or to relieve rich fools of their gold. A smile curved below the silk mask. He'd already lifted the gold of one fool. As he slipped the pendant into his pocket, his smile deepened. He was after a far richer prize from Elyse, something only she could give him.

~

Jerrold Barrington had chosen a satin frock coat Louis XIV of France might have worn. Imitating the posturing monarch, he'd affixed a heart-shaped beauty mark to his cheek and sported a wig of mountainous curls. It was his custom to dress as someone very powerful and wealthy. He considered himself at home among such company.

Now, with agitation, he glanced impatiently at the wide stairs. All his guests were present. Lady Winslow was chatting nearby with his father. He turned as a faint ripple of surprise moved through the crowd, lifting a thin brow at sight of the tall, lean figure dressed all in black silk. One by one, Barrington's guests parted as the masked man made his way across the crowded hall.

Jerrold's first impression was dismay, then shock. This had to be some joke. His fingers curled into hard fists at his sides. It was almost as if one of his guests were mocking him by posing as the Raven.

He pushed back his annoyance. After all, it was only a costume party, and he'd placed no restrictions on what his guests wore. But still, just the sight of that black outfit and the silk mask that were both well-known was enough to infuriate him.

He'd never seen the Raven, but his men had, when their ships were scuttled on the Barrier Reef or lured into traps among the small islands off the coast of New South Wales.

His losses to that thief over the past two years had practically driven Barrington Shipping to the brink of ruin. But his marriage to Elyse would bring renewed financial stability to the ailing company. Still his quarrel with the Raven wasn't entirely a matter of money.

It had become personal. The pirate's escapades had achieved a certain notoriety in England. Indeed, he now seemed almost a folk hero, one that had an uncanny ability to escape the authorities at every turn. And now, for some unknown reason, he had apparently gone into hiding.

The latest word he had from the captain of one of his ships newly arrived from New South Wales that had managed to arrive unscathed, was that there hadn't been any raids on Barrington ships for quite some time. But that wasn't good enough.

He didn't want the man to merely lie low. He wouldn't rest until the Raven was dead, or at the bottom of the Barrier Reef. He would stop the Raven, no matter what the cost. The smile Jerrold Barrington fastened on his face as he finally recognized his guest betrayed none of his thoughts. His voice was smooth as the silk of the man's mask.

"My compliments, sir. You've outdone everyone. You've caused speculation to run rampant."

Zach smiled. "I was certain you would enjoy a bit of humor as well as the next person. Do you think I resemble the Raven? I understand several of your crews have had an especially close look at the fellow."

"It's very clever, but the Raven is far too illusive to risk so much as to appear here. Still my compliments to you, and a bit of a warning." Jerrold added. "My men will have the Raven. Already his activities are greatly reduced. But let me assure you, if and when he chooses to strike again, Barrington Shipping will be waiting for him."

"The Raven doesn't strike me as the sort of fellow who would quit so easily, although I can see that he might become bored with it all. There is really no challenge to sinking ships." He deliberately goaded Barrington.

"Ah," Jerrold responded, "let me assure you there will be far more challenge in the future. I have joined forces with the Crown and made certain provisions aboard my ships. The Raven will find those he thought loyal, are not so when it comes to gold and silver to line their pockets. He won't know who the Judas is who will betray him."

"You seem to have considered everything. Undoubtedly, you've taken into consideration the loyalty of the colonists themselves."

"Naturally. And true to their convict ancestors, they all sell their souls for a handful of coins. The Raven will learn there is a price for loyalty," he continued. "It goes to the highest bidder. Do you still think you want to pose as a thief and murderer?"

Zach nodded. "It is, after all, only a costume."

Affecting a French gentleman, Barrington smoothed his wig. "You have an excellent sense of humor. I like that." He turned to his other guests. "Ladies and gentleman, Sir William St. James."

There were several raised eyebrows and mutterings of recognition among the fine gentlemen. An excited titter came from the ladies.

"You have the undivided attention of everyone in this room, and not one of these ladies' husbands will be on speaking terms with me after tonight. My congratulations, sir." The smile never reached Jerrold's cold eyes.

Zach saluted with the short sword, his gaze scanning the guests that were already there, wondering what costume Elyse might have chosen. He saw none that might have been her and seized a brandy from a passing servant. He felt a little like a cat toying with a mouse, or perhaps a rat. He raised the glass in a toast.

"To Lady Barrington."

Jerrold joined in the toast as a hushed silence fell upon the room. Barrington turned, his own glass halfway to his lips. Then he stopped. His eyes widened, and he inhaled sharply.

Zach turned at the sudden hush that fell on the large room as he followed the direction everyone was staring.

"Good heavens!" a surprised guest exclaimed. And another, "My word, isn't that...?" the comment was never finished.

Then, "Of course not, it's been over thirty years. But she is quite lovely."

Elyse had hoped to make a grand entrance, but this wasn't exactly what she'd had in mind. She felt the shock and dismay, even disapproval as stares seemed to go right through her. Then she caught sight of Jerrold's father, his expression could have turned the nearest person to stone, while Jerrold's expression was one of barely restrained anger.

Zach couldn't take his eyes off her. He felt as if a knife had been thrust between his ribs and twisted. He couldn't draw a breath. His fingers tightened around the glass he was holding until it seemed it would shatter.

'I'll wear it for you... ', the words burned his thoughts.

'You always wear your hair down... ' The words echoed back through some half-forgotten memory. And a smile, remembered as if it were only yesterday.

Zach's hands shook as he set the glass down. My God! Was he drunk already? Was he going mad?

And yet, as he stood there staring at Elyse Winslow,

dressed in that stunning gown that was the color of her eyes, he knew he wasn't drunk or mad. She was very real.

She could feel the tension in the air and saw the stunned expression on Lord Barrington's face as she entered the grand hall.

"What do you think that you're doing?" Jerrold demanded as she reached where he and St. James stood.

"Excuse me?" she asked. It was not the response she had expected.

"Of all the costumes..." he started. "Whatever possessed you to choose that gown?"

"It was in the room with the other costumes," Elyse replied, trying to understand what had caused his anger.

"A room full of costumes and you chose this!"

"Yes, since there was no note letting me know that I could not wear it," she replied with rising anger. "I saw the painting and thought it would be a pleasant surprise. I certainly didn't intend to offend anyone."

Zach ignored Barrington. He had eyes only for Elyse Winslow as everything and everyone else in the room seemed to fade into the shadows as if they were the only two people there.

"You're stunning," he told her.

She knew that voice behind the mask on St. James' face that covered one eye, his compliment soothing the wound from Jerrold's disapproval as speculation and whispered comments died down among the guests.

"Ah, champagne is being served," he commented, even though he'd never acquired a taste for it. But it was an adequate distraction.

Barrington's gaze snapped to his, and there was a moment where he was certain he would say something, then he perhaps thought better of it in front of so many friends.

"Of course, I am neglecting my guests." He momentarily turned back to Elyse, a cool expression on his face. "You will change into something more... suitable," he told her, then added, "I expect you to do as I ask." He turned abruptly and stalked back across the great hall, leaving them at the edge of the room.

She knew Jerrold had a reputation for being forceful with business associates, but this was far different, and she was stunned by his cruelty.

Zach fought to bring his own anger under control. He'd spoken out of turn, and he knew it, but that didn't matter. Nothing mattered except the wounded expression on her face that tore at him.

"I repeat what I said before—you are stunning. And Barrington is a fool."

Her hue had darkened with emotion. "I have no idea why everyone making such a fuss?" Her voice trembled slightly, but more from anger. "I thought it would be such a wonderful surprise." The surprise had been at Jerrold's outburst to the point of cruelty.

"Do you have a handkerchief?" Zach asked her as she blinked back tears.

She gave her head an angry toss. "I'm not crying."

"Good. I'm glad to hear that," Zach announced.

Why was she even discussing this with him? But before she could point out that it was none of his business, he grabbed a glass of brandy from the tray of a passing servant.

"It doesn't seem the best way to begin a marriage," he commented. "By the way, why are you marrying Barrington?" He held out the tumbler to her. "You're not at all suited for one another. You have too passionate a nature."

Passionate? She took a sip of the brandy.

"In answer to the first part, it doesn't concern you. In answer to your question, that doesn't concern you either. And as for your opinion about Jerrold... " She hesitated. If she was being perfectly honest with herself, St. James wasn't the first person to make that comment. Lucy had said the very same thing.

She'd dismissed it at the time. Still, it was odd that both St. James and her dearest friend had said the same thing about Jerrold.

"And my observations about your passionate nature?" he asked.

She refused to meet his gaze. "You're wrong about that too."

He reached up, his fingers warm beneath the curve of her chin as he forced her to look at him. "I'm wrong." His expression was no longer gently teasing. "I remember a very passionate creature in my bed two nights ago."

She bit back several comments, deciding that ignoring him was undoubtedly the safest course at this point. She didn't need to draw any more attention to herself. "You're mistaken."

"Am I? Let me refresh your memory." He traced her full bottom lip with his thumb and was rewarded by a faint tremble and the subtle change of color in her eyes.

She'd been embarrassed before an entire roomful of people; Jerrold was furious with her. His father would probably never speak to her again for reasons she couldn't begin to understand, and now this pompous fool was reminding her of something she would much rather forget. Worse still, she couldn't deny the pleasure that simple contact caused. She bit his thumb.

Zach's reaction was immediate. His other hand closed around her wrist, the hand with the wounded thumb, obviously not seriously wounded, slipped around her waist. He pulled her into the shadows of the shadows where the hundreds of candles in the great room failed to reach. She gasped at the contact with his lean, hard body.

"Did I ever tell you about my methods for taking revenge?" His gray gaze bore into hers.

"I don't believe we discussed that," she replied breathlessly.

A smile spread across his lips. "For revenge against being wounded I expect to be paid in triplicate."

"Three times?" Ridiculous for an injured thumb, she thought as she wedged her hands between them.

The last thing she needed was for one of Jerrold's guests to pass by and find her with the St. James. Or worse yet, that Jerrold would return.

"It makes the satisfaction so much greater."

He was serious! Elyse stared at him. Did he actually mean that he intended to bite her three times? She would have hardly any fingers left.

"Right now you're wondering if that means I intend to bite you as you bit me."

"Don't be ridiculous. I'm not thinking anything of the sort." He was close, too close. She could feel the warmth of his breath against her cheek.

She jerked her face further away from his, not trusting him one bit. He had an unnerving effect on her at a distance. This close could be dangerous as it had been that night after they left White's.

"You're lying," he threatened with something very near tenderness.

"Oh, for heaven's sake! It's ridiculous anyway. It was only a simple bite, and you deserved it. I have great faith in your powers of recovery." Her eyes widened as she vividly remembered his powers of recovery when he'd made love to her.

Amusement curved the corners of Zach's mouth. "But I still intend to pay you back three times." When her hand again came up against his chest to block the contact of their bodies, he seized her hand.

Elyse closed her eyes. If he was going to do it, she was powerless to stop him, but she wouldn't cry out. She forced herself to concentrate on something else, anything, except the punishment that was to come. Then, she opened her eyes at the contact of his teeth against the soft flesh at the tips of her fingers as he tenderly nibbled a finger then the next, then a third that she could only describe as tender.

"I should have known," she whispered a little too breathlessly.

"Yes, you should have. I would never hurt you." Zach continued the sensual assault at her fingers, until she cried and snatched her hand away to safety.

"You, sir, are too bold."

"A minor point after what we shared."

She took a step back. "I think we should be joining the others."

"Are you forgetting? You've been banned from the party," Zach reminded her. "I believe you were ordered to change your clothes."

"I'm not concerned about the party."

That gray gaze fastened on her. "Why did you agree to the marriage? Surely not because of undying affection for Barrington."

He was a bold one! "I agreed because..." When she would have defended her decision to marry Jerrold, she realized how empty that would have sounded.

"Because of your grandmother's friendship with Lady Barrington?" he speculated.

"No, of course not!" she blurted. "I've known Jerrold for a long time. He comes from an impeccable family, and until this evening I thought he cared a great deal for me." She looked at him then. "I'm not in the habit of discussing my personal life with strangers."

"Your description of Jerrold reminds me of the qualities one might look for in a good hunting dog. And as for our being strangers... I think you would agree that we are not," he pointed out.

She knew what he meant. "Is that the reason you came here? To embarrass me?" She whirled around to leave, to go somewhere, anywhere but here.

His hand closed around her arm. She was so beautiful when she was angry. "That's not the reason." He glanced looked over her shoulder as music drifted to them from the room across the hall. Someone, probably Lady Winslow, had had the foresight to have the musicians begin playing to distract the guests from the confrontation with Barrington.

"Actually, I came to ask you to dance with me."

He was insane. She tried to pull from his grasp. "I certainly don't want to dance with you."

"I thought you might say that. But, you see, I understand you. You're not afraid of anyone or anything. A little gossip certainly won't stop a young woman who parades around in men's pants and rides astride... or steals into a men's club to sneak a peek at what goes on there. As long as they're talking about you, why don't you give them something to really talk about."

"Such as?" She couldn't resist the temptation. Jerrold's nastiness had had a terrible effect on her. In truth, she didn't give a damn about what anyone else thought, except for her grandmother.

"Such as dancing out here with me in the shadows," he suggested with a devilish smile.

"My reputation will be ruined, and Jerrold will be even angrier. I should go upstairs and change."

"Like a good little girl." There was a faintly mocking tone to his voice. "Barrington is already angry, in case you hadn't noticed, and as for your reputation," he placed his hand over his heart. "I cannot tell a lie." He leaned in close. "I have already ruined it. What have you to lose?"

She should have been furious with him. Instead, all she could do was laugh. He was being ridiculous, and he was right. That was the most maddening part of it all.

"If I dance with you, will you leave me alone?"

"You have my solemn vow," he pledged, that hand still over his heart.

"As a pirate?" She couldn't resist. "Not quite trustworthy."

"As a gentleman."

"Gentleman?" she replied.

"Is there anything else you would like to add to your list of observations?" His warm fingers captured hers as he pulled her into his arms to begin the first steps of a waltz.

"As a matter of fact, there is," she replied as her steps matched his. "You're not old or infirm. You certainly don't seem to be afflicted with gout or trembling of the limbs. "And," she paused, "that costume suits you far too well. You seem more comfortable posing as a pirate than as a gentleman."

Zach flashed her a smile. "Did anyone ever warn you about offending a gentleman?"

"I think it's a little late for that." She rested one hand on his shoulder, the other held in his hand.

"It seems I've already offended one this evening, and now yourself."

"Impossible." He was enjoying the feel of her body as it brushed against his when they turned. Her eyes were an incredible shade of blue, mysterious, and a bit dangerous with their secrets.

"Impossible that you're a gentleman, or that you're offended?"

"Perhaps a little of both," he pulled her against him and watched the subtle change in her eyes at the intimacy of the contact.

"You have the oddest way of saying things, almost as if there were some hidden meanings." She laughed. "And you certainly don't seem to have much respect for anyone else."

"I have a great deal of respect when it's earned. But I'm not fooled by titles. They're just decoration and illusion."

"Like a mask?" she asked.

"Precisely." He smiled, enjoying their verbal sparring.

Her smile deepened with her little victory after the conversation with Jerrold. "I knew you were a pirate. It fits so much better than that ridiculous title you carry around. Sir William St. James. Is it a family name?"

Zach wasn't the least fooled by her. She was an intoxicating, beguiling little witch and she was subtly prying for information.

"I'll tell you someday." At the moment, he chose not to satisfy her curiosity. "Are you going to dance or talk?"

"Both," she announced, then recalled something that was bothering her. "I do hope you brought the pendant with you. There is still the matter of our little agreement."

"Ah, yes," Zach replied. "I believe it was something about a kiss in exchange for the pendant."

"You know perfectly well what the agreement was," she quickly proclaimed. "I would like to have the pendant now."

"Is that right?"

"Yes." They both looked up at the sound of voices to see a costumed couple emerge from the great room and walk in their direction.

She tried to step back. It would never do for Jerrold to find out she had been dancing with St. James when he'd thought her to be upstairs changing her clothes.

Amusement danced in Zach's gaze as the other couple walked past them, nodded a brief greeting, and continued on through large double doors at the end of the hallway that opened into the gardens.

"You were saying... about our agreement?" he completely ignored her glare of disapproval.

"I want my pendant back."

"I understand."

She glanced past him into the great hall. "Do you have it with you?"

He hesitated just long enough for her become suspicious.

"You don't have it?"

A devilish smile appeared below the mask. He was teasing her! She could have joyfully taken that sword that was part of his costume and run him through. The only problem was, then she would have to explain the body to Jerrold.

"Damn you!" she swore under her breath.

"I refuse to keep bargains with ladies who swear. I do have the pendant, and if you behave yourself and act like a proper lady, you might get it back."

When she would have called him several colorful names, he asked, "You do want it back?"

If a lady was what he wanted, a lady was what he would get. "Of course, I want it back."

"Then I am prepared to accept proper payment," he announced. His arm tightened around her waist, pulling her against him.

He towered over her, his face not more than a few inches from hers. Elyse panicked. If anyone else were to come out of that room, they'd surely be seen.

"Not here!"

"But you specifically set the terms of the agreement," he reminded her. "It was to be a public place."

"Not here. Someone might see us."

"That generally happens in a public place," he commented.

"I don't care what I said. It can't be here."

"Where do you suggest we consummate this agreement?" He chose his words carefully, thoroughly enjoying the play of emotions on her lovely face.

Elyse glanced across the hallway.

"Here," she announced, taking him by the hand and leading him to the library.

"This is not a public place," he reminded her, gazing about the room with several pieces of heavy furniture arranged in a sitting area. Framed pictures of every size almost obscured the walls.

He could be so exasperating, she thought. "It's a library."

He complimented her, trying to keep the smile from his lips. She'd unwittingly played right into his hands. He studied a portrait just over her left shoulder, noticing the Barrington name on the brass plate affixed at the bottom.

"I wanted a place where we wouldn't be seen. Jerrold wouldn't understand if he were to see us." For some reason she felt the need to explain.

"So, you chose an entire roomful of Barringtons to witness our little *agreement*."

She saw the direction he indicated.

"This seems to be some sort of family portrait gallery." He indicated the wall behind her. "All those paintings are of Barringtons. Impressive."

His tone suggested that he was far from impressed.

"Are we to keep the agreement or shall I leave?" she demanded.

"You will keep the agreement," Zach announced, his gaze fastening on her lovely face.

"I should like to see the pendant first, to make certain you do have it with you," she reminded him.

"Of course." He reached inside a boot and produced a small leather pouch. The diamond and pearl pendant tumbled into his hand. He suspended it from his fingers, turning it slowly.

"It really is quite lovely, if old fashioned. None other like it in the world." He tested her. Would she be able to tell the difference between the one he had and hers?

Elyse took the pendant from him.

"Does it meet with your approval?" He watched her carefully.

"Yes." She quickly turned to leave and immediately felt the pressure of his hand on her arm.

"There is the matter of your part of the agreement," he reminded her.

Elyse slowly let out the breath she'd been holding. She'd hoped to escape before he had a chance to remind her. She slowly turned around.

"Very well, and then you will keep the rest of your agreement."

He almost burst out laughing. She looked like the condemned being led to the gallows instead of a beautiful young woman about to be kissed.

He slipped one arm around her waist and pulled her against him. He forced back a smile as he felt her body soften into his. She continued staring past him with that vaguely bored expression. He wanted to wipe that expression from her face, to replace it with something far different, something glimpsed in the midst of a thunderstorm.

He caressed her cheek, then his fingers stole into the softness of her hair, heat spreading everywhere he touched. He sensed the subtle change in her breathing, the struggle for control. With the greatest tenderness, he bent over her, following his fingers with his lips. It was like a game, a delicious, wonderful game. He wanted to prolong it so that when he finally kissed her, as he intended, it would be so much sweeter.

When he'd kissed every place except her soft, full mouth, he hesitated, then smiled. Her eyes were closed, her lips were parted expectantly, her breathing was fast and softly sweet. Without knowing why, his gaze went to the wall behind her, to the array of portraits. He chuckled to himself. And she'd thought they wouldn't be seen. His gaze narrowed on the nameplate—Lord Clayton Barrington.

From the stable master he knew him to be Jerrold's grandfather, the man who'd had the black stallion Domino bred especially for his son. Seated beside Clayton Barrington in a portrait of him as a youth was a young woman with an infant in her arms—Lady Barrington and her son, Alex.

His gaze went to the next picture. It showed a tow-headed child of three or four years of age. Then the next, Lord Clayton Barrington again and the blond child, but with a different woman cradling an infant.

He stepped past Elyse, his silver gaze fastened on the family portraits—there were two sons. He'd heard nothing about another child.

Elyse recovered slowly. Her eyes slowly opening. She turned as he stepped past her and stared at St. James who had stepped in front of the paintings on the wall.

"Of all the... "She should have been relieved.

"Who are these people?" he demanded.

"I suppose they're all Barringtons, going back over the years," she coolly replied.

"I can see that." He moved along the wall, reading the nameplate under each painting. He stopped at the one that showed two young boys—one fair-haired, approximately four or five years old, and a dark-haired toddler.

"Alexander Nicholas Barrington and Charles Farragut Barrington. But his gaze fastened on the older boy with sun-bleached hair and soft gray eyes.

"Alexander Nicholas Barrington." Zach repeated the name. Somehow it wasn't right. He said it again, turning it over and over, unable to comprehend why it should seem familiar to him.

"There was an older child. What happened to him?" Zach asked.

"I was told that he died quite young—*Nicky*." She had no idea where that had come from. It was simply there, the name of a child.

She gasped as St. James seized her in a bruising grip. "What did you say?" Zach demanded. "His name? You said he was called Nicky as a child."

"I don't know... Perhaps something someone said that I remembered." She knew little about the Barrington family, except what her grandmother had told her about Felicia and, of course, Lord Charles.

"Tell me!" he demanded.

"I don't know!"

"Alexander Nicholas Barrington." Like a puzzle with thousands of pieces it slowly came together.

"Nicholas Barrington," he whispered.

"My God." Zach stared at the painting. "Is it possible?"

He turned and stalked from the room, leaving Elyse stunned and shaken. In that one brief instant, when he'd turned to her, there had been something in his gaze. It had seemed she was looking at another man... someone she knew!

It flashed across her mind like lightning, white-hot, blinding, there one instant, gone the next. She raced to the door, but he was gone. Staring into the empty hallway, she slowly opened her fingers. The pendant lay in her palm, still warm from his hand.

Who was he?

Twelve

Zach stormed out of the library. He needed to know about Alexander Barrington, and there was one person who might tell him. However, getting the man to talk would be another matter.

Long strides took him past the great hall where Jerrold Barrington entertained his guests. His gaze narrowed on Charles Barrington, the younger son in that portrait.

The room was brilliantly lit with dozens of candles. People, costumed like himself, were attempting to play out some make-believe charade. He turned and practically collided with the bewildered butler, a decanter of amber liquid almost tipping from the silver tray the servant held.

He grabbed the decanter from the tray. Then disappeared down the hallway to the doors that opened onto the gardens, and, like a phantom, he slipped out into the night.

Unless he missed his guess, the stable master was Irish, with a good appreciation of fine whiskey, or brandy. His boots crunched on the gravel that lined the driveway. A single light gleamed from one end of the stables.

The stable master was bent over a saddle, rubbing

the leather to a sheen. A pipe hung from his lips, fragrant tobacco smoke encircling his head. He looked up.

"Evenin', sir." He stood, wiping his hands on worn pants. "Is there somethin' you'd be needin', sir?"

Zach nodded. "Some conversation." He held the decanter aloft and saw the gleam that leaped into the man's eyes.

"Aye, 'tis a fine summer night."

"Then you'll join me?" Zach entered the stables, placing the decanter on the small table with the brushes and rags the stable master used. The man's gaze lingered on the amber liquid in the decanter.

The old man wet his lips as if he could almost taste the amber liquid. "The master doesn't approve..."

Zach nodded. "But the master isn't here, and we wouldn't want to waste this fine drink." He sat on the bench beside the stable master. "I'd like to hear more about that fine black stallion you were telling me about."

The man's gaze lifted momentarily from the bottle. "Ah yes, Domino. That was a long time ago."

"But I'm sure there must be a fine story to tell about him." He appealed to an Irishman's storytelling.

"That there is." The stable master wet his lips as if he could almost taste the silken fire of the brandy. "It might take a long while."

"It might take a long while to enjoy this brandy," Zach countered.

"It would be a pity to waste it." The old man passed a gnarled hand over the stubble of beard on his chin.

"A pity," Zach agreed. "And perhaps something of the family. I understand there were two sons."

"Aye, I remember the time when that black devil first came here to Fair View. He was almost two years old, but only partly saddle broke."

For the next two hours, he'd listened to the man's ramblings, plying him with more brandy and questions.

"You've spoken of Lord Charles," Zach commented. "Did he ride the black?"

"Lord Charles? No! He was afraid of the beast almost from the moment the old master brought him to Fair View. Could've been because he a bit younger."

Zach sat up, trying to keep the tone of his voice casual. "What of the older son?"

"Ah, yes, master Alex. The boy was a fine rider, could sit any horse. He had a way about him with the animals, including the black."

"What can you tell me about him?" Zach prodded.

The old man shook his head. "He was Master Clayton's first born, Master Alexander Barrington. And a finer young man there never was."

Zach nodded. "There's a portrait in the house of two young boys."

"As I said, there was never a finer lad."

Zach leaned forward and poured the man more drink. "I've heard little said about him," he casually mentioned. "You'd think a father would be proud of such a young man."

Rooney grunted as he took a healthy drink of the brandy. "Aye, you would," he agreed. "But that's not the way of it. They all want to forget." The old man emptied the glass in one swallow.

"What is it that everyone wants to forget? Was he wild and rebellious?"

Rooney shook his head, staring into the soft glow the amber liquid reflected through the glass. "If that was only the way of it, it would have been an easy matter. Such a sad, sad thing."

Zach's fingers tightened around the decanter. "What could be so bad?"

The old man looked up, fixing Zach with bloodshot eyes. "Murder."

. . .

Zach leaned against the frame of a tall window that opened onto the balcony outside his room, trying to think. He exhaled slowly, smoke from the cigarette curling about his head.

The empty decanter sat on the table beside the window. It had taken most of the contents to get what he wanted from the stable master. The old man finally had slumped over in a drunken stupor. Zach finished the rest of the liquor, desperately needing something to dull the painful truth.

He inhaled, the tip of the cigarette glowing fiery red. Murder, two sons born of different mothers, childhood resentments that festered into manhood, a favored first-born son, jealousy, rivalry for a father's love. Then the untimely death of Lord Clayton Barrington.

According to the stable master, some said it was an accident, others claimed it wasn't. There had been a dreadful quarrel, the house servants heard it. Then there was silence and a young servant girl supposedly found Alex Barrington standing over his father's body.

He was brought up on murder charges. The evidence supplied by the servant girl was damning, but there were rumors about her, too. Ah yes, rumors. The stable master knew the girl was caught more than once sneaking out to the stables with young Master Charles. She testified against his brother, then disappeared shortly after the trial.

And the sentence? Servitude and exile.

Because of his place in society Alex Barrington was spared hanging. He was ordered by the courts to serve a minimum sentence in prison and then be sent into per-manent exile. In the span of a few short weeks, Alexander Nicholas Barrington was transformed from the heir of one of England's wealthiest families to a con-vict. His title, his lands, his wealth were all forfeit in favor of the younger brother.

Nicholas Barrington. The words from an old journal his father had kept:

I began this journey into hell. One day I will return and have my day of justice for the crime of which I am accused... I shall now be called Nicholas Tennant.

His sentence became his hell. Nicholas Barrington was a man stripped of family, country, and ultimately his name.

It seemed impossible, yet in his soul Zach believed it.

The connection to the Barrington family had been there all along. Nicholas Tennant and Alexander Nicholas Barrington were one and the same.

I will reclaim my birthright from those who have accused me. I will return and have my day of justice.

The words from the journal haunted him. They were not words of regret or even denial—they were words of revenge.

Was it possible his father had been falsely accused? But why? And who would stand to gain the most if he was dead or prevented from inheriting? Charles Barrington?

The stable master had hinted as much but quickly let the matter drop and then wouldn't speak of it again. And there was the matter of the servant girl who'd testified at the trial, then disappeared afterward.

Nicholas Tennant had vowed to return. And what did it all have to do with Felicia Barrington? Zach rubbed the heels of his hands against his eyes.

He stared painfully into the blood red dawn. His head ached, but the pain helped clarify his thoughts. The hand he raised with a cigarette shook, but not with fear or weakness. The anger came hours ago in the stable and had slowly built until it was like a live animal clawing at his insides.

The mask was gone, as was the rest of his costume shirt. A fine sheen spread across his shoulders and back in spite of the cool night air that lingered. His hair was wild, unkempt, almost afire as the dawn fell in golden waves about his head. There was nothing of the elegant, sophisticated *William St. James* to be found.

As the walls seemed to close in on him, Zach threw the cigarette over the balcony and turned back to the room. He had to get away. If he remained another moment, he would go mad. There was nothing more to be done here. These people were powerful and respected. They would keep their secrets because the truth carried too high a price.

Whatever he chose to do had to be done away from here, where the odds were more evenly balanced. He stared at the walls that surrounded him. This had once been his father's home. He might have slept in this very room.

He turned and left, telling himself that Fair View meant nothing to him, held no meaning for him. It was only so much brick and mortar: rooms, hallways, and paintings. It had been part of his father's life, but not his. Those very same walls seemed to throw the lie back at him.

Zach hesitated outside the room at the end of the hall. He leaned into the door, the palm of his hand flattened against the smooth wood, and instinctively he knew. This was her room. Elyse was just beyond that door.

Memories of her in his bed flashed across his mind, memories of sleek, pale skin against his, the heat in her slender body that melted to passion as they came together. The anger that could flash in her eyes, then simmer to another emotion he knew she would deny —desire.

She belonged to Barrington, like one of his ships or Fair View, a possession he'd acquired by a stolen title. Whatever they might have shared began and ended that one night. His hand dropped to his side.

Downstairs, he went to Barrington's study. He

pushed aside the panel, exposing the wall safe. And just as he'd observed them from their meeting, the numbers fell into place beneath his fingers, the small door silently swinging open.

He pushed aside the odd pieces of jewelry, a thickly wrapped bundle of hundred-pound notes, other documents, and finally found the draft. He tucked it inside his shirt, then closed the safe. Let Barrington wonder what had happened to the draft.

～

"Where did you find this?" The black eye-patch fluttered in Jerrold Barrington's fingers.

His housekeeper, Mrs. Evers, shifted uneasily. "It was in his room, sir."

"And nothing else?"

"As I said, your lordship. It's as if he's disappeared." The woman's smile disappeared at the look in his eyes.

"A man doesn't simply vanish without a trace. We're not talking about ghosts or spirits, Mrs. Evers. What about the stables?"

"His coach and coachman are gone as well."

"Did Mr. Rooney say when he left?"

"He didn't know, sir." She didn't dare tell him Rooney had been found slumped over a table, snoring through a drunken stupor.

Jerrold slammed his fist down hard on the table, causing the silver tea service to rattle. His eyes narrowed.

Why would a man who'd lost an eye leave behind the item that covered that affliction? He'd thought the man a bumbling fool to be taken advantage of. It seemed he might have been wrong. But who was this mysterious stranger if not a nobleman? A muscle ticked in his cheek.

He looked up at the housekeeper." I want to see Mr. Lash."

Mrs. Evers' gaze widened. She didn't like Mr. Lash, no one did. He was a big brute of a man employed to handle *"private"* matters. Her hands twisted into knots.

"He's not here, sir."

Jerrold whirled on her, his eyes dark and piercing. "What do you mean he's not here? He should have been back hours ago." It wasn't like Lash to be absent. The man had an unnerving ability to attain perfection in everything. If he hadn't returned yet, then something must have gone wrong.

"I want to know the moment he returns," he told her.

"Yes, sir." She bobbed a curtsy and quickly left the room.

Jerrold Barrington paced the room. Suddenly he whirled around, his gaze fastening on the painting, the third from the left corner. It stood a fraction of an inch away from the wall.

Elyse stood before the portrait of Felicia Barrington that had been covered and stored away. Restless, unable to sleep after the dream had driven her from her bed, she'd come to this room. Now she looked at the portrait, her fingers gently clutching the diamond and pearl pendant in her hand. It was of the same design as the earbobs Lady Barrington wore.

She studied the painting, watching those eyes that stared back at her, reaching out to her from every angle no matter where she stood.

"1837," she repeated the year inscribed in the brass plate. "Your engagement portrait. What could have so drastically changed your life? You seem so happy?"

"She was happy."

Elyse whirled around, then smiled at her grandmother. "I thought the walls had started talking to me, or perhaps she had." She looked at the portrait of Felicia Barrington.

"Your maid said that I would find you here. I wanted to see the painting again."

"You've seen it before?" she asked with surprise.

Lady Regina crossed the room, her smile softened by memories. "Oh yes, just before it was finished. She was happy then, as radiantly happy as she looks in that painting."

"You said she was a very sad woman. She certainly doesn't look like it in the painting."

"She wasn't when this was painted. I've never seen a more vibrant woman or one more in love. But that was a very long time ago."

"The earbobs she's wearing, they're exactly like my pendant."

"Yes," Lady Regina answered without elaborating. She sighed heavily, thinking it was time for Elyse to know certain things about this family she was marrying into. Of course, she'd known that must be done one day, but she'd put it off. Now it seemed her dear friend Felicia had somehow brought it about.

"You may as well know, you'll hear bits and pieces of it anyway, once you're married and live here."

"Know what? Gossip, rumors, things people have no better sense to say."

"I'm afraid it's a great deal more than that, my dear." Regina looked up at the painting.

"Her parents were friends of your grandfather's, and she was only a few years younger than your father." She paused, then continued. "Your father went off to America and met your mother. Felicia met and fell in love with Alexander Barrington."

"Alexander...?" Elyse's gaze fastened on the portrait. "There were two sons?"

"Yes. Alex was Lord Clayton's son by his first marriage. He remarried after his wife's death. Young Alex must have been about four or five at the time."

"I didn't know," Elyse's dark eyes were troubled.

"It never seemed to matter," Lady Regina continued. "It all happened so long ago. It was all so dreadful and sad, something best forgotten. But when I saw Charles' reaction seeing you in that gown..." Lady Regina came closer to stand before the portrait.

"I never knew much about the two boys' childhood. I supposed it was like those of others. But as they grew older, there were rumors of problems. Alex was the firstborn, heir to Lord Clayton's title, lands, everything. Charles as the second son would inherit also, but to a much lesser extent."

"Alex grew to be a handsome young man," she continued. It was easy to see how Felicia fell in love with him, and he with her. This portrait was painted to celebrate their engagement."

It was warm in the room. Nevertheless, she felt as if something cold had brushed against her, and she shivered.

"She was engaged to Charles' brother," she whispered incredulously. "But how...?"

"It was such a sad thing, all of it." Lady Regina slowly shook her head. "The wedding was to have taken place just before Christmas of that same year. To this day, I don't think anyone knows exactly how it all began."

"Tell me!" Elyse insisted. But even as she said it, somewhere deep in her soul, she already knew.

"There was a violent quarrel. There were conflicting stories on how it began. When it was over, Clayton Barrington was dead. Alex was found standing over him, an andiron in his hand. The evidence was damning. Alex was brought before the magistrate on charges of murder. There was a dreadful scandal.

"Your mother and father had just married, and I had

gone to New York for the wedding and a long visit. It was all over when I returned. Alex was found guilty of murder on the testimony of a servant girl who claimed to have found him standing over Lord Clayton. He denied everything, but it didn't matter."

"What happened then?" Elyse's voice was faint whisper as she stood before the portrait of Felicia Barrington.

"He would have been hanged, but Charles pleaded for the court's mercy. In the end, Alex was given a sentence and exiled."

Elyse's fingers tightened. "Exiled? Where?"

"He was sent to the convict colony at New South Wales and forbidden to ever return to England. Felicia was devastated. I hardly recognized her when I returned from New York. It was as if she had suffered everything with him. I've never seen two people more in love, or two lives more shattered."

Elyse looked up, her eyes filled with tears. "She tried to go with him."

"Yes, but he wouldn't allow it," Lady Regina replied.

"He asked her to wait for him," Elyse whispered. "He said he would come back."

Lady Regina stared at her. "For two years she lived with that hope."

"Two years," Elyse murmured.

"And then without anyone knowing of it, without any plans or announcement, she married Charles Barrington." Lady Regina shook her head. "I never understood it. When I spoke to her once about it, she refused to say anything, only that what was done, was done. A few years after that, word finally came to the family that Alex had died in New South Wales. It was as if she died too. I think it was then she finally gave up all hope that he would return. She had Jerrold within a year after that, but she was never really well again."

Elyse stared at the portrait. She thought she could

almost see something alive in Felicia Barrington's eyes, something that wasn't in any of the other portraits at Fair View. If she reached out, would she feel warmth in those elegant fingers wrapped around the Remembrance Rose?

"She was so beautiful," Elyse sadly said. "And Lord Charles must have loved her."

"I believe he did, in his own way. But you must understand, she was a bright, sparkling thing when he first knew her. And Charles Barrington always liked to surround himself with bright, pretty objects."

"A possession," Elyse murmured, understanding only too well.

"Perhaps, but I think he was always secretly in love with her. But she had loved only one man, and when she couldn't be with him, her life became an empty shell. The woman you see in that portrait ceased to exist. It was as if she died when Alex died."

"How did it happen." Elyse asked.

"It was expected. And to be very honest, it was almost a blessing."

"A blessing? How can you say that? I think it's dreadful when any living thing dies. But especially someone so beautiful."

Her grandmother stroked her cheek. "I know you do, my dear. But that's because you're full of life and hope, and love." She added the last tentatively, then quickly went on.

"Life is not the same when a person doesn't have those. It's what gives it all a purpose, a meaning."

"I remember how I felt when I heard the news. It was just after the shipwreck. Ceddy and I were at Land's End. Everything was so difficult then. No survivors had been found in two days. The weather was frightful." Her eyes misted as she remembered that day almost twenty years earlier.

"Everyone said it was no use. It was the worst storm

anyone could remember in years. But I knew." She smiled lovingly at Elyse. "I knew, if they just kept looking..." Lady Regina composed herself. "I didn't realize it at the time, of course."

"Realize what?" Elyse held her grandmother's hand tightly. "It was afternoon. But I remember the sky was dark as night. The coachman had lit the lanterns. Ceddy tried to get me to go back to the inn. It was then that Quimby came over the edge of that cliff with a bundle clutched in his arms. The poor man was half-dead himself. But when they pried the bundle from his frozen hands, I knew I'd never seen anything so near death."

"Quimby found me," Elyse replied what she'd been told, her eyes going to the painting once more.

"Everyone thought he was too late. There didn't seem to be a breath of life in you. But I refused to accept it. We took you back to the inn. The doctor from the village looked after you." Lady Regina hesitated, her voice catching oddly.

"What is it?" It was a story she'd heard several times.

"You need to know. Perhaps it will help you understand how very special you are to me." Lady Regina looked up at the portrait.

"The physician said you were as well as dead." Her voice was hollow with remembered pain. "He said it was impossible that anyone could be in the water that long and survive. But I refused to believe it. I'd lost my son and your dear mother. I wasn't going to lose you as well. To this day I don't know whether it was a miracle or just your determination to live. But within days there was a change in you, and I knew you were going to live.

"I kept watch over you and I said countless prayers. You were still terribly weak, but the fever broke, and you were much stronger. It was then that we had the news from London that Felicia had died."

"It happened at the same time that you began to recover." Lady Regina looked at her granddaughter. "I'm not a superstitious woman, but I do believe that something happened in that moment when she was lost and you grew stronger. It was almost as if your life was beginning just as hers was ending." She patted Elyse's hand tenderly.

"Somehow it helped ease an old woman's grief. I'd lost a dear friend, but I'd gained someone very special."

Elyse looked up at the portrait. "Do you believe in love that lasts forever?"

Lady Regina pondered that question at great length. "I know I continued to love your grandfather after he was gone. Part of me still does."

"That's how I feel about mother and father. I don't remember very much about them. But I know they loved me and that I loved them. I'm talking about a different kind of love, one that happens only once in a great while but lasts forever."

"Well, certainly when we're young we tend to believe it will be love forever. And perhaps some do. There are no certainties about what happens when we leave this life. I'd hate to think there's nothing at all." Lady Regina smiled thoughtfully.

"I wonder if they found one another." Elyse's eyes softened as she stared at the portrait of Felicia Barrington.

"My goodness, what are you talking about?"

"Do you think Felicia and Alex ever found each other again?"

Her grandmother's eyes grew misty as she pondered that romantic notion. "If it's possible, they would find each other. They loved each other that much."

"He promised he would come back," Elyse added.

Regina stared at her granddaughter. "He did promise her that." She smiled uncertainly, seeing that Elyse seemed suddenly very sad.

"Whatever is wrong?" she asked. "I never meant to upset you."

Elyse slowly composed herself. "I'm just tired. I didn't sleep very well."

Her grandmother eyed her skeptically. Elyse did look tired. There were faint circles under her eyes. And she seemed so remote, distant. It wasn't like her to be over-emotional or moody. Yet, for a moment, she'd seemed a million miles away.

A chill of uneasiness ran through the older woman. She remembered that same expression on the face of a child many years before. It had made her feel as if she'd glimpsed something else very briefly. She had that same feeling now and shivered.

"Have you had the dream again?"

Elyse smiled. "Of course not," she lied, not wanting to alarm her grandmother.

How could she tell her? How could she possibly explain that it had started again, leaving her feeling an overwhelming sadness and sense of regret. It must be a little like dying she thought, then tried to push that idea from her thoughts.

"I'll be fine. Don't worry," she reassured her grandmother.

Lady Regina wrapped an arm around her granddaughter's shoulders, taking Elyse's hand in hers as she had when Elyse was a child. "It's probably just nervousness, with the wedding only a few days away. I thought it might be better for us to remain in London so that you could rest. Sometimes I question Jerrold's judgment. What you need is a good strong cup of tea."

She slipped her arm through Elyse's and together they walked from the room.

Elyse stopped and looked back over her shoulder at the portrait. She couldn't rid herself of the feeling that somehow, somewhere, she'd known Lady Barrington. It left her feeling confused and uncertain.

How could she possibly have known a woman she'd

never met, a woman who'd been dead for almost twenty years?

Damask linen, in a shade of soft gold, decorated the walls, and a pale cream-colored carpet covered the floor. The long dining table extended twenty-five feet, elegant Queen Anne lace trailing from its sides and ends, twenty-five gold place settings laid precisely on it. The mahogany chairs, all twenty-five of them, were richly upholstered in deep gold velvet, and hundreds of candles lit the room, winking from the multi-tiered chandelier overhead and the three magnificent gold candelabra on the table. At its center was an elaborate floral arrangement of delicate white rosebuds and yellow forsythia. The dining room at Fair View was aglow.

Lord Charles Barrington sat as host, Jerrold on his right. Elyse sat next to Jerrold, and her grandmother was to Lord Barrington's left. It was all very elegant, very proper, and she wanted to scream.

For the last two hours she'd listened to the casual conversation of those present. The local magistrate and his wife were there, along with the vicar, Mr. Beebe, along with others who attended for the weekend. And, for what must have been the dozenth time, she found herself watching the entrance. Then her gaze darted back to the conspicuously vacant chair in which there should have been another guest.

Her head ached and her skin felt icy. She smoothed her hands over the skirt of the pale-yellow satin gown Jerrold had insisted she wear. It was one of many he'd personally selected. She knew the reason he'd picked it. He had said that it would make her glow like a golden flower in a golden room.

At the time Elyse wasn't certain whether he was complimenting her, the room, or his own taste in selecting her clothes. She hated yellow and never chose the color. She had the distinct feeling that in the future she was headed for, she was going to be wearing a great deal of yellow.

She looked to the entrance again and swore to herself. She knew who it was she hoped to see there as Lord Barrington's voice cut through her thoughts.

"I am, of course, delighted that you could all join us in the celebration."

As he droned on, she nodded some vague response to the vicar, Mr. Beebe, at her other side. He was an ancient man with a monstrous bulbous nose and two tiny close-set eyes. His thinning hair was combed in a whorl around his head, to cover the bare spots. So much for godliness outshining vanity. But he seemed a kindly man, and he patted her hand often, remarking more than once that he'd performed several marriages for the Barrington family, though usually performed in church.

Elyse had only smiled vaguely in response. As always, Jerrold had made all the arrangements. They were to be married at Fair View, and she had no idea how many or whom had been invited.

She remembered his cool look when she'd suggested that the wedding be small. And then he'd continued to carry out his own plans, determined his wedding would be the grandest affair in all of London.

As the magistrate commented on some local poachers who were finally caught, Elyse noticed that her grandmother was involved in a lively conversation with a man she remembered only as the 'Colonel'.

He was resplendent in a red uniform with epaulettes and rows of gold braid. The sword belted at his waist had continually tripped him up, but he seemed fairly safe from it at the supper table, plying her grandmother and the other guests with his adventures while in Her Majesty's service. His gestures were wide, his voice booming. She almost expected him to seize his sword and handily fillet the roast pheasant when it was delivered to the table. The remainder of Lord Barrington's guests were no more than a blur to her.

Pheasant stuffed with apples and chestnuts was served. Baron of beef and poached salmon followed. Then there was roast dove with cream sauce and onions. The vegetables, fresh from the gardens at Fair View, were thinly sliced and had been briefly cooked in an herb sauce. As a finishing touch, they were sprinkled with slivered almonds and rose petals. And there were hot spiced peaches, apricots in sherry wine, and imported melons along with strawberries.

Red and white wine sparkled in crystal decanters. It was an elegant feast. But Elyse had little appetite. She took only the smallest portions, knowing if she refused anything she would offend Jerrold. She tried to swallow but found it difficult. She felt Jerrold's hand cover hers.

"Your grandmother mentioned that you weren't feeling well earlier. I hope it's nothing serious that will delay the wedding."

She looked up, surprised that he seemed so concerned. "I'm just a little tired."

Jerrold lifted his wineglass and took a sip. "I was beginning to think it might have something to do with our missing guest." His gaze indicated the conspicuously empty chair at the far end of the table.

"Did he leave without saying goodbye?" A faintly wheedling note came into his voice. "He seemed quite captivated with you."

Elyse pressed ice-cold fingers against her temples, trying to drive away the ache that had begun earlier and now throbbed.

"I've been meaning to speak to you all day," he continued in whispered tones. "Especially after that little episode last evening."

"It was a mistake to wear the gown, I realize that now. I apologized to your father." Elyse closed her eyes against the pain. "Must we talk about this now?"

"You've been shut away in your room practically the entire time, what with one excuse or another. I just want to be sure you understand certain proprieties. There are many things that will be expected of you when you become Lady Barrington and are mistress of Fair View. I shouldn't want a repeat performance of last night. And as for dancing out in the hall with St. James... well it just isn't proper! At any rate, I will no longer have that fellow to worry about."

Lord Barrington's voice boomed as he rose at the end of the table to propose a toast. "To my son and the future Lady Barrington." As he raised his wineglass in tribute, his guests did likewise.

Elyse whispered to Jerrold, "I don't know what you're talking about."

"Sir William, my dear. He's gone. I'm told he left very early this morning, before dawn. It seems he left this behind." He dangled the black eye-patch. "Obviously, he's not all that he appears. I'm having the local magistrate look into the matter, as well as the proper authorities in London."

The crystal goblet she'd reached for fell from her fingers, shattering against the gold plate. A sea of white wine soaked the table linen.

"Elyse, for God's sake get a hold of yourself!" Jerrold hissed as he came to his feet beside her. "Last night, and now this! What is the matter with you?"

She felt the scrutinizing stares of the others at the table as they gaped at her in stunned silence.

He was gone, was all she could think.

Elyse came to her feet, leaning heavily against the edge of the table. She felt a warm stickiness and raised her hand to stare at her cut fingers. There was no pain, only vague surprise as blood fell on the pristine white tablecloth, looking like small, perfect rosebuds.

Roses... red and white roses. She blinked back the tears that pooled in her eyes.

Her stricken gaze met the curious glances, seeing confusion and disapproval on the faces around her.

"I can't..." she murmured some vague excuse as she turned, gathering her skirts in her hands, and fled the dining room and the gaping stares.

~

Zach flexed his fingers against the sudden tingling. Elyse...

Memories of her flashed through his dark thoughts. How different things might have been had they met under other circumstances. But she was a member of London society and betrothed to another.

Barrington. The name and everything it stood for cut like jagged glass. He'd come to England for the truth. During the months at sea and the weeks in London, he'd prepared himself for whatever the truth about his father might be. He'd tried to imagine what he would discover.

A convict, according to those papers locked away for so many years. But what crime had he committed?

Zach had lived under English law and domination his entire life in the colonies, and he knew a man could hang for merely stealing a loaf of bread.

Murder? He refused to believe it.

The man Tobias and his mother had known was not a murderer. But then the man they'd known was not Alexander Barrington. He was Nicholas Tennant, a man who'd been convicted. Innocent or guilty, Zach knew no man could remain unchanged by what his father must have endured, first aboard the convict ship and then in servitude in New South Wales.

Convicts were no longer deported to the colonies. The practice had been abandoned several years earlier. But the stigma remained. Even as the colonies struggled to become a land of merchants, farmers, and tradesmen, they were branded by the dark part of their history. But many good men had once been convicts, and Zach needed to believe his father was one of them.

He rested his head against the seat back. He was bone tired, but his churning thoughts made sleep impossible. The coach lumbered and rolled along the road. Eyes closed, he concentrated on the grinding of those wheels, each turn taking him closer to London.

He drifted, not into sleep but numbness. The stable master had said there was a witness, a servant girl who'd disappeared after the trial. Rooney had given him her last known address in London. Zach wondered if she might still be alive.

As the coach clattered across the heavy-timbered dock, Zach pounded against the roof, signaling the driver. When the equipage rolled to a stop, he vaulted out.

The driver cringed at seeing his passenger emerge from the coach. The man was transformed without the black eye-patch he'd worn when he'd left London. Two haunted, deadly gray eyes pierced him through.

Zach paid the man well and sent him on his way. He'd been traveling all day, and it was after midnight when he walked up the gangplank of the *Revenge*.

"State yer purpose or lose yer head." The warning came sharply.

Zach smiled in response to the familiar voice, but it wasn't a smile anyone would have recognized. The man on guard laid the heavy wooden spar across his arm, in preparation to strike.

"At ease, Tris," Zach called out.

"Is that you, Cap'n?" The man on watch aboard the *Revenge* squinted into the glow of light from the lantern, relief flooding his face.

"Aye," Zach acknowledged as he reached for the railing and stepped down onto the deck. The sights, sounds, and smells were dearly familiar to him.

This was the *Revenge*. The gentle roll of her deck,

the creaking of mooring ropes, the slap of water against her hull reminded him of who he was. In the last days, he'd almost forgotten.

But something wasn't right. The light from the lantern pooled across boxes and crates of supplies to be stored in the hold, scattered across the deck, splintered open, their contents spilling across planking. A rope from the rigging was slashed, its frayed ends dangled.

"What happened here?" he demanded as he crossed the deck, then came back. Barrels of fresh water were smashed. Sacks of grain, beans and flour were cut open their contents making lumpy masses in combination with the water. He whirled on the night watchman.

"They came at us from seaward, sir." He jerked his head to the opposite side of the ship. "Must've been two dozen or so, and they were armed. They were after the cargo and cut down anyone who got in their way. But we gave 'em a good fight, sir. We put at least a dozen or so overboard. Some preferred to jump." The man stroked the wooden spar that was crusted with dried blood.

"There's a good many won't be returnin' home tonight, or any night for that matter."

Zach frowned. What he saw wasn't cargo, but damage left behind as others had searched for it. "There was no cargo still aboard... What of the warehouse?"

"They hit the warehouse after they were here. We tried to warn Sandy and the others, but we were too late."

"The wool?" Zach's expression hardened as the anger came. It wasn't the wool he cared about. It had been only a disguise for what was hidden deep inside several specially marked bales, and the only ones who'd known about the gold hidden inside were himself, Tobias, and Sandy. Neither man would betray him, he'd bet his life on it.

The seaman nodded. "Seems they weren't after the

wool at all. They set fire to several bales, then tore open the rest."

Zach cursed. While he'd been in the country playing social games with Barrington, the man had been clever and had struck first. Barrington had been stalling, keeping him away from London long enough to steal the gold.

The money will be paid as soon as my man has the gold. Barrington's words rang in his ears. Without the gold, the draft was worthless. That had been Barrington's game all along.

He had to have time to think of an effective counterattack. "What about the men?"

"A few injuries. Nothing that won't heal."

"Have you heard from Tobias?"

"We sent word round to the house. Mr. Gentry got here right away. He's in your cabin, sir."

"Good." Zach turned toward the gangplank. He intended to talk to Sandy, to find out if there was any hope of finding the men who'd attacked the warehouse.

"And there's the man we got down below." Tris informed him matter-of-factly.

Zach turned. "What man?"

The seaman grinned, his smile crooked in the roundness of his badly swollen and bruised face.

"He doesn't talk much. A big giant of a fella. But he seemed to be the leader. I had him taken below. I thought you might want to ask him a few questions." The bruised smile deepened.

The light in Zach's eyes darkened to something deadly. "Very much so. Send word to the warehouse. I want to see Sandy as soon as he comes aboard." He turned and went below. He would have his answers, and he'd have his gold. Then he would repay Barrington several times over.

Zach called out in response to the knock on his cabin door as Tobias sat, red-eyed, in a chair beside his desk. The second mate came in and stood silently before him.

"I've got men searching every street and back alley of London right now, sir. We'll get your cargo back." Determination gleamed in the man's visible eye. The other one was no more than a white slit in a mass of bruises.

"I hope you gave them equal to what you got," Zach observed, pouring a full glass of brandy and shoving it across the desk to his man.

Sandy eyed him skeptically, then took the drink, tossing it back in one quick motion. "That we did, sir."

Zach nodded. Sandy had been with him for a long time. He was the best there was. He would keep his promise. "What is the damage to the ship?"

"Very little, sir; a few broken crates and smashed barrels. There was some riggin' lines cut. Nothing that can't be set right and ready to sail."

"I want an exact accounting of the damage and of the injured men. Replace any lost supplies. Make all necessary repairs. I want her seaworthy by nightfall. And I'm going to need at least a half-dozen able-bodied men, the strongest among the crew."

"Sir, I'm sorry..." The second mate started to apologize.

Zach waved it off. "I should have expected as much. But it won't happen again."

"Yes sir," his man agreed.

"The wolf has been careless, and I know where his lair is."

"Sir?" Confusion clouded Sandy's gaze.

Zach smiled at his second mate. "I know where the gold is to be delivered." He flexed his bruised and swollen hand.

He was fortunate that he hadn't broken every bone in it. But the prisoner had given his name and a great deal more. Mr. Lash had held out a long time, but they had finally come to an agreement.

Zach knew where the gold was to be taken and hidden until Barrington returned from an extended trip after the wedding. By then, the man probably assumed the furor over the stolen cargo would have died down and that Zach would have departed. But he had something else in mind.

"The gold is to be stored at a pre-arranged location. It's to be delivered there tonight under cover of darkness, and we'll be waiting for it when it arrives."

Sandy let out a long, low whistle. "The gold and the money?"

Zach nodded. "Payment for Barrington's treachery. After all," he added, "a gentleman must abide by his agreement or pay the penalty. Wouldn't you say, Sandy?"

"Aye, sir." Sandy's eyes narrowed appreciatively. "But what if the bastard gave you the wrong information?"

"I think it's safe to say the man now believes in telling the truth. But if he's lied, then he dies," Zach stated coolly. He glanced at the ship's clock. It was nearly four-thirty in the morning. It would be daylight in another hour.

"It's a full day's ride back to Fair View. When Barrington's man doesn't arrive within a reasonable amount of time to tell him of their success, he will send someone to check up on Mr. Lash, or perhaps come himself.

"I'll wager," he continued, "that he'll do the latter since the wedding is scheduled for day after tomorrow." He ignored the tight feeling in his chest at that part of it.

"That means the earliest Barrington could possibly arrive back in London would be tomorrow morning. And by then the gold will be safely back in our hands, as will full payment for this." Zach held the legal bank draft aloft.

"He'll send someone to the docks. But the *Revenge* will be gone. As soon as the gold arrives, I want for us to be well at sea." He rounded the desk and approached the map on the far wall. He pointed to the English coastline.

"You'll sail to this point, then anchor offshore at Dover," he instructed his second mate. "According to Tobias, there's a small cover, here." He indicated the meeting place.

"What about you, sir?"

"There's someone I must find before I leave London. I may not even be able to locate her. She disappeared over thirty years ago. But if I'm not at that cove by first tide two days from now, you're to sail without me. I'll find you later. Is that clear?"

Zach saw the momentary hesitation that passed between Tobias and his second mate. "That is an order," he said firmly.

The two men muttered that they understood.

"Good." Zach turned to Sandy. "See to the provisions to be brought aboard. Then we must plan how we're to retrieve the gold. We don't have very much time." His mate nodded curtly and left. Zach turned to Tobias. "You look like hell. Get some sleep."

"What about you?"

Zach shook his head. "I have to make plans."

"What about Lord Vale's house?"

"Go back only for what you can carry. The rest stays. No one is to be suspicious. I want everything to seem normal. The servants must know nothing. Tell them you have several appointments and an engagement, then return to the ship. I want you aboard when the gold arrives."

"You think you can get it back?"

He turned to his friend, laying a hand on his shoulder. "I'll get it back and I'll get Barrington's money as well."

"That's not the real reason you risked all this. Did you find out what you came for?" The old man studied him. In the three hours since Zach had returned, he had not spoken of what he'd found out about his father.

"Aye." There was pain in his light gray eyes. "It's not

what I hoped for, Tobias." He stood, staring at the new dawn through the porthole window. "But then, I suppose life is never what you expect." He turned and smiled at his old friend. "I'll have everything I want before I leave."

"What about the woman?"

Zach's anger resurfaced, tightening inside him. "What about her?"

"You can't just leave... "

He cut his old friend off, not wanting to discuss Elyse. "She belongs with Barrington. I'm certain they'll be very happy together."

"You need to talk about it, boy, all of it, whatever you found out about the Barringtons and her."

"I don't have time to talk now," Zach bit off sharply.

Tobias clamped his mouth shut, knowing Zach wouldn't tell him anything until he was good and ready.

"All right, but you'll have to talk about it sometime. You can't just hold everything inside, eatin' yerself up with it."

"Enough!" Zach ground out the warning, his patience gone. "I need to get back to the Vale manor."

Tobias crossed the cabin. He paused at the door, one hand on the latch. "Try to get some sleep first," he added. "You look like hell."

Thirteen

He had a name, and an address that was almost thirty-five years old.

Like a man possessed Zach searched through the squalor and stench of London. He saw pain in the eyes of the beggars who stretched out their hands to him and wondered what had brought them to this existence.

He began to think it was hopeless, and time was running out. He'd started just after dawn, no longer dressed as a titled nobleman but like the sea captain he was. Rich clothes and a title would only have put these people off. They would close their doors and mouths to him because of the barrier of fine silk, satin, and jewels.

Zach spared no amount of money in trying to find Lydia Robertson. If he didn't find her today, he would have to leave without knowing what she had really seen happen between his father and grandfather that day so long ago. As it was, if he did find her, there was every possibility she might refuse to tell him no matter how much money he gave her.

"Hey, Cap'n."

He whirled around in response to the insistent tugging on his cuff. The toothless beggar he remembered from earlier that morning grinned up at him revealing not teeth but gums. He was bald, the knitted cap full of holes pulled down over his head. He looked as if he probably wouldn't remember the last time he'd bathed, and he smelled like it.

Zach had paid him a full half-crown that morning for information about Lydia's most recent whereabouts. Like the other addresses he'd been given, it had produced nothing. He'd felt certain that the man had lied because no one at that place had known anything about Lydia.

"What do you want?" Zach ground out. London was like Sydney. No different. Thievery, hunger, and poverty could be found in any city. He'd seen enough today to make him ache for the pristine wildness of Resolute. God, how he wanted to be away from all of this!

"A half-crown, Cap'n. No less," the man demanded with all the audacity of the thief he was. "And I have the information you were askin' about."

"I paid you this morning and got nothing for it."

"I gave what ye asked for, no more and no less. It's not on me head if it was for naught. Didn't find her, did ya?" His dark eyes looked up at Zach.

Definitely a *bandicoot*, Zach thought. With his pointed nose and sharp dirty claws, the little man reminded him of the rabbit-like creatures found in abundance in the valley at Resolute. He idly wondered if the beggar used that snout-like nose to sniff out his next meal, then dug it out with his claw-like hands.

"No, I didn't find her, but then you knew I wouldn't." Zach seized the man with both hands, twisting the front of his moth-eaten coat.

"You didn't find her, 'cause she weren't there," the little man gloated.

"I'm in no mood for games," Zach replied. "There will be no more money until I find her. Now, what do you know?"

The man drew back at the dangerous glint in the stranger's eyes. He had the look of a sea captain, but there was something in his bearing that suggested he was more than that. And the bulge of coin in his pocket suggested wealth. The beggar knew he couldn't physically take the money from this man, so he'd decided on a different tactic, though he'd cringed at the thought of being honest.

"You can insult me all you wish, Cap'n. Words never hurt the Snipe." He pounded his chest for emphasis. "I've learned to survive without kindness. This isn't exactly the sort of body that draws friends, or ladies for that matter.

"I came after you," he continued. "I knew you wouldn't find her this mornin'. I found out where she's been livin' the past year."

"And, of course, there is the matter of that other half-crown," Zach suggested, keeping a careful eye to the street about him.

It wasn't unusual for someone like the Snipe to work with someone else in his thievery. Often the cohort was a street urchin. Without family or the ability to work, the child became a willing accomplice.

"Ain't nothing free in this 'ere life, Cap'n. But then I suppose you're a man who would understand that. A half-crown will do, but I really ought to charge you more." He ran a gnarled hand, minus two fingers, across his grizzled chin.

Zach studied the beggar carefully. Undoubtedly the man was lying, but what did he have to lose? He'd followed every lead, knocked on the door of just about every shop, eatery, and whorehouse within a twelve-block radius. He'd begun with faint hope this morning, telling himself that people rarely moved far beyond their beginnings. But as the hours wore on, he'd been forced to admit that, after thirty-five years, Lydia Roberts had either disappeared or she was dead.

It was late, time was running out. In another hour he'd be forced to return to the *Revenge* to make the final plans for the raid that evening. After that, everything would move quickly. There would be no time to search again. Having done what he had planned, he would have to leave London forever. Like his father, he would be an exile, but a willing and very rich one.

"Very well, but you had better be telling the truth." He grabbed hold of the front of the man's moth-eaten coat. "If you're lying, I'll take you back to my ship and chain you in the hold. Then, when we are well out to sea, I'll cast you to the sharks. They're not picky about their next meal."

In all his years, the beggar had never known fear. But he did fear this man, and the gleam in those steely gray eyes. If ever he'd looked death in the face, he was doing so now.

"If you do me in, how can I take you to Lydia?"

As silent understanding passed between them, Zach set the man back down at the pavement. "Take me to her and there's a full crown for you. Lie to me and I'll cut your throat."

"Right yer are, Cap'n."

Zach was hard pressed to keep up with the man as he wove his way expertly through the mass of humanity at the open market they passed, and then a tavern, several brothels, and a smithy's shop.

"Here we are, Cap'n," the snipe announced.

Zach gave the bandicoot a look that could have split a man's head in two. "Why didn't you tell me about this place this morning?"

"Because I didn't know of it. Lydia moves around. She has to."

Zach eyed him sharply, wondering what line of business Lydia had taken up over the last years. The beggar indicated a long flight of outside stairs leading up the side of the building that housed what was obviously a fish market. With his other hand, he indicated it was time for payment.

"Stairs," Zach grunted out. "Clever. And by the time I return, you're gone. Not likely, my friend." He spoke the last words coolly. Amidst loud protesting, he dragged him up the stairs with him, and knocked at the door.

After several minutes, a slender young girl peeked from behind curtain. They heard the bolt at the door slide back, and she poked her head out.

"What yer doin' here, Snipe?" the girl exclaimed.

"This here's the one I was tellin' you about. He's come here to see Lydia."

"Gor!" the girl breathed out. "I thought you was twistin' me arm. But she can't see no one. She's real bad today. You know how she is when she gets one of her spells. It's all I can do to keep her quiet. I can't afford to be put out of this place if they hear her cryin'."

"He's got gold coin, Tilly," the Snipe informed the girl, his eyes widening for emphasis. "He just wants to ask her some questions. That's all. What harm could it do the poor soul and then good coin to ease her misery?"

"All right." The girl named Tilly stepped reluctantly aside. In spite of her manner, the small room was clean though sparsely furnished, and what smelled like a stew simmered at the coal stove. A cloth decorated with hand stitching covered the table set with two chairs, a rocking chair with two slats missing from the back was set before the fireplace, and a door at the back led to another room.

"I'll take that full crown now," the Snipe told him.

"I want to see Lydia, first." Zach turned to the girl, not wanting to frighten her. "I just want to ask her some questions about someone she knew a long time ago. That's all, and I'd be more than willing to pay for her time."

She laughed. "That's all Lydia has nowadays. She's a good soul, but I warn you, it's a bad bargain." She made a circling motion at her head. "She's not herself, know what I mean?"

"Crazy?" Zach asked.

Tilly shook her head. "She likes for people to think she is. But I see a look in her eyes sometimes—not dangerous or anything like that. She has some strange ideas, but yer can talk to her if you like." The girl's gaze fastened on the bulge of coin in his coat pocket.

"I'll be right back. Then maybe we can find something else you'd be liken', Cap'n." She hinted as she disappeared into the other room.

"Cap'n?" the Snipe prodded.

"You'll have your money afterward."

The Snipe grumbled something about not being able to trust anybody, then focused on the stew.

"She'll see ye," Tilly announced when she returned. "She's making herself decent, then go on in."

He stepped into the room and let his eyes slowly adjust to the half-light that spilled through a slit at the curtains. An hour later he emerged. He wasn't surprised to find the beggar still there. The girl looked up at him expectantly.

"How long has she been like that?" he asked.

"A long time. Her memory comes and goes, always in bits and pieces. I can't make much out," Tilly answered with a shrug.

"Are you her daughter?"

"Daughter? No!" The girl made a guttural sound, then softened her words. "Me and Lydia teamed up about three years ago. She weren't so bad then. Lived in this little place over a few blocks. I needed a place to stay, and she needed somebody to help pay the rent. Her money didn't cover expenses."

"How did she make a living?"

"Lydia never worked the streets if that's what ye mean. She has money that comes in, but she was always spendin' it as fast as she got it. On all them fancy gowns and things that don't mean much in a place like this."

"Gowns?" he didn't understand what this had to do with anything.

"Yeah, like she was a grand lady or something. Called herself Lady Barrington."

Zach sat in the chair before the small desk in his cabin aboard the *Revenge.* He'd made his final plans for that night with Sandy and his crew. Now he tried to sleep, but found it impossible. He rested his head on the desk. The ship was cool and quiet, his men either topside seeing to last-minute details before they put to sea, or ashore with Sandy. Tobias would come aboard later.

The ship creaked as it rolled restlessly in calm harbor waters. It was as if she were as eager as he to be at sea again. Soon, he thought as he closed his aching eyes. He'd had no sleep in the last two days, and he'd have none for at least two more. But instead of fatigue, he felt the restlessness of the ship around him, the straining at the mooring ropes.

Lydia Roberts. A madwoman who fancied herself Lady Barrington. He'd been doubtful at first just how much he could believe. But the girl had confirmed enough.

Perhaps Lydia was mad, or perhaps she'd only re-treated there where she knew no one would bother her. But as long as he lived, he'd never forget the look in her eyes when he'd entered the room and opened the cur-tains to let in light.

Bedridden, clinging to the elegant satin shawl about her shoulders, she'd stared at him, a half-lucid, half-crazed expression frozen on her face. Then her hand had flown to her mouth.

"You!" she'd cried. "It's you." And immediately she'd begun to cry, tears streaming from eyes decorated with cosmetics, and trickling down brightly painted cheeks until the colors of her makeup ran together, making her more pathetic than she'd first seemed.

"You've come back!"

She'd stared at him, her mouth moving, but no words coming out for the longest time. And when she finally spoke, she was in another time and place. She clung to his hand, begging his forgiveness, vowing her love, telling him things too fantastic to believe.

But Tilly had known the truth. She'd heard it countless times from Lydia in the woman's saner moments, and then, of course, there was the stipend that appeared each month, hand carried by a uniformed servant. He arrived, delivered the envelope into Lydia's shaking hands, then disappeared. And they lived for another month. Tilly supplemented the income from sewing she took in and from other more obvious activities.

She'd grown fond of Lydia. She listened to the stories, the rantings and ravings, and held the older woman when the tears came. One day she'd followed the uniformed servant back to his employer—Jerrold Barrington.

From Lydia's fragmented memories and what Tilly had told him, Zach knew he had the truth at last.

Lydia was a naive young girl of fourteen when she went to work at Fair View, the Barrington country estate. There she was trained as an upstairs maid by her aunt, who'd long been in the family employ. Once a pretty little thing, it was not long before she came to the attention of both Barrington sons, Alexander and Charles.

The older son, Alex, was favored by Lord Barrington. He had fair hair and eyes the color of quicksilver. Lydia loved him the minute she saw him. It was not so with Charles, who was four years younger. Perhaps that was the reason Charles pursued her.

So, while Lydia longed for a glance or a touch from her beloved Alex, she received those and more from Charles. With the ruse of a note purporting to come from Alex, he lured her to the stables and there took her innocence and her dreams. With youthful naiveté Lydia had hoped for Alex's love and had suffered for it.

The younger son turned her love for Alex against her, viciously blackmailing her into his bed. When he summoned her, she was forced to go to him or have Alex and Lord Barrington confronted with the truth. She thought her heart would break when she learned Alex was to marry Felicia Seymour

Zach shook his head. Felicia had once been betrothed to his father. That explained the passages in the journal. Lydia had remembered the pearl and diamond pendants, and the day she discovered Alex preparing to give them to her. Lydia had fled the room in tears, Alex not understanding the hurt he'd brought to the poor girl.

But Charles Barrington wasn't satisfied with luring Lydia away from Alex. He was driven by jealousy, anger, and the consuming greed of his own mother, Lord Clayton's second wife.

Alex was the favorite son, the firstborn. He would inherit the business, all the land, the title, practically everything except the small estate in Northumberland Lord Clayton had set aside for Charles. And Alex was to have the lovely Felicia as well. It was more than Charles could bear.

At this point in her tale, Lydia had gazed guardedly toward the door, as if she feared someone would do her harm. But then she'd again lapsed into the past. Clinging to his hand and calling him by his father's name, she'd begged his forgiveness for her lies.

His thoughts churning, Zach had faced the truth. This woman had given evidence against his father regarding a crime he hadn't committed. Her testimony had damned his father to imprisonment and permanent exile. Zach wondered if he could believe her... if he wanted to believe her?

In the end, Zach had known Tobias was right, that he'd come too far, risked too much, not to see it through after he'd found the one person who could tell him what had happened.

Lydia had sobbed out her grief, her tears falling onto his hand as she'd clasped it to her breast. That fateful day, she'd begged Charles to meet her in the library at Fair View. She was with child and needed desperately to talk to him about what was to be done. She'd stepped into the shadow of a bookcase as she heard him approach with Lord Barrington.

She heard the argument that followed, the violent words, the threats, and recriminations. She knew the moment the argument became physical, Lord Barrington striking his son for accusing him of favoring Alex. And she heard the final blow and saw Lord Clayton fall to the floor.

She'd watched, horrified, as the young man bent over his father. Looking up, his gaze had locked with hers, and Lydia had been certain she'd seen her own death in those dark, evil eyes.

Terrified by what she'd witnessed, she was easily convinced to keep quiet. The bribe Charles had offered was marriage and respectability. And so, Lydia had become his accomplice. Her statement had convicted Alex. For her reward, she'd expected to be Lady Barrington, but Charles had other plans. He had acquired almost everything once promised to his brother, but he wanted it all, including Felicia.

Sobbing, Lydia had collapsed back against her pillow, unable to tell him more. But Zach was now able to fill in the missing pieces.

When the trial was over and Alex was exiled for life,

Charles Barrington had set out to win Felicia's hand. And he had. It seemed one Barrington was as good as another to that mysterious lady. As for his father, Zach knew that he'd never stopped loving her. Why else would he have kept that journal and the pendant all those years?

Now it was Jerrold Barrington who kept the family secrets, paying Lydia handsomely every month for her silence. The child Lydia had conceived by Charles Barrington had died shortly after birth. She'd never mourned its loss, feeling that it was really a blessing. And she'd continued to live her sad life, half-insane because the lie she'd told had sent the man she truly loved into exile.

Zach didn't hate her. He pitied her. Her life, like so many others, had been irrevocably changed by Charles Barrington's greed. And Jerrold Barrington was a willing participant in the cover-up of his father's crime. Why not, when the entire Barrington fortune and his right to inherit depended on his cooperation?

He had left Lydia to her memories and her madness. He'd paid the Snipe handsomely for taking him to her, and he'd given Tilly enough to put food on the table and coal in the stove for some time. She would no longer have to sell herself to make ends meet. Whatever was left to Lydia in this world or in the shadows of her mind, she could now afford to live in peace, free of Charles Barrington.

Zach was certain he'd dozed only a few minutes, but the dreams came anyway. In the last weeks, he'd been haunted by images out of his father's journal—the trial, the first months in New South Wales, the struggle to build a life at Resolute. The journal was his only link to the man his father had once been. And the dreams were so real that he could almost reach out and touch the things his father had described.

Lys. A dream? A memory?

Zach jerked awake, the memory slipping into the dark corners of his mind. His senses cleared slowly.

He rose and stretched, frowning at the time on the ship's clock as the sound came again. Sandy and the others must be returning early. He'd thought it would take them longer to make the necessary arrangements.

Stepping into the passageway outside his cabin, he heard it once more. The sound seemed to come from the forward hold. He walked to the end of the passage. There were two storage areas—one forward, one aft—to give the *Revenge* more even keel in the water. With the loss of the wool, both were now empty except for supplies they would need for the voyage home. But still the sound came from inside.

Zach unbolted the door and pushed it open, shining the lantern into the hold. It was cool, dark, and faintly musty. Light pooled on the smooth sides of the ship. A ladder reached high overhead to the closed hatch. The gold would be stored there when it was safely aboard.

He returned to his cabin and splashed cold water over his face. He stared into the small mirror above the washstand, searching for answers in the eyes that stared back at him.

Ever since he'd begun his voyage, he'd felt compelled to pursue something. It went beyond finding out the truth about his father. There was more. He sensed it, but didn't understand it. He threw the cotton cloth down beside the basin of water. By morning he would have taken the first step in his revenge against Barrington for his father.

The night was steeped in darkness, the moon being obscured by a thick layer of clouds. There was no light to mark the passage of the two heavily laden transport wagons bearing the markings of the Argosy Freight Company.

The guards that rode in the back were quickly silenced, their limp bodies slumping to the street. Others took care of the drivers.

The Raven emerged from the shadows with his men, only the flash of a dangerous smile revealed any of the emotions among the pirates.

Quick, efficient hands affixed new signs over the company emblem and name. And six unconscious forms were bound, gagged, and placed into the two identical Argosy crates sitting in a third wagon. A new driver climbed aboard; two new guards took their places at the back of each wagon.

The seventh man gave a silent signal and watched as each wagon took off in a separate direction, disappearing into the darkness. Their destination was the same, but for safety they would take separate routes. Satisfying himself that they were well out of sight, he pulled on the bell rope at the loading dock.

The Argosy foreman had been expecting the signal. He opened the small side door and peered out, a frown lining his forehead.

"Eh? What's this? There were supposed to be two crates." The last man, tall on the straight wagon seat, dressed all in black, nodded and gestured back to the two crates.

The foreman came down the steps and looked into the back of the wagon. He grunted his satisfaction, then gestured to a man inside to set the pulley of the large gate in motion. It creaked open.

Urging the horses forward, the driver reined them to a halt inside the warehouse.

"Have any trouble?" the foreman inquired.

"None." The reply was merely a grunt.

"Where are the others?"

"Tavern. It was a long night."

"Can't say as though I blame 'em," the foreman commented. "I don't like workin' late meself. All right, just sign here that you delivered the shipment." The man handed the driver the bill of lading. He chuckled at the description of the contents—building materials.

A signature was quickly scrawled. The foreman looked up as the man jumped down from the wagon and silently walked toward the big door.

"Hey, where you goin'?"

"Tavern."

For the second time in as many minutes the foreman shook his head. He didn't understand where the boss got people like that, and furthermore he didn't want to know. He vaguely wondered what had happened to Mr. Lash, not that he particularly liked the man. As a matter of fact, he was glad he hadn't come this time.

The foreman looked down, his brow wrinkling. "Hey! What kinda signature is this?" he yelled after the man, but the driver had already disappeared. He looked back down at the scrawl. The man must be joking with him. Raven?

"Yeah, and I'm the Archbishop of Canterbury," the foreman mumbled sarcastically.

Within hours, the second mate on the *Revenge* had the cargo secured in the hold. As the still night air gave way to the whisper of a good sailing wind just before dawn, mooring ropes were cast aside.

The harbor tugs labored to turn the majestic clipper about, nudging her graceful prow toward the open channel. Gulls cried overhead in a lavender sky as Tobias stood beside the man at the helm. He was glad to be putting London behind him.

At a sharply barked command the sails were unfurled. They billowed and caught the wind. Their course was set, south to Dover.

Elyse rubbed her throbbing temples. The dream had come again last night, but she didn't remember very much of it. What she did remember, she didn't understand. She'd slept badly after their hasty return to London two days earlier.

Pleading important business that simply couldn't wait until after the wedding, Jerrold had insisted they return immediately. Elyse had gratefully agreed. But she hadn't been prepared for the ride back.

The driver had practically ruined the team of horses, and Jerrold had pushed him to such a dangerous pace on bad roads, they'd broken an axle. She'd never seen Jerrold so furious. And now this.

She threw the stack of legal papers down on the table in her grandmother's drawing room. The wedding was this afternoon. There were still countless things to be done, including the final fitting of her gown. Now Jerrold had sent his solicitor round with a stack of legal documents she'd never seen before.

"I simply can't read through all this. There isn't time. If you'll just hold onto them, I'm certain I'll have more time after the wedding."

After the wedding.

Why did she feel such a sense of dread? What the devil was wrong with her anyway? Her grandmother was treating her like some sort of invalid, and Katy was avoiding her altogether.

She thought of how sharply she'd spoken that morning and suspected that might be the reason. Then, too, she'd heard Lady Regina talking to Katy in the dining room before she'd joined them the evening before.

Bride's blues, her grandmother had called it, attributing it to fragile nerves. God's nightgown! She'd never had a fragile nerve in her life, and she couldn't stand people who did.

If everyone didn't quit treating her like some innocent invalid or helpless person taken with a case of nerves... Elyse tried to shake off her mood. She had nothing to be upset about, she told herself. She was marrying the most eligible man in all London, and her grandmother had known his family for many years.

St. James mocking words came back to her—Sounds like something one might look for in a good hunting dog.

"Miss Winslow...?"

Once more, she tried as diplomatic as possible to explain. Her grandmother had raised her to be astute and well informed. She simply would not sign these documents until she had thoroughly read them and had them looked at by Ceddy.

"I quite understand your concern, Miss Winslow, but I assure you, an agreement of this sort is quite normal when two people from families of substantial means marry."

"I'm sorry, but I have no knowledge of this. It will have to wait."

The solicitor tried again, meanwhile pushing his wire-rimmed glasses back up the length of an incredibly crooked nose.

Elyse closed her eyes, praying for divine intervention as the man repeated his instructions.

"It is customary for the bride to sign over her properties prior to the marriage, or in this case any properties you will inherit. According to English law, everything would then be the property of Master Jerrold."

"I have no properties," Elyse tried to explain for the third time.

"What is this about?"

Both turned as Lady Winslow swept into the room.

The solicitor cleared his throat and began again.

Lady Winslow held up a hand. "My granddaughter's wedding is in just a few hours. She must dress and has no time for legal matters. I'm certain my solicitor can take care of everything if you will just leave those with me."

The man shuffled the papers uncomfortably. His

instructions were explicit, he was to have Miss Winslow sign the documents. It appeared that this was not to happen.

The man backtracked. "Very well." He quickly stuffed the documents inside his leather case, donned his hat, and made his way out the front entrance.

"I wonder what that was all about," Lady Regina commented. "I certainly would like to have seen those documents. What could Jerrold possibly be thinking? I've never heard of anything so outrageous."

Elyse thought the same but didn't have time to ponder as Katy charged past the room, stopped, and retraced her steps.

"Here you are. You gave me a fright. I was afraid you had decided to take a late morning ride, today of all days." Katy bustled across the room.

She fixed Katy with a penetrating gaze. Already, it seemed her freedom was fast disappearing. What would it be like when she actually was Lady Barrington?

"Quimby and Mr. Quist have been polishing up the coach for days, and the groomsman has been working with the horses. They've promised to be ready on time. I can't say the same for you."

"Katy, darling," Elyse gave the maid a soft smile, "did it ever occur to you that you might make someone a good wife?"

"Whatever on earth for? Besides, I haven't found a man good enough yet." She nodded as she seized Elyse by the arm and propelled her toward the stairs. "When I decide to marry it will be to a man who offers me the sun, the moon, and the stars, takes me breath away and makes me toes curl—a man who steps right out of my dreams."

Elyse stopped in the middle of the doorway. "Makes your toes curl?" A smile teased at her lips. "I had no idea you thought of such things."

The maid drew back with feigned shock. "I have me dreams too. Just like you."

"Dreams." Elyse repeated with such wistfulness that the maid looked at her with concern.

"Why so sad? This is supposed to be the happiest day of yer life."

The shadows at Elyse's eyes betrayed the smile on her lips. She didn't believe in dreams anymore.

Lady Winslow followed them to the foot of the stairs. She frowned at the exchange. Today should be the happiest day of Elyse's life. Why did she have the feeling it wasn't?

Three hours later, the coach pulled out of the long drive of Winslow House. Pinned into her seat by layer upon layer of elegant, white silk and satin, Elyse struggled to sit forward. This was the last time she would look at that house and feel that she belonged there. When she saw it again, she would be Lady Barrington. That thought pushed her back onto the cushioned seat and made her silent for the remainder of the ride to the church.

Zach refused to be seated in the outer office of the agent of Barrington Shipping Company, Lionel Hodge, the young man behind the desk.

Once more Zach had donned the clothes of a gentleman, the black eye-patch firmly in place. He gazed at Hodge when the man's thin voice broke his train of thought.

"My instructions were that I would honor the draft only when the shipment was delivered."

"Precisely." Zach nodded his agreement. His eyes scanned the office, noting the dust motes stirring in the late morning sunlight. It was still comfortable in the bookkeeper's office, but beads of moisture, were popping out along the man's forehead. Zach was cool as ice.

"My man should be here any moment," he said, forcing a pleasant expression. "Would it be possible to have a cup of coffee while we wait?"

The little man jumped up, practically upsetting a pitcher of water. "Of course. I'll just inform my assistant." As if relieved to have an excuse, Lionel Hodge rounded the desk and disappeared through a glass-paned door.

Zach could hear lively discussion behind the glass. Seizing his opportunity, he immediately went to the file drawers along the opposite wall. Unless he missed his guess, he'd find what he wanted there.

The third drawer contained leather-bound ledgers. Seizing one, he began a quick review of the entries. His eyes narrowed with satisfaction as he scanned the last ledger and found what he was looking for.

Argosy Freight Company was a subsidiary of Barrington Shipping. Entries had been made for an impressive list of shipments. Undoubtedly, this was a little side business Barrington had gotten into. He tore one page of entries from the ledger. Quickly folding it and placing it in the inside pocket of his day coat, he replaced the ledger just a moment before the pasty-faced Lionel Hodge stepped back into the office.

"My assistant will bring coffee. Our offices are closing at noon today." Hodge's lips twitched into a smile and his eyes darted about the office, looking anywhere except directly at the imposing man standing before his desk. "Lord Barrington is being married this afternoon."

"Yes, the social event of the season, I understand," Zach replied, his eyes narrowing. Both men looked up as a knock sounded on the outside office door.

"Ah, that should be my man now," Zach announced smoothly.

He stepped across the office before Hodge could

round the desk, opened the door, and stepped back, allowing Tris to enter, a reluctant companion in tow.

The foreman for the Argosy Freight Company gave Tris a sullen glare. His arm was twisted at an awkward angle behind his back, preventing escape, and he didn't immediately look at Lionel Hodge. Indeed, he seemed reluctant to do so.

"What is the meaning of this?" The bookkeeper was flustered.

Zach smiled. "You have the draft signed by Jerrold Barrington for payment in full for the gold. This gentleman can verify that two cartons for that shipment were delivered to his warehouse." He turned to the discomfited foreman. "I believe you received that shipment last night."

The stricken man seemed to have been rendered momentarily speechless. Deciding that he had temporarily lost the power of speech, Zach supplied the necessary information. "Last night a shipment was delivered to the Argosy Freight Company. Is that correct?"

The foreman looked helplessly to the bookkeeper. There'd obviously been no plan to cover this unusual development. Tris jerked the man's arm upward when he answered too slowly.

"Aye," the foreman grunted out painfully, his face going from pale to crimson.

But Lionel Hodge wasn't about to be so easily maneuvered.

"What has any of this to do with Barrington Shipping?" he asked.

Zach smiled. He'd been waiting for Hodge to ask that question. "Isn't it true that Argosy Freight Company is part of the Barrington holdings?"

Hodge smiled like a satisfied little mouse who'd just grabbed the cheese out from under the cat's nose. "You are mistaken, sir. And since the shipment has not been received, I cannot honor the draft," he announced with thin-lipped satisfaction.

"I see." Zach nodded to Tris. A copy of the Argosy bill of lading was presented. He laid it on the bookkeeper's desk. "This proves the gold was delivered last night."

Hodge was undaunted. "That proves nothing." He gave the paper a perfunctory glance. "Only that Argosy Freight received a shipment of gold."

The *cat's* paw came down on the *mouse's* tail as Zach retrieved a piece of paper from his coat pocket. "And this is a page from a ledger of accounts. Notice the lettering at the top." He indicated the gold-embossed Barrington name at the heading of the page. "Barrington Shipping Company, and the name of the subsidiary company—Argosy Freight. I believe, Mr. Hodge, we have established that Barrington Shipping, in fact, has received the gold."

Recognizing the ledger page, Hodge finally nodded and turned toward the file drawers. The third one sat conspicuously open. He turned back to Zach, the white of his face beginning around his mouth and climbing into his hairline.

Zach cut him off with an impatient wave of his hand. "I am quite correct, Mr. Hodge. Now, if you will please sign the draft and come along with me. I believe the bank will be open for the remainder of the day. But I do wish to be quick about it. It's been pleasant doing business with your employer."

"I will have to notify Lord Barrington." Hodge nervously shuffled the papers on his desk. He reached for the bell pull that would summon his assistant from the adjacent office.

Zach's fingers closed over the man's hand. "I don't think you'd really want to do that. After all, Lord Barrington is to be married today. He would be most displeased if you were to interrupt him with such a trivial matter."

The flustered bookkeeper looked from Zach to Tris and back again. The perspiration along his upper lip glistened. "Yes, of course."

Zach smiled. "Now if you will come along with me, we can conclude this business." He donned his hat, and seizing the bookkeeper by the arm, pushed him out the door and down the steps to the waiting coach.

In less than an hour, the transaction was completed. Several hundred thousand pounds sterling of Barrington money had been transferred to an anonymous account at the Bank of Zurich.

Zach approached the coach, shoving Hodge onto the seat beside the Argosy foreman. Tris sat opposite them, a pistol leveled at his prisoners, a long-bladed knife across his lap.

"What should I do with 'em, Cap'n?"

Zach removed the watch from his vest pocket and checked the time. It was one o'clock in the afternoon. In another hour it would all be done.

"Leave them where they won't bother anyone for the next several hours. Then get to the ship."

"What about you, sir?"

Zach looked up. The gold was safely aboard the *Revenge* at Dover. It could be sold to any buyer. The money was now safe at the Swiss bank, though a portion of it had been placed in an account under the name of Lydia Roberts.

He hoped the money would in part make up for the woman's suffering. She'd been cruelly used by Charles Barrington, then set aside with a small pension to guarantee her silence. She deserved a portion of the money.

Zach should have been pleased. Everything had gone according to his plans. He'd outfoxed the fox. Like the others in the colonies, he would continue the fight against Barrington and the Crown when he returned to New South Wales. But there was a hollow feeling deep inside him.

He'd wanted the truth about his father and had found it. But the large amount of Barrington money he'd put in that bank account could never make up for what his father had lost. That was more than gold or money. Alexander Barrington had lost his identity, his family, his honor. What price was there on that?

His eyes narrowed, and the muscles in his jaw worked back and forth. He wanted revenge. Barrington had to pay for what his father had suffered. And no amount of gold would equal that. In any case, Barrington would merely send more men and more ships to try to recover the gold. Zach looked at Tris, his expression hard. There was something of far greater value to be had from Barrington, he decided.

His men had instructions to sail from Dover on the next tide. There was still time to achieve the ultimate revenge. He nodded to Tris and slammed the coach door shut.

"I'll join you at the appointed time. But first, I have a wedding to attend."

Fourteen

The Anglican church was small. It had been the site of royal weddings since the time of Henry VIII. Elyse vaguely wondered if Jane Seymour had once stood in this same small anteroom contemplating her fate.

At least Elyse wasn't plagued by the thought of a former wife going to the guillotine as Seymour had been with Anne Boleyn. Still, she felt an overwhelming uneasiness, almost as if her life were ending. In a way it was. After today she would be Jerrold's wife, Lady Barrington. Strange, in all the months of their betrothal, she'd never consciously thought about that. She'd pushed back her nagging doubts.

She silently tried to bolster her confidence, telling herself all brides must feel this way. Then she looked over to Lucy and experienced a wave of envy. Lucy hadn't been nervous the day of her wedding, she'd been ecstatic. Elyse wished she could at least feel happy excitement, but she just didn't.

Lucy turned from the door, her blue gown a shimmering dark contrast to Elyse's pale blue one Jerrold insisted she wear.

She took the long velvet case and opened it. She gazed down at the perfect blue sapphires and diamonds in the gold necklace, and groaned.

"It's beautiful." Lucy sucked in her breath.

"They're gaudy," Elyse declared with a touch of pique.

"They go with your gown," Lucy pointed out.

"They should. Jerrold insisted on approving the fabric as well as the design." Snapping the lid to the case shut, Elyse sank down onto a nearby chair.

"Oh, Lucy! What's wrong with me? Why am I so critical? Everything Jerrold says or does irritates me. It shouldn't be this way," she moaned hopelessly.

Lucy sank down in front of her, grasping her hands. "Maybe it's just a case of nerves. Want to talk about it?"

"About what?" Elyse rested her forehead on her arm.

"Oh, handsome mysterious strangers, an unexplained night that you didn't spend at my house," Lucy suggested.

Elyse's head came up. "I'm marrying Jerrold. The rest is over, done with. Good heavens, it never even existed. It was just a... "

"An affair?"

She stood and paced the floor. "Tell me I'm doing the right thing."

Her friend hesitated.

"If that's what you want to hear, then I'll say it—you're doing the right thing."

Elyse repeated the words she'd been reciting to herself over and over again all morning. "And everything will be all right."

Lucy shook her head at this foolish game Elyse was playing with herself. "Everything will be all right," she repeated.

With a panic-stricken look on her face, Elyse whirled around. "When?"

Lucy crossed the room and put her arms around her friend.

She wanted to be truthful. But she didn't, instead she lied brilliantly, knowing that was what Elyse wanted her to do even as she knew her friend was too smart to be deluded by lies, even the ones she'd been telling herself all these months.

"You'll feel better after the wedding. It happens to all brides."

"You weren't nervous," Elyse said accusingly, remembering Lucy's and Andrew's wedding. It had been such a joyous occasion.

"I was marrying someone I loved completely. Can you say the same about Jerrold?"

"Oh, Lucy, there's a church full of people, and Grandmother..."

"She wants only your happiness," Lucy finished for her. "Why are you being so stubborn about this? For God's sake, you don't love Jerrold Barrington!" She was practically screaming at her friend. They both turned in surprise to the insistent knocking at the door.

"It's time to go," Elyse whispered softly.

Lucy threw up both hands in frustration. "If you're determined to ruin your life I might as well be there with you. But if you ask me... "

"Lucy, please." Elyse hugged her friend. "Just be happy for me."

"I guess I have enough happiness for two. But you should have your own."

Lucy turned her around, not able to meet her friend's eyes. "I'll fasten the necklace for you." She picked up the discarded case.

Elyse shook her head as she stepped away. "No. I prefer to wear the pendant Grandmother gave me." When she turned, her eyes spoke volumes.

"Jerrold will not be pleased," Lucy warned.

Elyse smiled. "Perhaps he'll leave me standing at the altar as punishment." The smile faded.

Lucy's brow wrinkled into a rare frown. "If you're not certain... "

Elyse cut her off. "I know what I'm doing."

But did she? Was this what she wanted?

"What the devil is happening?" Jerrold Barrington's explosion caused everyone among those present to jump. He turned on the hapless employee of Barrington Shipping, who'd arrived only moments earlier.

"Mr. Lash was found only about an hour ago." The man twisted his hat in his hands.

"Where?" Jerrold snapped.

The man swallowed hard. "At a tavern, called the Hog's Breath Inn, down by the waterfront." He smiled. "He was with the innkeeper's daughter."

"Fool! Three days! Three days and not a word from him. What did he say when you found him?"

The man, reduced to mumbling, was immediately seized by his jacket front. "Where is the shipment?" Jerrold demanded.

"He said they got the shipment just like you ordered. He had the men deliver it, and Jones reported the ship is gone. They must have left early this morning. Everything has gone as you wanted."

Jerrold threw the man from him. "I'm surrounded by fools. Lash tells you the shipment was delivered?"

"Yes, sir!" The underling straightened his coat. "I verified that with the foreman this morning, just like you said. I saw the two crates myself, sittin' there."

Jerrold's fists slowly relaxed at his sides. Perhaps everything was working out in spite of what had happened to Lash. Still...However, there was no more time to consider checking further. A knock at the door signaled that the ceremony was about to begin. He turned to his employee.

"Get back to the warehouse and have the crates inspected. I want the contents verified. When that's done, report to me here. Do you understand?"

The man nodded, then went out a side door. Jerrold

turned to leave by the other door. Of course everything had gone as planned, he told himself. Lash had merely taken it upon himself to do a little celebrating after the success of the raid.

And yet, even as he stepped from the room and walked the short distance to the door that opened near the altar, he felt a prickling of uncertainty along his nerve endings.

At the back of the church, Elyse tried to smile as she took Cedric's arm. He'd been both father and grandfather to her for as long as she could remember. It was only right he should stand at her side now. Her hand was ice cold, her fingers trembling as he placed his large hand over hers.

"Ready, my dear?" He gazed down at her quizzically, perhaps sensing some of her own uncertainty.

Elyse nodded and smiled, though her face was pale and drawn.

Lucy followed behind as they walked down the long aisle, passing row upon row of guests, friends, and acquaintances and relatives turning discreetly, to catch a glimpse of the bride.

Elyse saw her grandmother amidst the sea of faces and focused on that one beloved face and forced herself to be strong.

She felt the faint pressure of Ceddy's hand and looked up. They'd reached the end of the aisle. Jerrold was waiting for her. Ceddy inclined his head faintly as he extended her hand to Jerrold's.

She looked for a smile, something in Jerrold's eyes, a look or a glance. Anything to show even the slightest affection. She saw only a momentary flash of disapproval as his gaze fell on the sapphire and diamond pendant she'd chosen to wear instead of his choice for her.

Nothing was ever good enough. It angered her,

causing vivid color to spread across her cheeks in what would undoubtedly be mistaken for bridal radiance.

It should have been different. Her gaze met his and she immediately looked away, not wanting him to see her true feelings. How had she become so certain of them so late?

It wasn't a matter of knowing what she wanted, but what she didn't want. But now it was too late. What could she do? Turn around and inform everyone present that it was all a mistake? Laugh it off as a foolish charade?

I can't do this, she thought. *I don't love him!* She wanted to scream it at the top of her lungs.

She thought of her grandmother and everyone who had campaigned for this marriage, the perfect match several had told her.

Everything swam before her as the Anglican priest's words droned on and on, intoning the ancient rite that would join her to this man forever.

Forever! the word screamed at her.

She couldn't breathe.

It was as if a great weight were pressing down on her. All feeling seemed to seep out of her. She wanted to make it all stop.

Zach watched from where he stood, for a moment caught by the solemnity of the marriage ceremony. Then his gaze fastened on Elyse. She was so beautiful, he thought. Her gown was pale blue, tightly cut across the bodice and slender waist before falling into a slender skirt. The sleeves were tight fitting to the wrist, the neckline cut low across the swell of her breasts.

This is what she apparently wanted, he thought. But even as he felt anger over her obvious scheming to be Lady Barrington, he couldn't suppress his surprise at the simple but elegant diamond and pearl pendant she wore and wondered at the reason she had chosen it.

The church was softly lit by row upon row of candles, and a dozen more set before the altar that was draped with a crimson tapestry embossed with the sign of the cross.

The priest's words echoed off stone walls as light shimmered throughout in colorful reflection from the stained-glass panel behind the altar. Then, all eyes focused on the somber beauty of the bride.

Behind the altar, all was steeped in shadows. She glimpsed the robed figure emerge from the left of the altar, bearing the rings that were to be blessed. It will soon be over, Elyse thought, yet briefly wondered why the man had the hood pulled low over his face. Just as quickly, it was forgotten. She heard the priest call for the rings a second time and looked up as candlelight from the altar glinted off the long, curved blade pulled from beneath the heavy robe. It slashed through the air, but she was too stunned to move.

She heard Lucy's startled gasp. Beside her, Jerrold muttered a curse, "What the devil?"

The figure moved toward them, and a hand closed over her wrist. Before she could think, before she could react, she was pulled past the startled priest, then pulled back against the heavily muscled chest of the man beneath the robe. With his other hand, her assailant pressed the blade against her throat.

"No one moves!"

Finally recovering from the intrusion, Jerrold took a step forward as if he meant to pursue the man. "Let her go."

"One step further, Barrington." At the warning, the blade was pressed more firmly against Elyse's throat.

She could feel the faint sting of the blade pressed into her flesh. But whoever this man was, if he intended to kill her, he would already have done so.

"Please," the priest implored with outstretched hands. "Let her go. Surely you can't mean to harm her."

Zach hesitated. Yes, he thought, it would be the perfect revenge against Barrington. He turned the blade on the priest.

"Please, continue," he ordered.

The priest was confused. "I don't understand...?"

He immediately ceased protesting when the blade returned to Elyse's throat.

"Finish the ceremony, but... with one small change. I will take Lord Barrington's place."

Elyse heard her grandmother's stunned response, along with that of others who had gathered.

"Do it, now!"

"I cannot." The priest stuttered. "What you ask is sacrilege."

"Listen to me, priest," Zach warned. "I don't give a damn for your rules. She's coming with me, and neither you nor anyone else can prevent it. If you're so concerned with honor, consider hers once I take her from here."

"It would be a sin in the eyes of the church, a bride abducted and forced..." The priest was incredulous, but prevented from making further protest.

Zach waved the sword at the priest. "Do it, now!" he repeated. "Or she will die."

The priest's hands trembled. "This is madness!" he whispered brokenly. "May God have mercy on your soul for what you do."

"No!" Jerrold told the priest. "You will not do this!" He lunged forward, then abruptly halted, his eyes fastened on the blade pressed against Elyse's throat.

"If you do this," Jerrold threatened, "there is no place on Earth where you will be safe!" he choked out. "I will hunt you down and see you hanged for this!"

Undaunted, Zach told the priest, "Continue."

Within seconds it was done, the priest ending the marriage rites begun such a short time before.

Elyse had whispered a faint 'yes', the blade held against her neck. Her captor had given his assent, and the final words were spoken. She thought that she recognized his voice. Was it possible?

This couldn't be happening! It wasn't real, she thought.

Zach motioned with the blade. "Everyone, stand away! And don't be foolish enough to attempt to follow."

She was pulled back and tripped on the hem of her gown. She expected to feel the blade press more painfully against her neck. Instead, his arm tightened around her, preventing the fall.

Hope flickered as she was pulled through the darkened hallway that led from the altar, that her captor might release her as the sound of someone running came from behind them. It was Andrew Maitland.

"Good God, man! Whoever you are, let her go! Then leave and be done with this!"

Her assailant raised his head briefly and tossed a folded note at his feet. Then Elyse was picked up and thrown over her captor's shoulder as a half-dozen others rushed after them.

She couldn't see anything in the darkened hallway. She wanted to scream, but it was impossible with his shoulder pressed against her ribs. Then he suddenly stopped and grabbed her by the arm, pulling her behind him.

She stumbled on the flagstones underfoot and almost fell, only to be hauled back to her feet as she was pulled through an archway, a door creaking shut behind them.

She struggled, she fought, she clawed at those hands that seemed to be everywhere, then half-fell down a short flight of wooden steps, gasping as her knee was bruised on the bottom step. Then she was dragged around a corner and flattened against a wall, stones in the wall poking painfully into her back as she was pinned by the muscular body clothed in a priest's robes.

A warm hand smothered any sound she might have made. She was hopelessly trapped by a deranged maniac who seemed to be taking great pleasure in the close contact of their bodies.

Voices came from the passage, then just as quickly passed by. Elyse slumped back against the wall as the voices receded.

Gathering her strength, Elyse turned and thrust a hand against her captor's chest, momentarily freeing herself. With one hand, Elyse slashed at his shadowed face, her nails removing a fair amount of skin. Her wrist was immediately seized by a strong hand.

There would be only one chance as she took a deep breath. The scream died in her throat as his other hand closed over her mouth.

His hand came away from her mouth as he struggled to capture her wrists.

She could vaguely make out the shapes of barrels and boxes in the small chamber. It was a storeroom at the back of the church.

The monk's hood fell back, and Elyse stared up into a face now shadowed only by the single patch that covered one eye. Golden hair fell, unkempt, about his head. The planes of his face were sharply etched by shadows and an unreadable expression. Then the expression on his face shifted dangerously, his mouth curving in a mocking smile that revealed a flash of white teeth.

"What have you done?" Elyse choked out. But before she could say more, his head came down, his mouth bruising hers to silence.

"Damn you!" he hissed, jerking away from her. His lip bled where she'd bit him.

Fingers tightened on her wrists as he jerked her arms high over her head, pinning them to the wall.

"Let me go!" Elyse seethed. "Just what do you think you're doing!"

Holding both of her wrists with one hand, Zach wiped the trickle of blood from his lip. His gaze locked with hers.

"Exactly as I please," he informed her, his fingers bruising her chin as he jerked her face up.

His mouth crushed down on hers, his lips forcing hers apart, his tongue plunging between. He lowered one hand to her waist. Then his fingers pressed through the layers of fabric until they dug into the curve of her bottom. This too was an assault but of a different kind.

Elyse felt as if she were drowning. What was happening? What was St. James doing here? Why had he abducted her and why had he insisted on that ridiculous ceremony?

There were more questions, but no answers as his body pressed hers against the wall, her hands imprisoned by his. Confused and shaken, betrayed by her own body, Elyse she gasped as the kiss abruptly ended.

"I'm certain it would be far more enjoyable staying here with you all afternoon, Miss Winslow. But we must be going."

Going? Where? Her protest was quickly muffled beneath his hand.

"Lovely, lovely Elyse. You wanted so much to be Lady Barrington. Sorry to rob you of that moment, but if Barrington is the fool I think he is, he may still want you when I've finished with you." He momentarily released her wrists.

Confusion filled Elyse's eyes. What was he talking about? Surely he didn't mean to hold her to that farce of a ceremony.

"You make a lovely bride, but this will only slow us down." He seized the bodice of her gown and tore it from her, leaving her clad only in the thin silk chemise.

Elyse's confusion gave way to humiliation, then anger, and she managed to call him several names.

"Such language for a lady," he said mockingly. "You must do something about it." Then, added, "But you may be quite right. And if Barrington is half the man I think he is, he'll come after you. And that is exactly what I want."

Now she felt the fear. It spread, cold, across her skin. Why was he abducting her? Where would he take her? Then she thought of her grandmother. What must she think?

Dear God! Let this be a nightmare and she would awaken from it all. But it was frighteningly real. When she tried to reason with him, his hand across her mouth was replaced by a cloth stuffed into her mouth. Then she was plunged into complete darkness as a thick blanket was drawn over her head and shoulders. A grain sack! Then she was lifted, flung over his shoulder once more, and carried.

"Nothing? What do you mean you found nothing? They must still be in the church! I want her found and found now!" Jerrold stormed about the small anteroom where those closest to the bride and groom had gathered with the priest.

Cedric squeezed Regina's hand reassuringly "This is getting us nowhere. We've searched every passage, room, and chamber in this church. She's not here. I think we would do better to notify the authorities."

"Ceddy is right." Lady Regina slowly came to her feet. "While you're standing here ranting and raving, that lunatic has fled with my granddaughter. Something must be done now!" She turned to the stricken priest.

"There is no point in keeping the guests here any longer. There will be no wedding today."

"I think there has already been a wedding," Lucy Maitland observed.

"What do you mean, there's already been a wedding?" Jerrold turned on her. "That ridiculous little charade is completely meaningless." He turned to the priest for confirmation.

"Tell them."

The priest shook his head. "I'm afraid I can't."

"What are you talking about?" Jerrold demanded. "Elyse was forced to participate in that charade. Everyone saw that."

"Everyone saw a wedding ceremony, performed by a priest. It appeared that Miss Winslow was reluctant and yet..."

"Damn you! What do you mean by that?" Jerrold leaned threateningly toward the priest.

Lord Charles stepped between his son and the priest. "You go beyond yourself. You would do well to remember where we are." He then turned and apologized to the priest for Jerrold's outburst.

"Under the circumstances, it is understandable. But the truth is the ceremony is binding," the priest acknowledged. "If you will allow me to explain," he continued, "the ceremony is binding. But if one of the parties should petition for annulment, the marriage could be set aside. But there is the matter of intent... " His voice was heavy with regret.

"Intent? What the devil do you mean by that?" Jerrold's voice was filled with cold rage.

"If the man who abducted Miss Winslow is determined to carry out this marriage, then it may prove harmful to her to pursue annulment."

"You can't mean..." Jerrold was furious. "I'll take care of this myself."

"I think you should read this," Andrew Maitland handed Jerrold the note he'd been given him by the man who had abducted Elyse.

"What the devil are you talking about?" Jerrold snapped. "What is it?"

He unfolded the note and scanned the contents:

There is a special place in hell for thieves and murderers
—the Raven

His face went ashen then flushed red. "What the devil is this supposed to mean?"

"It was left by the man who took Elyse," Andrew told him.

Before he reached the chapel doors, a hesitant voice called out. Jerrold whirled around.

"Mr. Hodge! What the devil are you doing here?"

"Sorry, sir, but I thought you would want to know. It seemed important to you before, and I did try to follow your instructions."

"Good God, man! Speak up and be quick about it."

"It's the gold, sir," he whispered.

"It will have to wait."

"Beggin' yer pardon, sir. That fellow came for payment."

"What fellow?" Jerrold crossed the room and pulled his man aside.

"The man you told me might come by," Hodge explained, twisting his cap in his hands.

"And, of course, you handled it just as I instructed," Jerrold replied.

The man nodded. "I tried, sir."

"Tried?" Jerrold seized Hodge by the front of his coat and pulled him out into the hallway beyond the anteroom. "What are you talking about?"

"He came for payment, just like you said he would..."

"And?"

"He forced me to sign the draft, then go to the bank with him to transfer the money."

Jerrold's response exploded. His grip on the man's coat tightened. He longed to feel bones snap, but he felt a restraining hand on his arm and looked into Lord Charles' face.

"Get a hold on yourself," his father told him.

"Tell me! All of it," Jerrold demanded.

"I had to do it," Hodge replied. "He brought along the foreman from the Argosy Company. Right there in the office, he proved Argosy had received the shipment, then he threatened to bring in the authorities.

"What else could I do? I knew you didn't want anyone knowing about the gold," Hodge added.

Jerrold thrust him away. St. James had made off with his gold and his money, and with that note it was obvious that he'd also abducted Elyse. St. James was the Raven.

~

After leaving the church, Zach carried her to the waiting horses. A cart or wagon would have been more comfortable for her, but they needed to leave quickly before Barrington put out the alarm.

He checked the rope that bound her, then eased her across the saddle, and swung up behind her. Instead of heading for the east end of London and the docks as Barrington would assume, he turned south. There was a long ride ahead.

It was just after dark when Zach reined in at a roadside inn. He paid the man for a room, then pulled Elyse from the back of his horse.

She thrashed and squirmed as he carried her up the stairs. If the innkeeper thought anything of it, he said nothing and returned to his own bed with a good amount of coin in his pocket.

Once inside the room, Zach tossed Elyse down onto the bed. He loosened the rope that bound her. She fought and struggled, then tumbled to the floor. He knelt beside her and eased the cloth from her mouth.

"Bastard!" she screamed at the top of her lungs.

"Possibly, but that won't help you," he told her.

She was completely disheveled, her hair tangled, and furious. Considering the long ride they'd made, he was impressed even as he put the gag back into her mouth.

She continued to fight him, kicking out with her legs, and thrashing wildly about, her head connecting with the leg of the bed with a faint crack. Everything went dark.

Zach removed the gag. When she didn't stir or so much as open an eye, he made her as comfortable as possible on the bed, then gently probed the bruise on her head. For the first time since that last night at Fair View, he allowed himself to look at her, really look at her.

She was beautiful and, try as he might to hold on to it, the anger slipped away. He stroked her cheek and smoothed back her hair that had come loose when she'd struggled at the church.

She was clad only in a chemise, her slender body curled under the blanket. There was regret as he bound both her wrists to a bedpost and slipped the scarf back over her mouth. Then he stretched out beside her.

If only things were different, he thought.

It was still dark when he slipped out of the room and wakened the innkeeper, and learned they were still some distance from Dover. The innkeeper wrapped food for the rest of the ride and was well paid.

Elyse had wakened when he returned. She stared at him with a wary expression. He untied her ankles, leaving the rope around her wrists, then walked her down the hall to the water closet that was nothing more than a small room with a hole in the floor, a bucket with fresh water and a cloth. He held onto the rope while she took care of necessary things, the wariness in her eyes now a glare of anger.

She'd been abducted, bound and gagged, thrown over the back of a horse for hours, then tied to a bed God knows where, and now the insult of being held at the end of a rope while she relieved herself. If she wasn't still bound and gagged, she would have seized the bucket and hit him with it.

Back inside the room, he removed the gag so that she could eat and have a drink of water.

"If you cry out, the cloth goes back inside your mouth," he bluntly told her." Not that the innkeeper would pay much attention. I suspect this isn't the first time he's seen this sort of thing."

She glared at him as she downed a biscuit and hard cooked eggs, then drank water. Her throat was raw from the past hours with the cloth in her mouth. "I hate you," she whispered.

"You're entitled to that," he told her.

"Whatever you hope to accomplish..." she drank more water. "You will fail."

"That is always a risk, but I'm willing to take it."

"Why?" she croaked.

"An old score to settle," he replied as he gently probed the bump on her head. She was going to have a good bruise there. She pulled back as if she'd been struck—the look in her eyes went straight through him.

"What old score?" she demanded. "What can you hope to achieve?"

He answered with just one word. "Revenge."

She fought him again when he slipped the gag back into place.

"I'm sorry," he told her, but it was time to leave. Her eyes filled with anger.

. . .

Zach knew that everything afloat in London harbor would have been searched by now. Barrington would realize he'd chosen another route, or would think he still remained in London, possibly to ask for ransom. But he was clever and with the *Revenge* no longer in London, it was possible that he would figure out that he'd gone to Dover.

They'd been on the road several hours as a breeze stirred. They'd made better time than the night before, with him leading the second horse with Elyse astride, wrapped in the blanket and bound to keep her from falling or trying to run off.

The midday sun rose over the headland that jutted out into the channel, and he pulled the horses to a stop. In the cove below, the *Revenge* rode the gentle swells of a restless tide. Glancing at the small stretch of beach, he saw a longboat and guided the horses down the path alongside the sea wall.

He dismounted, then helped her down as Sandy and Tris beached the longboat and ran toward them.

"We thought you might not make it, Cap'n." Sandy fixed a narrow gaze on him. "We heard that was quite a wedding you attended."

Zach nodded. So word had already reached Dover. "What else did you hear?"

"Seein's how it's goin' to be a long voyage home, I let some of the crew stay in the village last night. We got word just a little while ago that Barrington is apparently sendin' search parties to every port up and down the coastline." Sandy looked over at Elyse, wrapped in the blanket with the gag at her mouth.

"You wouldn't know anything about that now?" Sandy asked.

"Not a thing," Zach replied. "See that our passenger gets aboard. And be careful." He winked at his second mate. "I wouldn't want her bruised any more than she already is."

"Aye, aye, Cap'n." Sandy saluted as he carefully carried Elyse to the rowboat. Zach removed saddle and bridle from both horses and turned them loose. He then turned to Tris.

"Is Tobias aboard?"

"Yes sir, and he's none too happy."

Zach nodded. "I expect he's not."

His gaze scanned the ocean. Sandy signaled from the longboat as they approached the ship. The tide was fast turning. Shading his gaze against the rising sun, he scanned the *Revenge*. She looked like a proud, powerful bird, her wings slowly expanding, ready to take flight.

"When we get aboard, set our course south by southeast with the wind. And run up the Portuguese colors."

"Lisbon, sir?"

"Lisbon." Zach nodded. "There's a man I want to see about some gold."

Fifteen

"No mercy! Lash 'em to the yardarm!"

Elyse groaned as she slowly awakened, the words jarring through her.

"Keel haul the bloody swine!" was followed by a string of colorful curses.

It had to be part of a nightmare. And yet, as the words pushed their way through the haze, she had a nagging suspicion it wasn't.

Her throat was so dry it was paralyzed, and something was bound across her mouth. Coming more fully awake, Elyse jerked her head to the side, and immediately winced.

It seemed as if every muscle ached.

"Lash 'em to the yardarm!" The screech helped her focus despite the pain. She felt as if she had been lashed to a yardarm and left for days. She forced herself to relax. Whoever had been shouting had stopped.

It's all right, she told herself. It's just a bad dream. In a few minutes you'll wake up and it will be over.

It didn't work.

She tried moving her arms, but her wrists were bound together. Good heavens! Where was she? She rolled onto her back. Staring overhead, she tried to make out shapes in the meager light, but everything blurred into soft gray. A thin sliver of light a few feet away and down low caught her attention. The light came from beneath a door!

She tried to swallow; her throat was so dry. Trying to sit up, Elyse felt the restraint of the rope across her shoulders. She was tied to the bed! She twisted and turned as much as the ropes would allow, then fell back.

As she breathed in slowly, her senses sharpened. St. James had been the one in the shadows at the church. That phony ceremony, being abducted at knife point! Where had he taken her? And why?

Please, let this all be a bad dream, she thought, but instinctively knew that it wasn't.

Then she felt the slow, back and forth roll of the bed beneath her and the room. And the faint sound of water. She was on a ship!

"You can't just leave her in there!" Tobias argued, in spite of the glare that could have cut a man's head in two. "It's been hours since we left Dover. Has she eaten anything in all that time? And what about water?"

"She's all right!" Zach closed the ship's log on the desk. "Tris made certain the ropes weren't too tight. At any rate she's still asleep. Tris checked on her a few hours ago."

"A few hours? For God's sake, man, what are you tryin' to do to the girl?"

"I think you underestimate Miss Winslow," Zach replied. "At any rate, it's none of your concern! Leave it be!" He hadn't slept. He was weary of arguing, but Tobias wasn't about to let the matter rest.

"As this ship's doctor, I demand she be well treated well! That doesn't include being tied and gagged. Where the devil would she go?"

Zach saw the determined expression on his old friend's face.

"I'll have the ropes removed. She'll be given everything she needs to make her comfortable. It was never my intention to mistreat her."

"Is that so? What about bringin' her here? I'm certain you just didn't walk into that church and extend a formal invitation for an ocean voyage. And I'm equally certain if you had, she would have refused!"

"Enough!" Zach's fist came down on the desk.

Undaunted, Tobias tried another direction. "What are you going to tell her about all this?"

"As little as possible. I think it's better that way."

Tobias stared hard at him. "Is that all there is to it?"

Zach's head came up. "That's all. There are things that you don't know. She's aboard this ship and confined to her cabin until I say otherwise. It's safer for everyone."

"You'll have to talk to her sooner or later," Tobias argued. "She doesn't strike me as the type to calmly accept bein' shut up in that cabin. She's undoubtedly goin' to have a lot of questions and she deserves answers."

"I'll take care of it when the time comes." Zach put him off, at the same time knowing full well he was only delaying the inevitable. He couldn't very well keep her bound and gagged for the entire voyage to New South Wales.

Tobias frowned. "Have it your way. But you need to know I don't agree with any of this."

"I intend to have it my way. I am captain of this ship," Zach reminded him.

"Aye." Tobias nodded thoughtfully. "Now, I think you'd better tell me what you found out."

Something had happened when Zach was at the Barrington estate, and he meant to know what it was. He didn't understand the change in his young friend. And what part did the girl play in all this? Why was

Zach goading Jerrold Barrington into a confrontation he probably wouldn't survive.

"It's about your father, isn't it?" Tobias speculated. "It has to do with whatever you found out about him and Felicia Barrington."

Zach rolled his head back wearily, his eyes closed. Then laughter rumbled deep in his chest. It was mad, insane. Hadn't Elyse said that in the church? He came out of the chair, slowly pacing the cabin, laughter rolling out of him until his shoulders shook, leaving him weak, unable to talk. He'd come to England for the truth. Well, by God, now he had it.

He came up against the far wall of the cabin and braced his hands on either side of the open porthole. Tobias had a right to know. Slowly, he told him what he knew—a story of half-brothers, a story of greed and betrayal that led to murder, the trial that followed, and the lives that were destroyed. And he told him about Felicia Seymour the beautiful, innocent pawn of one man's hatred against his own brother.

When he again looked at Tobias, the anger had won. It was there in the hardened line of his mouth, the coldness of eyes, void of anything except the burning light for revenge.

"Alexander Nicholas Barrington was my father."

Tobias shook his head. "I can't believe it!"

All at once he felt old, very old. He rubbed his fingers against his forehead. "All those years I knew yer father, and not a word. Not one! There was only that one letter from her." Tobias sat back heavily in the chair.

"I need a drink." Zach stood, staring out the open porthole. Rolling waves spread away to the disappearing coastline in the afternoon sunlight. He frowned slightly at the sight of dark clouds on the horizon. Then he came away from the porthole.

He was tired. His body screamed for sleep, but his

mind refused it. He wished a drink were all it would take to wipe his mind blank. Then maybe he could sleep.

Tobias reached for the bottle between them. He held it poised over the tumbler and hesitated. Without warning, he came out of the chair with the energy of a man half his age and hurled the bottle against the far wall, the best brandy that could be stolen or bought running down the side wall of the ship.

"You're mad! You know that, don't you?" He turned on Zach. "Bringin' her aboard will see us all hanged! What in God's name were you thinkin'?"

In all the years he'd known Tobias, Zach couldn't remember seeing him quite so angry, drunk or sober. "This will bring the Crown down on us. Barrington will come at you with everything he has."

Without so much as drawing a breath, Tobias continued his tirade, jabbing the air as if he were striking at somebody or would like to. Zach had no doubt as to the target.

"Suicide! Plain and simple. That's what it'll be. Don't you know that Barrington has ships and men in damned near every port? He controls everything. He gets things done with just the snap of a finger." Red-faced, he then turned on Zach and leaned against the edge of the desk, bracing his weight on white-knuckled hands.

"Where can you hide?" he shouted.

"I don't intend to hide. I want him to find me."

Tobias stared, dumbfounded. He was quickly finding out he didn't know Zach Tennant at all. He had once, when they'd begun this voyage. Could the man have changed so much?

Zach's voice was low, deathly quiet. "He has to be stopped."

"And you're using that girl for your revenge," Tobias accused.

"Yes!" Zach bit off. "Charles murdered their father,

but Alex paid the price!" He came crossed the cabin. "He paid with his life, with everything he valued. Exiled, a criminal sent to Australia! Made to pay for a crime he didn't commit. But even that wasn't enough for Charles Barrington. He had to have *her*."

Felicia Seymour.

"She was nothing but a possession to him." Zach was losing control. He could sense it but couldn't stop it. He stood, hands gripping the desk. "He took her just as he took everything else. She didn't love him! He knew it, but it didn't matter. And, in the end, he destroyed her too."

"And now you want revenge, no matter who it hurts," Tobias finished for him.

Zach never looked at him. "Someone has to pay for what they did to him."

"Well, I won't be part of it," Tobias announced. "That girl is innocent. She had nothing to do with this, and I won't be part of your scheme. Neither would your father if he were alive." Tobias turned toward the cabinet. Opening it, he seized a bottle of brandy and tucked it beneath his arm.

"I'm going to get drunk, very drunk. And I hope like hell you've come to your senses when I'm sober again."

The cabin door slammed hard as Tobias left. In frustration, Zach doubled his fist and drove it against the cabin wall. He welcomed the pain.

Then he dropped his hands to his sides. Tobias was right. For hours he'd refused to go near the cabin just across from his, unwilling to face her and confront what he'd done. He'd used one excuse after another.

Coming away from the wall, he seized the key from his desk and crossed the companionway. Key in the lock, he hesitated. Then, thinking better of this move, he called down the companionway for Tris.

Elyse worked the rope binding her wrists to the sideboard of the bed. Then, she laid back as she tried to breathe around the gag that cut into her mouth. The motion of the ship had changed. Locked in the cabin, she still sensed they'd encountered stronger waves. That could only mean they must have put to sea.

She thought of her grandmother and Cedric. Dear God, what must they all think? Her grandmother was a strong woman, but she'd already suffered the loss of a husband, a son, and Elyse's mother.

Tears of frustration streamed down her cheeks. She remembered how happy Regina had seemed on the ride to the church.

The ceremony at the church! Elyse thought of Lucy Maitland. She could almost imagine Lucy might have had something to do with all of this. She'd been so opposed to her marriage to Jerrold. But Elyse had to admit, even Lucy wasn't capable of so elaborate a scheme.

Her thoughts were scattered. How long had she been in that cabin? How long since they were at sea? What was St. James going to do with her? She stared at the single lamp that swung overhead as the sound came again. A key in the lock?

The door swung open, and a tall man was briefly illuminated in the doorway. Then he turned toward the narrow bed. Elyse instinctively shrank back into the shadows.

He leaned over her briefly, his large hands scraping against her skin as he untied the ropes. She was too stunned at the sudden freedom to pull away from the heavy odor of sweat and salt sea air about him.

Trying to rub feeling back into her wrists, Elyse cautiously sat up. Clad only in the thin, silk chemise she grabbed for the coarse woolen blanket and clutched it against her.

"Get out of here!" she ordered indignantly. Then as the man turned, seemingly to follow her request, she came up off the bed.

"Wait!"

Elyse wrapped the blanket around her. It would do her no good if the man left. Who could know how long it might be before someone returned? If anyone did... And she wanted some answers.

"Where is St. James?" she demanded, bravely tilting up her chin. "I demand to see him at once."

The man turned slowly, his dark eyes watching her speculatively with no small amount of confusion. "Who?"

Elyse shifted uncomfortably. "Sir William St. James." If that even was his name, she thought.

"He brought me here," she added.

The man's gaze slipped over her, head to toe. "Captain Tennant is captain of the *Revenge*."

"*Revenge?*" Elyse repeated slowly. Her gaze fastened on the man's unreadable expression.

"Very well. I want to see the captain."

"No."

"I demand to see the captain."

"The captain will send for you when he wants to see you." He gestured to the tray and the wrapped bundle he'd set on the table.

"You have water, food, and clothes."

That was all. Water, food, clothing, and no answers. She crossed the small space separating them, the blanket wrapped around her body.

Seizing the wrapped bundle, she threw it across the cabin. Then she seized the pitcher of water he'd brought with the tray of food. It crashed against the far wall. Then she picked up the tray of food.

Zach heard the curses in an angry feminine voice, then the crash of dishes, followed by more curses. Only this time they were different as Tris emerged from the cabin across the companionway as if he'd been shot out of a cannon. He turned, meeting his captain's questioning gaze.

Emerging from the far end of the passageway, Tobias stared at Tris, who was plastered, head to foot, with what looked like the evening meal.

Another crash was heard, quickly followed by another. The curses were muffled but nonetheless distinct. All three men were treated to a very colorful tirade.

"Sir, I..." Tris tried to explain, but he winced and stepped away from the door as something hit it from inside.

"That does it!" Zach said coming down the companionway. "Stand aside!"

"This should be most interesting." Tobias nodded to Tris as the man squeezed by him to head toward the crew's quarters in search of clean clothes.

"I demand to see your captain!" Elyse shouted. "I won't be kept prisoner any longer! Do you hear me!"

She whirled around at the sound of the door to the cabin being opened.

"You!" she gasped incredulously. Then, as realization set in, she took deadly aim with the supper tray.

" Stop this, now!"

Zach was across the cabin, his fingers closing over her wrist.

"Stop it!" he warned. "I can break it with one simple twist."

Elyse slowly recovered from her first shock as she stared at William St. James.

"This is your ship?"

"My ship!" Zach replied. "And I don't particularly want it broken to pieces in the middle of the ocean."

She was stunned then livid with anger. "Damn you!" She lashed out. "It was you all along!"

"Yes! Now if you'll just behave yourself."

"Behave?" She was furious.

My God, the man must be mad, she thought. Without thinking, she doubled her fist and punched him as hard as she could.

Surprised by the blow, Zach immediately released her, his hand going to his bruised eye.

She lunged past him and out into the companionway. Not wasting a moment, she scrambled up the ladder to the top deck.

He reached the companionway just in time to see her bare feet disappearing over the top rung of the ladder.

"Why didn't you stop her?" he yelled at Tobias.

"How?" Tobias snapped. "I don't have a rope," he added sarcastically.

Zach vaulted up the ladder. Rain pelted him through the open hatch. It blew across the ship in great billowing gusts, making the decks slick and dangerous.

Water ran over the deck as the bow dipped through the next wave, then spilled down the open hatch. He saw Sandy at the wheel, shouted, then turned in the direction his second mate indicated.

Elyse stumbled along the deck, rain plastering the chemise to her body, wind whipping at the blanket.

She was only a few feet away, but on the rolling deck of a ship that seemed like miles. Zach lunged after her. If she lost her footing, she might easily be swept overboard with the next wave.

She heard her name, then the wind whipped it away. She turned and saw him coming after her. She wanted to run, to get away from him. But the wind and rain lashed at her, stinging painfully, making it impossible to see.

A strong hand closed around her arm. She clawed at his hand, trying desperately to break his hold.

Zach pulled her against him, the blanket gone, her hair streaming down her back.

She collapsed against him. He grabbed the line at the center mast, his other arm encircling her waist. There was nothing gentle in him as he pushed them both toward the open hatch. His fingers bit into her arms as he almost threw her down the opening.

She grabbed at the top rung of the ladder and made her way down slowly, her hands cold and clumsy, her arms shaking.

Zach shouted to Sandy, saw his mate's thumbs-up sign, then climbed down after her, slamming the hatch into place. He stepped down into the companionway and turned on Elyse. She was soaked to the skin, water puddling at her feet. Bruised from being battered about, she was in no mood for his anger.

At that moment, Zach was too furious to speak, but the expression in those gray eyes could have turned the water she was standing in to ice. He looked first to Tobias, then to Tris and the half-dozen other men staring at them from the crew quarters, who were now on their way topside.

"I don't remember this being a pleasure cruise," he snapped. "All of you have something to do."

Every man except Tobias immediately went about his business. Tris headed for the galley. The others scrambled toward the ladder.

"Well?" Zach turned to Tobias.

The older man was certainly not the toughest sailor aboard, yet he seemed completely unaffected by Zach's temper. His eyes narrowed as he looked from Zach to Elyse.

"I'll be interested to see who wins this round. If you need any help, just give a shout." He turned back to his own cabin.

Zach's hand closed around Elyse's wrist as he pulled her down the companionway. He stopped at the door to her cabin. It was a shambles. Food was plastered on the near wall. Pieces of glass and the metal tray littered the floor.

He pulled her in the opposite direction, kicking open the door to his own cabin, and thrust her inside.

Slamming the door behind them, he turned on her. "I'm captain of this ship. My orders will be obeyed and that includes you!"

Tears of anger slipped down her wet cheeks. "Why have you brought me here?"

He was angry, tired, and she'd just scared the hell out of him. Zach grabbed her by the shoulders. "If you ever try anything like that again..."

Whatever she'd planned to say was cut off.

"You little fool! Don't you realize you could've been killed!"

"A lot you would care. You abducted me, kept me bound and gagged, then dragged me here on the back of a horse."

"It was necessary!"

"Necessary? For whom? You? And who are you?" Water dripped off her, creating an expanding puddle at her feet. She silently dared him to come closer. She'd like to blacken his other eye.

"That's of no importance to you!" Water dripped from his hair. He wiped at it angrily.

"No importance?" The absolute nerve of the man! Anger goading her beyond all caution, she pulled back her arm. Her clenched fist shot out and was easily caught.

"I'm in no mood for games," he said coldly.

"Games?"

"No mercy! Keel haul the bloody bastard!" From somewhere down the companionway, the voice she'd heard earlier screeched above the storm. She went white at those words. Her teeth had begun to chatter violently, but not from the cold.

"I suppose you're going to torture me." Her voice was strained as the screeching continued.

He turned from her. "Damned if that isn't what you deserve. But Sebastian doesn't give the orders around here. I do." Going to the chest of drawers along the side wall, he took out a towel and threw it at her.

"Sebastian?" What sort of character he might be, she wondered. Undoubtedly another pirate.

"He's a bird, and a damned bossy one at that. I may just decide to have him served up for supper one of these nights. Now, get out of that wet thing yer wearing and dry yourself off. I won't have you catching your death of cold simply because you were foolish enough to go up on deck in the middle of a storm."

She caught the towel, her eyes narrowing, and threw it back at him.

He whirled on her, patience gone. There was something dangerous in his voice that warned she may have pushed him too far. She refused to cower or back down.

Zach should have known better. But he was tired, and angry. He saw her stubbornness as defiance, pure and simple. He crossed the cabin and with a single move, separated the fabric of the chemise that had clung to her like a second skin.

Shock, and then anger came. First her wedding gown, now this. She couldn't run, and she couldn't hide. She wrapped her arms about her to hide her nakedness, anger burning through her.

Her defiance was like sand in a wound. Zach pulled her against him, his gray gaze meeting brilliant blue as he stripped away the last of the clinging silk. Seizing the discarded towel, he bent down, roughly rubbing her bare legs dry. It was practically his undoing.

Swearing, Zach came to his feet and threw the towel into the far corner. His angry gaze bore into her. Then he turned and pulled a dry shirt from the drawer. When he turned back, the sight of her completely naked, dripping wet and shaking, sent everything spiraling out of control.

She stood there proud and angry, her arms crossed

over her breasts, vivid color on her pale cheeks. But she didn't pull away or try to hide from him.

'I hate you!'

She wanted to say it, but couldn't, her throat aching as he walked toward her and she felt herself being pulled into that gray gaze, the anger slipping away no matter how hard she tried to hold onto it.

'Touch me', the words whispered between them.

Had she said it, or had he? She didn't know, as his fingers gently brushed her cheek, and his lips brushed hers.

Her hands closed around the front of his shirt, holding on, eyes closed, as the warmth, the taste, moved through her, taking away the anger, taking her away to another place, another night...

Who was she, Zach thought again? Why did he want her again, with an ache so deep and so painful that he could hardly breathe. He tasted the wind and the rain on her lips, and something that waited in the shadows of his mind, something that pulled at him, like a deep hunger that would always want more, like the air he breathed.

"Lys." A name out of the past...

He stepped away from her and wrapped the shirt around her.

"It's several hours before daybreak," he told her. "It's safer if you stay below deck."

Then he was gone.

Sixteen

Zach rose before first light. He'd spent the remainder of the night in the crew's quarters after making certain that all was well with the ship.

He slipped into the galley and grabbed a cup of hot coffee. It burned into his stomach, steadying, fortifying. He nodded to Sandy.

"How did we fare?"

"She took the storm real good. I've got Jalew topside at the wheel. We were only a few degrees off course when the storm cleared. I made the adjustments and we've more than made up for the lost time."

"Good. When do you think we'll make Lisbon?"

Sandy shrugged. "Late tomorrow, if the wind holds. I went ahead and posted extra men at the watch, just in case." He stood, shrugging off the fatigue of a long night.

"I was just headed topside to relieve Jalew. He's been on for a couple hours now."

Zach drained the cup. He knew the "*just in case*" referred to El Barracuda, Juan de la Vasquez Vimeiro. A Spaniard by birth, he'd turned pirate several years ago and now considered the waters of Spain his private hunting ground. Lisbon was quite a ways north of his usual territory, but they'd heard rumors he'd attacked merchant ships as far west as the Gulf of Cadiz. And with a cargo hold full of gold aboard *Revenge*, Zach couldn't risk an encounter.

"Get some sleep. I'll take over." He turned toward the companionway, practically colliding with Tobias. His friend fixed him with bloodshot eyes.

"I won't ask how you spent the night." Zach nodded.

"Good. I wouldn't remember anyway." Running a hand over his heavily bearded chin, Tobias forced his bleary eyes to focus.

"How's our passenger faring this morning?"

Zach frowned. "No screaming, no broken dishes. I imagine she's still sleeping." He didn't bother to add that she was in his cabin.

Tobias accepted a cup of coffee, frowning when the cook waved aside his suggestion of a draught of brandy. "Dang fool man. I don't see why you keep him on. He's belligerent and disrespectful," he muttered as he followed Zach to the companionway.

"I keep him on because he's the best damned cook on anything afloat or ashore. And as for respect, I suggest you put away the bottle and try to earn it."

"I'll remember that the next time he comes to me with a burn or cut." He narrowed a red-rimmed eye. "I may just let the wound fester awhile."

"Fortunately for us all, my friend, you enjoy eating almost as much as you enjoy drinking. He'd get back at you by putting something in your food."

Tobias nodded. "I'll try to remember that." He hesitated, wondering what kind of response his next question would get. "About last night...?"

Reaching the ladder, Zach stopped. "What about last night?"

"I'm not askin' for details, but I gotta tell you, boy, you're playin' with fire."

"Go on."

Tobias shifted uncomfortably. "She was supposed to marry Jerrold Barrington. You abducted her and forced her aboard this ship. If you've given her any reason to believe..."

"To believe what?" Zach asked.

"Damn man!" he hissed, leaning forward so his words wouldn't be heard by the rest of the crew. "You can't just use her like that and then set her aside. I don't care who she's to marry. It's not right! You can't be playin' with her feelin's."

Zach studied him for the longest time, then turned back toward the ladder. "You're absolutely right." And he knew that he was. He'd come to that very same decision when he'd left his cabin.

"Therefore, you may inform Miss Winslow that she may have the use of my cabin for the remainder of the voyage. She'll be more comfortable. I'll take hers." He started up the ladder.

Elyse awakened slowly, her eyes fixing on the porthole. It took a few minutes for her to remember where she was, then she wished she hadn't. She scrambled to the edge of the bed. St. James hadn't returned.

She came off the bed, determined not to think about it. She would put her mind on food, the weather, anything else but that. Her clothes had been picked up, folded, and placed atop the cabinet. Captain Tennant, no doubt. The man was full of surprises and contradictions.

Crossing the cabin, she dressed. Catching a brief glimpse of herself in the shaving mirror above the basin, she cringed and immediately borrowed the soft-bristled horsehair brush. She carefully worked the tangles from her hair.

She made the bed and tucked in the heavy quilt at the edges. She smoothed the wrinkles from the quilt and a memory surfaced—she had done this before, just this way, and the fragrance of the bed linens...

A knocking at the door brought her around. Captain Tennant wouldn't bother to knock, she was certain of it. That could only mean it was one of the crew. She wore the shirt and a pair of pants that had obviously once belonged to a smaller member of the crew. She rolled back the cuffs so that she wasn't at risk of tripping, then smoothed her hair back.

"Come in."

The door opened slowly, and a graying head poked tentatively around the edge of it. Elyse recognized the man she'd seen in the companionway the day before when she'd tried to make her escape. Now he looked as if he expected a plate or cup to come flying at his head.

"I promise not to throw anything." She decided she'd much rather gain some information before her captor came back. After all, where was she to go in the middle of the ocean? She wanted to know where she was and where they were going.

Faintly reddened eyes twinkled back at her, and the man came around the door and fixed her with a disarming smile. He reminded her of Cedric.

"Tobias Gentry is the name—ship's physician."

Now that she saw him in the full light of day, Elyse's eyes widened. "I know you."

"Aye, we've met before. But at the time, I was dressed a little fancier than I am now."

"You were at the supper party. If memory serves me correctly, dressed as a Spanish marquis."

Tobias winced. "It wasn't my idea. I would've come up with something a little more original."

"Such as Tobias Gentry, ship's doctor?" She suggested, amusement dancing in her eyes. It was good to be able to talk to someone without feeling anger or the need for confrontation.

His eyes narrowed, but the twinkling remained.

"Zach said you weren't the shy type. I can see he was telling the truth."

"Zach?" she asked.

"I suppose there's no harm in your knowing. Zachary Tennant is captain of the *Revenge*. And a fine ship she is. If you like ships. I don't care much for them myself. But if a fella has to sail, this would be the one to sail on."

The beginning of understanding lit Elyse's soft blue eyes. "So, you're a reluctant passenger as well. Were you were abducted?" she paused. "Or did you come aboard willingly?"

Tobias rubbed his chin thoughtfully. "I suppose I would have to say that I came aboard willingly."

"You must know Captain Tennant well," she commented.

"Fairly well, I darn near raised the boy—me and his mother." He stopped, realizing the game she played. His eyes narrowed.

"Yer a clever one. I'll have to be careful or you'll have the whole crew mutiny to yer side."

"I don't see how that's possible since I'm being kept prisoner."

"Not at all," he replied. "You may come and go as you please during the day, so long as the *Revenge* is at sea."

Then I'm not to be locked in here?"

Zach was right. Elyse Winslow wasn't the fainting, simpering type. She was as proud as she was beautiful, and stronger than most any woman he'd ever met, considering what she'd been through.

He cleared his throat as he broached the delicate subject. "Zach said you were to have the use of the cabin. He thought you would be more comfortable here. He'll take the other cabin, once it's been cleaned."

Elyse smiled at him gratefully. She found herself liking Tobias Gentry, in spite of his choice of friends.

"Well, if I'm free to move about as I please, is there any possibility of acquiring some breakfast?"

He nodded. "I thought you might be hungry. The sea air does that to a person. And cook saved some of his best ham and biscuits for you. They're the best outside of Minerva's at Resolute."

She looked up. There was a name she hadn't heard before. "Resolute?"

"Home, for these wanderin' seafarers. And I assure you, it will do these old eyes good to see it again." He took her gently by the arm and closed the cabin door behind them.

"Is it far away?" she asked.

He smiled at her and gave her a wink. "Not so far for some."

She gave him a confused look.

"In good time, Miss Winslow. In time," he assured her.

"Is that where I'm being taken?"

That question brought him up short. She certainly did have a way of going right to the heart of matters. He squinted at her in the meager light of the companion-way. Lord, but she was a beauty with those large blue eyes that took your breath away. And she wasn't full of herself like so many proper young ladies were. Then he wondered what the hell she saw in a pompous ass like Barrington.

Zach was certain it was the title and the promise of wealth. But that didn't fit this young woman who was completely unaffected, and quite comfortable wearing a man's shirt and trousers instead of fine satin and laces. And that forced him to admit that he liked her.

How the devil was he supposed to let Zach carry out his ransom plan now. He took the easy way out, avoided a direct answer and felt the coward for it.

"You'll have to ask the captain about that."

It was obvious that she and Tobias might exchange

pleasantries and casual conversation, but his loyalty was unquestionable.

"What about those biscuits? I'm starving."

Reprieved from more questions, Tobias beamed. Now food was something he could talk about and enjoy with her.

Elyse had been up on deck for hours. It was wonderful, exhilarating. And it was freedom of a sort that she'd never known.

The weather had cleared. The sky overhead was a brilliant blue, broken only occasionally by the few clouds. The wind was strong, and the water slipping past them with amazing speed was faintly tipped with whitecaps.

She saw him the first moment she stepped from the forward hatch. His golden hair caught and held the sun, his broad shoulders loosely covered by a stark white shirt, the sleeves rolled back to expose his forearms. He stood at the wheel of the ship, completely absorbed in the sails overhead, the direction of the wind, and the ship.

She inhaled the tangy sea air, luxuriating in her freedom. In spite of the small cabins below, *Revenge* was a large ship. She was astounded by the amount of sail that billowed overhead. She had heard one of the men say they were running before the wind, with every last inch of canvas set. Her gaze swept the center mast.

She turned to Tobias. "A Portuguese flag?"

He nodded. She was observant, more than most. "Aye."

"Then the *Revenge is* a Portuguese ship?" Elyse concluded. "But there are more English accents than anything else among the crew."

"There's not an Englishman aboard this ship," Tobias informed her, taking a long pull on the pipe he'd lit earlier.

Elyse turned to him, with a perplexed expression. "Why do you say that?" How much would he tell her?

He pointed with the stem of his pipe. "Kimo, the big black fella over there is from Africa. He was nothin' but a boy when he was taken off a slaver fifteen years ago." He pointed to another man. "Mano over there is from Colombia, South America!' He recited backgrounds of a half-dozen other crewmen; including a Chinaman from Whampoa, a swarthy little man from Madagascar who greatly resembled a monkey and the man known as Sandy who was second mate aboard the *Revenge.*

"Sandy is from the north countries. Swears his ancestors were Vikings. I believe it. The man has an almost uncanny instinct for water and wind. Like Zach. And Jalew over there is an Abo."

He gestured to a stocky man who was almost as dark-skinned as the giant Kimo.

"Abo?" Elyse was well studied, she'd traveled considerably with her grandmother, but she'd never heard of this.

"Aboriginal. A native from down under. He was born at Resolute." Tobias took a thoughtful pull on the pipe. Fragrant smoke caught on the wind, then was whisked away. He decided there was no harm in telling her a few things.

His smile softened. "The land down under, at the bottom of the world." Clamping the pipe firmly between his teeth, and drawing an imaginary circle at a nearby map with his fingers.

"This is the earth as man has come to know it."

She watched fascinated as Tobias Gentry continued his geography lesson.

"Europe is here. Over here you have India, Russia, China, and down here, you have Africa, Kimo's native country." The geography lesson continued "And over here... "

"North America, central America, and South America," Elyse interjected.

"Very good." He smiled, complimenting her. "Up here are the Arctic regions, down here the Antarctic. And here is the continent of Australia, the land down under."

Her startled gaze met his, "Australia? But these men?"

"They're from a dozen or more countries, they hold fast to as many cultures, but Australia is the port they call home when they're not at sea. They're a wicked lot. But any one of them would give his life for Zach. Each one is more than a brother to him.

"He gave them freedom, dignity, and a good life," he continued. "You wouldn't know it to look at these men, but most of them are very comfortable financially. Some have families in New South Wales, but for others the sea is as much woman as they want."

"And the captain?" She asked, wanting to know more about him.

Tobias nodded thoughtfully. "He was born at Resolute. He's equally at home on land or sea. But I think he prefers it there. It's in his blood."

She considered this latest bit of information. "He speaks perfect English."

"When it suits him, and thanks to me. Only a faint bit of brogue slips through now and then. That came from Megan, his mother. She was Irish and a very fine woman. She's gone now."

"You said you helped raise him. But you're not his father?"

He didn't answer her right away, but looked out at the sea.

Tobias took another pull on the pipe. It was natural for her to have questions. But he forced himself to remember who she was. How much did she know or suspect? Still, there was nothing in her gaze to indicate anything but simple curiosity.

"I helped raise him. He was a handful. But no, I'm not Zach's father. His father and I were friends many years ago, in the early years."

"Early years?"

"Aye, when we first went to the colonies as young men, a very long time ago. Zach never knew his father. He died shortly before Zach was born. Me and Megan raised him at Resolute."

Jerrold had said more than once that the colony was filled with convicts, and she knew that many had been sent there. "But you're a doctor, obviously well educated, and Captain Tennant is a well-educated man."

"As I said," he replied gruffly, "it was all a very long time ago." He studied the pipe in his hands, then frowned as he knocked the bowl against the railing, loosening the smoldering tobacco.

"It must be a lot like the United States," Elyse commented as she digested what he'd told her. She knew England no longer transported convicts to Australia. The practice had ceased years ago. Tobias certainly wasn't a convict, nor was Zachary Tennant for that matter. She realized her impressions of the Australian colonies had been shadowed by Jerrold's contempt for that faraway place.

"I should like to see it someday. It must be a vast, wondrous place to be filled with so many different people, cultures, and languages. Does Captain Tennant speak other languages?"

Her last comment had the effect of completely disarming Tobias. What a wondrous creature she was, completely uninhibited, with an openness and curiosity that was rare among women raised in proper Victorian England.

"Aye, that he does." He beamed at her with the pride

any father might have. "He speaks any of a half-dozen other languages as fine as English."

"And I suppose that includes Spanish as well."

"A fair amount."

She broadsided him with her next question. "But why a Portuguese flag, if the captain and crew are from Australia?"

He shrugged. What harm would it do for her to know? There was a great deal she was going to find out before this was all over.

"It serves a purpose. Right now," he said, and gestured with his pipe out across the expanse of ocean, "we're off the coast of Spain. They won't bother with us."

Her eyes widened. She'd heard of such ships and crews... *Pirate ships!* But surely not... And yet as she looked at the crew, it did seem a very real possibility.

"Why not an English flag when in England?" she asked.

Tobias stiffened. "Never an English flag! Zach would scuttle the *Revenge* and send her to the bottom of the sea before he'd allow the bloody Union Jack atop her mast!" Then, as if suddenly remembering himself, his expression softened.

"Australia is a Crown colony," he explained. "We have our own flag and occasionally must fly another flag, for protection."

He was obviously very upset about her mentioning the English flag, but why? She smiled as she tried to smooth over the moment.

"And perhaps an American flag?" she suggested.

Tobias glanced over at her and couldn't resist that smile. "Aye, we've flown it more than once."

"My mother was American."

Tobias watched her thoughtfully. So, this was something about Miss Winslow he hadn't known before.

Elyse turned, leaning casually back against the railing, her hair catching in the wind. "My grandmother still calls the United States, the Colonies, even though they haven't been colonies for over a hundred years.

"I was born there, but I don't remember very much about it. I came to England when I was very small. My parents died, and I've lived with my grandmother ever since. England is the only home I've ever known. It's easy to love something when you've never known anything different. People often think of me as a foreigner."

She didn't mention that Jerrold once suggested he was making a great sacrifice in marrying her. He'd quickly dismissed her American-born mother, emphasizing her father's side of the family when introducing her to family and friends as if it was something to be looked down on.

It was late afternoon. A shadow swooped across the deck and Elyse looked up.

"Gulls," Tobias informed her.

She frowned. "But I thought they stayed close to shore."

"Aye, they do." He nodded to her.

Her gaze met his. "But I don't see land."

"You won't for a few hours. But the wind has been good, and we'll be there soon enough."

Elyse turned. Shading her eyes, she strained to see something other than rolling ocean on the horizon. Tobias pointed over her shoulder. "You'll be able to see it there first. The Spanish coastline. We should make it by tomorrow if the wind holds."

Zach adjusted the wheel of the *Revenge* with the subtle change of the wind. He should have insisted that Elyse stay below decks. But Tobias' request that she be allowed some freedom had seemed harmless enough.

He was surprised at how much he knew about her. She loved the freedom of a stolen ride in the early morning hours, dressed as a man so as not to draw attention. He could envision her riding in the Woods, perhaps in search of Jane's Folly, her hair whipping out behind her. Or, sneaking through backstreets and alleys with him, in nothing more than a man's shirt and coat.

She loved her freedom, and he could imagine her frustration at her imprisonment in the small cabin measuring no more than ten feet square. She'd managed to let them all know just what she thought of her situation.

He looked for her, his gaze searching the deck where she'd just been with Tobias. Her long dark hair streaming in the wind. Earlier, he'd allowed Tobias to convince him that she would be perfectly safe up on deck. He now realized that had been foolish on his part.

She was the only woman aboard a ship with a full crew of men. They were good men to the last of them, but still they were men and a woman, even one dressed in long pants and a shirt could mean trouble.

Zach cursed under his breath as he turned the wheel over to his second mate.

He had several matters he wanted to discuss with Miss Winslow, and it was better done below decks. It was best to establish that now.

She made a beguiling sight, her face turned toward the sun, the wind in her hair. Too beguiling, Zach thought as he joined her and Tobias.

"I'm certain you find all this quite enjoyable, Miss Winslow," he commented. However, this is not a pleasure cruise. You will go below."

Her mouth dropped open. She'd felt him before she'd heard him, known the exact moment he came up behind her, and had sensed something in his hesitation. She was grateful that he'd kept his distance from her and hoped it would continue. Apparently not.

The picture Tobias had painted was certainly not of a ruthless, unfeeling man. He was responsible and caring toward his men. She'd seen it in the easy camaraderie they enjoyed as he spoke to them and worked alongside them. Why was the anger so easy with her? What did he want from her?

It was Tobias who broke the emotionally charged air. "There's no harm, and it's beastly hot in those cabins."

"Nevertheless, she's to return to her cabin," Zach replied.

Elyse stiffened. So, now she was a prisoner again.

"If you object to my request, Miss Winslow," he continued, "I can always have you removed, forcibly if necessary. One way or the other you will go below."

Why was he being so hateful to her?

Tobias muttered under his breath, out of earshot of the crew. "There's no need for this. She wasn't doing anything wrong."

"I make the decisions about what's right or wrong on my ship, and about who comes up on deck."

She wanted to slap that arrogant expression from his face. But she knew only too well where that had gotten her before, and she wasn't about to give him the satisfaction of humiliating her in front of his crew.

She thanked Tobias for his kindness, then turned, walked past Zach Tennant, and climbed down the ladder that led back down to the cabin.

What did he want from her? He'd refused to tell her anything. And the little she'd been able to learn from Tobias hadn't answered any of those burning questions.

Zachary Tennant was a mass of contradictions—not a nobleman as he'd pretended but a sea captain and pirate. And he was clever. Whatever he was about, it was part of a plan that included posing as someone else, so that he could come and go among those in London. But for what purpose? Did it have to do with the business he'd had with Jerrold and Barrington Shipping?

She tried to think through everything Tobias had told her. Very little of it made sense. She was certain of only one thing—that she was being held prisoner aboard this ship, a ship that flew under many flags, using them as disguises—a pirate ship. And according to Tobias, they were now approaching the coast of Spain.

She halted at the cabin, refusing to go in willingly. He had followed her and reached around her, his left arm lightly brushing hers as he pushed open the door to the cabin she'd first occupied.

She had two choices—she could stand there with him so close that she felt the heat from his body, or she could go into the cabin. There was no place she could escape. She walked into the cabin.

"I apologize."

The apology and the surprising quiet in his voice had her turning around. She wanted him angry, as angry as she was. But he wasn't.

What was he up to? There had to be a reason he'd risked so much to abduct her. Only one thing would make anyone risk so much.

"What is the price?"

"The price for what?" he asked.

She leveled that brilliant blue gaze at him, fighting back the anger. She hadn't thought for a minute this would be easy, nothing about this man was.

"You know perfectly well what I'm talking about," she continued. "What ransom have you demanded for me?"

So that's it, Zach thought appreciatively. She didn't miss a thing. She was smart and it hadn't taken her long to arrive at the obvious conclusion. But the obvious one wasn't necessarily the correct one.

He studied her, the way she stood, arms folded across her breasts, the shirt too big over her shoulders, the tangled mane of her hair falling down her back. She'd been stripped of all the fine trimmings of a lady. She'd been bound, gagged, and bruised, regrettably by him. Yet at that moment she was the most beautiful woman he'd ever seen. And the most desirable.

It was something he'd felt from the beginning. He'd wanted to hate her for what she was, the perfect, well-bred young Englishwoman groomed and molded to be Lady Barrington. But she'd turned everything against him with something he didn't understand.

She'd been angry up on deck and he'd prepared himself for the confrontation he'd known would follow. Remembering Tris' experience the day before, he'd quickly made an inventory of all loose objects within her reach as they reached the cabin. Now she stood before him, demanding answers. There was no reason not to tell her.

"There is no demand for ransom."

His words sank in slowly. No ransom? It made no sense. What game was this?

"You wouldn't risk so much without thinking you'd get something for it in return," she replied. "You must surely know that Jerrold will send people to find me," she reasoned. "But if you tell me now what the ransom is, we can be done with this, and you can release me when we reach Portugal." She waited.

Zach leveled his gaze at her. No more disguises, no more pretense. Everything stripped away between them. Nothing but the truth. Could she accept it?

"As I said, there is no ransom."

She laughed, that soft, smoky laugh that was both incredulous and defiant. "Don't you understand? It doesn't matter what precautions you've taken, or how fast this ship is. He will find you."

She could only guess what that would mean for him and his crew. Knowing that, it suddenly seemed horrible to her.

"I know."

Elyse stared at him. He was mad! To just stand there and calmly admit that he knew exactly what would happen and yet act as if he didn't care.

"How much? Ten thousand pounds? Twenty? Name the price. I know we're to arrive in Lisbon soon. Arrangements can be made to give you the money then, and we can be done with this."

"I told you once before, it's not that easy."

"What are you talking about? Your kind always asks for money."

Amusement curved his mouth. "And just what is my kind, Elyse? I'm curious as to what you think."

"A kidnapper, a pirate, the sort who always has a price."

"Husband?" he suggested.

Elyse paled. "Surely you don't refer to that ridiculous ceremony. No one would accept it..." She stopped, trying to bring her emotions under control. "It doesn't mean anything. I did not give my consent."

His smile deepened. "Of course you did. Everyone in that church heard it."

"You're insane! I was forced. It would never stand," she argued even with the doubt that crept in.

"What purpose does it serve? You don't want to be married to me, and I certainly don't want..."

She was cut off as Zach held up his hand. "I don't take money for what I do. I work for no one. And as for abducting you..." He paused then continued. "The ceremony serves my purpose. Barrington has been publicly humiliated. His bride has been stolen right out from under his nose, and by a man he hates more than anyone else in the world. You, my dear, are the perfect lure for the perfect trap."

She stared at him. He was deliberately trying to confuse her. The perfect lure for the perfect trap? And why the devil should he hate Jerrold when they'd only just met? She didn't understand any of this. It didn't make any sense.

"You're nothing but a thieving pirate!" she flung at him.

"That is an interesting possibility," he admitted.

"Then, you don't deny it."

"I don't deny or acknowledge anything. You're the one making the assumptions."

She groaned. This was getting her nowhere. If money didn't seem to interest him, then maybe the thought of hanging from a rope would get through to him.

"There's no place you can hide. You'll be found and made to pay for your crimes."

"Elyse, do you really believe I didn't know that when I abducted you from that church?"

No, she thought, he isn't the sort of man who does things without knowing full well the repercussions.

"Jerrold will come after you," she whispered, incredulous now, trying to reason with him. That gray gaze met hers.

"I want him to find me."

His simple admission stunned her. He was inviting his own death. She shook her head in disbelief. It was hopeless. Those few words had told her there was no hope for her release.

"Why are you doing this?"

"In a way, Elyse, there is a ransom. You are the ransom. I knew Jerrold would come after you. His pride wouldn't let him do otherwise. I've even made it easy for him. I left him a note. He now knows who abducted you and where you can be found."

"I don't understand."

Zach smiled, but his voice was filled with bitterness. "It's a family matter, an old score has to be settled." He turned and headed for the door.

"You could be killed." She followed him to the door and tried to reason with him.

"Would that matter to you?" he asked.

Would it? "I don't want anyone to be hurt. I just want to go home," she replied.

"As Lady Barrington." His voice was tight, raw. His hand came up.

She took a step back.

Zach saw her reaction and winced. Did she really believe he would harm her? He reached up and touched her cheek. He saw the confusion in her eyes. If only things could have been different between them, if they had met before all of this... Something tightened inside him, and he pushed the thought away.

How could he be so cruel at one moment and so gentle the next? she thought. It was like a weapon he used, and she couldn't let him know how he affected her. She refused to meet his gaze, afraid he would see it in her eyes.

Elyse breathed out shakily. This wasn't how it was supposed to be. She wanted to hate him. "You are mad!" she whispered.

"Undoubtedly so," he replied. "Why else would I sail to England and abduct such a troublesome hostage?" The expression in his eyes changed, making her shiver. "But it will be ended soon enough."

"Jerrold will kill you when he finds you." The expression on his face wasn't what she expected. There was no fear.

"He will try." Then the coldness in his eyes changed, his expression closed, revealing nothing. "Tell Tris if you need anything."

Elyse slammed the door after him, then collapsed back against it.

What was she going to do?

Seventeen

"**D**amn!" Tobias muttered as he lowered himself down the ladder.

Zach turned from his cabin to find the older man waiting for him.

"Did you have to be so cruel?"

"It was necessary."

"Yer treatin' her like some sort of criminal. Zach, for God's sake, she's done nothing wrong!"

"You've been like flesh and blood to me, boy. But I can't accept what you've done to that girl."

"Enough!" Zach was tight-lipped as he tried to push past his old friend. But Tobias wasn't to be put off.

"How long do you think you can keep her on board this ship without answering her questions?"

Zach turned to him. "It's not like you to interfere. Why now? What the devil do you care? If I didn't know better, I'd think you were drunk."

The older man's hands shook, but from something far different than the effects of the drink. "I wish to God I was. Then maybe I wouldn't be considerin' what I am at this moment." His own anger very near matched that of the young man standing before him. He hesitated.

"What the hell," he exclaimed. "You deserve it!" Quicker than either man had time to think, Tobias slammed a fist into Zach's left eye, staggering him back against the wall of the companionway.

Zach looked up at his friend, his expression one of complete shock. He pushed away from the wall, gently probing his eye. "If you were twenty years younger..." he threatened.

Tobias flexed his hand. "Hard-headed as you are, I've probably broken some bones." He smiled with grim satisfaction, thoroughly enjoying the swelling of Zach's eye.

"I won't apologize. You deserved it!" That part of him that was a physician thought to check the eye. Instead, he made an obscene gesture at Zach and headed in the opposite direction toward the galley.

For a man of his age, Tobias had one hell of a punch. Somehow Zach didn't mind. He had it coming, and he knew it. He headed toward the ladder.

They would make the port at Lisbon near daybreak. He had business there. He wanted to be done with it and unload the gold. Then they could be on their way. But he also had to check with the harbor master to find out if there'd been any unusual activity on the part of Barrington ships. At best, he knew he had the advantage of two days' sailing time. He needed that extra time to make Sydney and set his final plans in motion.

It was late when Elyse finally slept. Then the dreams came—she saw herself as a little girl, the chaos and terror of the shipwreck, then the young woman she'd seen in that portrait and a man with sun-streaked hair...

"I have a gift for you," he whispered.

"You've already given me a gift," she told him.

He reached up to touch the diamond and pearl earbob at one ear. Its twin dangled from the other ear. In his other hand, he held two roses—one blood red, the other white. "This rose is my passion for you, this one is my promise that I will love you forever."

"Don't go..." she whispered as they disappeared.

Zach sat there for the longest time watching her.

He'd walked the deck for hours, restless. And then there was the regret at what he'd put her through.

Sitting there now, watching over her, somewhere between the last of the night and daybreak, the regret was sharp, almost painful.

He refused to think about what would actually happen when he and Barrington finally met. He knew what the outcome must be.

She was his wife by that ceremony at the church. His wife!

Even now he didn't understand what had made him do it. It would have been simple enough to abduct her. That would have been enough to send Barrington after him. But he'd wanted more...he wanted her. For reasons he didn't begin to understand. That one night in London?

It was there, he wanted more.

"What are you doing here?" she asked, then noticed the color that had come up at his other eye.

"What happened to your eye?"

"In answer to the first, I heard you call out. In answer to the second, a minor disagreement," he replied.

Elyse slowly smiled. She had heard a bit of that 'disagreement' earlier.

"I wanted you to know that I'll be going ashore to take care of some business in Lisbon."

She moved to the edge of the bed, wearing the shirt she'd worn earlier. "Must I stay aboard?"

He'd treated her badly, he knew that and could well understand that she wanted to go ashore. But there was more to it. She was intelligent and stubborn.

She might well try to escape and approach the authorities in Lisbon. He couldn't risk that. For her sake, or his.

"You'll be safe enough here," he said, not unkindly, but his decision was final.

~

Hours later, Elyse watched from the railing as the small boat carried Zach and those who were going ashore, the Port of Lisbon in the distance. She joined Tobias, who had chosen to remain aboard.

"I've seen it all before," he told her, his pipe clenched in his teeth as the *Revenge* rolled gently at anchor.

"It's the same in every port, and I need to be clear-headed when the crew returns. There's always a few bumps and scrapes to attend."

"I was surprised to find the guard gone from my door this morning," she commented without adding that Zach had been there, strangely just watching over her.

"Aye, Zach let him go ashore, since there's little danger of you bein' swept overboard and drowned while we're in port. "

"Free to come and go, so long as it's not ashore," she commented.

"He's got his faults, God knows he does," Tobias replied. "And I don't agree with his methods, but he's got his reasons. I trust that, and he's a good man."

"He obviously had his reasons for not wanting me to go ashore."

Tobias nodded. "That he did. And that is the reason." He gestured over her shoulder.

He pointed to a large ship that road high in the water, with a half-dozen cannons positioned along the deck.

"Her name is *Sultana,* and her captain is Juan de la

Vasquez Vimeiro, more commonly known as El Barracuda."

Elyse shaded her gaze as she took a long look at the *Sultana*. The rigging was intact, but the hull was badly scarred, several efforts at repair overlapping each other. It had apparently encountered a good number of confrontations and though it seemed to ride in the water surely enough, it was obvious that no great care had been given the ship. In contrast, the *Revenge* gleamed like a polished black pearl in the morning sun.

The sleek schooner's hull was freshly painted, and the wood deck was spotless. The tall masts, also painted black reached into the blue Mediterranean sky. The sails had all been lowered and neatly secured, the lines tied. Every bit of brass, and wood gleamed, and high above, at the center mast, the Portuguese flag fluttered in the breeze. The ship reminded Elyse of a gleaming black bird, hovering over the water, ready to take flight. And like the man who captained her, she was lean, strong, and beautiful to look at.

"Who is El Barracuda?" she asked, retreating from those thoughts.

"The worst cutthroat that ever sailed," Tobias replied.

"A pirate?" she stared at El Barracuda. The *worst* pirate, according to Tobias.

"What makes him different from the others?"

"He's a man with no honor," Tobias stated flatly.

"Honor? Among thieves?"

"Aye, even among thieves," he replied. "But not that man. It doesn't matter who he hurts or the destruction from those cannons. He's a bloodthirsty fellow. Makes my blood run cold just to see that ship here. That means he's pirating the Mediterranean."

"Why do the authorities allow him to come in?"

"As long as he's not caught at thievin' and abides by the law inside the harbor, they allow him to come in for supplies. His money spends like everyone else's, no matter how ill-gotten. Zach has had a few encounters with the man, one particularly bad. El Barracuda has never forgotten it. That's another reason Zach kept part of the crew here and took some of the men with him."

This was something else she hadn't known about Zachary Tennant. Her gaze went back to the *Sultana*.

"What happened?"

"El Barracuda decided he wanted a cargo Zach was carryin'."

"He attacked the *Revenge?*"

"That was his first mistake," Tobias commented. "The *Revenge* is not as big as most ships, being only a schooner. But she's heavily armed, and fast." He gestured down the long decks to the cannons.

"It was the only time El Barracuda ever lost a cargo he was after. It cost him half his crew, and a great deal of pride. He swore he'd see Zach sent to the bottom for it. That's why Zach is careful, especially with you aboard."

She almost laughed at that. He didn't want to lose his hostage.

"When will they be returning?" she asked.

"The men will probably stay ashore for the night, before we continue on to Sydney. It helps them relieve a bit. Even the best seaman gets cabin fever. Zach will probably return after he's completed his business."

Sydney? Australia? Halfway around the world! She had to find a way to get off the ship.

She looked up at Tobias, afraid he might have read her thoughts. She thanked him for the coffee he'd shared.

"You're welcome," he said thoughtfully, watching her.

She turned toward the hatch that led below deck, and quickly descended the ladder. Once inside her cabin, she went to the porthole that she'd opened earlier for fresh air.

If she tried to leave from the deck, someone would surely see her. She looked at the porthole again. It was small, but it was her only chance to escape unseen.

She found a knitted cap in one of the drawers. She yanked it down and tucked her hair underneath.

The shirt and pants she'd been given would have to do and would help with the disguise when she reached shore. That thought raised the question, what she would do when she reached it? She needed money.

She felt like a thief. But it couldn't be helped. Though she still had her diamond and pearl pendant, she was reluctant to part with it, even to buy her way home. She crossed the companionway to Zach's cabin and searched through drawers there.

She found a pouch with a substantial amount of gold coins inside. Surely she would be able to purchase passage to London and possibly some clothes. She tucked the pouch into the waist of the pants, then turned to the porthole.

She looked out again. Now that her decision was made, the drop to the water seemed miles away instead of only several feet. But there was nothing to be done about that, and the water would break her fall.

She carefully wedged herself out of porthole, held onto the edge to get her bearings, then dropped to the water below.

The water was surprisingly warm compared to English waters. She kicked her way to the surface and swam away from the *Revenge*.

At any moment she expected the warning cry to go out from one of the men who had stayed behind. But there was nothing, only the screech of seabirds overhead and the water. Still, she couldn't rid herself of the feeling that she had been seen.

She'd learned to swim as a child and had always been a strong swimmer. It took longer than she anticipated, but she finally reached a landing with steps that led up to the dock.

Dockside, people bustled about. Ships moored there were loaded and unloaded, wagons delivered cargoes and carted other cargoes away. The pier was a noisy, buzzing confusion of workers, seamen, and merchants. No one noticed as a bedraggled figure stepped up onto the landing, then the dock.

Elyse gave a long look back over her shoulder. The *Revenge* was beautiful, like that large, graceful bird she had imagined earlier. Something tightened deep inside her at leaving the ship. She didn't try to understand it.

Eighteen

Lisbon reached out to the sea from the estuary of the Tagus River. The city, made up of seven coastal hills, reflected the ancient cultures that had once been there.

It was an international port. Its intricate, winding cobblestoned streets provided access to houses of soft pink, turquoise, and white, with tiled roofs and iron balconies accented with flowers.

This city's heritage had been greatly influenced by the Moors, but it dated back to prehistoric times and was rich in history, culture, and trade.

Elyse had visited Lisbon two years earlier with her grandmother. They'd stayed at an elegant villa high in the terraced hills overlooking the city, and had made trips to ancient castles, fortresses, churches, and museums. The Lisbon she knew was a mixture of cultures and fascinating.

She'd enjoyed watching the brilliantly costumed dancers on warm evenings, and she'd ridden in a carriage through the Alfama district, had seen the lovely Arabic palace, the Catelo Sao Jorge, used as a fortress by the Visigoths in fifth century.

In the marketplace could be found gold and diamonds from Brazil, ivory from Africa, spices, silks, and porcelains from China, ginger and pepper from the Malabar Coast.

She had discovered it all with her grandmother. But that was the Lisbon far different from the port with its rolling ships, and cargos that waited for wagons.

Still exotic and fascinating, this was the province of merchants, traders, and seafarers. She dodged past tall black sailors who reminded her of Kimo. Stripped to their waists, they wore great gold rings looped in their ears, and brilliant bracelets adorned their heavily muscled arms.

She dodged away from more than one seaman fascinated with the *'lad'*, as they called out to her, who possessed such fair skin. Following the direction of their stares she quickly found the reason. The front of her shirt was plastered to her body, leaving little to doubt. Arms folded across the front of the shirt, she continued her explorations.

She knew just enough of the language to ask for the local merchant who might sell garments and smiled her relief when she found a street vendor who spoke English.

He was selling all manner of goods, from fresh lobster, prawns, and crabs to brightly woven baskets, hats, and a few items of clothing. She quickly selected a hat with a wide brim and a colorful cape of the type she'd seen some men wearing. It would help conceal her until her clothes dried, and not draw attention to her. To complete her purchase, she chose a pair of leather sandals.

As Elyse held out the gold coins, the merchant's eyes shown almost as bright as the gold. He seized one. Then, after biting down hard to see if it was real, he held out his hand for more.

She hesitated. These coins were all she had. She hoped to send a telegram to Paris, where she might be able to contact friends of her grandmother, or possibly buy passage home but it could be days, before her departure from Lisbon could be arranged. She handed the merchant one more coin. His fingers automatically signaled for two more.

She firmly shook her head. He shrugged his shoulders, then turned to another customer.

She pushed back the suspicion that she'd probably paid double what everything was worth. She donned the cape and hat and strapped on the sandals. Now she had to see about getting out of Lisbon.

She was sweltering. Her clothing had long since dried, and beads of perspiration ran between her shoulder blades. She'd already learned what Zach meant by thieves and cutthroats. Twice she'd seen men attacked by street thieves.

She had kept out of the shadows. She'd also learned to watch for the crew of the *Revenge*. In one shop she passed, she saw a large African buying colorful cloth and recognized Kimo. She immediately ducked around the corner when he turned and came out of the store, the cloth tucked under his arm.

And she was tired and hungry. It seemed that she had walked for miles on the cobbled streets that wound through the area near the wharf. She passed second-story dwellings overlooking shops and businesses, laundry draped along their balconies or hung from lines strung between open windows.

And in countless shops she asked about boat passage. She got everything from disinterested shrugs to blank stares. In one market, she had a pomegranate stuck in one hand, a smelly mackerel in the other, while the merchant held his hand out for money. He got the pomegranate and the mackerel back.

By late afternoon Elyse collapsed wearily onto a chair at a small sidewalk restaurant. Too tired to go on, she was also too hungry to ignore the wonderful aromas that came from inside. She ordered food and a huge loaf of bread still warm from the oven. A request for water, ended up being wine. The Portuguese loved their wine.

It wasn't food prepared at Winslow house or aboard the *Revenge,* but nothing had ever tasted so good. She paid with one of the gold coins. The attendant had no other customers at that time of the afternoon and struck up a congenial conversation while Elyse tried to decide what to do next. Since the young man hadn't attempted to cheat her for the food and spoke such good English, she decided to trust him.

"I need to arrange passage to London. Do you know where I might book passage?" At first her question brought only a faint shrug, then the man paused.

"The Green Dolphin. You might find someone there who could arrange it."

"The Green Dolphin?" she repeated.

He nodded, stroking his chin thoughtfully as he removed her empty bowl and cup. "It's not far from here, on the Rua do Carmo. My wife's cousin works there. He hears things, he may know of such a ship. But he works at night and sleeps during the day."

"How far is it?"

He pointed past the small square. "Three streets. Turn right, middle of the street with a large sign with a green dolphin." He smiled at her.

As she rose to leave, she felt gentle pressure on her arm.

"Be careful," he told her. He continued with a warning. "Many of the men who go there, are from the ships. There is much drinking, sometimes fighting. It is not a place for someone as young as you. It is not a good place to be if there is trouble. There, a man takes his justice with a knife."

Elyse nodded, thanking him. Zach's warning of thieves and cutthroats immediately came back to her.

Stepping from the restaurant, she looked at the late afternoon sky. She still had a few hours before she could find Santo at the Green Dolphin. Until then she would just have to keep out of sight.

~

His sale of the gold concluded, together with the arrangements for its transfer before sundown, Zach stepped out of an office in a building located in the Baixa, the central business district in Lisbon.

He'd sold the gold for a substantial sum. Payment would be transferred to his account in Zurich. He'd done business with Esteben Bautano and knew the man could be trusted, unlike other people he'd dealt with in the past.

He nodded to Sandy to be quick. He was anxious to get back to the ship, but his second mate wanted to make a few purchases in the open-air market that lined the waterfront.

Their last time in Sydney, Sandy had spent most of his time with the daughter of an Irish merchant. Zach suspected his friend thought himself to be in love. Taking advantage of the cool shade outside the shop, he waited, leaning back against a stone wall.

He watched as a beggar worked the opposite side of the street, cup clutched in an outstretched hand. The man wandered, apparently blind, tapping his way along with a cane.

Zach smiled to himself as he watched the man who seemed to have an uncanny ability for picking out the passersby with coin in his pockets.

The port was full of passengers arriving or departing for some foreign port. Several coins dropped noisily into the beggar's cup.

The man continued along the street until he rounded the corner. Then he became noticeably more surefooted. His pace quickened; the cane was forgotten as he slipped to the middle of the alley. The cup was up-turned, the coins quickly stuffed inside the pocket of his pants. It wouldn't do for him to leave too many coins in the cup.

The man dropped the cape back into place, resumed his hunched, shuffling gait and tap-tapping, and returned to the street. Such was life in the street.

A group of boys caught his attention. They scattered down the street, begging for money, imitating the blind beggar, and stealing fruit from a sidewalk vendor. A particularly small lad, undeniably the youngest, boldly approached him.

Feet planted squarely, one hand placed on a hip covered by pants that had obviously known several owners, the boy peeked up with large dark eyes from beneath the rim of a soiled cap. The little beggar mimicked the common street phrases the others had used, holding out his hand.

He was getting started young, Zach thought with regret. The little fellow probably had six or seven brothers working the next street over, bringing home a good income for their family. Still, Zach never was able to turn his back on a child, especially not one as young as this.

He pulled a coin from his pocket. Holding it out, he spoke to the boy in his own language. The child snaked the coin from his fingers, mumbling a quick thank you, then starting to dart away, but something about him caught Zach's attention. A wisp of glossy, long hair slipped from beneath the boy's cap.

Quicker than the child could leap away from him, Zach reached out. With one hand he caught a wrist. With the other he swept the cap off from the child's head. A torrent of long silky hair cascaded down, transforming the boy into a wide-eyed, little girl.

She was a dark-eyed little temptress, part vixen, part

alley cat. She struggled at first, until Zach reprimanded her. Then she hung back warily, bracing herself away from him on firmly planted feet. Her head turned, huge brown eyes like liquid amber contemplating her next move.

Zach dropped down into a crouched position to meet her at eye-level, and slowly drew her to him. He reached out, taking black silken hair between his fingers.

"So, you're not a boy at all," he commented and smiled when she looked over her shoulder, obviously looking for her companions. But they had already disappeared down the street. Her wary gaze came back to his.

"Why are you begging in the streets?" he asked in Portuguese.

"My mother and sisters are hungry," she blurted out.

Zach shook his head. "I don't think so," he continued in Portuguese. "Your cheeks are not sunken. I think your mother and sisters are well provided for and wondering where you are right now."

In spite of her initial wariness, the girl found herself warming to this tall, gray-eyed Anglo with hair like the sun. And when he smiled, he made her feel very special.

"So, why then are you begging in the streets where it is dangerous?"

A somber expression came to her face. She didn't know what this stranger would think or do to her. But the soft light in his eyes betrayed his stern expression. She looked up at him from beneath the sweep of long, lustrous lashes.

"To see if I could do it." She shrugged her slender shoulders, an impish light leaping into her dark eyes.

Zach threw back his head and laughed. He laughed until tears filled his eyes. Then he looked at her, really looked at her. It was the same, that slightly brazen stance, the slender shoulders squared as if she'd take on the whole world if necessary. It was in the challenge in her eyes. She reminded him of Elyse.

"You should be home with your sisters, wearing pretty dresses, learning how to be a lady."

"Why would I want to be a lady?" she replied. "It's boring. All they ever do is sit and gossip and eat pastries. They all grow fat, but I will never be fat." She laid a hand against her chest as if making a solemn promise.

"I want to be slender, so that I can run fast like the boys. I do what boys do, I like boats and horses and fighting."

"Ah." Zach sighed, taken by her. "But you are a girl nevertheless, and that can be quite a marvelous thing. Don't you know you will one day break many hearts?"

She seemed to consider how that might be accomplished. "How?" she asked.

Zach lifted a strand of her hair. "With lovely long hair worn loose about your shoulders, pretty dresses in every color, and your smile."

She frowned. "I don't like dresses. My mother always makes me wear pink ones with lace. It itches." She rolled her eyes. "I wouldn't mind if she would let me wear clothes like Antonia."

"Is Antonia your sister?"

She nodded. "She would like you."

"Would she now?" Zach thought on that, thoroughly enjoying such a lovely creature even if she was no more than seven or eight years old. She was laughing and teasing, and even a little flirtatious. It seemed so easy for this little one. Her feelings were unguarded, unpretentious.

"What color dress does Antonia prefer?"

Her eyes widened. "Oh, she likes bright ones—red, blue, green. Pretty full skirts, and blouses with short sleeves made of satin and silk. My mother has a woman make them for her."

"What would you choose if you could have something pretty to wear?" Zach played along, genuinely interested in the workings of this young, but decidedly very feminine, mind.

She thought very long about that. Closing one eye, she placed a finger against her chin and pondered. Then her eyes widened, and she pointed over his shoulder.

"That is what I would choose." Her eyes sparkled with childish delight, as she slipped from his grasp and darted behind him to the small shop Sandy had entered earlier.

Zach followed her gaze. There displayed in the window was a magnificent silver and white knitted shawl. It was meant to be worn long over a woman's dress, woven of most delicate threads in a pattern of interwoven flowers. At first it appeared to be white in color, but as the sun shone through the glass, sparkling at the silver beads that had been intricately worked into the design, each flower bloom was silver. It was quite beautiful and no doubt very costly.

"That is what you want?"

"Oh, yes!" The little girl stood beside him now. "It is something a boy would give a girl he cared very much about. My sister has such a shawl."

"Does she now? And does she also have a special young man in her life?"

"Sí, Jorge. They are to be married. Then I can have her room all to myself."

He laughed at her charming innocence, and then he sobered, his smile softening. "Thank you for telling me about your sister."

"Do you have a special lady?" She lifted those large dark eyes that would one day hold a man's fate in their depths.

"You should," she decided. "No one who is as handsome as you should be without a lady." Then she looked up at him, struck by a sudden idea. "Would you like to meet my sister, Josefina?"

He smiled down at her. "I'll be leaving soon."

He couldn't remember when he'd enjoyed a *lady's* company so much, except perhaps that morning and the night before with Elyse. Odd how she and this child were so much alike.

"But if your sister is only half as beautiful as you are, then she will have no trouble finding a young man." His little captive immediately blushed, but Zach didn't notice. He was staring at the exquisite shawl.

"Come on. You shall have your shawl." Taking her hand in his, he led her into the store.

He made several purchases. The white shawl he'd seen in the window was for his little apprentice thief. The second shawl he chose was very similar, with delicate hand-worked yarn and silver beads, but it also had tiny seed pearls woven into the design. He had them wrapped separately. Along with the shawl, Zach chose several brightly colored skirts and blouses. His little companion took great delight in picking the colors.

Zach accepted the wrapped items and paid the shopkeeper. Then he turned back, one last purchase in mind. He eyed the many clear glass jars containing candies of different sizes and shapes. What better way to sweeten a little girl's disposition? He let the little thief select her favorites.

Sandy, who had long since completed his purchases, stood waiting outside, a curious expression at his face. Zach held out his hand to his little companion. "Good day, *senorita.*"

She dimpled, flashing him a devastating smile that surrounded several pieces of candy.

"*Uuilo obrigado.*" She turned and would have run away with her horde of candy. His voice stopped her.

The little thief turned, and Zach started to present her with the package containing the shawl she'd seen in the window. For a moment he held it just beyond her grasp.

"You must promise you will wear a dress at least one

day each week, and when you wear it, you will wear this also."

She nodded, her large round eyes adoring. *"Muito obrigado,"* she exclaimed and then scampered away. But a few yards down the cobbled street, she stopped and turned back around.

"What is it?" Zach's eyes smiled his pleasure at giving her the gift. Truly, he felt as if he'd received the greater gift; he'd purchased something for Elyse, something he felt she would truly enjoy.

"How old are you?" she asked with bold curiosity. In another three or four years she would blush even to speak with him.

Sandy had been watching their exchange, and he could contain himself no longer. He burst out laughing.

"I think, Cap'n, your little *senhorita* has plans for you. You'd better watch out or she'll be taking you home to meet mama."

"If I were ten years younger and you were ten years older, I would never be able to leave Lisbon," Zach told her.

She thought on that. "You are very old," she told him." When I am a woman like my sisters, you will be as old as my father. I do not think I would like that. I want a young man who is very strong and fast. He must at least be able to sneak apples away from old Gonsalves' cart without being caught."

Zach laughed. "You're right," he told her. "He must at least be able to do that." Then, growing very solemn, he placed his hand over his heart as if it were truly breaking.

"I will never forget you."

Suddenly the child revealed the breathtaking beauty she would one day be. She smiled shyly, her lashes sweeping low against her cheeks.

"I will never forget you, *senhor."* Then she fled, her

bundle clutched tightly under her arm, candy in her cheek.

"Ah, Cap'n." Sandy shook his head appreciatively. "You've a way with the ladies."

Zach frowned slightly, wondering if another young lady would be as pleased with his gifts. He found himself wanting to say there was only one young lady who mattered to him, but he didn't. He merely nodded gruffly at Sandy.

"Let's get back to the ship. I want to be there when that broker arrives for the transfer. The sooner that gold is off my hands, the happier I'll be."

Sandy nodded sternly, but the light in his eyes danced. "Aye, aye, Cap'n."

It was almost an hour later when they crossed from the landing to the *Revenge* in the small landing boat. Zach nodded to his man as he climbed the ladder and stepped onto the deck.

It was already early evening, shadows slipping across the water of the harbor. He'd hoped to be able to tie in at the dock to unload the gold more easily, but this was a busy time of year in Lisbon. At any rate, a man he'd dealt with before had two steam driven ferries he used to transport goods up and down the nearby Tagus River.

One was tied up not too far away, having just brought in a shipment of wine casks for delivery to clients in the city. The broker was to meet the ferry captain and they would be along first thing in the morning. Zach looked up as Tobias came up from below. His old friend greeted him with a nod.

"Any trouble?" Zach glanced meaningfully back over Tobias' shoulder in the direction of the *Sultana.*

"Not a whisper. El Barracuda is not aboard, and a good many of the crew are gone as well. There's just a skeleton crew keepin' an eye on things. They've been takin' on supplies most of the day."

"What about our supplies?" Zach took the supply manifest Tobias handed him.

"Everything you ordered is aboard. Tris and a couple of the other men finished securin' everything earlier. They're eager to be ashore themselves as soon as the others return."

Zach nodded, scanning the manifest Tobias handed him. Tris was trustworthy. He could be certain they had most of what they would need for the voyage to Sydney. Extra stores of fresh water and perishable food would be obtained along the way.

Their course across the Mediterranean to Suez and through to the Red Sea would take them across the Arabian Sea to India. From there they would skirt the coast of Ceylon en route to Singapore, head on to New Guinea and into the Coral Sea off the coast of Australia. It was not the easiest route, but it was the shortest, if a man knew the waters, the reefs, and the small, scattered islands that could offer shelter.

Zach looked up, his gray eyes scanning the deck. He'd left instructions that Elyse was to have the freedom of the ship, and at this time of day, when the sun no longer beat down on the decks, he expected to find her enjoying the cool evening air.

"Was there any problem today with our passenger?" he inquired.

Tobias shook his head. "She was up on deck earlier, but she's spent the afternoon below." He noticed the package Zach held under his arm. "What have you there?"

Zach glanced up, shoving the manifest back at Tobias. "A very pretty young lady in Lisbon reminded me that a gift might help tame an angry lady." He started for the companionway.

"She's been quiet down there most of the day." Tobias puffed at his pipe as he followed Zach back down the ladder.

A furious shout greeted Tobias as he stepped down into the companionway. His gaze swept the cabin when he reached it. All was neat, orderly, everything in its place.

"Search the ship!" Zach ordered, sending Tobias and the crew that remained aboard into the various parts of the ship.

The entire ship was searched. But he already knew what they would find, as he stared out the porthole in the cabin. Nothing.

"Father in heaven!" Tobias muttered as he crossed to the porthole and stared down at the water below. "How on earth did she manage?"

Zach swore as he came away from the porthole.

He had a dilemma. He assumed Elyse had been gone most of the day, at least- since midmorning, when Tobias had last seen her. The crewmen who were ashore still had not returned. They were due aboard at any time.

Though he'd given them strict orders to be aboard by now, Zach knew they would trail back one by one. Ashore, it would be impossible to find them, and with the gold still aboard *Revenge* awaiting the finalization of the transaction, he dare not take any of the remaining crew to search for Elyse. It was much too risky with the *Sultana* and El Barracuda nearby in the harbor.

He quickly made a decision and dispatched Tris to the landing with the landing boat. As soon as any of the crew returned, he was to immediately bring them to the ship. Zach would set out to find Elyse himself.

Didn't she realize the danger of being alone in a seaport without protection? A woman was a vulnerable target. That thought brought him up short. His mind filled with images of the little girl he'd met in the plaza, dressed like the little boys who begged in the streets.

Elyse wouldn't be dressed as a woman! The only

clothes she had were the pants and shirt he'd given her. She didn't even have any money...

A thorough search of his cabin confirmed his suspicions. He couldn't see that any clothes were missing, but the bag of coins he'd kept in the desk was gone.

When he returned topside, Tris had returned, along with Kimo. Zach quickly ordered Tris to prepare to take him back, then he told Tobias to send others as they returned to help in the search. He brushed past Kimo, not seeing the puzzled expression on the African's face.

"The little girl is gone? I wonder if dat might have been her we see in the marketplace."

Zach turned and seized the man by the shoulders. "Where?"

He was six foot four inches; Kimo towered over him. But Zach had a special bond with this loyal seaman. He'd taken him off a slaver with almost sixty others, and he'd delivered them to Sydney where they were given their freedom and the choice of returning to their native land or staying in Australia.

Kimo chose to stay with the *Revenge*. It was as if this large, gentle man had found his home on those oak decks. Zach had taught him English and how to read and write. For his part, Kimo was as loyal as the rest of the crew. And the huge African knew Zach's secrets, but he would die before he would give them to anyone. There was nothing he wouldn't do for Zach.

"I'm prob'ly wrong, Cap'n. But today in the marketplace I saw a young man. He was small and I only saw him for a minute, but he had fair skin, and eyes like the color of the water on the Barrier Reef."

"Where?" Zach replied. Maybe fair skin wasn't a sound enough reason to think Kimo had seen her, but those eyes. And hadn't Zach's exact thought been that they were the color of the water off the reef?

The African thought for a moment. Then a wide smile split his face from ear to ear.

"It was outside the shop where I bought this silk for Annie back home."

"I need more—the name of the shop, a location, something different that you remember."

The man's smile broadened even more. "The shop-keeper was a black man, like me. Tall, from the Zulu tribe. He was taken like I was and managed to get his freedom and come here!"

Zach clasped him at the shoulder. It wasn't much, but it was something. There couldn't be many black men who owned shops in Lisbon, much less from the Zulu tribe. Zach went below. When he returned, he tucked a gun into his belt.

"I go with you, Cap'n," Kimo told him.

"No, I want you to stay aboard with Tobias and Sandy. If there's any trouble, they'll need you." Zach looked up at his friend. "It's all right. I know my way around Lisbon."

Then Zach had a thought. "When did you see this boy?"

"It was late afternoon. We stopped at a small tavern to eat, then came back here."

"How far a walk from the docks, and in which direction?" Zach was trying to get a bearing on the general area where Kimo had seen her.

Kimo turned to look back at the curve of the city as it spread away from the docks. "There." He pointed a long finger to the south of the landing. "We stopped to eat near the shop, then walked to the docks. It was a short walk."

Zach was grateful to learn that at least mid-afternoon Elyse had still been in the waterfront area. That greatly narrowed down their search. But it was a dangerous area. Something nagged at him. Trying to find her would be like trying to find a needle in a haystack, and he was fast losing daylight. He went to the rail.

"I don't know how long I'll be gone. But I want all the men aboard by midnight."

"Aye, Cap'n." Kimo nodded.

"Why do you bother?" Tobias asked. The look on his face was hard, as if he blamed Zach for her escape.

"Forget it. Barrington doesn't know that she's escaped and he's not likely to. You'll have that bloody confrontation you've been wantin' and she'll be well out of it."

"What the hell is that supposed to mean?" Zach demanded.

"It means that you've brought the girl nothing but grief. She was nothing but a pawn to get to Barrington anyway you could, you said so yerself. Why not just leave it be? Save yerself the effort. She means nothin' to you."

Zach stepped back from the rail. His hand buried in the front of Tobias' shirt. For a long moment they just stood there locked in a silent battle of wills, one having spoken the truth, the other refusing to accept it.

He slowly let go of Tobias, regret sharp. There had been a lot of regret lately. His hands closed gently over the man's shoulders. "I'll be back." He turned and climbed down over the side. Tobias watched as he left. It was a small victory, but he'd take it.

When he reached the docks, Zach made his way along the familiar back streets and alleys, fear driving him. She must have been really angry and desperate to leave like this.

He silently cursed himself. He'd been a fool to believe she wouldn't try. Hadn't she asked him time and again to release her? And everything had been so bad between them when he'd left that morning.

She was stubborn, defiant, and strong willed. He'd gotten no less than he deserved, and he knew it, but this time he was afraid she didn't know what she was getting into.

This wasn't London, where her grandmother was

well connected, and the Barrington name could protect her. This wasn't a morning romp to Jane's Folly in the Woods, or a prank like slipping into a discreet men's club. This was Lisbon, dangerous, deadly, and no place for a young lad, much less a young lad who wasn't a lad at all.

Elyse eventually found the Green Dolphin Inn. Now she waited across the way.

It was dark. The oil lamps at the corner cast soft shadows a few feet down the street, then everything was plunged into darkness. The Green Dolphin's door had opened as two men stepped out.

Others had emerged, unsteady on their feet, assisted by friends or alone, had staggered a few feet then become violently ill. Elyse pulled back into the shadows of the building across from the tavern. Above, in second-story windows, lights glowed.

She heard voices as people passed, the squall of a cat, the cackling laughter of the woman whose shadow appeared briefly at a window, then disappeared as arms reached for her, pulling her from view once more.

In spite of the warmth of the cape, Elyse shivered. The waiter at the restaurant had warned her this was not the place to be. But it was where his wife's cousin worked, and hopefully the man would know of a captain who might be bound for England.

It seemed to Elyse she'd waited for hours. The cool night air, damp from the sea, had given the wool cape a heavy musty smell. She couldn't wait any longer, and quickly walked across the street, her sandals noiseless on the cobbled road.

The interior of the Green Dolphin hit her in a wave of smells. This was life at its lowest, drunken and perverse. If she'd feared the darkened streets of Lisbon, likening them to her worst nightmares, this was like no nightmare she'd ever experienced.

Tables sat about the tavern, surrounded by chairs. All were occupied by men: sailors, wharf riffraff, and a sprinkling of the scourges of humanity. Somewhere in this sea of human flotsam was Santo.

Elyse asked for him at the end of the long bar, keeping her eyes downcast. A burly, black-haired man with a sweeping mustache was pointed out to her. She worked her way around the edge of the tavern, quickly stepping out of the way of a drunk customer, pushing another away when he careened toward her, and ducking beneath the swinging arm of a balding pirate who had taken aim at his companion's face. His companion was a garishly made-up woman whose stained bodice gaped away from mammoth breasts.

"What will ye have?"

"Information, please." She realized how ridiculous such proper language must sound in a place like this. The man behind the bar obviously thought the same.

"We don't give that away around here. Whatever you want, ya gotta pay for. If you want a drink, pay for it."

"I want to talk to Santo."

The man looked at her carefully. Elyse lowered her head, shielding her face. The man shrugged.

"Hey, Santo," he shouted in a poor mixture of Portuguese and English. Then he turned back to her. "You can talk, but not at the bar. I got payin' customers."

Elyse nodded as the man Santo came up beside her, giving her a questioning stare. He wiped his hands on the apron tied around him. *"Sí?"* He watched her warily.

"Your cousin's husband said I should see you." Again, that guarded look. "He said you might know of someone with a ship going to England."

"England?" With a noncommittal shrug of the shoulders, he turned away, crossing the tavern to serve the drinks. When Santo came back, she asked again.

"I need passage, on a ship to England."

"I understand," he replied.

"Do you know of someone?"

He looked at her speculatively. "Such a thing would cost a great deal of money. Where would a boy like you get that?"

Elyse started to say she had it with her. But looking around she hesitated.

"I can get it," she replied.

Santo only snorted as he moved behind the bar, nodding to a customer at the far end. Elyse's gaze followed him as he took a bottle to the customer. Her eyes widened. If there were such things as pirates on the high seas, this man surely was one.

He wore bright red pants, a sash wrapped around his waist with a broad black belt that barely controlled a belly that was bulging through the strained buttons of his soiled white shirt. The long, leather vest he wore hung practically to his knees. His girth almost matched his height, with black leather boots, cuffs rolled to just below his knees.

He was bald except for a matted fringe of hair that grew around the perimeter of his skull and fell past his shoulders. His gleaming forehead set far back on his head, and was accentuated by what should have been black, bushy eyebrows. Instead, they were just one continuous, shaggy brow that grew out of the area above his eyes. And those eyes frightened her.

They were like narrow slits, pig eyes in the flat face, pink rimmed, without lashes. They were cold eyes, gleaming with strange lights in spite of the fact that the tavern was dimly lit.

He reminded her of a great black bear she'd once seen dressed in fine clothes at a fair in London. But fine clothes hadn't kept the bear from breaking its tethers in a fit of rage and turning on everyone within reach.

Now, as Santo spoke to the man, the man shifted his

gaze to her. The pig eyes narrowed, and fear tightened her throat.

"So, little man." With this gruff acknowledgment, the bear shifted his weight and came toward her. "You are looking for a ship bound for England. I might be setting a course for England, if the price is right." Then he leaned toward her, his stench preceding him so that Elyse was forced to hold her breath.

He laughed again, a humorless sound. "But it doesn't look as if you have the price, little one."

Elyse's head came up. Zach had called her that; the nickname had seemed endearing on his lips, a casual caress spoken as he'd made love to her. Dear God, how far away all that seemed now, and in spite of the anger that had sent her from the *Revenge,* she found herself longing for that safe haven. Elyse swallowed hard. She hid her pale, small hands beneath the cape, lest they give her away. She was here and must see this through.

"I have the price," she boldly informed him, lowering her voice as much as possible.

"Ah! So the boy can speak. I was afraid you might be a mute." The bear roared with laughter. "Like the last one I had." He turned and nodded to men at a nearby table. Were they friends, fellow sailors?

"So what do you say, my little friend." The bear clapped her so hard on the back he almost sent her to the floor. Then he patted her, his hand squeezing down cruelly at her shoulder.

"You are soft, little one. I would almost think there was a girl beneath that cape you wear. But I don't mind the softness. So, tell me, if I were to risk my ship and my crew on this voyage to England, what would you pay us?"

Elyse straightened, pulled the hat more securely down atop her head and lowered her voice once more. "I can pay you and there would be more when we reach England."

"Ah, more." He winked a pig eye at a companion nearby. "But what if you are lying? What if you only have a few coins or none at all? I make the trip for nothing, at great expense to myself and my crew. But if you have something more to offer..." he suggested.

"When we reach England," she repeated. "I have nothing else."

A smirk distorted the bear's face. "There is always yourself, little one."

Elyse gasped. Had the man seen through her disguise? Was some of her hair hanging below the hat? My God, what should she do now?

"I am sorry," she apologized. "I will look elsewhere," she mumbled, backing away from the bar. Neither she nor the grinning bear paid any attention to the shadowy figure that moved into a darkened corner of the Green Dolphin.

Zach had arrived in time to hear the last of the exchange. He'd tracked the *'boy'* with those exceptional blue eyes from the shop where Kimo had purchased the silk, to the cafe, then to the Green Dolphin.

No one had so much as turned to glance in his direction as he slipped in through the front entrance. Those present were too enthralled with the conversation between the young 'boy' in the bright-colored cape and the man at the bar.

Zach's hand settled over the pistol at his belt. He was dressed all in black, like a pirate, and far more dangerous.

He knew sooner or later his crewmen would come here in their search. A quick look around the dimly lit tavern confirmed that they hadn't arrived yet. Whatever he decided, he was on his own.

From where she stood near the bar, it seemed the entire tavern erupted at once. Deciding that she would have to look elsewhere for someone to take her to England, she stepped back and tried to get past the *bear* and make it to the door.

She screamed when he lunged for her. From somewhere over her shoulder she heard a sharply barked command that was oddly familiar, then her name as the bear tried to grab her.

Zach! She almost cried out, she was so glad to hear his voice. But it carried a sound of urgency. Looking up, Elyse saw the danger.

The bear was descending on her. She ducked, losing her hat, then heard a loud exclamation as her hair tumbled to her waist. She seized that momentary advantage of surprise as she glanced in the direction she'd heard her name.

Curses filled the air. Elyse was grabbed from behind, an arm closing around her neck. Then she saw him, and no sight had ever been more welcome.

Zach left the shadows at the wall, the expression on his face more frightening than anything she'd ever seen. He raised the gun and aimed it at her. Elyse screamed as the gun discharged. Instead of feeling a bullet rip into her, she felt the arm at her throat loosen, and the weight of the man who'd been holding her suddenly drop to the floor.

Zach grabbed her and pulled her behind him. He fired at several other sailors who lunged toward them. With a hand on her wrist, Zach propelled Elyse toward the small room at the end of the bar.

"Get out of here!" he shouted at her. "There's a door out the back, through there." He fired two more shots, and two men fell at his feet.

Elyse felt as if she were fastened to the spot. She couldn't run and she couldn't scream. Then she saw him, the great bear of a man who'd attacked her. He slowly rose from the splintered wood that had once been a table, drew an equally long blade from his waist. Immediately the wall of men descending on Zach fell back and the bear pushed his way through. A vicious smile appeared below the pig eyes.

"So, Zachary Tennant, we meet again."

"Leave off, Vimeiro."

"Even if the girl gets away, I will still have you. There are at least twenty of us and you... are alone. A fatal mistake, my friend."

"Only for you, Vimeiro. As it was once before," Zach reminded him. If it was possible, the pig eyes narrowed.

"Only you would be so daring to remind me of that. But in truth, I have never forgotten it. Now, you see, the situation is reversed. I am in control, but I can be generous."

Keeping up the conversation with Vimeiro, Zach slowly backed Elyse to the door of the room.

"I am an honorable man, Zach Tennant. I will give you a chance to fight for the girl."

"Why should I fight for her when she's already mine?"

The bear snorted at the arrogance of the man. "But only yours if you can succeed in getting her out of here and away from twenty men. On the other hand, if you were to fight for her and win, I would be forced to allow both of you to go unharmed."

Zach laughed, a cold sound. "That is, of course, assuming that you are honorable, which everyone here, including your crew, knows that you are not."

Her knees practically buckled beneath her. What was Zach trying to do, provoke this bear into attacking?

"Whatever happens, you get to that door," he whispered. "Don't stop. Get to the ship."

"I won't leave you."

"You can't do me any good!" Zach hissed at her, his body a protective shield between her and the man known as Vimeiro.

"Get out of here."

"Right," Elyse muttered, knowing full well she wouldn't. He'd risked his life in coming after her. She might be foolish, but she wasn't ungrateful. She backed up a few steps, glancing over her shoulder to the closed door and praying it wasn't locked.

"All right, Vimeiro. I'll fight you and I'll beat you again," Zach told him.

"Agreed. We'll fight with cutlasses, like true pirates. And we'll both turn our guns over to my men, for safe-keeping." The man was already gloating.

"She gets the gun," Zach told him.

Elyse stared at him. She hoped that he knew what he was doing. She'd never so much as laid hands on a pistol before.

"I may as well warn you, Vimeiro. She's a dead shot. I taught her to handle arms."

"As fond as she seems of you, I'm surprised she hasn't used a pistol on you. I will agree. This could be most amusing."

Zach thrust the pistol into her hands.

"If anyone moves, shoot them!" he bit off curtly. Then, transferring the cutlass to his right hand, he pre-pared to face Vimeiro.

The bear had the advantage of weight, and he was strong. But he was slow to move and was forced to yield and change position constantly as he lunged and found nothing but air where Zach had been a moment before.

They grappled, they slashed at one another, then backed away searching for a weak spot. Then they lunged, each trying to catch the other off guard and to strike a deadly blow. Zach was strong and much quicker, but he was hemmed in by men who owed allegiance to Vimeiro. Any one of them could cut him down. He had to keep moving.

Vimeiro, acted the part of the bear Elyse thought he resembled. He stalked, lumbered, grunted, and stalked again, wearing Zach down with swipes and lunges that weren't necessarily meant to draw blood.

She called a warning to Zach. Vimeiro's men were closing in on him.

"Just as I thought," Zach hissed. "You don't know the meaning of the word honorable," he told Vimeiro. "Therefore, I will be forced to kill you." He lunged, missing; quickly recovered and lunged again.

This time, Vimeiro side-stepped at the moment of contact, swung around with surprising agility, and lunged, his cutlass aimed at Zach's shoulder.

Elyse screamed but quickly recovered. She aimed the gun at Vimeiro's men.

"You cannot kill all of us," one of them taunted.

"You will be the first," she replied, hoping that she could carry out the threat if it came to that.

The bear lunged after Zach. Instead of moving out of the way, he side-stepped, spun, and brought the cutlass down across the back of Vimeiro's head as the huge man stumbled to the floor.

Vimeiro lay crumpled, unconscious, on the floor. A deathly silence hung over the tavern as his crew stared at him. Not waiting for them to recover, Zach grabbed her by the hand and pushed her through the door of the small room.

They were obviously in some sort of storeroom. Hundreds of bottles lined the floor-to-ceiling shelves; casks and wine barrels stood about.

Elyse had a quick glimpse of the woman she'd seen earlier. She was sprawled on a wooden countertop, her bright red skirt riding high over her waist. The bodice of her gown had been pulled down, revealing massive breasts that fell to either side of her body. She looked up at the interruption.

"Hey, what's this? Who the hell do you think you are, barging in on a lady?"

The man bending over her wasn't the least disturbed. He silenced her with a growl as he thrust at her.

Zach pushed Elyse ahead of him to the back of the storeroom. Another door blocked their escape.

"Go!" Zach ground out.

"It won't open!"

"Here!" Zach shoved passed her. He tried the lock. When it wouldn't open, he took the pistol from her, aimed and fired.

A deafening roar filled the storeroom, followed by a creaking groan as the door opened, and they were out of the back of the tavern. But Zach slowed beside her, and she practically went to the ground as he sagged onto her, putting one arm around her shoulders.

"What is it?"

He braced himself against the wall of the building, his breath coming in uneven gasps. He pulled her close as footsteps sounded in the alley. Elyse held her breath as someone passed by.

Dear God, she hadn't counted on some of Vimeiro's men coming around to the back of the tavern. She could hear cursing from inside the storeroom. They had to get away. Zach took her hand and pulled her to the street. A lamp overhead shown down as they emerged. They could hear voices heading the opposite way. It would take only a few minutes for the men to start searching this direction.

She had no idea what direction led to the docks.

Zach chuckled. "So now you're willing to go with me."

"I hardly think this is the time to discuss it," she said sarcastically, still scared out of her wits. "Come on!" she prodded.

"Not until you say it."

"Say what? For heaven's sake, Zach, they'll find us. Do you want to have to fight Vimeiro again?"

"Say that you want to go with me."

He spoke with a lazy drawl. What was wrong with him?

"All right. I want to go with you."

He smiled faintly in the lamplight and reached out to stroke her cheek. "I don't think I'm going to make it." He braced himself against the side of a shop.

Elyse's head came up, her alarm sharpening. "What are you talking about? We have to get back to the *Revenge!*" His arm was around her shoulders, holding her against him. When she pulled away to look up at him, she gasped. A wet, stickiness soaked his shirt.

"You're hurt!" She stared at the stain spreading across at his shirt.

"We have to get you back to the ship." She pulled his arm around her.

"No," Zach groaned.

Elyse cried out softly, turning into him. "You can't die! Not here!" Nothing she'd said made sense, and she knew it.

"There's a place near here."

"Where?" She wiped the tears from her eyes.

"Zamora's," Zach whispered. "An old friend."

Zamora. The name conjured up visions of another friend of his, the one she'd met in London at Jerrold's club—Fatima. She wondered if Zamora was the same type of friend, then quickly pushed the thought from her mind. It was none of her business; they needed help.

"How do we get there?"

"It's not far." He winced, inhaling sharply as she took his weight against her. "Two blocks down, then to the right, at the sign of the half-moon over the door."

"Oh, so you're familiar with this neighborhood. You really should pick your friends more carefully." That got a rise out of him.

"I suggest you be quiet and start walking. I'm not sure how long I'll be able to stay on my feet."

She wasn't certain how they accomplished it. They

stopped and started many times, night sounds sending them into darkened doorways. But Zach seemed to know where they were going.

Now she was frantic. They'd follow his directions, she'd searched every door, the few numbered signs, name plates.

He kept insisting this was the street and finally she found the half-moon carved at a doorway. She pounded at the door. Whoever this woman was, Elyse desperately hoped she was home.

"She's always home. This is her place of business."

Elyse gritted her teeth and knocked again. After what seemed an eternity, a bolt was released inside, the door opened a crack, and a boy appeared.

"I don't understand what he's asking!"

Beside her, leaning against the doorframe, Zach inhaled sharply against a new wave of pain.

"He wants to know who it is," he explained and then groaned to the small voice.

Zach suddenly grabbed for the doorframe as he felt himself going down. The last thing he heard was Elyse crying out as he fell through the open doorway.

Nineteen

"*Cristo!*" the boy exclaimed and whistled softly as he bent over Zach. Then he turned and ran through the house. So much for friends, Elyse thought angrily.

As soft light struck the walls of the small hallway, she looked up. A bent form in a long shawl crept toward them, followed by the boy and two men who looked no better than the ones they'd just left. Elyse raised the pistol.

The bent figure halted, holding a lantern up high, and Elyse could see it was an old woman. Zamora?

The light from the lantern slipped up Elyse's body until it revealed her face. The old woman mumbled something, and the boy quickly came around and whispered back to her.

The woman made a soft clucking sound; then, completely ignoring the pistol Elyse held, she pushed past her and once again held the lantern aloft. Light spread over Zach and the pool of blood beneath him.

Elyse immediately dropped to Zach's side. When the old woman held out the cane and would have poked at the dark wet stain at his shirt, Elyse batted it away.

"No!" she hissed, the one word she knew was easily understood.

It immediately brought a response from the boy as well as the two men.

She wasn't about to let them come near. He'd risked his life by coming after her. It was her fault he was hurt. She owed him this much.

One word from the old woman halted the others.

It was difficult to believe that this was Zamora. The look on Zach's face when he'd mentioned the woman's name was secretive, almost tender. Surely this wasn't Zamora. But Elyse had to know if she could help them.

She tried to make herself understood, speaking very carefully and slowly. "I need to find Zamora."

Elyse groaned. Her knowledge of Portuguese was limited. Her Spanish was hardly better, but she decided to try it.

She pointed to Zach's shirt. *"Sangre. Mucho sangre. Por favor...*We need to find Zamora." She stared at them, tears of frustration in her eyes.

"Por favor!" Please, she thought desperately. *"Ayuda...?"*

The larger man moved her aside as if she were nothing more than a bothersome insect. The other man joined him and, together, they lifted Zach and carried him up the stairs at the end of the hallway.

"You are brave, *senhorita*." The old woman spoke perfect English.

Elyse stared after them in confusion. If this was where Zamora lived, then where was she? Zach was carried to a bed in a room at the top of the stairs.

Orders were given in a rapid flow of Portuguese. Then the two men quickly left the room, and the small boy took up the lantern. The old woman carefully unbuttoned Zach's shirt, pulling the shirt away from the knife wound.

"Take the lantern," she curtly ordered Elyse. To the boy, she said, "Fresh cloths, hot water." He bounded out of the room.

Elyse held the lantern aloft, though her hands were shaking. The old woman looked, up at her briefly. "He has lost much blood."

Elyse nodded mutely. "We were attacked at the Green Dolphin. Where did those two men go?"

"Do not concern yourself with them." She glared at Elyse. "We must think of him."

The boy returned.

"Hold the light steady!" she growled, then muttered to the boy, "Take the lantern from her before she drops it." She jerked her head toward the lad.

"You must help me!" She looked up at Elyse. "And quit shaking. You will do him more harm than good. Are you afraid of a little blood?"

"No!" Elyse snapped, not caring if that offended her.

The old woman chuckled. "So, you are spirited as well as brave. Amazing for one so small. Are you a girl or a boy?" She gestured to Elyse's clothes.

"Shouldn't we bandage him before he bleeds to death?"

The woman turned sharp eyes on her. They were old eyes that had undoubtedly seen much, but they were as alive as the boy's.

"Is that important to you?"

"Of course it's important!" Elyse blurted out. "Why else would I have brought him here?"

The old woman only shook her head, then began applying bandages. They quickly turned crimson beneath her wrinkled hands.

"Where is Zamora?" Elyse asked. "He wanted me to find Zamora."

"I am Zamora."

When she recovered from that, Elyse moved beside Zach pressing the thick pad against the wound as the old woman directed, applying pressure until the muscles between her shoulder blades ached.

"It is no good," Zamora announced, drawing Elyse's

startled glance. "The bleeding will not stop. The wound must be closed."

"What are you talking about?" Elyse's startled gaze locked with the old woman's. "You have to help him. Surely there is something else that can be done. Perhaps more bandages?"

The old woman shook her head. " Even now the bandages you hold are filled with blood. If the wound is not closed, he will die. I have done it many times for my own people, but there is great danger."

"What danger?"

"There is the possibility that the knife may have done more damage inside. If I close, he may continue to bleed inside. Then it will be only a matter of time until he bleeds to death." Zamora drew a heavily veined hand across her forehead, smoothing back a strand of silver-streaked hair.

"There is only one way to be certain. I have seen this many times. My people are very good with knives."

Elyse swallowed back the fear that tightened inside so that she could hardly breathe. "Then you have to close the wound inside as well."

The old woman nodded her agreement. "But I cannot do it."

Elyse paled, her throat going completely dry and making it almost impossible to swallow much less speak. "You have to do it! There is no one else!" Her voice grew stronger. "He asked me to bring him here. He said you could help! I thought you were a friend!" she accused, her eyes glistening fiercely.

The woman shook her head. "I am a friend, more friend than you will ever know. But there is only so much old Zamora can do. Do you think I like what I tell you?" She came out of the chair, her skinny arms waving through the air in a gesture of helplessness. Gold and silver bracelets flashed through the silence. "I owe him my life!" She flattened a hand against her breast.

"There was a time when I hoped he would take my daughter to wife. But they are too much the same— volatile and dangerous when angry. They would have torn each other apart. Still, I look upon him as a son. But I cannot do what you ask. I would do him more harm with these old hands."

Elyse hung her weary head, too tired to understand everything the woman was saying. "You said that he'll die if the bleeding isn't stopped. I won't let that happen, simply because you're afraid to try." She fought back tears of fear and frustration. Breathing past the constriction in her tight throat. She thrust her hands back through her disheveled hair, as she tried to think. Then her head came up. Her eyes were hard and determined.

"Tobias!" she whispered as if the name were a prayer.

The old woman's eyes narrowed. "That old man is here?"

Elyse nodded. "Aboard the *Revenge* in the harbor." She breathed more easily as relief washed over her. Tobias would come! He would do what was necessary to save Zach.

Zamora spat out contemptuously. "The old fool is probably drunk. You'd be killing him to let Tobias touch him."

Elyse eyes riveted on the woman. "It seems I have no choice!

At least hc's not afraid to try." She didn't voice her own fears. It was true. She'd seen Tobias several times when he'd had more than his share to drink. But in his sober moments, his hands were steady. She trusted him, and she knew that Zach did as well.

"We must send one of the men to the ship."

"No!" the old woman replied. "It is too dangerous. Those who did this will still be looking for him."

Elyse slowly stood. "Then I'll go myself!" She met the woman's gaze defiantly.

"He might die while you're gone."

"You won't let that happen," she replied. "You said yourself that he is like a son. Would you let your son die?"

"You have the fire and spirit of a Gypsy," The old woman cackled. "Stay with him. I will send the boy."

"It's too dangerous!"

"The boy will be all right. He knows the streets of Lisbon. They are only dangerous for those who do not know them. Besides, I would not risk him any more than I would risk this one. The boy is my grandson." She called to him and rapidly gave instructions. He nodded, then bounded from the room.

It seemed they waited an eternity. Elyse kept pressure on the wound, until Zamora pushed her aside and took her place. Then she couldn't keep still.

She paced, and she constantly checked the window. Then she turned at the sound of footsteps on the stairs. She picked up the pistol from the table beside the bed.

"Do you think my sons would let anyone else come into this room?" Zamora asked.

Tobias came through the door, followed by Sandy and Tris. Elyse thought she would collapse, so great was her relief. Tobias' gaze immediately went to Zach, then found her as he rounded the bed.

"Are you all right?" he asked.

"Yes," she whispered brokenly, causing him to look up.

"Can you help him?" Doubt washed over her. Still nothing but silence, and that deepening frown on his face as he checked the wound.

"Tobias?"

"He's lost a lot of blood," he said without looking up. "And his pulse is weak." But there was a faint twinkling in his eyes. "I've seen him take worse." He fixed a speculative gaze on her. "Does it matter to you?"

She hesitated. She'd been certain of her feelings at the Green Dolphin when he'd first appeared, and she'd been certain when she'd thought Zamora's sons might hurt him.

"Yes."

Tobias smiled faintly. "Good." It was only a beginning, but it would have to do. "I'll need help, and I don't trust that old woman with her herbs and potions." He gestured to Zamora. His remark brought a glare from the old woman, but she held her tongue.

I'll do whatever I can."

"Bring my bag, then wash your hands thoroughly. And have that boy step closer with the lamp. My eyes aren't as good as they used to be, and we've got some work ahead of us." He nodded to Tris and Sandy. "Make certain we don't have trouble."

They nodded and took up places, one just outside the door, the other downstairs with Zamora's sons.

As long as she lived, Elyse would never forget the next hour as Tobias gently probed the knife wound, washed the wound with alcohol in the form of whiskey, then took the first stitch. Both hands were bloodied to the wrists in a very short time, and Elyse constantly blotted blood from the wound so that he could see what he was doing.

Time and again, she poured whiskey over the wound as he'd instructed her. And time and again, she was certain she could stand no more—no more blood or cut flesh, or the frightening shallow rise and fall of Zach's chest as he breathed. She fought the screams at the back of her throat, closed her eyes, and could still see blood. How was it possible to lose so much blood and still live?

She'd lost all sense of time. Her back ached from bending over for so long and her arms had long since lost all feeling. She felt like some sort of mechanical creature, obeying Tobias' commands, handing him scissors or needle, cutting the thread he stitched, wiping the perspiration from his forehead so that it didn't run into his eyes. And always there was the blood.

Elyse was certain as long as she lived, she would see it every time she closed her eyes. It was as if her own lifeblood were soaking the cloths and staining everything. And then, miraculously, there was no more blood. She wiped the wound and stared at the bandage Tobias bound at the wound. Her startled gaze met his.

"Aye, we're done. It's closed and the bleeding has stopped." He wiped his hands across the front of his shirt. It too was stained with blood.

"Will he live?"

The physician straightened against the stiffness in his back. "He's strong and he's a fighter. But perhaps Zamora could answer that better than me." He turned to the old woman whom he obviously held in mutual contempt.

"What do you say, old woman? What do you see with those old eyes of yours? Or perhaps you could brew up some tea and ask the tea leaves?"

She came out of the chair where she'd been watching everything with dark eyes. "Be careful, you old sea turtle, or I will throw you in a pot of boiling water and make soup of you. I've always thought that would do you a great deal of good," she snapped.

"Ah, enough of your kind words, Zamora. I'm tired and the girl is about ready to collapse. He can't be moved. So, it seems you have house guests at least until morning," Tobias informed her, undaunted by the old woman's threats.

"They're welcome to stay. But I should throw you out for your insults."

"Then who would tend to his wound, should he awaken?"

Zamora's eyes narrowed as she took a step toward Tobias.

"My medicine is as powerful as yours, maybe more powerful."

"Then why didn't you use it?" Tobias was weary, his eyes were red rimmed, his usually even manner was fast fading.

Zamora sniffed indignantly. "Because she repays my kindness by insisting that I send for you. But I understand what is in her heart. It speaks what her words will not say. And because of that, I am willing to do as she asks. Now, plague me no more, you fool!" She thrust a crooked finger toward the doorway. "You can sleep in the boy's room. He will not mind, and he will not be inclined to slit your throat." She turned to Elyse.

"I'll stay with him," Elyse announced. She had no idea why there was such animosity between Zamora and Tobias, and she didn't care. She just wanted to be with Zach if he should wake.

The old woman shrugged her shoulders as if to say it made no difference to her where Elyse slept, but her keen eyes watched as Elyse dropped into the rocking chair beside the bed, then pulled it closer and laid her head on her arm beside him.

She had dozed off. She wakened suddenly at the pressure of a hand at her shoulder.

There was confusion at first, waking in an unfamiliar place, then her gaze fastened on Zach, and she immediately came upright in the chair. Zamora's wrinkled hand was gentle on her shoulder.

"He is all right and still sleeps."

She slowly relaxed. A single lantern cast a faint glow in the room. It was still dark. How long had she slept?

Zamora waved a hand toward the small table, where bowls had been set. Streamers of steam curled lazily above each, and Elyse thought vaguely of the tea leaves

Tobias had mentioned earlier. She hesitated, wondering if the woman really was a Gypsy.

"You must eat," Zamora told her. "How can you care for him if you are weak? Come. There is nothing you can do for him. More than anything, he needs rest. There may be fever, and then you will work very hard."

Elyse rose slowly, a hand-stitched blanket falling from her lap. She picked it up, slightly confused. She didn't remember having the blanket earlier.

The old Gypsy smiled. "It gets cold at night so close to the water." She motioned to a chair. "You were restless and did not sleep well."

"I kept seeing things."

Zamora's eyes narrowed as she placed a basket of bread on the table. "Ah yes, he dreams. Sit and eat." She took the chair opposite, positioning her small body on the chair seat as if she were a small watchful bird.

"What about the fever?" She glanced back over her shoulder at him. He seemed to be resting peacefully enough.

"The fever will come when his body fights off the poison that comes from the wound. I have seen it many times." Zamora smiled as she gestured to the bowl of steaming liquid. "It will keep the hunger away."

Elyse thought nothing had ever smelled quite so delicious. Chunks of meat and fresh vegetables filled the well-seasoned broth, with long strands of noodles and chunks of a rich dough. It made her think of the ensopado she'd enjoyed at the restaurant the day before. Was that only the day before? It seemed a lifetime.

As her questioning gaze met the old Gypsy's, she wondered what other ingredients might be in the soup. It was as if the old woman read her thoughts.

"I am a good cook. My grandmother taught me." She smiled. "There is nothing in the soup that will harm you."

"It's delicious," Elyse told her. "My grandmother's

cook would pay handsomely to know what you've put in it." At the thought, a wave of sadness washed over her as she thought of her grandmother and others, not knowing her fate. Her eyes filled with tears.

Zamora watched her with keen eyes, instinctively understanding there was a great sadness in this young woman. "I know you have come a great distance and I would gladly tell you what is in the soup. It is made with a little of this and a little of that, a pinch of herbs and whatever else can be found in my kitchen."

Elyse smiled through her tears. "No magic Gypsy potions?"

"Bah!" Zamora exclaimed. "That old fool Tobias would have you believe I chant incantations over a witch's brew and fly about on a broom." She gestured about the small room. "Do you see a black caldron?"

"I see a pot of soup," Elyse confessed.

"Yes, and you must remember everything is not always as it seems." Zamora pushed the basket of warm bread toward her.

Aware of the old woman's keen gaze, Elyse commented, "Everything is not always as it seems. That pot of soup just might be a witch's caldron."

"Only to that old fool of a man." Zamora laughed with her. "Being a Gypsy is my heritage, not my profession. He would have you believe we ride around in brightly painted wagons, make campfires in the hills, and steal from rich travelers."

"But you don't," Elyse surmised.

Zamora fastened that dark gaze on her. "I am too old to ride around in a wagon, and my bones feel the coldness of the earth around the campfire. Why should I travel about to steal from rich travelers when that can be done right here?" Her lips curved into a teasing smile so that Elyse wasn't certain whether she lied or played at some joke.

"And you tell fortunes with tea leaves?" Elyse replied.

"Tea leaves! Bah!" Zamora shook her head, sending silvery, waist-length hair swinging back and forth at her hips. "That is for silly old women with nothing better to do, and superstitious old fools. I am neither, in spite of what that old dog tells you." She poured two earthenware tumblers full of red wine. Then her smile returned. "Tea leaves are unreliable."

Elyse smiled as she took a sip of the wine. She liked Zamora.

"Do you make the wine as well?"

"It was made by a friend. He brings me more than enough wine to share with friends."

"Is Tobias a friend?" Elyse broke a piece of bread off.

Zamora laughed, the throaty sound coming from deep inside. "Yes, in spite of himself. He is a friend. That is all that matters. And I respect his skills as a physician. I would never have attempted such an operation. His skills have stopped the bleeding. Now Zamora's skills will defeat the poison that will come with the fever. It is not necessary that we like one another, only that we respect each other."

Elyse was surprised by the woman's candor and astuteness.

"And he respects you."

Zamora nodded. "He would rather die than admit it is so, but whenever the *Revenge* is in Lisbon, Zach comes to see me. And he always asks for my special healing herbs. I am not fooled. I know it is the old man who asks for them, but he is too proud to do so himself." Zamora winked at her.

"He is afraid to admit that an old Gypsy knows more than he when it comes to healing potions. That knowledge is handed down through the generations of Gypsies, unlike the ability to foresee things which comes to only a few."

Elyse's gaze came up, her soft blue eyes darkening. Zamora smiled knowingly.

"Even now you wonder how I know that you have come a great distance."

Elyse shrugged. "I was aboard the *Revenge,* and we only just arrived."

Zamora nodded. "I do not speak of the *Revenge.* I speak of another journey, the one you made a long time ago."

"And now you want to tell my fortune?" She'd once had her fortune told by a Roma woman in a traveling caravan that camped on her grandmother's country estate. She was only a child at the time, but she'd quickly learned the woman's technique of drawing out pertinent information with innocent conversation, then turning it around to make it seem she actually was able to know about other people's lives.

"What do you see in me?" She slowly drank the wine.

Zamora's eyes narrowed as she realized that she didn't really believe her. Still there was something about this one. "I do not tell fortunes. Only you can know. I am merely the one who sees, like a window that you look through. But you mock me. You think that I lie." She laughed.

"Always it is the same with those who refuse to believe what I know, in here." She pointed to her head, to her sleek hair bound back by a blue silk cloth. "And what I feel here." She laid a hand over her heart. And I know that you have traveled a far greater distance than the one on the *Revenge.* "

Elyse shook her head. She was tired and in no mood for the woman's ramblings. "I suppose, you can tell me where my journey began and will end."

She immediately regretted her sharp words. Whatever Zamora was or pretended to be, she had been generous with her house, her food, and her care of Zach. Elyse had no right to criticize her.

But Zamora had known countless people who'd doubted her, at first. She nodded. "I cannot tell you. Only you can know that. But I will show you what I mean." Zamora opened her left hand and extended it across the table.

"Each of us has lines on our hands. And these lines mean something. This one," she pointed to the one crossing the top of the palm from just below this finger. "The same line on my hand is long, but broken in many places. I will tell you what I have told no one else." She leaned closer as if sharing a secret.

"I have had five husbands and at least that many lovers. I have loved many times, but never deeply and only for a short time."

Elyse had finished the soup and bread. A warm comfort filled her. She leaned against the edge of the table and sipped the wine that slipped soothingly over her senses.

"The heart line."

"Exactly so," Zamora concluded. "I knew this as a young girl, but I chose to ignore it. Had I heeded the teachings of my great-grandmother and the knowledge I was born with, I would have taken greater care."

Elyse opened her fingers and stared down at her own hand. The exact same line was deeply etched and unbroken. But with everything that had happened, what did it mean?

She thought of the turn her life had taken in the last weeks. Did the heart line account for abductions?

"I don't know what to believe," she softly told the woman. "What about the other lines at my hand?" Elyse became more curious as the soft glow of wine spread through her.

The old woman smiled. "Their meaning comes from the different parts of a life. The happiness a person will know is indicated in the line very near the heart line."

Elyse laughed with the old woman. "Are there others?"

Zamora shrugged. "Yes. One indicates health and another indicates whether you will know great riches or poverty." Her eyes twinkled. "But wealth can be measured in many ways, can it not? It is not always measured in the amount of gold in one's pocket."

"Tell me more."

Zamora placed another stick of wood on the fire. "You do not believe an old woman."

And oddly enough she did. She just didn't understand all of it.

Zamora stirred the fire, frowning. She'd sensed something in this one the moment she'd laid eyes on her. It was that knowledge of her great-grandmother's that allowed her to see, and there was something about the girl, something otherworldly in spite of the innocence, something sad and almost mournful in her eyes. Ah, yes, Zamora thought, in spite of the youthful beauty, there is a very old soul in this girl.

Elyse extended her hand. "I want to know what you see."

The old woman's eyes narrowed. She sensed that the young woman was being completely honest. She didn't believe in Zamora's powers, but she did not disbelieve either. An open mind was a place to start.

"Very well." Zamora smiled at her. "I will tell you a Gypsy's tale of great love, wealth, and travel to foreign lands."

She filled both their cups with wine, then sat in the chair across the table. With great ceremony, she smoothed back silver strands of hair and the ornate bracelets on her arms. She opened her mind and closed out everything else except this room, the table, and the young woman sitting across from her.

"Give me your hand," she commanded softly, her dark eyes hooded. Her slender, aged fingers were warm from stirring the fire. She cupped Elyse's hand in hers, gently spreading the fingers, until they were relaxed, and then she stared at her palm for a very long time, the silence drawing out in the room.

"No riches, travel, or the love of a handsome stranger?" Elyse said with faint amusement.

Zamora slowly looked up at her. Her dark eyes were filled with a strange light. They were old eyes, ancient, and filled with the secrets they saw.

She wanted to doubt this young woman. It was too impossible, part of an ancient legend handed down from one generation to another of her people. But as she again looked down at the slender hand in hers, she knew it was true. She must find a way to make the young woman understand.

"What do you see?"

Zamora frowned. Again that feeling of coldness seemed to fill the room. But it wasn't the cold, empty feeling that usually came with the forewarning of something dreadful. It was like the mist shrouding the harbor in winter that eventually burned away. No, she thought. There is too much doubt. She will not accept the truth.

"I see wealth, happiness, and travel to a distant land," she stated simply and rose from her chair.

Elyse was certain that she had sensed something almost within her grasp, and then it was gone like the visions in her dreams. She'd thought to humor the old woman, but her own sense of loss was almost unbearable. She couldn't disguise the disappointment in her voice. Perhaps it was that she desperately needed answers when there were none.

"You didn't see anything else?"

Zamora poured water from a huge urn into the simmer pot, then cut up more vegetables and chunks of meat to feed her sons and grandson. She turned, fixing the girl with that penetrating stare. Perhaps this one really did want to know.

"What more could you want than wealth, love, and happiness?" she asked.

"I want to know what you see?"

The old woman returned to her chair. She took both of Elyse's hands, her dark eyes boring into hers.

"Perhaps it is time that you understand." Her hand tightened over Elyse's. Slowly she spread the fingers apart, exposing her palm once more.

"This as I told you, is the heart line." She stopped, staring down at Elyse's hand. "That is very strange. For most people it is often broken. But yours runs very deep. It is long and unbroken. That means you shall have one great love." Zamora hesitated.

"Please, go on. I want to know everything," Elyse persisted.

The old Gypsy nodded and continued. "Here is where the lifeline is usually found." She drew her finger in a wide arc from the inside of Elyse's hand just above her thumb down to the heel of her palm. Then she stopped. Where she indicated, there was no line, only the smooth unbroken plane of smooth skin.

"I don't have a lifeline, and yet here I am, very much alive."

Zamora looked up at her, those old eyes seeing beyond the present moment, into past moments, years, and... lifetimes.

"The lifeline does not tell whether a person lives or not, but the length of one's life."

"How can you measure something you can't see?"

The old woman stared at her. "You already know the answer. You have always known it. It is only that you would not accept it." The old woman gently released her hand.

"How can you measure something when you don't know where it begins or ends?"

There was no other choice now that the path had been chosen. She must tell the girl everything, or she would be lost forever.

"My great-grandmother told the story of a man she once knew. This man had no such line on his hand. But he had the ability to recall another life in another time and place. Those who knew him said he'd always had those memories since he was a child.

The old woman watched her as she continued. "He knew this life, down to the most precise detail. He knew the names of people and places from a hundred years before—things he could not have known unless he'd seen them. These things would come to him in dreams. He spoke of leaving one life and entering another." Zamora leaned far over the table, her gaze boring into Elyse's.

"The line measures the beginning and the end of a life," she explained. "This man, I speak of, had no such line across his hand because his life had no beginning or ending."

Elyse stared at her. "What you're saying is impossible! A person is born, lives, and dies. That's all!"

"Can you deny that even now you are troubled with dreams you do not understand?" Zamora went on to tell Elyse what she already knew.

"You've had them since you were a child, and always they are the same. And there will come a time, perhaps already, when the dream is real. It is a memory of another time, another place, another life."

"It can't be," Elyse whispered.

"You may deny it with every breath, but you know it is true. I see it in your eyes."

"You know nothing about me... " Elyse pressed her fingers against her forehead as if she could wipe it away. But she couldn't.

"I am not wrong." Zamora confronted her.

Elyse refused to meet that dark gaze, afraid of what she might see.

"Are there others?"

Zamora nodded. "There is another," she answered simply.

"I have known of one other in my life."

Elyse looked up, following the line of the old Gypsy's gaze to the bed against the far wall on which Zach slept.

She looked up at the old woman. "What are you saying!"

"I am saying that there are many things in this world that neither man nor God can explain. There are those who live many lives, perhaps searching for something, or... someone. It is there in your hand. It began long ago. The truth is there, you have lived another life. This life began when the ship was cast upon the rocks."

Elyse was stunned. There wasn't any way for the woman to know these things. "You expect me to believe this?"

"I expect nothing of you. You asked me to tell you what I saw, and I have told you. Whether you choose to believe it or not is up to you. There is a reason only you can know, fate has brought you two together again. But I warn you, if you ignore what I have told you, you may never find each other again."

Zamora rose then, suddenly very weary. It was always the same when she used the gift.

"I must feed my sons. Check the bandages," she told her with a look over at the bed. "Make certain there is no bleeding. And then you have a choice. You must decide whether to accept what fate has offered you, or not.

"You have a chance at happiness that was taken from you, that only a few will ever know. But only you can decide." Then she was gone, a bowl of soup in each hand, the door slightly ajar as she made her way down the darkened stairway.

Surely the woman was mad, Elyse thought. What she suggested was unbelievable. Yet, how was it possible for the old woman to know so much about her?

She was unable to sleep after the old woman left. Everything she'd been taught and had believed told her that what Zamora told her was impossible. People didn't live one life and then simply drift into another.

But even after the old woman returned and made her bed upon a pallet of blankets before the hearth, the doubts remained. It would have been so easy to ignore what she suggested, to dismiss it as nothing but foolishness... except for the dreams.

Always there were the dreams, filled with visions and images she didn't understand. The only thing she was certain of was that those images were not from her own life.

Another place and time? What if it was possible? What if the old woman's words were true? What if she had lived more than one life and Zach had somehow been a part of it?

She crossed to the bed on which Zach lay. Gently, so not to wake him, she took his hand in hers.

She stared at his hand, then at her own. They were the same, there was no life line.

'I knew you'd come back to me.'

The words she'd first spoken that night returned. This man had haunted her dreams. His was the face that looked back at her through the mist, his arms were the arms that reached for her. Tears pooled in her eyes.

A choice, the old woman had told her. She could leave, walk away from all of it. He was powerless to stop her. It would be so easy to do just as she'd planned when she'd left the ship. She still had the gold coins. She could easily slip away, return to England, and... But what if it is true?

"Who are you, Zach Tennant? Who am I?" She rested her head at the edge of the bed.

He was certain he was dreaming. He tried to sit up, but weakness forced him back.

This wasn't his cabin aboard the *Revenge*. He tried to move again and felt the warmth of a hand on his, and he remembered—Lisbon and the Green Dolphin. He'd gone there to find her.

His head went back. She was here, she was safe...

Now, many hours later, Elyse felt his hand at her cheek. She slowly sat up, untangling her hair from his hand. She pushed to her feet and quietly made her way across the room. The first light of dawn slipped through the shutters at the window.

The house with a carved moon at the door was quiet, everyone was still asleep as she slipped out the room. She'd made her decision.

Still, she hesitated. What was it that held her back, refusing to let her go?

Leave, she told herself. And she did, out into the street, through the mist that rolled up from the harbor as tears slipped down her cheeks.

Zach suddenly wakened, in that way that had become habit aboard the *Revenge*, listening, feeling the steady roll of the ship around him. But he wasn't aboard the *Revenge*.

He slowly pushed himself up from the bed. He was drenched in cold sweat, then burning with heat. His fingers curled seeking the cool silkiness of her hair, but there was nothing there.

He looked around. The room was vaguely familiar. This was Zamora's house! But how? And where was Elyse?

He clenched his teeth against the pain as he forced himself to his feet. He crossed the room, leaning heavily against the table.

She had been here, he remembered, he had felt her, the warmth of her hand in his, the coolness of her hair as he had drifted off again.

He opened the door to a narrow hallway and moved toward the stairs.

Lys!

Twenty

S he made her way toward the waterfront.

There, she told herself, she would find a ship returning to England as she had originally planned. Twice she thought she saw crewmen from the *Revenge*. Each time she turned down another street to avoid them.

Then down another street that took her closer to the waterfront, where workers already swarmed the wharf, small landing boats bobbing in the water as they set out with crews returning to their ships.

Out in the harbor, the *Revenge* gleamed in the early morning light.

Head down, determined to find a ship that could take her back to England, she didn't see the shadow that crossed hers until it was too late. She screamed as a grimy hand clamped over her mouth and an arm went round her waist, and she was hauled up against the bulk of a foul-smelling man.

"Look what we got ourselves here, Chappy." A grunt of approval came from the shadows as Elyse struggled to free herself.

"Hey, ain't it the boy that started all the trouble at the Green Dolphin?" the one called Chappy commented.

"One and the same." A face loomed over her, the foul stench of filth, fish, and body sweat made her stomach lurch.

She squirmed helplessly under the hand that prevented her from crying out. Beads of sweat broke out between her breasts and trickled down, molding the dampening shirt to her. If they hadn't already guessed, they'd soon see that she wasn't a boy at all.

She freed one arm and swung hard, hoping to throw her captor off balance, then tried to escape.

"No you don't!" the first man grunted as he grabbed for her and pulled off the cap on her head. The cap gone, her hair tumbled to her shoulders.

"What the hell!?" He exclaimed.

She lunged away a moment too late, crying out as his hand closed around her hair and he pulled her back.

"This ain't no boy at all!"

Elyse was spun around. Bile rose in her throat as she was drawn up against the man, her body forced against his.

"Get your filthy hands off me!" she screamed at him.

"Spirited, eh. El Barracuda will be interested to know why you're wearing those clothes. But I think he cares for young boys as much as he cares for them whores he visits in port. Yer thin. Maybe he won't like you at all."

His accent was thick, but she understood all of it and his meaning was obvious as he ran his hand down her back, then over the curve at her bottom. She lunged away from him, only to be brought up short when his hand twisted painfully in her hair.

"Eh, Chano, you may be right. But she may be able to tell him what the Raven is carryin' in the hold of that ship. Hurt her and she won't be able to tell him nothin'."

The man called Chano grunted as he seemed to consider what his companion had said. "We'll take her to the ship. He might let me have 'er when he's through."

When she tried to kick out at him, he slapped her. When she screamed, he stuffed a foul-smelling rag in her mouth.

"That's so you don't draw no attention before we get you to the ship."

The air was slammed out of her lungs as she was thrown over his shoulder.

For two days Zach had the streets of Lisbon searched, and for two days his men returned with the same answer. There was no sign of Elyse. She had completely disappeared. He insisted on returning to the *Revenge*.

He was fighting off the effects of the wound and the herbal medicines Zamora had been giving him. He tried to stand, felt the floor shift beneath his feet, then heard his friend cursing explosively.

"What are you putting in that brew of yours, old man?"

"Somethin' you've used a time or two yourself. Now, you've got to stay put or that wound will open up." Tobias warned.

"Has there been any word?" Zach winced as he stood.

They both looked up as the second mate suddenly appeared in the doorway. Kimo was with him, pushing a man ahead of him. He was small and filthy with frightened eyes that grew larger when he saw the Raven.

"This one followed me. He was sent with a message." Kimo threw the little man to the floor of the cabin. "Tell him," he ordered the man, standing over him with crossed arms and a knife in his hand.

"Tell me!" Zach leaned heavily against the chart table. "What do you know? I just may let you live."

"El Barracuda knows about the cargo you carry. He

will give you the woman for what is in yer hold," he blurted out. "But not here. He says to come to the island if you want the woman to live."

Tenerife. El Barracuda's home port.

Zach knew it well enough, as most who sailed these waters, to have avoided it in the past. Those who made the mistake of sailing those waters and reaching the island were rarely seen again. Or, if they managed to escape, there were stories of the bloody end for their crews.

He nodded to Kimo.

"Can you swim, little man?" He asked the man who squirmed as he held him aloft, then dragged him from the cabin.

Zach looked at his second mate. "The Sultana?"

"Put to sea this mornin', under heavy sail."

Zach nodded. "Prepare to get under way now."

A look passed between Sandy and Tobias.

"Now," Zach repeated."

When Sandy had gone to carry out his orders, Tobias looked at him sharply. "You're in no condition to do this." He knew what it meant, a bloody confrontation with El Barracuda, if they could catch him.

"The gold isn't even aboard any longer." Tobias knew well enough that Zach had it transferred under cover of darkness.

"What will you do, buy it back? And go to your death to do this?"

Zach fixed him with a long look. "You are my friend and more, as much a father as I have ever known. God knows, I owe you my life for your care, but this is something I will do. If you cannot, I understand, and Sandy can have you taken to the docks."

"Is she worth it?" Tobias demanded, but he knew the answer even as he asked it. He saw it in those eyes that darkened like a storm over water.

Orders were given to the crew. A late morning

breeze picked up, and it filled the sails as they were unfurled. They hoisted the anchor and *Revenge* moved like
a swift bird across the water toward the open sea.

Elyse squinted at the glaring light thrust in front of her
face. She cried out as she was pulled to her feet, tripped
from ropes that bound her ankles, and fell to her knees
in the slime-filled water in the bowels of the ship.

She tried to break her fall with her bound hands, her
fingers sinking into the filth and sludge at the bottom of
the hold. Then she was pulled upright by a hand at the
back of her shirt. Always it was the same—no food, only
foul water, and only the crudest means of relieving
herself.

"Now, missy, we'll try again," came the voice from
behind the hand that held the lantern.

"Tell me about the gold aboard the *Revenge?*"

Elyse shook her head. The same question had been
asked countless times, and she had given the same
answer.

"I don't know," she croaked from between dry,
parched lips. She was so exhausted, but she'd give them
no satisfaction.

"I don't know anything." She'd die before she'd tell
them the truth, and she was certain death would come.
She was so weak she could barely stand. She hadn't eaten
since she'd left Zamora's, and the crew of the *Sultana*
weren't about to offer her anything.

Her thoughts blurred, but she tried to hold on to
just one. If she gave in to the bone-aching weariness she
might let something slip and tell them—that the gold
was no longer aboard the *Revenge.*

She'd been a fool to leave the old woman's house.
She knew that, but it was small comfort to her now.

El Barracuda. She'd heard the name before. The
man was the worst sort, a pirate feared by other pirates.

His men had almost killed Zach at the tavern. She wouldn't give him any information. It was a small revenge, but she was determined to have it.

She forced back the sob that would have been so easy as she thought of Zach. Was he still alive?

In the two days since she'd been taken captive she'd thought of nothing else, with Zamora's words tormenting her.

"There will come a time when the dream becomes real... another time and place, another life. You must choose what you will believe."

The light from the lantern glared in her eyes. She was so tired. The questions had been constant, never allowing her more than a few minutes' rest before starting again.

The faces of the two men blurred and then disappeared and she was sinking into a place where there was no more hunger or bone-aching weariness, only the sound of the water and the darkness that wrapped around her. She shivered. It was dark and she was so cold.

'Don't leave me!' She didn't know if she said it or dreamed it. She was a child again and it was so dark, and there was water everywhere...

"I will find you..."

Then Zamora's words whispered through the darkness. *"If you refuse to believe what I have told you, you will never find each other again, not in this or any other lifetime."*

There were other memories—the night of the party, the trip to Fair View, a portrait and a stained-glass window, blood everywhere and she was screaming...

It would all go away, her grandmother told her. But it didn't.

Was it possible? Could Zamora be right? Had she and Zach known one another in another place and time?

'If you refuse to accept what I have told you, you may never find each other again, not in this lifetime or any other'.

She had to get out of there. Somehow, she had to find him, she had to know.

She was stiff and sore from sitting in such a small space in the hold of the ship. The ropes had been removed, her feet bare except for the leather sandals she still wore, her hands free.

Had it only been two days since she'd been brought aboard the Sultana?

She stretched her arms and legs as she leaned against the hull of the ship, sea water washing over her feet. Something brushed against her ankles, then disappeared, her companions the rats that scurried about.

Her shoulder bumped into something—a box or crate? With only water to drink the past two days, she was weak, but managed to climb atop the crate, pulling her legs under her.

She tried to think, to try and find a way out of there. But where would she go?

The hull of the Sultana shuddered around her as several loud blasts rumbled overhead, followed by more blasts from some distance away. She clung to the ropes that bound the crate as the *Sultana* lurched and began a slow turn. Another round of blasts followed her.

They were being fired on!

She frantically searched the surrounding darkness and finally found a sliver of light at an overhead hatch.

She had to feel her way around crates and barrels in the hold, losing her grip on a rope as the Sultana lurched, then moving again toward the hatch as more cannon-fire roared from the deck above, and was then answered once more by distant fire.

She reached the ladder and pulled herself up until her head brushed against the hatch.

As the ship shuddered, she fought to maintain her

precarious hold. What would she find up on deck? Would El Barracuda's men throw her back down into the hold?

Another deafening blast exploded as she pushed against the hatch. It slowly lifted, and she slipped her hands into the opening. She peered out onto the deck. Another blast rocked the ship, a heavy cloud of smoke blinding her. She pushed again and raised the hatch enough for her to crawl out onto the deck and soon realized that the smoke wasn't from the cannons but from a fire that burned overhead where the main mast had been blown away.

The crew of the Sultana fought to cut the lines of the severed mast, while other men adjusted the remaining sails as the ship groaned and slowly came about once more, men scrambling below decks as more cannons appeared along the port side.

She took advantage of the confusion and chaos and ran to the railing. Out across the rolling blue-green water was another ship. The *Revenge* was returning fire.

Was Zach aboard? How was it possible?

The schooner was lighter, faster, and more maneuverable than the bulkier *Sultana*. Elyse watched as the gleaming ship cut across the course of the frigate, immediately trimming sail as she prepared to come back around. The *Revenge* was also turning and bearing down on the Sultana. Cannon fire exploded from the deck of the *Revenge*.

The ship had sustained little damage that she could see, yet, as orders were shouted around her, she knew the danger. El Barracuda was in an almost perfect position with six cannons on each side.

Favoring his bandaged side, Zach moved to the helm. He looked to the center mast and checked the trim of the sails. He motioned to Tris to have extra line pulled in.

"They're coming into position, sir," Sandy called out.

Cannonballs burst overhead. Zach ordered the schooner brought about sharply, and then gave the command to return fire. The move unexpected, several well-placed shots caught the *Sultana* broadside and overhead at the mast.

He gave new orders, had the sails trimmed even more and heeled the schooner hard to port, bringing her sharply about to make another run. But the *Sultana* had maneuvered as well. Her starboard guns now had a clear target.

"Cut sharply," Zach gave the order. "Set her on a direct path across the bow of the *Sultana*.

"They'll cut us to pieces, Cap'n." Sandy warned, but Zach was already yelling to his men to turn the guns.

"Look!" Tris shouted and pointed. Everyone aboard *Revenge* turned to stare at the *Sultana*.

The lines at the mainsail sagged and the center mast had been blown in half. The crippled ship had begun to list badly as the churning sea rolled over her bow.

Zach gave the orders, and the *Revenge* was brought about, hard astern of the frigate. The *Sultana* was hopelessly crippled, the prize El Barracuda had hoped for was lost as his crew fought to save themselves.

"She's going down, Cap'n!" Sandy shouted again as the frigate's bow nosed downward. The damaged lines and sails flapping in the wind, the Sultana rolled and her crew with her. Water surged over the railing, taking crew, shattered mast, and everyone with it.

Elyse was thrown into the water. She could see light above her as she was pulled under. She fought it... fought as she had as a child a long time ago, as the ship crashed upon the rocks and was then torn apart.

She was falling. The water closed around her, filling her mouth as she tried to scream, choking her...

Revenge came about.

"Cap'n!" Kimo pointed out across the water as the crew of the Sultana released lifeboats while others scrambled over the side of the sinking ship as what was left of the center mast swung crazily over the deck, sweeping everything, including a slender figure, overboard with it.

"Lower the landing boat!" Sandy ordered as Elyse was plunged into the water and disappeared beneath the surface.

Tobias shouted when Zach would have gone to the landing boat. "You've lost too much blood, you'll never make it." He shot a glance past Zach to Kimo. Before Zach could argue, his crewman was already over the side of the *Revenge*. He didn't wait for the boat, but instead swam toward the Sultana, then dove beneath the surface.

Kimo surfaced, and then went down twice more. The next time he came to the surface he had her and swam toward the landing boat as it rode the waves close by.

"She's alive," Tobias announced once Kimo was able to bring her aboard the *Revenge*.

He didn't understand how it was possible. From the time she was swept overboard until the time Kimo brought her to the surface was too long. He'd know of men who drowned in less time.

She was alive, but barely, full of more sea water than the Sultana, he would wager, as he stepped into the role of physician once more, gently peeling the clothes from her, then wrapping her in warm blankets with Zach standing over him, about to collapse from what they'd been through.

"You'll do her no good if the bleeding starts again," Tobias told him as he turned Elyse on her side so that any remaining water would be brought up. He'd already made a quick examination and determined that she had no outward injuries from her time in the ocean or in the hands of El Barracuda.

"Leave," Zach replied. "I'll care for her myself."

Tobias shook his head, he didn't leave. By his experience, she would probably never waken, but he wasn't about to argue the matter with him and have another dead patient on his hands.

He stayed with her when he wasn't topside seeing to the running of the ship. He bathed her, gently eased the soup past her lips that cook prepared, and held her.

"Lys."

It was a whisper at first. Like a breath of wind that filled the sails, or water gently lapping against the hull of the ship.

It slipped through the darkness, back across the years, across time. A memory so strong he could almost touch it.

"Come back to me," he whispered.

Twenty-One

The Red Sea, the Arabian Sea, and then along the southern tip of India. For weeks they sailed, making port only when fresh water and food was needed.

Now, they'd left land far behind three days earlier. The next land they would see, weeks ahead, would be the coast of the Australian continent. The ocean was vast, filled with tiny phosphorescent creatures that glowed in the waves at night, forming a soft, blue-green cloud in the water about the ship. Flying fish played about the ship, along with porpoises and dolphins. Exotic Portuguese man-of-war often floated on the surface. And, of course, there was Sebastian, the brilliant green and red macaw who screeched obscenities.

It was a place apart, a small private world aboard the *Revenge,* where faces and smiles had become dearly familiar.

No one spoke of it, but Elyse knew by the way Zach drove the crew that Jerrold was there—a rumor, his ship seen—relentless, closing the distance. Days, weeks, but he would come. She found herself watching for sails on the distant horizon along with the rest of the crew. And all of this was happening because of a need for a revenge that she didn't understand.

With Tobias' care, Zach gradually recovered from the wound he'd received in Lisbon, and she recovered from sinking of the Sultana.

There were parts of it all that she still didn't remember, and other things that were so vivid from her time in the water that it was almost frightening, as if it happened all over again, the same as when she was a child. No matter how much she wanted to deny the things Zamora had told her, there was so much of it that simply could not be explained away.

She returned to the cabin she had occupied before. Zach made no protest, but she often found him watching her, his gaze fastened on her as if he was searching for something that she knew they both struggled with—something that would explain all of it—another life, another chance, but where would it now end with Jerrold determined to hunt them both down.

Repairs were made aboard *Revenge* from the confrontation with the Sultana, even as they put more and more ocean behind them.

There was little for her to do, and she had taken to the most mundane everyday chores simply to keep herself busy: picking up cast off clothes that needed to be laundered, clearing the chart table of plates of food where Zach met with Sandy, or pulling a book from the shelves behind the chart table to read.

She was surprised at the variety of books she found there. There were two by Herman Melville, including *Moby Dick.* She'd read it years earlier and started it again. With much time on her hands, she read a lot.

There were also books written in French and Spanish, which she couldn't begin to read, and an entire series on the history of England, not surprising since Australia, was a Crown colony. But she was surprised at the extensive papers and volumes on the American colonies, one titled *The Birth of a Nation, American Independence,* and several others including a thick volume by Thomas Jefferson, and a plain, leather-bound book she found by accident.

Opening it, Elyse discovered that it was a journal. She stared at the words on the first page, and the name of Zach's father, Nicholas Tennant.

Dare she read it? A journal was a private thing, not meant to be shared with everyone, much less a stranger. But she wasn't a stranger. Her fingers trembled as she turned the first page.

London, England
  June 7, 1839

I begin this journey into hell. One day I will return and have my day of justice for the crime I am accused of.

I will reclaim my birthright from those who have taken it from me. And, God willing, Felicia will be waiting for me.

I shall now be called Nicholas Tennant, a new name for a new life.

Elyse stared at the words she'd read at least a dozen times.

Felicia. He could mean no other than Felicia Barrington!

She didn't want to continue. It was almost as if she was afraid of what she would find. But Zamora's words whispered at her, and she slowly turned the next page.

She read on, feeling all the desperation and futility that poured forth in those words. Then, she read about Resolute. The struggle, the daily fight to carve a home from the wilderness of New South Wales. She sensed the iron-willed determination of Nicholas Tennant in his descriptions of that new life. She saw frustration in his bold, short strokes, and calm acceptance of a small victory when an entry recorded the number of lambs born that first spring.

And she read about Felicia—the longing in words so private that she had to close the journal several times, of letters sent that went unanswered, then the news that arrived by ship—and another entry written by someone else, Zach perhaps, that Felicia Seymour had wed. She was Felicia Barrington, the scrawled angry words that gave way to a sad acceptance that reached deep inside her and left her crying.

Felicia Seymour had loved only one man—Alexander Nicholas Barrington, who took the name, Nicholas Tennant. Alexander Barrington was Zach's father!

"My pendant," she whispered as she finally understood. There had always been two of them—the earbobs Felicia had worn for the portrait. Alexander Barrington had given them to her when they were engaged to be married!

For the longest time, she sat there, too stunned to think, to even move. Zach's father had been engaged to Felicia Seymour, and then the crime he was accused of, tried for murder, and sent to Australia banned from every returning to England.

What had happened to Felicia? What was she told? That he was dead?

She had eventually married Charles Barrington, and Zach's father made what he could of the life that was left to him. All those unanswered letters, the questions, the wounds that never healed when two people were torn apart.

Elyse closed her eyes at the pain and anguish that must have brought them, felt all over again, deep inside, as real as when it first happened. She looked up. Zach watched her from the doorway of the cabin, then looked down at the journal in front of her.

"Now you know," he said, crossing the cabin. "That journal is all I have of him."

"Jerrold's father... " she whispered.

He nodded. "He took the one thing that meant more to my father than anything else."

"And Felicia..." she whispered.

Tears streamed her cheeks. "She died the day of the shipwreck when my parents were returning to England." She looked up at him then.

"Zamora said..." she closed her eyes as she struggled with what the old woman had told her.

"The dreams; that I had lived before. I don't understand all of it, but she said that it was here," she opened her hand and stared down at it. She looked at him then, "She said that I was waiting for you to find me..."

Then still struggling with all of it, she rose and replaced the journal on the shelf. When she turned to leave, he stopped her, a hand at her arm.

"Lys," he whispered.

Alex Barrington's nickname for Felicia, the woman he had loved and lost. He whispered it again as his hands cradled her face. He wiped the tears away with his fingers. Then the whisper of his lips against hers.

Then there were no more words as he touched her as if he was seeing her for the first time, memorizing her, each touch as he slowly removed one of the blouses he'd purchased for her, her hands covering his as, together, they pushed the pants from her hips, and, together, removed his pants and shirt, her fingers lightly brushing the wound that still healed at his side.

His hands clasped with hers as they slowly came together, his lips whispered against her, his body caressed hers, then he pulled her to him as if he would pull her inside him and never let her go. "Beautiful Lys," he told her as they lay together afterward. Mine, he thought. Always and forever.

"What will happen when Jerrold finds us?" she asked

through the shadows of the cabin, as he held her against him.

"It will be settled once and for all, the way it should have been."

"And what if...?" The words wouldn't come but they were there—what if he didn't come back to her.

Zach held her tight against him. "You're mine. Nothing can ever change that."

Hands stroking, breathless, urgent sounds, then the sounds of dreamless sleep as the cocoon of the ship wrapped around them. They didn't speak of it again.

They had left the Bass Strait behind the day before. Sydney lay just ahead.

Elyse stood in the middle of the cabin she'd shared with him these last weeks. It was strange how she'd become accustomed to the movement of the ship. Now, the balmy weather and the slow, rolling motion of the *Revenge* was the same as it had been at Lisbon and she knew they were near Sydney Harbor.

Zach had told her that she was to go ashore. Tris would take her, then take her on to Resolute. He would wait for Jerrold.

She knew what he was doing, preparing for. She didn't want to go. But she also knew that this needed to end, for both of them. She also knew that he would never allow her to stay.

"No," he had said gently the past night as they lay together, in a way that she knew she couldn't change his mind.

"But what if...?" He had silenced her fears with his fingers against her lips and then made love to her. Now she packed the few clothes she had in a carpet bag, including the skirts and blouses he'd purchased for her in Lisbon. Then, she watched him on the deck of the *Revenge* as Tris took her ashore in the landing boat. Tobias chose to remain with him, his care still needed for Zach's wound.

She looked for him again and found him still there as Tris made arrangements for the driver who would take them the long way to Melbourne, still silent as the driver pulled away the following day from the inn where they stayed the night and turned south toward Resolute Station. But the fear was there, that she would lose him all over again.

Twenty-Two

Zach checked the night watch, nodding to his man as he passed by. All lights aboard the *Revenge* had been extinguished. They couldn't afford to give themselves away, even though there had been no sign yet of Barrington.

Fraser Island was actually a small cluster of islands separated by shallow inlets that popped up at a moment's notice. The waters throughout the chain could be treacherous if a navigator didn't know his way through them. Zach knew these waters well. And it was for just that reason he'd chosen to anchor the *Revenge* at Fraser when he wasn't in port.

Over the years, the islands had provided an excellent hideaway when he wasn't raiding. All ships leaving Sydney Harbor were forced to turn into the wind, directly in the path of the islands. But Zach knew as few others did, that the sea breezes around the islands could be traitorous. They blew contrary to most winds, causing more than one captain inexperienced in these waters to founder on the rocky shoals that crisscrossed through the chain, or to run up on the deadly reef just a little to the south when the wind suddenly died, leaving sails slack.

Zach had first ventured to these islands with the old

man, a Scot, who taught him to sail. He'd learned to sail by stars, the currents, and the wind. Sailing had become second nature to him. Now, as he watched the last light of day on the western horizon, he thought of Elyse.

He felt it again, that vague prickling of warning, an uneasiness he couldn't quite name. The ship lay quietly at anchor, water lapping gently at her hull, and the men had prepared and quietly took their turns at the watch.

Somewhere below, *Sebastian* squawked and was then silent, probably with a piece of bread rather than the dull blade he deserved. Two of his men nodded as he passed them by. Nothing seemed out of the ordinary. Still, he couldn't rid himself of that feeling.

Over and over again, he told himself this confrontation with Barrington was unfinished business and, after it was settled, he'd go home to her. If, that was not to be... He couldn't forget the look in her eyes when she'd begged him not to go.

He couldn't think about it now. There would be time enough later to try to understand it all. For now, he could only think of Barrington. He'd waited a long time for this.

The English commander stood at the bow of the heavily gunned frigate, his feet planted firmly on the gently rolling deck as the vessel slipped through the night.

He hoped to hell Barrington was right about all of this. If not, they'd come a long way on a fool's errand. And earlier that day he'd begun to believe it was just that.

He was risking a great deal slipping out of Sydney Harbor without orders and then turning south toward Fraser Island, off the coast of Melbourne. Barrington had received word that the man known as the Raven was there. He looked at Jerrold Barrington now, at the bow beside him.

"You had better be right about this. I don't mind telling you the admiralty is gravely concerned about our inability to bring the Raven to justice."

"Have no fear, Commander," Jerrold assured him with confidence. "The man was well paid for the information."

Word had it that Tennant's ship had been seen in Sydney Harbor only days earlier. And according to the information he'd paid handsomely for, there was one place where the man known as the Raven would be waiting for them, hoping to take advantage of the element of surprise. But surprise would be on their side. And this time there would be no escape.

The blood red dawn washed the decks of the *Revenge*, mist slowly rising from the water.

Moments before, the guard had changed, when a signal light was seen from the small island just north of Fraser Island, a dot of an island at the mouth of the inlet to the other islands.

Jerrold Barrington waited aboard the Royal Navy frigate. He was using his own ship as the decoy, but he wasn't about to be in the line of fire when this began. He wanted to be in a position to watch the slaughter when the Raven took the bait and came out into the open, thinking they were evenly matched.

The wind came up sharp and strong, buffeting *Revenge's* flags against the center mast as she slipped from the cove, her black hull slicing through the dark water, the rising sun gleaming off her decks. The sail at her center mast caught the blood red of the sun, and overhead the red flag bearing the emblem of a black raven snapped in the wind.

All aboard were ready, their eyes trained on the lumbering Barrington frigate. She rode low in the water, coming slowly about on a windward tack. It was then, as *Revenge* first became fully exposed with the wind against her, that the cry went up.

A blast rocked through the chain of islands, the sound echoing off the rocky peaks and cliffs. And in that instant, Zach knew the frigate had been the bait.

Revenge was running before the wind, Zach's original intention to come about and square off with the frigate. Now he took over the helm, realizing a trap had been laid. Cannons roared from the cloistered islands on the leeward side.

He knew these islands as no other and used that to come about and gave the signal to fire *Revenge*'s cannons. A roar split the air as the cannons were fired, and he had the schooner already coming around to fire off the starboard side.

He watched the water, sat the wind that slipped across the surface and cut across the path of the first frigate, stealing his wind.

His best hope was to outmaneuver the heavier ships, slip past them through a narrow passage through the two farthest islands then come about and wait for them to follow.

Revenge slipped through the passage and, as he brought her about, the crew trimmed the sails. They came about, the cannon on the leeward side ready and aimed for the first frigate to follow. It was Barrington's ship, his personal flag at the main mast from the main as the frigate made the fatal mistake of trimming their sails and barely made it through the narrow passage over the coral reef.

Sails trimmed, the frigate was slow in coming about as the crew scrambled on her deck. Zach gave the signal and cannon fire exploded from *Revenge* and echoed off the rocky islands.

Three of the cannons fired found their target, the frigate shuddering under the blows as the second frigate briefly appeared at the mouth of the passage, then slowed, the English Union Jack wobbling crazily. Unfamiliar with the outer islands that were of little consequence except for seabirds and whales, the second frigate had gone aground on the coral shelf that lay along the sides of the passage.

With the second frigate of no more concern, Zach's attention swung back to Barrington's ship. Temporarily becalmed, the crew working furiously to adjust the sails, Zach took advantage of the wind that swept off the westernmost island to bring the *Revenge* about. Cannons loaded, he waited until they were parallel to Barrington's ship and within range.

"Cap'n?" Sandy asked as they waited, holding their position within range for now.

"Run up the flag. I want Barrington to know exactly who we are."

The flag with the Raven was sent aloft, snapping in the wind.

Zach gave the order. "Fire!"

The narrow channel between Fraser Island and the mainland looked as if a major sea battle had taken place. For years afterward the residents of the small hamlets and fishing villages on the island would tell tales of the battle.

One frigate was heavily damaged, and the crew abandoned ship. The crew made their way ashore in rowboats. Some swam ashore. It was said that the master of the ship, a man by the name of Barrington, perished as the ship broke apart.

A second frigate, a ship of the line, was stranded on the coral shoals, slowly battered beyond repair, All survived.

The only ship to escape unscathed was a schooner, sleek and fast, that swept past them both and headed for the open sea, flying a flag with a black raven.

Epilogue

RESOLUTE STATION, N.S.W.

Among the people whose culture was centuries old, it was known as the *Dreamtime*, that linked past with present and the present with the future.

Elyse found the truth of the past in that Dreamtime. She and Zach had always been together, in other times and places known by other names, but always together, destined to be together once more, in this life.

She still had the dreams, but they were different now—fragments, bits, and pieces she was no longer afraid of but accepted as the memories of those other lives. And he was always part of it, just as he was part of her life now.

Four days she waited at Resolute, made welcome by the people there, watching the road, waiting just as she had waited before.

There was telegraph in Melbourne several miles away, and Tris was the one who brought word from Melbourne that all were safe. Two days later, with fair winds the *Revenge* arrived in port. It was another day before Zach and those who were returning to Resolute, including Tobias, arrived home. Others remained aboard ship for the time.

Sandy, an able second mate, was made the new captain, in charge of moving cargo and passengers between Melbourne and Macau, or the longer voyage to the United States.

Now, Elyse walked back alone from the small cottage not far from the large, sprawling house at Resolute. She listened to the night sounds, so different yet familiar.

In those first days, alone except for Tris, she had made several visits with Jimmy Nymagee's wife, Sara. The power of the Dreamtime was strong in her family.

Usually only the men were allowed to sit under the stars at night, building the fires, chanting the ancient messages connecting them to those other lives. But Elyse was allowed to watch from the edge of their circle.

Afterward she felt at peace, and content, more of her questions about those other times and places having been answered. It helped her to understand and accept her special gift that Zamora had first told her about.

Zach's bitterness over the betrayal that had exiled Alex Barrington to this land so many years ago ended at Fraser Island.

She knew the rest of the story. A servant girl had been forced to lie to the court about what she'd witnessed between the father and the brothers. After Jerrold was lost at Fraser Island, Charles Barrington disappeared. The courts in England had been petitioned on Zach's behalf and a decision had been handed down. With no heirs, the Barrington title, Fair View, Barrington Shipping, all passed to Zach.

He had promised Elyse that his pirating days were over. Now that he controlled Barrington Shipping, he could practice another form of resistance to the Crown, one within the bounds of the law.

Elyse had sent letters to her grandmother explaining everything and promising they would visit her. She was anxious about how Regina had taken the news of her 'marriage', in fact, to the man who'd abducted her. But when Lady Regina wrote back, she'd been more concerned with receiving an invitation to visit the land 'down under'. She and Ceddy would be arriving sometime in the spring for an extended visit that was also a belated celebration. They'd married shortly after receiving Elyse's letter.

About time, Elyse had thought, delighted that Ceddy was now officially part of the family. And by the time the older couple arrived, they would officially be great-grandparents. She laid her hand over the growing firmness at her stomach.

As far as she could determine with everything that had happened, she had conceived aboard *Revenge*, when both could no longer deny the truth of their past life together. The child was now part of this new life together.

She loved the feel of the child within her. A son, Sara had assured her, he was an affirmation of life, this life. In a way she supposed that made all life unending. But she silently wondered if this son of theirs would understand their secret.

Would he have a lifeline on his hand or would he, as they had, be part of some past life? And what of the future?

Elyse could accept whatever it offered, for she knew that, when this life as they knew it ended, she and Zach would find each other again.

She approached the gardens at the west side of the house, and hesitated as she saw a shadow move along the side of the house. She couldn't see it clearly. Then it lengthened and came toward her.

Zach stepped from the darkness into the soft glow of light that spilled from the windows. Usually, he let her go alone to the meeting place of Jingo's people, but tonight he'd waited for her.

"Did you travel with the dreamers tonight?" He

greeted her tenderly, his arm slipping around her waist. In spite of his teasing, she knew that he respected the ancient culture of these people who were so closely bound to the land at Resolute, just as he was.

"Only for a little while." She smiled up at him. "I wanted to be with you." She shivered faintly. The night air had turned cool, the different scents of this place that she, drifted on the evening breeze.

Zach's arms tightened around her as they stopped in the garden beside a large eucalyptus tree, the leaves fragrant with that uniquely pungent smell. He pulled her back against him, his hands sliding from her shoulders, down where their child lay within her.

"Are you keeping my son warm?"

Elyse laid her head back against his shoulder, sighing as his mouth slipped down the side of her neck to the top of her shoulder. Heat spread through her, settling below where the babe rested.

"Our son is nice and warm." She laughed softly as through the soft fabric of her dress, Zach's hands closed over her disappearing hipbones. He pulled her back against him.

Could she ask him now, when she knew he would promise almost anything?

"Zach?" She called him that because it was his name, in this life.

"IImmm?" he murmured against the back of her neck, inhaling the sweetness of her unbound hair.

"Come with me next time."

Silence.

Until now, he had let her go alone when she felt the need to understand more about the other lives. But always with that silence afterward. Was it the same now?

"I'll go."

She let out a slow breath and turned in his arms.

"You're certain?" she asked.

He laid a hand at her cheek, his thumb brushing her lips.

"Yes." He reached up, stroking back a tendril of hair from her cheek.

She was so beautiful—this woman, his wife, the mother of his child.

He didn't know what she wanted or needed to hear. He only knew what he felt each time he looked at her, that they had been together before, lost each other, and then found each other again. Being with her was like coming home.

How many times? He didn't know. He only knew that it was true, that when he left this life, he would find her again in the next one.

His obsession with Felicia Barrington was ended, quite simply because he knew that she *was* Felicia. It came in small moments—the turn of her head, a certain smile, a look that was for him alone. It was undoubtedly what had drawn him to her that first time so many months ago in London. She had been waiting for him then.

"I'm not a religious man," he tried to explain. "I never felt the need for it. I still don't. And there are so many things I may never understand. But I know that there's something stronger than life and death, something that goes on and keeps two people together."

He brushed his lips across hers. "I've always loved you. I love you today, I'll love you tomorrow, and forever."

Her eyes were wet with tears as she laid her head against his chest, feeling the strong beat of his heart. The arms around her, the strong hands caressing her, were from her dream and now they were real. She'd found him again. He'd come back to her.

"Look!" she said, pointing across the garden that Alex Barrington had planted years before.

There, bright and luminous in the evening lit by the

moon and stars, the white roses of Resolute bloomed among the red, fulfilling a promise from that other lifetime.

"The red rose is for passion. The white rose is my promise that my love is forever."

<h1 style="text-align:center">Also by Carla Simpson</h1>

Angus Brodie and Mikaela Forsythe Murder Mystery
A Deadly Affair
Deadly Secrets
A Deadly Game

Merlin Series
Daughter of Fire
Daughter of the Mist
Daughter of the Light
Shadows of Camelot
Dawn of Camelot
Daughter of Camelot
The Young Dragons, Blood Moon

Clan Fraser
Betrayed
Revenge

Outlaws, Scoundrels & Lawmen
Desperado's Caress
Passion's Splendor
Silver Mistress

Memory and Desire
Desire's Flame
Silken Surrender

Ravished

Always My Love
Seductive Caress
Seduced
Deceived

Join Carla's Newsletter